CORNELIA

Other Books by Dan Armstrong

Taming the Dragon
Prairie Fire
Puddle of Love
The Open Secret
Chain of Souls
The Eyes of Archimedes Book I
The Siege of Syracuse
The Eyes of Archimedes Book II
The Death of Marcellus
The Eyes of Archimedes Book III
Zama

CORNELIA

The First Woman of Rome

A Novel

Dan Armstrong

Mud City Press

Eugene, Oregon

Cornelia: The First Woman of Rome
Copyright © 2017 by Dan Armstrong

Published by
Mud City Press
http://www.mudcitypress.com
Eugene, Oregon

This is a work of fiction. Names, characters, places, and incidents are either the product of the author's imagination or are used fictitiously.

The image on the book's cover comes from the Wikipedia Commons. The original is a painting by the Swiss artist Angelica Kauffman (1741-1807) titled "Cornelia, Mother of the Gracchi." The image on the back is also from the commons. The artist is unknown.

ISBN-978-0-9993219-0-4

Printed in the United States

To Judith

AUTHOR'S NOTE

The episode in Roman history described in this novel takes place between the years 136 B.C. and 121 B.C. and represents a critical, but rarely discussed, period in the evolution of the Roman Republic. The Republic was first established in 509 B.C. Rome at that time was governed by a senate populated exclusively by members of the Roman aristocracy (the patricians). Over the next three hundred and sixty years, this early plutocracy begrudgingly transformed, one law at a time, into an increasingly democratic system, though the upper class always maintained a firm grip on the levers of power.

Cornelia: The First Woman of Rome follows the lives of the Gracchi family—Cornelia Scipionis and her three children Tiberius, Gaius, and Sempronia. Over a fifteen-year period, Tiberius and Gaius were central players in Roman politics and installed a series of laws designed to give the common citizen (the plebeians) a larger part in the process of governance. Unfortunately, the progressive politics of the Gracchi led to an unexpected turn away from civility in Roman discourse, and despite the goodwill of the brothers, marked the beginning of a tumultuous one hundred-year devolution of the Roman Republic into an empire. The story of the Gracchi family is one of the lesser told chapters in the history of ancient Rome, though it might also be one of the most telling. At the very least, it is an important cautionary tale for all aspiring democratic nations and merits repeating.

*

The many Latin, Greek, and other foreign names used for the characters in this novel are listed alphabetically at the back of the book for the reader's convenience. In addition, a family tree located before the prologue provides the ancestry of the central characters in the story. A glossary containing words specific to ancient Roman culture follows the list of characters.

Although a concerted effort has been made to be faithful to a very complex episode in the history of Rome, simplifications were made for the sake of readability. In the end, this is a novel. The story is an embellishment of the existing literature.

"A woman, serious
about future and past,
I peruse Greek scrolls,
weave Latin wool and toughness.
But I never asked for heroes.
Some jewels would have been enough.
In my salon I thought and spoke
poetry only till politics took over."
                -Susanna Roxman, from poem *Cornelia*

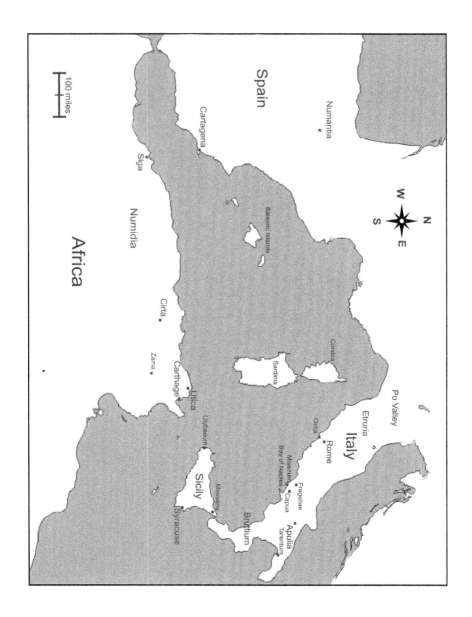

Western Mediterranean

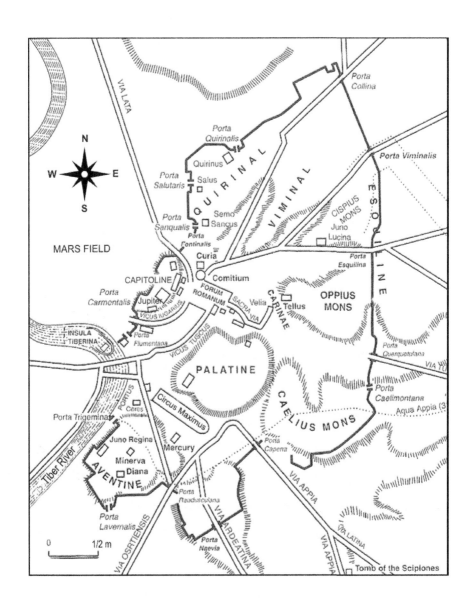

The City of Rome

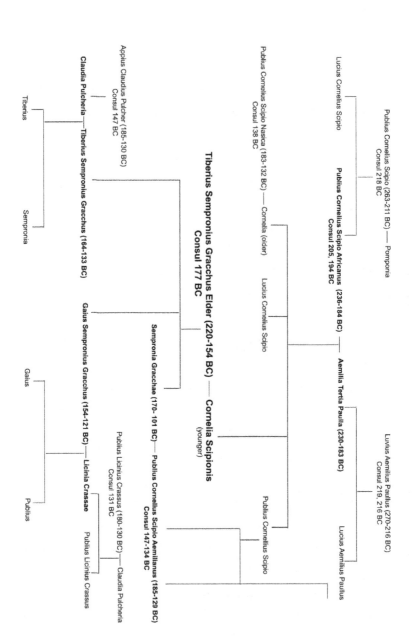

Cornelian/Gracchan Family Tree

PROLOGUE

I, Sempronia Gracchae, daughter of Tiberius Sempronius Gracchus and granddaughter of Publius Cornelius Scipio Africanus, can now say I have witnessed the first few steps in the collapse of the Roman Republic. After nearly four hundred years, the most stable democracy in the world has succumbed to thuggery, undisguised corruption, and demagoguery. I no longer recognize the society in which I live. The situation so grieves me, that even though I am a woman and my opinion counts for little, I feel compelled to write a history of this demise, a demise that broke the heart of the most respected woman in Rome, my mother Cornelia Scipionis Africana, and would bring tears of rage and anguish to my ancestors. While the heroes of my story are surely my brothers, Gaius and Tiberius, my mother provided the foundation upon which their characters and intellects were allowed to flourish. For me, all begins and ends with this woman. I write to bare my soul in hopes of relieving hers.

Life in Rome changed dramatically in the years after my grandfather defeated Hannibal. Rome became the dominant nation in the world. Ambitious Roman consuls found reasons for military campaigns anywhere treasure might be plundered and humans shackled. Armies were dispatched throughout the Mediterranean region and into Gaul making one conquest after another. Wealth flowed into Italy by the boatload—gold, silver, artwork of all varieties, and tens of thousands of slaves. What had once been a nation of farmers, a people who prided themselves on hard work and austerity, transformed into a culture of excess and financial extremes. The rich had more and the common citizens less.

My grandfather saw the beginning of this. He became so cynical that he quit the Senate ten years after his triumphant return from Africa to live out the remainder of his life in isolation. The story of what happened in Rome afterward can best be told through the life of his daughter, my mother Cornelia, as elevated and capable a woman as her father was a man. She is nearly seventy-five years old now. She and

I, two widows who never remarried, share her villa in Misenum. I have yet to show her what I am writing, but I have only just begun.

As the daughter of Scipio Africanus and Aemilia Tertia Paulla, Cornelia was born into the highest ranks of the Roman aristocracy. Her father and mother emphasized education, particularly the study of Greek literature and philosophy. Although Africanus died when Cornelia was seven, Aemilia provided Cornelia with world-class tutors and access to Rome's best private libraries. At a young age Cornelia possessed a worldliness gained through education and her social milieu entirely unknown among Roman women.

At seventeen she married my father, Tiberius Gracchus, then forty-five. He was from the plebeian class but of the highest character, twice a consul, once a tribune of the plebs, and once a censor. Though Africanus and Tiberius were never friends, Tiberius gained the family's favor when, as a tribune, he twice vetoed Porcius Cato's legal attacks against my grandfather and his brother Lucius. Those vetoes earned him the valuable prize of my mother's hand in marriage.

Cornelia came with the unheard of dowry of fifty talents of silver and her patrician name. Despite the age difference, Tiberius was a good match for her, and my parents loved each other in a way that was uncommon among arranged marriages. They had twelve children in their eighteen years together, but only three lived past the age of five.

I was the first surviving child. I was born with a twisted ankle, called by some a clubfoot. Female newborns, especially the second or third in a family, are often left out to die in Roman culture. It is the same for a male child born with a deformity. After losing three children in thirty-six months, and my brothers not yet born, my mother, perhaps concerned she would not bear another living child, went against all social norms and nursed me through my early months despite my being both female and deformed.

My father was on a campaign in Cisalpine Gaul at the time. He never knew about my ankle. Cornelia wrapped my foot every day from the moment I was born, gradually straightening and strengthening it. By the time I was a youth, I could walk without a limp. Hidden beneath the hem of my stola, my twisted foot was never noticed or mentioned—not even to the man to whom I was promised, my cousin by adoption, Publius Cornelius Scipio Aemilianus.

My father died of an illness when I was sixteen. My brother Tiberius was nine. Gaius, my mother's third surviving child, had just been born. I was married the following year.

My ankle, which I had learned to endure in my early years, began to ache when I passed the age of thirty. Walking with any kind of grace became increasingly difficult. My husband, Aemilianus, could not help but notice. An overly proud and critical man, he felt my imperfect gait reflected badly on him. That my four pregnancies had not produced a surviving child only added to our troubled relationship. The situation became so trying that I began to believe my mother had made a mistake allowing me to live. In moments of weakness I would recall what she had told me when I was nine and first asked about her decision to nurture me when I was an infant.

"Your body was not perfect, Sempronia," she said, "but I never doubted the clarity of your mind. I saw it in your eyes right away. My mother granted me the gift of education, and I wanted a daughter of my own to educate and with whom to share my fondness for literature and art. You are that lovely girl."

Yes, this sweet memory provided me with strength, but it was one thing for my mother to educate my brothers for an active life of military service and politics and another to educate me. Why educate a woman when she will have no duties other than managing her house slaves? There is, of course, the appreciation of knowledge for the mere beauty of it. Which is surely something in itself; a form of wisdom as Cornelia would say. But education also inspires—and empowers—and a woman with ideas can be a problem if she has nothing to do. So now, after fifty-five years of unanswered promise, I have decided to write this history.

The events I chronicle occurred over a period of fifteen years, beginning twenty years ago when Cornelia was fifty-four years of age and her reputation was at its greatest. I was present in Rome for almost all of those fifteen years, but much of what I describe came to me secondhand through interviews and casual conversations. Because of the prestige of my husband and my mother, I had access to almost all the important players in my story, sometimes through close familial ties, sometimes during social gatherings, sometimes when my sources had too much to drink. In a few instances, I have expanded one or two key pieces of information into dramatic scenes far beyond what I might reasonably know. If you feel my imagination or my unabashed bias compromises a history's need for accuracy and objectivity, please forgive me. What was it the Greek playwright Menander said? "Teaching a woman to write is like providing poison to an asp." Should any members of the Roman Senate read this book, I suspect they will say I have proven Menander right. I offer only one excuse; confessing to murder is never easy, as many of those same senators might also attest.

PART I

TIBERIUS

"The plebeians and Senate of Rome were often at strife with each other concerning the enactment of laws, the cancelling of debts, the division of lands, or the election of magistrates. Internal discord did not, however, bring them to blows; there were dissensions and contests within the limits of the law, which they composed by making mutual concessions, and with much respect for each other."

-Appian of Alexandria, *Civil Wars*

CHAPTER 1

My history begins at a time when I still believed in the gods. My brother Tiberius had just returned from military duty in northern Spain. He was twenty-seven and had already shown the promise of his heritage. I had a dinner for him at my home on the east side of the Palatine Hill. It was just family. Tiberius, my brother Gaius, my husband Aemilianus, and Tiberius' recently widowed father-in-law, Appius Claudius Pulcher, reclined on couches on three sides of the table. My mother Cornelia, Tiberius' wife Claudia Pulcheria, and I sat in chairs opposite the men. Gaius had just turned seventeen. I was thirty-four.

The dinner was a celebration. Tiberius had accounted well for himself during what had been a difficult campaign in Numantia, serving as the quaestor for the current consul Gaius Hostilius Mancinus. Rome was all abuzz with several versions of what had happened—not all of which were good. We were anxious to get it directly from Tiberius, but no one more so than Aemilianus, arguably the most powerful man in Rome at the time, both in wealth and political influence.

The meal began with a tray of olives and another of oysters and prawns sprinkled with cumin. The men drank wine from Apulia. Claudia, Cornelia, and I drank posca, apple cider vinegar diluted with water.

Tiberius was in good spirits and, much like my mother, maintained an assured composure when he spoke, projecting confidence without conceit. Even on this evening, when relating the events in Numantia that had catapulted him into the public eye, his manner was calm and thoughtful. "We struggled in combat with the Numantines from the moment we arrived. I wouldn't fault Mancinus. It just seemed that everything that could go wrong did."

Aemilianus, who had already heard some of the early reports, lounged stoically at the head of the table. Of all of us, only he was not outwardly enjoying the evening.

"Toward the end of the summer," continued Tiberius, "we were beaten badly east of the Duero River, not far from Numantia. Mancinus felt the campaign was in danger of becoming a complete failure and evacuated our camp in the middle of the night, leaving much of our baggage behind." Tiberius was a handsome man with curly brown hair, a clean-shaven face, and deep, penetrating brown eyes. He shook his head recalling the situation. "Their scouts saw us leaving. They looted our camp in the morning then put two separate armies on our tail. By noon they were attacking the rear of our train.

"A lot of men were lost, as well as what little baggage we had with us. Combining these attacks with artful maneuvering, the Numantines pinned us into a small valley. Mancinus saw, as every one of us did, that we had little hope of escape. He sent his legates to the Numantine leaders with the intention of negotiating a truce."

"You mean a surrender," said Aemilianus soberly.

Tiberius nodded. "It was either that or having twenty thousand legionnaires surrounded and slaughtered. But their leaders rejected Mancinus' envoys, saying they would only speak to me—because several of them had known our father." He glanced at Gaius and me. "He had shown the Numantines leniency twenty years earlier."

Cornelia smiled at this. "So you became the mediator, Tiberius?"

"Yes, Mother, they trusted me. That's what made the settlement possible. But once we had begun our march back to Italy, I realized that the ledgers I kept as part of my duty as quaestor had been left behind in our camp. Knowing they would be important for documenting what had happened, my friend Laetorius and I rode back to Numantia to see if we could recover the books. Although we were uncertain how this request would be received, we were welcomed at the gate. They returned the ledgers and asked if there were anything else I might want that had been lost. Eager to return to our troops, we asked for nothing more, but when we began to leave, they invited us to a feast with their leaders. Not wanting to insult them, we stayed for the meal, where again they spoke of our father with the highest praise."

Again this pleased Cornelia. "It's always been my desire that you and your brother would follow his example. It seems that you have,

Tiberius." She turned to my younger brother. "And I have no doubt that Gaius will as well."

Aemilianus, a resolutely serious man with a narrow, hawk-like face, sat up from his reclining position. He had said little all evening and had let the rest of us dominate the conversation, but he clearly had something to say now. "Do you believe this is something to be proud of, Tiberius? Surrendering to barbarians?"

"Proud of, sir? No, but we saved the lives of some twenty thousand Romans."

"Twenty thousand men, but they weren't Romans. They were cowards. The reputation of our military is sullied when we openly surrender to uncivilized peoples like the Numantines." He glanced at Gaius to make sure the young man understood, then looked directly at Tiberius. "The review will be tomorrow. The entire thing will be judged dishonorable. Expect the senators to annul your treaty. If they follow precedent, Mancinius and some, if not all, of his officers are likely to be sent back to Numantia as prisoners of war."

Tiberius' wife Claudia visibly paled. Her father, a high-ranking senator and a noted member of the populares, the progressive faction in Roman politics, nodded. "Yes, I'm afraid Aemilianus is right."

Tiberius already knew this was true. The review would be difficult, and he would have to testify.

Cornelia spoke up. "You mean Tiberius could be sent back to Numantia as a prisoner?"

Aemilianus treated no other woman with the respect he gave my mother. She was his aunt and a few years his senior. He had known her all of his life and had done everything for our family after my father's death. "It's possible, Cornelia."

"And what will you say? Your opinion will count for a lot."

"I will say just what I said to Tiberius. Roman armies don't surrender. I will support having the treaty annulled. And I will focus the responsibility on Mancinus, saying he's unqualified to lead an army. I'll request that his imperium be taken away and that he be sent back to the Numantines in chains."

"But, sir, there must be more than one way to look at what happened." Tiberius could disarm you with his openness. "Rome needs soldiers."

"Brave soldiers."

"Of course, sir, but these men were brave. The situation was untenable. Why accept butchery when it's avoidable? Especially when we're so short on legionnaires."

"What do you mean?"

"On the way back from Spain, coming south out of Eturia, I noticed that there were very few small farms owned by Roman citizens. Wealthy men have bought up the little farms and consolidated them into plantations. They use huge teams of slaves to do the work—the same hard farm work that makes Romans into good soldiers. Now those displaced farmers live in Rome with little to do. How can we build our armies when our legionnaires have been moved off the land?" Land ownership meant everything in Rome. Only a man who owned land, no matter how large or small a piece, could enlist in the army. This was Tiberius' point. He looked around the table at the others. "We'll be reduced to hiring mercenaries."

Aemilianus sat back. He knew his cousin, twenty years his junior, was an exceptional young man, but his firmness and conviction had surprised him. "I think I understand what you're saying, Tiberius. Raising citizen armies gets harder with each passing year, but even if you're right, the principle you're defending isn't. Roman armies don't surrender."

Cornelia addressed Aemilianus and Appius. "I haven't done the traveling Tiberius has, but I have witnessed the increase in slaves in the city. Could there be a problem with having so many slaves on our farms?"

"Absolutely," said Appius. "A slave revolt has been going on for months now in Sicily, and we've seen several minor slave uprisings here in Italy. I think Tiberius is right. We depend too much on slaves for our farm work. It undermines the fundamental strength of the state."

Aemilianus lifted his chin haughtily. "I've seen the increase in slaves also. But that isn't what the Senate will be talking about tomorrow." He turned to Tiberius. "Expect a rough day for Mancinus."

Tiberius, Appius, and I were the last to leave the table. The plates of uneaten food had yet to be collected, and the lamps were low on oil, casting the room in wavering shadows. Appius, then in his mid-fifties, leaned up close to the table. He had a long, jowly face, with bright blue eyes and once fair hair gone white.

"I think you touched on something very important this evening, Tiberius." He glanced at me, then back to Tiberius. Appius respected my intelligence in same way that others respected my mother's. "The people are steadily being pushed off the land. The number of slaves working the farms increases every day. Something needs to change. We need land reform of some kind."

Appius tapped a finger on the table. The lamplight flashed in his eyes. "Do you intend to have a political career, Tiberius? This is an issue that could attract a lot of attention. Providing land for displaced farmers would generate some much needed leverage for the populares and significant political influence for you."

Tiberius allowed a smile. "It's more than politics to me, Appius. My concern is for the security of Rome. I haven't really thought about land reform, but maybe I should."

"You could be a tribune of the plebs," said Appius.

I agreed. "No one speaks as well as you, Tiberius."

Tiberius tilted his head in thought. "Yes, I guess that's something to consider."

And that was when the idea first came up. There were ten tribunes of the plebs. They led the People's Assembly and acted as intermediaries between the Senate and the plebeians. The most important positions in the Roman government were the two consuls, the two censors, and the ten tribunes of the plebs. I had no doubt that Tiberius would make an excellent tribune.

CHAPTER 2

At dawn, the morning after my dinner, Hostilius Mancinus gathered a contingent of his officers, including Tiberius, at Mars Field, the military exercise grounds west of Rome. The consul led the men and two of his personal slaves, all on horseback, four miles east along the base of Rome's massive south wall to the temple of Bellona, just east of the city proper. The officers, wearing full battle armor, dismounted beside the obelisk that stood before the temple and gave their horses' reins to the slaves. A crowd of citizens had gathered next to the temple. They moved in close to get a look at Mancinus, expecting him to be rebuked. Something less than the full three hundred senators were fanned out on the temple stairs in their togas talking among themselves.

Publius Scipio Nasica, the pontifex maximus, floated down the temple stairs in a white hooded robe to meet Mancinus, who was already striding across the yard, his purple consul's cloak pinned to his shoulders, a gilded gladius at his hip. The two men exchanged a few words beside the brazier adjacent to the temple altar. Mancinus returned to his officers, and Publius Nasica signaled to a priest standing at the edge of the yard. The man lifted a flute to his lips and began to play. The crowd hushed to silence as a young woman in a white gown, one of the Vestal Virgins, came out of the temple with a torch lit from the sacred flame of Vesta. She used the torch to light the kindling in the brazier. When the fire had taken hold, she sprinkled wine and incense into the fire, causing the flames to jump and hiss, then she backed away to the edge of the group of senators. The crowd around the yard parted and two minor priests, flamines, led an elaborately groomed calf with red fillets tied to its ears and tail to the altar.

Publius Nasica said a prayer to the goddess Bellona, sprinkled some mola, a mixture of wheat and salt, on the calf's back, then used an amphora to dribble a few drops of wine on its head. The pontiff nodded to the priests, and they flipped the squealing calf on its side. One held it down. The other cut its throat with a flint knife. All watched the animal bleed out on the ground. The priest with the knife then slit the calf's belly open from the genitals to the top of its chest. The other priest held the incision open while the one with the knife sorted through the glistening pink entrails. He withdrew and cut free the lungs, the heart, the liver, the kidneys, and the gall bladder, handing them one by one to Publius Nasica, who turned them over in his hands, looking for abnormalities. After a short time, he placed the organs in the brazier and announced, "The Goddess of War has granted us permission to hold this military review. Will the senators lead us into the temple."

Mancinus and his officers were the last to enter the temple. It was a large, very old temple. The review would take place in the windowless central chamber, the cella. Huge oak beams spanned the ceiling. Twenty torches on the walls provided light. The floors were polished marble, laid out in an ornate design of triangles and circles. A mural painted with scenes from famous battles in Rome's history wrapped in a band around the top of the walls. War trophies—shields, helmets, bloodstained swords, lances of all varieties—were mounted throughout the room. A fourteen-foot marble statue of Bellona stood at the north end of the cella. She stood on one foot, the other upraised, with a sword held over her head set to deliver a blow. The senators formed a semicircle at the base of the statue. Marcus Aemilius Porcina, Mancinus' co-consul, sat in his curule chair in front of the senators, wearing a bright white toga trimmed in purple. He would lead the review.

Mancinus walked to the center of the room and faced his peers. He was well aware of what was going to happen. Tiberius and his other officers stood behind him, squeezed in around the perimeter of the room along with the citizens who had come in to watch. Many more were outside, looking in through the doors.

Mancinus told the same story that Tiberius had told our family the night before, but he elaborated heavily on the dire nature of the circumstances, being trapped in a small valley and surrounded by a greatly superior force. "Our choice was to surrender or be cut to pieces," said Mancinus as he concluded his report to a chorus of catcalls from the audience and a smattering of the senators. Amid the commotion, one of the senior senators, Quintus Pompeius, stood and called out to be recognized. Aemilius Porcina raised his hand for quiet, then gave Pompeius the floor.

"Unacceptable, Consul," stated the senator, playing to the crowd. "Surrender is unacceptable under any circumstances. And you must know that the circumstances you described were created by your own poor decisions. I recommend that the Senate annul the Numantine treaty and repeal Mancinus' imperium."

Another elder senator, Titus Annius, wearing an orange, ill-fitting wig, spoke without being recognized. "Mancinus and all of his officers should be shackled and sent back to Numantia. We have no need for these men in Rome."

Several more senators stood to continue the abuse. One demanded exile, another execution. The audience's approval rose with each admonishment. The insults and vulgarity targeting Mancinus knew no limits of decency. Several ripe vegetables sailed through the doorway, splashed on the floor, and slid in a wet mess to Mancinus' feet.

Mancinus was a proud man. He held his polished silver helmet at his side and stared straight ahead through it all. He understood the situation. If his actions were deemed un-Roman, he would accept the judgment in an entirely Roman manner.

Aemilius Porcina stood and again raised his hands to quiet the demonstrations, then asked Mancinus if he had anything to say in his defense.

He answered no.

Porcina addressed the officers in the audience. "Does the consul's staff have anything to add before the Senate votes on the annulment of the treaty?"

None of the senior officers came forward. There was a long ugly pause. The dishonor of the controversial surrender hung in the air like defeat after a battle. Unable to bear the disparagement of the military action he believed was justified, Tiberius, a junior officer, pushed out of the crowd onto the floor.

Aemilianus was seated with the other senators. He had already spoken with several of them prior to the review. He had assembled a majority who would vote to censor Mancinus and exile him to Numantia, but not the rest of the officers. Aemilianus was as rigid as any senator in Rome. He would have sent the entire army back to Numantia, even his young cousin whom he loved, but he had softened his stance out of respect for Cornelia. He had intended to voice his opinion, but deferred when Tiberius came forward.

To Aemilianus' dismay Tiberius repeated what he had said at the dinner table the night before. He recounted what he had seen in Eturia and other parts of north Italy, and how the disappearance of the small farms was making it hard for Rome to fill her legions. "You might call what Mancinus did un-Roman. But I was there. Mancinus saved twenty thousand experienced soldiers at a time when we don't have them to spare. Surrender may have been a crime to our ancestors, but today, in these circumstances, one could easily argue that what he did was in the best interests of the state. He deserves no reprimand."

A peculiarly profound silence followed, not because so many of those present understood the reality of the problem Tiberius was trying to address, but because his brief delivery was so captivating. It wasn't even what he said. It was the character and the clear-seeing mind behind his words that impressed them. No one uttered a peep until he had returned to the cluster of officers along the perimeter. Then mumbling began to percolate around the room. Mancinus stared straight ahead the entire time.

Aemilius Porcina gave Aemilianus the floor. He recommended that the Senate vote to annul the treaty and to place the responsibility entirely on Mancinus. The other officers were not to be punished. Mancinus alone had created the situation and failed to respond properly. He should be sent back to Numantia in chains. Despite many contrary views among the senators, and the disappointment of the audience, Aemilianus' proposal passed and the review was completed.

CHAPTER 3

After the review, while the senators and some of the audience were outside the temple milling around and talking, Aemilianus sought out Tiberius and took him aside.

"That was unwise, Tiberius," he said angrily. "I'm not sure what you were trying to prove in there, but that little speech of yours nearly undermined all my efforts to prevent you from being sent back to Numantia with Mancinus. Fortunately, I had a motion on the floor before any of the other senators got a chance to lash out at you."

Tiberius' first military campaign had been under Ameilianus' command. He respected no man more than my husband, and his words hurt, but Tiberius still believed he was right. "But what I said was true, sir, and needed to be said. We have populated Italy with slaves and don't have enough citizens with land of their own to fill our legions. It will kill the Republic."

The retort only enraged Aemilianus further. "What will kill the Republic are armies filled with cowards."

"But you do recognize what I'm saying is true. Some portion of those at the review did."

Aemilianus clenched his fists in frustration. He had no children of his own. Tiberius was like a son to him. "I won't argue that with you," he said in exasperation. "But you were sticking up for a man about to be exiled after I had spent the morning convincing my colleagues that he alone was responsible. You made me look like a fool."

"I was Mancinus' quaestor, sir. I was standing up for my senior officer. It's what a good officer does."

"And while you were so intent on cutting your own throat, I was trying to protect you."

Tiberius hung his head. He knew he had embarrassed Aemilianus and taken a huge risk by stepping forward. But he also felt strongly about what he had said and that he had needed to say it.

Aemilianus turned away and left Tiberius standing by himself at the edge of the crowd. Appius Claudius had been watching from a distance. He was an outlier in his own right. Eight years earlier he had asked the Senate for permission to celebrate a triumph for his defeat of the Salassi, a barbarian tribe in foothills of the Alps. When one of the tribunes of the plebs vetoed his request, he decided to celebrate the triumph anyway. As soon as Appius entered the city with his troops, the tribune tried to physically stop him. Appius' eldest daughter, one of the Vestal Virgins to whom the law gave special protection, stepped in between the tribune and her father like a human shield. The tribune backed off and the triumph continued. It was the first time anyone had ignored a tribune's veto—and it was only the sacrosanct position of the Vestal that allowed it to happen.

Appius approached Tiberius and put his hand on his son-in-law's shoulder. "Let me guess what that was about."

Tiberius nodded gravely. "He was right. Speaking out for a man on a skewer can be dangerous."

"True enough, Tiberius, but did you see how the audience reacted to your insight about the land?"

Tiberius smiled. "Yes, particularly in the eyes of those around the perimeter of the room. Not all of them understood, but many did—even with the little I said."

Appius nodded. "You might want to do some research on the subject. Right now your ideas are based on too little observation. And be aware that this idea has been touched on before—by Aemilianus' friend, Gaius Laelius."

"I didn't know that."

"You were probably ten or eleven years old. Laelius tested the Senate with a plan for land reform. It got nowhere and he gained quite a few enemies. The wealthy plantation owners like having their land. And your cousin saw that firsthand."

Tiberius nodded.

"Get the opinion of others, Tiberius. Then go out into Italy. See for yourself. Ask questions. Find out who owns the land and what it's being used for."

"It's possible the problem only exists in the north."

"Find out. I'd like to know more about this myself. Tell me what you discover. I see land reform as a good way to make our side of the Senate relevant again."

CHAPTER 4

Tiberius followed Appius' advice. He began by inviting Diophanes of Mytilene and Gaius Blossius of Cumae to meet him at Cornelia's home in Rome. Both men were tutors my mother had hired for our educations. Diophanes taught rhetoric, and of all our tutors, he surely had the most influence on us. Because of him we could speak clearly and convincingly. Blossius, a stoic from the school of Antipater of Tarsus, taught us history and philosophy. He turned us all into populists, which I am sure was what my mother intended. Both men were in their sixties now. Diophanes was frail and mostly bald with a long white beard. Blossius was too heavy, given to leisure, wine, and strong opinions. I was at the house that day visiting my mother when the two men arrived. Tiberius was in the library. His personal slave, Helios, a brown-skinned Cretan who had attended to him since childhood, waited outside on the street.

Tiberius opened the discussion by describing what he had seen while traveling in north Italy, then posed the idea of land reform. Both men grasped the significance of the situation immediately.

"Brilliant insight," blurted out Blossius, who had already served himself a cup of wine.

"And critical to Rome's future," added Diophanes in his perfect orator's voice. "No army fights better than one of landed citizens. It's the foundation of Rome's military success."

Tiberius nodded, pleased by his advisors' response. "So, if I were planning a political career based on a platform of land reform, where would I start? What actions should I propose in order to engage the people?"

Again Blossius was first to respond. "Offer to give the landless citizens small pieces of property. Enough to raise and feed a family, say twenty or thirty iugera."

"But where would that land come from?"

"The public land," answered Diophanes. "There's a lot of it, all over the peninsula, won by the conquests of the last one hundred years—most of it yet to be distributed in any way—some of it still held by those Rome took it from. Not all of it's farmland, but quite a bit of it is."

"And those large plantations you saw in the north, Tiberius." Blossius refilled his cup from an amphora on the table. "Isn't there a law that limits how much land a man can own?"

"That rings true."

"Absolutely," said Diophanes. "Two hundred years ago Lex Licinia Sextia established limits for both land—five hundred iugera—and livestock—I believe, one hundred cattle and one hundred sheep."

"And many of the wealthier Romans have surely exceeded those limits," said Tiberius. "Whatever land they have over that limit could be reclaimed and given to those without?"

"But most of those large landowners are senators," said Diophanes.

Blossius ignored the comment. "So you're talking about a massive redistribution of both public and private lands."

"Yes," stated Tiberius. "Yes."

Cornelia and I were seated on a bench in the atrium when the men's rapid exchanges caught our attention. Cornelia stood and motioned for me to follow her.

"I'm sure the senators will be very pleased when you offer to give their property away," said Cornelia, gliding into the conversation. In most Roman homes this would have been considered inappropriate. Women did not join the men in serious discussion—except in my family, where debate was always open to anyone with an opinion.

Tiberius welcomed us with his usual graciousness. "What are you saying, Mother?"

Blossius was stretched out on a one-armed couch. He lifted his cup to Cornelia. Diophanes, standing, acknowledged her presence with a nod and a smile. Both men had long respected my mother for her intelligence and insight.

Cornelia came all the way into the room. Always well-dressed in an understated manner, she wore a white tunic beneath a white stola, with an overfold at the waist, held in place by a gauzy saffron sash. A matching pala draped around her shoulders and arms. Her fair but graying hair framed her face from ear to ear in an elaborate fan of cylindrical rolls, a style she tended to maintain as part of her matronly image, that also excluded face paint and jewelry. "Expect some resistance, Tiberius. That's all I'm saying."

"But wouldn't the senators see the reason for it, Mother? Both Aemilianus and Appius do—and certainly they have more land than the law allows."

"Yes, I'm sure they understand the need, but you haven't told them it's their land you want to give away. Be prepared for a different response."

"We could start with the unclaimed land. I have looked into that somewhat. It's as Diophanes says. There's a lot of it—with huge pieces used as open pasture for cattle and sheep. The ownership is unclear at best."

"But at some point you'll have to redistribute land that has been claimed?"

"Only if the owner has more than the legal limit," said Blossius. "There must be some equity in the ownership of land. Democracy is weakened when too few have too much. The addition of slaves makes it worse. Land reform will only work if it's portrayed as being good for the state."

"He's right, Mother. We have just punished Mancinus for being un-Roman. In my view, Rome is on the verge of becoming un-Roman."

"I understand the problem, and I, like both your wise advisors, agree with what you're saying. Land reform is necessary." She looked at each of the men, and then to me. "But if you're planning a political strategy, part of it is knowing who the opposition is before entering the arena. Your preparation must include talking to a few large landowners prior to announcing your platform. Aemilianus, Appius, Publius Crassus, and his brother Mucius Scaevola—these are all important men with lots of land. They're also men who respect you and will listen to you. Find out what they think. Once you have their support, talk to others, people you know might resist."

"Appius was the first to suggest land reform to me. I know what he thinks. He believes as we do."

"One thing Greek history has taught us," said Blossius, "is that those who stand up to men of power suffer the consequences."

"Maybe in Greece, but not in Rome," stated Tiberius. "Men have argued viciously in the Senate for four hundred years and never has it come to blows."

"Besides," added Diophanes, "this is legislation that will appeal heavily to the populace. There is power in this kind of political action. Mobilizing the common man is at the heart of all real democracies. What you've got here in Rome is a bunch of wealthy senators handing the consulship back and forth among their friends, hardly the democratic ideal."

Cornelia laughed. "Very good, Diophanes. But we have a real world to deal with here. Will you also put a limit on the number of slaves a man can own? Would that not also be necessary?"

Tiberius looked around at his friends.

"Of course," I said. "Slaves are a big part of it, Tiberius. You've said that from the beginning."

"But you wouldn't want to limit the number of slaves right away," said Cornelia. "You'll have to do one thing at a time to have any chance of success. Work out the details of what you want to do, come up with a well-thought-out policy, and know that your biggest obstacle will be a handful of the wealthiest and most powerful men in the Senate."

"Sound advice, Cornelia," said Diophanes. "What fool thought to keep women out of the discourse?"

"Only a man who had not met my mother," said Tiberius.

CHAPTER 5

Cornelia was the fourth and last surviving child from one of Rome's most famous couples. Her father Africanus had defeated Hannibal; her mother Aemilia came from one of Rome's five original families. Their offspring were considered to be among the chosen. All were given the advantage of wealth and a superior education, but only Cornelia excelled as a student and made a point of carrying on our family's dedication to literature and art.

Publius, Cornelia's oldest brother, twenty years her senior, was born sickly and never achieved either military or political distinction. Married with no children into his late thirties, Publius adopted my future husband Aemilianus, then died two years later, the same year that I was born. He was forty.

Her brother Lucius, three years younger than Publius, seemed to have more potential, earning the cognomen Asiaticus for minor military success in Syria where he was a praetor. But Lucius fell victim to the luxuries of the Asian lifestyle and gained a reputation for intemperance and debauchery, something entirely anathema to my grandfather's way of thinking. When Lucius returned to Rome after his time in Syria, he was immediately accepted into the Senate, only to be cast out two years later because of dissolute living. Lucius, who never married, died two years after that at the age of thirty-four. He was considered a black mark on a family that had always been among Rome's finest.

My mother's sister, another Cornelia, was twelve years her senior and like Publius was not of robust health. She married her cousin Publius Cornelius Scipio Nasica at the age of eighteen, had two nonsurviving children, then died at the age of twenty-two giving birth to Cornelia's nephew Publius Nasica, a man who plays no small part in this history.

Of the four children, Cornelia was the only one who was exceptional in any way. Being the youngest child, and only seven years old at the time of her father's death, she received special attention from Aemilia, who took a more active part in Cornelia's education than she had for the other children. Cornelia flourished under her mother's supervision and immediately showed an aptitude for language, learning to read and speak Greek by the age of ten. It is a shame that Africanus, who was so disappointed with his two sons, did not live long enough to see Cornelia blossom into the woman she became.

One story I heard from my grandmother when I was very young, presumably to inspire me, spoke to Cornelia's remarkable intellectual maturity as a youth. Upon learning Greek, she promptly fell in love with Homer and quickly read both *The Iliad* and *The Odyssey*. One evening when Aemilia had a large dinner party, in which Cornelia was included though only twelve, one of the guests asked Cornelia to demonstrate her Greek. She stood from her chair, and without the presumption of a precocious child, recited the story of Odysseus and the Cyclops with unusual poise and humility. The image of my mother, as a young girl, holding a room of much older men and women spellbound with her perfect Greek, never left me, and even when she was older and well into her sixties, I could always imagine that somewhere inside her was that confident young girl—who I had always hoped to be.

CHAPTER 6

Several days after the discussion of land reform at Cornelia's home I brought up the topic with Aemilianus. We had eaten the evening meal together in the triclinium. As was too common, neither of us had said a word during the meal. He was about to leave the table when I stopped him with a question.

"Do you think wealthy plantation owners are pushing plebeians off the land? Is that really a problem?"

Our marriage had never been a good one. I had a hard time getting pregnant. Three times I had miscarried before six months had passed. We also lost an infant in the child's first year. My painful ankle and now noticeable limp only made things worse.

Aemilianus hesitated for a moment, as though considering whether he would deign to answer me. He stood up and straightened his tunic. He was a big man, imposing and stern, with a weather-hardened face from a career as a soldier. "No," he said with force, and some irritation, before turning away to leave the room.

I stood up with difficulty. "Truly? You seemed to agree with Tiberius that night we had my family over for dinner."

Aemilianus glared at me. "I hadn't had time to think about it then. Why would you care?"

Too many of our conservations went this way. He treated my mother with deference, but not me. "It came up the other day when I was at my mother's villa. Tiberius was talking about it with Diophanes and Blossius. They agreed with him, even added to his argument. He wants to pursue a platform of land reform."

"That would be foolish. Laelius tried that fifteen years ago. It nearly ruined his career." Aemilianus continued out of the triclinium, signaling the conversation was over. I followed him into the atrium.

"Isn't there a lot of unclaimed public land that could be given to citizens without?"

Aemilianus turned on me with an ugly look, his way of shutting me up.

"What about the law that no citizen should own more than five hundred iugera?" I persisted. "Certainly many of the wealthier senators have accumulated more than that?"

He ignored the question and walked across the atrium to the library.

I called after him. "I think Tiberius is right. I think something needs to be done."

"Who would care what you think, Sempronia?"

And that ended it. My husband's response reminded me of what Cornelia had said about trying to take land away from the rich and powerful. Our land holdings were much greater than five hundred iugera, and Aemilianus, one of the most progressive men in the Senate, was already hedging his bets.

CHAPTER 7

In the elections that winter, Aemilianus, considered the best military mind in Rome, was elected to the position of consul for a second time, specifically to go to Numantia to put the "impudent barbarians in their place." He went to Spain in the spring. My brother Gaius, then entering his first year of military service, went with him as an equestrian in one of Aemilianus' four legions. Tiberius had gone to Africa with Aemilianus twelve years earlier. Now Gaius had the opportunity to spend time in a military camp with Aemilianus as an extension of his education.

But Aemilianus was more than a soldier. Following in the tradition established by my grandfather, Aemilianus was an advocate of Greek knowledge and education in general. He owned the largest collection of Greek scrolls in Italy, something he had inherited from his natural father Aemilius Paullus, who had brought the collection back from Greece after defeating the Macedonian king Perseus. Thirty thousand scrolls now filled Aemilianus' library, making it the most renowned in Rome. Aemilianus invited scholars from all over the world to come to our home to discuss literature, philosophy, and science. The library was a big part of it. The Greek historian Polybius lived in Rome and was a fixture at these gatherings, as were the playwright Lucilius, the stoic philosopher Panaetius of Rhodes, and the tragic poet Pacuvius. Cornelia was present at many of these gatherings, and so was I.

During Aemilianus' time in Spain that year, such was Cornelia's esteem among Rome's intellectual elite that she took on the role of organizing these roundtable discussions that took place in Aemilianus' library. At the third gathering with Cornelia acting as hostess and facilitator, King Ptolemy VIII of Egypt, who was in Rome for business, made a surprise appearance at the circle, arriving in his gold embossed carriage with ten slaves and ten bodyguards.

Egypt at this time existed as two Roman provinces. King Ptolemy VIII, known as Physcon—an allusion to his large girth—ruled the western province of Cyrenaica, his brother the eastern province of Ludaea. In the year after my father's death, Physcon was nearly killed in an assassination attempt by his brother. Physcon immediately came to Rome to demand that the Senate remove his sibling. Although his plea was dismissed, he met my mother at a dinner party while he was in Rome. She was thirty-five years old at the time, still a very attractive woman, and widely known for her intelligence and grace. Physcon, then twenty-seven and not unhandsome, made an effort to court Cornelia. One of the wealthiest men in the world, he had a certain charm and spent many afternoons with Cornelia talking about history and literature. What intimacy they might have shared I never knew, but just before he left Rome for Cyrenaica, he asked Cornelia to marry him and share his crown. It was a huge honor, and many of her friends advised her to accept, but out of respect for her recently deceased husband, she had already pledged not to remarry and declined the king's proposal. A man accustomed to getting what he wanted, Physcon was uncommonly gracious, but he hoped Cornelia might change her mind with time, and for nearly twenty years now he visited her whenever his business brought him back to Rome.

Since his last visit two years earlier, he had married twice, both times to his sisters. The day of the second marriage he had his brother murdered to consolidate his power in the two Egyptian provinces. Then to make sure there was no male heir, he had his other sister's twelve-year-old son killed and sent to her in small pieces. Cornelia was aware of all of this and, of course, found it unsettling.

She was in the peristyle with me cutting flowers for that evening's gathering when my Numidian housemaid Nadia came out to the garden. She was an unusually quiet woman, ten years younger than I, with dark skin and curly black hair that she kept in a long thick braid. "The King of Egypt is here to see your mother," she announced.

Cornelia enjoyed Physcon, but his visits were invariably unannounced and always put her on edge, this one all the more so because of the recent regime changes. I remained in the garden so she could have some time alone with Physcon. She greeted him in the entrance hall with her bouquet of freshly cut flowers.

"Flowers for me, how thoughtful," said the king with a tip of his head.

Cornelia waved the flowers at him as though she were going to hit him. "They're not for you. We're having a circle this evening. You're welcome to stay. I believe you know most of those who'll attend."

"Yes, that's why I'm here. Polybius told me about it. I came early so that I might have some time with you."

"We have until the guests begin to arrive."

"Then I'll get to the point." He smiled. "You know there is no woman in the world I consider more beautiful than you." He embraced her and kissed her on both sides of her face.

"Your eyesight must be going, Physcon."

"No, not at all. You have a radiance well beyond ordinary vision."

"That must be why it doesn't show in my mirror."

"You're making fun of me when I'm being serious." He gazed at her, drawing air through his mouth, always being a little short of breath. He wore a long robe of red velvet, embroidered at the neckline, cuffs, and hem with gold wire and dotted here and there with tiny pearls. Its voluminous size disguised any sense of the shape of his body except that there was more of it than before. "There is a word that comes from the Far East, India I believe, *darshan*." He struggled down to one knee. "It means to bask in the radiance of a holy person. That's how I feel in your presence."

Cornelia knew exactly where this was headed.

Physcon opened his hand, revealing a brilliant blue sapphire atop a ring of white gold. "Will you marry me, Cornelia? It's the only way I can ever be happy."

"You already have a wife, Physcon. Why are you doing this?"

"She's my sister. That's no marriage. It's politics. And something I can dissolve with the snap of my fingers. All I need is a reason." He allowed her to give him a hand as he rose to his feet. "And you are my reason." He had large expressive eyes, full round cheeks, and a mischievous smile. He had to know she would say no, but his smile denied it.

"Nothing has changed. I still intend to honor my husband." Cornelia walked away, headed back to the peristyle.

Physcon followed her through the atrium. It was a warm day in early summer. Sunlight shone through the portico casting shadows in wide stripes across the glazed terracotta tiles. "If you won't marry me," he said on drawing up alongside of her, "could we at least make love?"

Cornelia would have slapped any other man, but she knew Physcon too well and simply ignored him. "I'm surprised you're here for the circle. Last I heard you threw all the intellectuals out of Alexandria. I know you didn't do that to please me."

Physcon took a deep breath. "It wasn't because of what they were teaching. It was their politics."

"Almost all of them were Greek scholars. You've no need for democracy in Egypt?"

Physcon smiled sadly. "I can't fool you, Cornelia. I never could."

The sound of others coming into the house stopped their conversation. Nadia announced Polybius and Blossius. Polybius was lean and angular; Blossius, a somewhat smaller version of Physcon, already had a cup in his hand. As they gathered in the atrium, Cornelia introduced her guests. "King Ptolemy, I believe you know these men."

Each man gave the slightest tip of his head.

"I prefer the title of pharaoh, Cornelia."

"My apologies, Pharaoh. Let's go into the library. Maybe we can open your mind to philosophy again."

"I'm more interested in what your son is doing," quipped Physcon.

"You're thinking of land reform in Egypt?" asked Polybius.

"Only that which her majesty the Nile chooses."

"I can tell we're in for an interesting gathering," said Blossius, slopping wine out of his cup as he led the way to the storied library. "It's a shame Aemilianus can't be here. His wit will be missed."

I heard their voices and went to the front of the house to join them. My home was one of the grander villas on the Palatine Hill and suitably decorated with the many trophies and pieces of artwork Aemilianus had brought back from his military campaigns. Like most of the homes of the Roman upper class, the house was laid out around the atrium, in our case an expansive two-story rectangular enclosure, defined by its portico of hand-painted columns and open to the sky for light. An ornamental pool caught rain in the center of the atrium and rooms of varied uses—the triclinium for dining, a small sewing and weaving room for making clothing, and several bed chambers for guests—lined the east and west sides. The south side opened onto the peristyle and a garden. On the north were the home's main entry and a thick plank door leading out to the street.

Aemilianus' library was the largest room off the atrium. Its thirty thousand scrolls were stored on three walls in three-foot deep, floor-to-ceiling wooden racks, four scrolls to a niche, their ivory or ebony umbilicuses protruding just enough to pull them out. To prolong their life, the papyrus scrolls had been anointed in the oil of the cedar tree and filled the room with a sweet camphorous scent. Two walls were devoted to works in Greek, one wall to those in Latin. A small stool was available to help reach the highest racks. A bust of my grandfather sat on a pedestal in a cutout on the west wall. A portrait of Aemilius Paullus hung opposite it on the east wall. A large wooden table with four wooden chairs sat in the center of the room for unrolling and reading the scrolls. Slots cut high on the east wall accessed light from the atrium in the morning. Two oil lamps provided light the rest of the day.

One of the most fascinating objects in Aemilianus' library, beyond the collection of rare scrolls and the knowledge within, was a device that Aemilianus referred to as a terrella. About the size of a round of cheese, it sat on a shelf in the corner of the library and invariably caught the attention of anyone entering the room. Physcon was immediately drawn to it.

"This looks interesting," he said, approaching the large bronze globe encircled by seven smaller globes on wire hoops.

All of us but Physcon knew the story behind it. Polybius the historian did the honors. "It's a model of the solar system, Pharaoh, as imagined by the Greek Aristarchus of Samos. It's unique because he places the Sun at the center instead of the Earth. The Sun's the large globe. The planets and the moon are the smaller ones." Polybius gave the globe a spin with his hand and all the smaller globes moved around it in their orbits.

"The Greek mathematician Archimedes of Syracuse made this terrella a hundred years ago. Claudius Marcellus brought it back from Sicily after his siege of Syracuse." This was all material covered in Polybius' latest book, which detailed Rome's rise to world power. He had completed the massive history the previous summer. It was immediately called genius. He was considered one of the wisest men alive. He had been one of my tutors. I considered him a friend, and felt fortunate to know him.

"Aemilianus," I said, "received it as a gift from Marcellus' grandson after the fall of Carthage."

The king pointed to the ceramic tank that stood beside the terrella. "What's this for?"

"It's filled with water," said Polybius, "and attached to the globe by this small waterwheel." He touched the tiny connective gears, then pulled an empty bucket from the shelf below and positioned it on the floor. The tank had a stopcock. Polybius opened it, allowing a stream of water to pour over the waterwheel and into the bucket. The large globe began to rotate—along with all the smaller globes—like a fantastic water-driven toy. Physcon was mesmerized, as were all of us—and I had seen the device in action scores of times.

Physcon stood back. "Where are the stars?"

Polybius looked to Cornelia and smiled, apparently the circle had begun. "When Marcellus returned from Syracuse, he returned with two large spheres. He kept this one at his home." He touched the big bronze sphere. "He placed the other, also made by Archimedes, in the temple of Virtus as a gift to the state. Have any of you seen it?"

Cornelia had, but none of the rest of us.

"That one is a blown glass sphere with the stars painted on the surface—to create a map of the heavens. The placement of the stars is based on charts made hundreds of years ago by Babylonian astrologers. Archimedes got the idea from the Greek geometer Thales of Samos. It's large enough that the terrella could fit inside. Try to imagine that. The bronze spheres inside would rotate as they do here, while the glass sphere would turn at its own rate on the outside. We might consider that a rough model of the universe—our solar system surrounded by a halo of stars."

Physcon put a finger to his lips, tilted his head, and pondered Polybius' description. After an extended silence, he nodded. "Yes, I think I can imagine that. But what goes on outside the sphere of stars? How far does the universe extend beyond that?"

Polybius laughed. "That's not a question a historian can answer."

"Then who can?"

"Only a very brave philosopher," replied Blossius. "And there are probably as many of them as there are answers to the question."

CHAPTER 8

During the next six months, Tiberius surveyed the Italian countryside and talked to landowners. As he had assumed, there was a lot of undistributed public land. Much of it had been farmland, but now it was mostly open pasture, especially in the south. Local ranchers moved their herds through these pastures with the changing seasons at no cost, making cattle and sheep considerably more profitable than growing wheat or other grains. Herds well into the hundreds were not uncommon. The Lex Licinia Sextia livestock restrictions appeared to have been ignored as thoroughly as the land limits. Enforcing this seemingly forgotten law would have to be addressed as part of land reform.

When Tiberius returned to Rome, he went straight to Diophanes and Blossius to discuss his findings. He also enlisted the advice of his father-in-law Appius Claudius and Publius Crassus, whose daughter was promised to Gaius. Both men were influential senators connected to the populares and knew Tiberius' talents. They were as eager to see Tiberius get into politics as his tutors were. Crassus' brother Marcus Scaevola, also a senator and one of Rome's best legal minds, sat in one afternoon with Appius and Crassus to help Tiberius write the first draft of the bill. Now with a plan to promote, he could begin his campaign to become a tribune of the plebs.

The tribune position had been created three hundred and fifty years earlier as a reaction to the aristocracy's control of the government. When the Republic was first formed, all of the most important positions in Rome, religious and political, were restricted to patricians, men of the highest class. Fifteen years later, the entire population of plebs took over the Aventine Hill, refusing to move until they had some kind of representation in the process of governing. As part of the ensuing compromise, the position of tribune was created to act as a intermediary between the people and the Senate. When first enacted, the People's Assembly, a voting body restricted to plebeians, elected two tribunes. Two hundred years later it became five. Currently ten men are elected annually to form what is called the tribunate.

Any single tribune or collection of them can call the People's Assembly together. One or all can convene the Senate to discuss legislation that will later go to the Assembly for a vote. A tribune can also veto a public action or remove a magistrate from office. A tribuneship is a powerful position and is considered sacrosanct. Interfering with a tribune in any way can result in being exiled from Rome. When Appius' daughter stepped between her father and a tribune to stop his veto, it was unprecedented—one protected individual confronting another. Surprisingly no criminal charge was made against Appius' daughter, something that would become an important issue in the near future.

When Tiberius told me he was going to make his first public appearance, I decided to attend. It would be in the comitium, the sunken amphitheater at the west end of the forum. He would announce his candidacy and present his platform of land reform. He was an excellent orator. That was something Cornelia had demanded of all of us—that we could speak clearly, accurately, and with force. As a woman, I never had any use of this in public. It was worth even less in my marriage—Aemilianus' word could not be questioned—but because of Diophanes, I was capable of appreciating a good speech when I heard one.

Women rarely go to the forum. I rarely went out at all. With my ankle it would be a challenge, but I was determined to go—and to go alone and not in my litter, so as not to be noticed. It was a somewhat dangerous thing to do, so I borrowed Nadia's hooded, raw wool cloak to disguise myself, and as discreetly as I could, made my way across the city to the forum.

The forum is a large, rectangular plaza that stretches from the temple of Vesta at the east end to the base of the Capitoline Hill at the west end. Near the center is a large black rock that marks the tomb of Romulus, the founder of Rome. Stores, banks, and other commercial buildings line the north and south perimeters.

When I reached the comitium, Tiberius stood off to one side of the speakers' platform, waiting for a man who had an audience of less than twenty to say his piece. The platform itself is a bit of Roman history. It was made from six brass rostra—ramming beaks—taken from ships sunken two hundred years earlier at the battle of Antium. The rostra and the Senate building, called the Curia, sat directly opposite each other on the upper lip of the circular comitium so that speakers on the Curia steps or at the rostra could address those in the huge bowl-shaped amphitheater below.

It was October. The sun was out, but it was cool and breezy. The large white clouds in the west were overhead by the time Tiberius finally stood up to the rostra to address whoever would listen. He took a moment to survey his meager audience. Then he looked off at the men moving about in the forum whom he hoped to draw in. He had no idea I had come to watch.

"How many of you own land?" Tiberius called out to those who could hear him.

None of the men in the amphitheater responded. Tiberius shouted the question again, louder. A few men in the forum standing close to the comitium perimeter turned to look at him.

"How many of you have known a soldier's life?" Tiberius asked his audience.

Most of the handful of men in the amphitheater shouted back that they had. Several others standing around the amphitheater perimeter did the same. One man yelled back, "What of it?"

"There is an honor to being a legionnaire," Tiberius answered. "And there's an honor to being a Roman citizen, and it comes with the pride of owning land and supporting your family off that land."

Several of those few who were listening responded with a mixed chorus of agreement. A single man stood up. "So what's that mean for those of us without land? Are we not citizens?" A second man followed with, "Are you saying we're nothing?"

"No, not at all," answered Tiberius. "I'm saying just the opposite—that you should have land. And that every citizen deserves a piece of land to call his own. Some of you might have had land when you enlisted, but have since sold it or have so small a piece of land it can't support your family. That's a problem in my opinion."

And it was. As men sold their land or lost it to economic pressure, they were no longer eligible to serve in the military—the greatest honor of being a Roman citizen. Several of the men along the amphitheater rim began to filter down the stairs and take seats. They were not sure where Tiberius was headed, but he had gotten their attention.

I worked my way through the crowd to the edge of the comitum so that I could hear Tiberius more easily. He appraised his growing audience then continued, speaking louder and with more passion. "The beasts that prowl about Italy have holes and lurking places where they can make their beds. But many of you who have fought and suffered injury for Rome enjoy but the blessings of air and light. These alone are your heritage. Landless, perhaps even homeless, you wander to and fro with your wives and children with little more than the clothes on your back."

More people gathered along the top edge of the amphitheater, drawn in by the tone in Tiberius' voice. This was how it always was. A speaker had to be provocative enough to gather an audience, and Tiberius was fully aware of that.

"Our generals are in the habit of inspiring their soldiers to combat by exhorting them to repel the enemy in defense of their tombs and ancestral shrines. The appeal is an idle prompt to most of you. You cannot point to a paternal altar to protect. You have no ancestral tomb. You have no land at all."

The hubbub increased. More seats began to fill. Tiberius' opening lines rang of something that they knew was true but had never really thought about.

"And yet you are still willing to fight and die so that a very few might accumulate land and wealth," Tiberius continued. "We Romans are called the masters of the world, but there is no clod of earth that you can call your own. Isn't the man who has a stake in his nation—a piece of its land—more likely to be devoted to the security of the state?"

"Yes, of course," shouted a man at the back of the amphitheater, "but what do you intend to do about it?"

"Give land to every man without."

Several of those in the audience laughed as this audacious answer, but it also drew more in. *Who was this man? And what was he talking about? Giving land away?*

"How can you possibly do that?" came out of the gathering crowd that now filled more than a quarter of the comitium.

"There's plenty of undistributed land all over Italy, and there are also men with more land than Roman law allows. These same men have been steadily buying up your small farms and using slaves to do the work that you or your father used to do. You've all seen it. You know what I'm talking about. It's the reason your grandfather or your father or you yourself sold your property and moved into the city."

Tiberius went on to lay out his plan for land reform. By the time his speech was drawing to a close the entire comitium was filled. But the audience was not just old soldiers and the landless denizens of the street. Here and there I recognized noted senators in the crowd, most of them frowning, uncertain what to make of this man at the rostra.

"If what I've said makes sense to you," called out Tiberius in conclusion, "if it rings true, remember the name Tiberius Gracchus when it comes time to elect this year's tribunes. Given the opportunity I will find a piece of land for every landless Roman in Italy. It will give purpose to your lives and at the same time increase the size and loyalty of the Roman army. What's good for the people is also good for the Republic. Long live Rome," he shouted, then left the rostra.

Many of those in the audience surrounded Tiberius as he made his way from the rostra to the forum, asking him questions and patting him on the back. Tiberius responded as best he could as he pushed his way ahead, knowing he had accomplished what he wanted.

After Tiberius had broken free from the crowd, I trailed after him as he headed east across the forum. I wanted to congratulate him, but with my ankle I was losing ground. All of a sudden our cousin Publius Nasica, the pontifex maximus—the highest position in the Roman religious hierarchy—and some twenty years older than my brother, came out of the crowd right in front of Tiberius so that he had to stop and face him.

"Bold words, Tiberius. But foolish. What you're dangling before the masses will never happen." He was a short thick man, with a full beard and an arrogant manner. "Take some good advice from your cousin. Forget your radical politics and give up your false promises."

Tiberius was a powerfully built man with a reputation as a more than capable soldier. While in Africa with Aemilianus, he had been one of the first wave of men to surmount the walls of Carthage. But Tiberius was not a hothead and he responded without undo emotion or bluster. "What I am proposing, Publius, is not a radical idea. It's what Rome must do to maintain her supremacy in the world. Yes, some men, perhaps like yourself, who have bought up more than their share of land, will have to give some of it up, but they should be proud to do so as part of their patriotic duty."

Publius Nasica glared at him. "I don't think so, Tiberius. I've invested a lot of money and labor into my property. No one's taking it away."

"Yes, that's the case for almost every large landowner. But the law limits land holdings to five hundred iugera. This is not an idea built in the clouds. It's part of our constitution. Distributing private land won't be easy, but men like you will be compensated. And our nation will be stronger for it."

Tiberius attempted to move past the pontiff and continue on his way. Publius put his hand on Tiberius' shoulder. Those around them in the forum sensed the tension and backed away creating a ring around the two men. Tiberius was not intimidated. Instead of forcefully taking the man's hand from his shoulder, he embraced the pontiff, and whispered into his ear, "Let's save this for after I'm elected, cousin. Then we can have our discussion properly on the floor of the Senate."

Tiberius then released the pontiff and continued on through the crowd, leaving Publius Nasica frustrated by how easily his cousin had diffused the situation. By this time I had caught up with Tiberius. As soon as he walked away from the confrontation, I pushed the hood off my head and called out to him. "Well done, brother." I came up alongside of him, trying my best to keep up.

"Sempronia! You heard me! Thank you for making the effort." He slowed his pace seeing that I was having trouble.

"I saw you with our cousin. I think he was looking for something more than an embrace."

Tiberius laughed. "My task will not be easy. Publius is just one of many who will have strong objections. But with the promise of land, I will have solid support from the populace. You were watching. You saw their response. It needs to happen."

I smiled at him. "You don't need to convince me. I understood the wisdom of land reform from the beginning. But even men like my husband are unsettled by the idea of giving up anything they feel they have earned."

"You've spoken more with Aemilianus?"

I nodded. "He's knows the difficulties you're going to face. I think he's worried about you—and his property."

Tiberius took a deep breath. "I need him on my side. Can you help him understand that?"

"My opinion doesn't count for much, Tiberius. You listen to me, but Aemilianus doesn't."

"You seem to be in pain, Sempronia. Are you all right?"

"I can manage. It's fine."

"You're not fine," he said, then waved to a man leading an empty carriage and paid him to take me back to my house. When I got home, I could barely make it from the carriage to the front door. I went to my bedroom to look at my ankle. It was badly swollen and beginning to turn in on itself, much as it had when I was an infant.

Nadia heated some water and put it in a bucket for me. Aemilianus had returned from Numantia a few weeks earlier, so I soaked my ankle until the time I expected him to come home. Then I wrapped the ankle with linen bandages for support and strapped on my sandal.

CHAPTER 9

After announcing that he would run for tribune, Tiberius began posting tracts that described his platform throughout Rome and the nearby villages. Aemilianus entered the house one night with one of them gripped in his hand. He stormed through the atrium and cursed to Jupiter at my "foolhardy" brother. The sound of his arrival brought me from the peristyle to the atrium.

"Did you see this?" He held out the poster and shook it in his hand. "Tiberius seems to have lost all the sense I once thought he had. He's going to end up dragging me into this mess. I should have let them send him back to Numantia with Mancinus."

I knew about the posters, but I had not read one yet. Aemilianus threw the balled up piece of papyrus at me. It landed at my feet on the tile floor. I had to bend over to pick it up. My awkwardness and pain were obvious. Aemilianus glared at me. "What's wrong with you?"

Up to this point I had disguised the extreme difficulty I was having. When he had first commented on my limping, I told him I had turned my ankle. Now as I stood and regained my composure he was staring at me. "I turned it again, Aemilianus. It's still very sore."

He waged his head in frustration and stomped off to the library. I could not tell what infuriated him more, me or Tiberius' platform.

Aemilianus came to my bed the next morning at sunrise. I had yet to bear him a child, and despite my repeated failures, he was determined to keep trying. It was obligatory on his part and cold duty on mine. I had lost all affection for the man long ago. Our marriage had never been good. After eighteen years I rejoiced in his absence and cowered in his presence.

His visits to my bedroom were never announced. He would pull back the blankets and mount me from behind with little ceremony or outward pleasure. There had been a time when we gave sacrifices to

Venus and prayed to the lares—the little figurines in our household that protected the family. Now it was a seed deposit, nothing more, often awkward, and always difficult at the beginning.

When Aemilianus entered the bedroom on this morning, he wore a tunic with nothing beneath. I could see from his profile that he was already erect, meaning there would no foreplay. I quickly spit on my fingers and slipped my hand between my legs to lubricate myself somewhat before he set himself to the task.

He ripped the covers from the bed, taking no heed of what I was doing. He had seen it before and made no comment, but he chanced to see my bare ankle in the dim morning light. He gawked at it as though disgusted. "This isn't some accidental twist of your ankle." He made a terrible face. "It looks like some kind of deformity."

"It's just a bad day, Aemilianus. My ankle's been troublesome of late."

He glared at me. "Perhaps we've been lucky you're barren. What kind of child would we get from the likes of you? I have no desire for such offspring." He turned away from me as though I was a leper and left the room angry. I rolled over and burst into tears.

CHAPTER 10

My marriage to Aemilianus had never been more than an arrangement between families, but at seventeen, I had been excited to marry this handsome military officer, fifteen years my senior. I had known him my entire life and had even lived at his home with my brothers and Cornelia in the first year after my father's death.

Aemilianus' career took off six years after our marriage. Rome's third war with Carthage was going badly, and there was a groundswell for Aemilianus to take command of the war. Some of this was because of his heritage and some because of his early showing as an officer. Although not yet forty years old and too young by law to be a consul, such was the uproar, the Senate made an exception. Aemilianus was elected to his first consulship and went to Africa where he promptly turned the war around and ultimately besieged and destroyed Carthage. He returned the most popular man in Rome.

Despite my troubles with him, Aemilianus was not a bad man and was known for his populist leanings. He appreciated the fact that I was educated, and though we were never close, he treated me well enough during the early years of the marriage. But my inability to produce a child and Aemilianus' growing concern that he might not have a son put a huge strain on our relationship, and as time went by I became more a piece furniture in our home—that he occasionally used—than a favored wife. I was fortunate that as things grew more difficult at home Aemilianus spent more time on military campaigns. When he was in Rome, I found reasons to visit my mother.

For all the public's admiration of Cornelia for her intellect and her once seemingly perfect marriage to one of Rome's most respected and virtuous statesmen, she was also recognized as a role model for Roman mothers. And when things were the most difficult, that is how I saw her, someone who was always there for me, someone I could open my heart and cry to if need be.

A few days after Aemilianus' tirade about Tiberius' posters, I spent an afternoon with Cornelia, who lived just a few blocks from my home on the Palatine Hill. We sat in the peristyle at the back of her villa where she maintained a formal garden. Three colonnades of stark white limestone defined the space. Cornelia loved flowers and did all the work in her garden. We shared an alabaster bench that faced her favorite bed of roses, and though it was winter, the sun was out and the sky was a brilliant blue. I wore a bleached wool mantle around my shoulders. Cornelia wore a white linen stola over a wool tunic and had wrapped herself in a lavender palla.

"I noticed when you came in, Sempronia, that you're limping again. How is your ankle?"

"I'm having a lot of trouble with it, Mother. Every few days I misstep and it folds over on me." I lifted the hem of my stola to show her.

She gasped at the sight of my swollen ankle wound up in the straps of my sandal. "I'm surprised you can walk at all." She was fifty-five, but still very beautiful, just a radiant woman, with subtlety and intelligence in every glance of her eyes—which were blue like mine. "Have you seen a physician?"

"I haven't. As long as I don't do too much and take the time to get off my feet, it's all right." I let my stola fall back over my ankle.

"You need to see someone, Sempronia. I'll arrange it for you."

"I don't think there's much that can be done."

"Don't be so sure about that," she assured me. "I'll talk to my friend Asclepius."

I agreed to see her doctor, then changed the subject. "I was at the forum when Tiberius gave his first speech."

"I hear he speaks well."

"He learned it from you, Mother."

"And Diophanes."

"But it was mostly from being around you." I put my hand on hers. "What do you think of his platform?"

Cornelia looked off momentarily as though thinking, then faced me. "I think it's good. What he wants to do is right and in the best interest of the Republic. He will get some resistance." She tipped her head. "I believe that's already begun."

"Aemilianus thinks he's making a big mistake."

"Because he's shaking up the aristocracy?"

"The whole thing seems to embarrass him. Have you seen the posters Tiberius is putting up?"

"Yes, he asked me to read one before he started spreading them around. It all makes a lot of sense. I'm proud of him."

"Aemilianus brought one home balled up in a wad. He was furious. I'm not sure if he's worried he'll have to give up some of his land or if he's just disappointed it's his cousin that's behind it. You know how much he used to brag about Tiberius."

"But he's really upset about this? I was hoping Tiberius might get some support from Aemilianus."

"He said he should have let the Senate send him back to Numantia with Mancinus. He was very angry at the time. Maybe he didn't mean it. But that was how upset he was."

Cornelia could not disguise how much this troubled her. "Maybe I should talk to Aemilianus. He might listen to me."

"Please do. You know he doesn't listen to me."

"What has he said about your ankle?"

I had not wanted to bring this up. My relationship with Aemilianus was not something I talked about. Few Roman women talked openly about their husbands. But his words that one morning had hurt me. I blurted out what I should have kept to myself. "He called it a deformity. He said it was fortunate I was barren. He wouldn't want children from a cripple." I hung my head and tried not to cry. "He hasn't come to my bed since." I lifted my head. "Not that I want him there."

Cornelia put an arm around me and drew me close. "Sempronia, I'm sorry. I thought we had beaten that ankle long ago."

"I'm fine," I said.

She knew I was not and looked at me so sadly I regretted saying anything at all. "I feel badly that Aemilianus has not been the kind of husband I wanted for you. I was the one responsible for making the match. I'm to blame." She shook her head. "At the time I was certain he would make a good husband. Though he never knew my father, Aemilianus always spoke highly of him and wanted to hear stories about his life and military exploits, many of which related to Africanus' regard for the integrity of women."

Someone entered the house. We heard footsteps coming from the atrium. It was Gaius. He smiled immediately upon seeing us and strode out to where we were sitting. He had the same build as his older brother, but with more width and less height. Like Aemilianus he was back from eight months in Spain. It had been his first campaign, and he proudly wore his military tunic with a wide leather belt but no armor or weapon.

Cornelia and I both stood to accept his embrace. When he released her, he turned to me. "Sempronia, it's been a long time."

"Almost a year." This was my baby brother. Now a soldier. I put my cheek against his. "I like your beard."

I was sixteen when he was born and had helped my mother with him throughout the first two years of his life. Tiberius was a fine brother. We had been tutored together, and we were good friends. But Gaius was my favorite. He was the only child I had nurtured and seen grow from an infant into an adult.

He self-consciously stroked the downy hair on his face. "I let it grow in Spain. How are you? With child?"

Cornelia gave him a look and shook her head.

"No," I said quietly. I knew he was not trying to be cruel. It was a legitimate question for any woman in Rome, but me. I deliberately changed the subject. "Have you spoken to Tiberius?"

"Yes, he told me he wants to be a tribune. I told him he was crazy."

"Why's that?" asked Cornelia.

"Politics, Mother. I prefer the clarity of a soldier's life. None of this dickering and backstabbing. Politics is ugly business."

"With that I agree, Gaius. But what do you think of his idea of land reform?"

He shrugged. "I haven't given it much thought."

"You should," she said like a mother to her youngest.

He laughed, then lunged forward on one foot, extending his right arm to stab an imaginary enemy. "Technique and practice, Mother. That's all I have time for."

She shook her head in mock anger. "What about between your ears? I hope some of that education I gave you is still bouncing around in that head of yours." She said this in Greek.

He responded in the same by quoting Socrates. "I know nothing but the fact of my ignorance."

We all laughed, Cornelia the loudest. I loved being in my mother's home and seeing my brothers.

Cornelia became serious. "You've been back from Spain a few weeks now. Have you set up a time to visit Licinia?" Arranged marriages are always closely managed in the months prior to the wedding. The couple is introduced when the future bride reaches thirteen years or older. Then a year or so is given for the bride and groom to get to know each other. Licinia, Publius Crassus' daughter, had recently turned thirteen. It was time for Gaius to meet her. They would marry in a little over a year. The first meeting always took place at the bride's home.

Sometimes these arrangements worked out. My mother and father had always felt fortunate to be paired. The same was true for Tiberius. He was uncommonly thoughtful and made a good husband. Claudia had given him a son and a daughter—Tiberius and Sempronia. They were happy together and had a loving marriage. You already know how mine worked out.

"I haven't set anything up yet," said Gaius. He was an outgoing and energetic young man, but he had been reluctant to begin this part of his life. I knew his bride-to-be and thought highly of her. I expected them to get along, but how couples engage is not a science I can pretend to know.

"I've saved you the trouble," said Cornelia, watching Gaius twist and turn before her. "Go to Crassus' villa two days after the elections. You will spend the afternoon with Licinia and her mother."

It was the last thing in the world Gaius wanted to do. He made a face at me like he might vomit. He had that kind of animal humor common to younger brothers.

Cornelia shook her head at him. "Be there at midday, Gaius."

"I will. Thank you for arranging the visit. I might never have done it."

Cornelia reached into the overfold in her stola. "Give Licinia this ring." She handed Gaius an iron ring. She watched him inspect it. "It seals your engagement."

Gaius glanced up at her.

"I look forward to talking to you afterward." She slipped me a wink.

Gaius kicked one foot with the other. "I can barely wait."

"Nor I," she replied.

CHAPTER 11

Cornelia came over the next morning with Asclepius, a Greek physician whom she trusted. He inspected my ankle with the usual sad head shaking. He squeezed it and turned it this way and that.

"Your ankle will steadily deteriorate, and there's nothing anyone can do to stop it. Eventually you will not be able to walk on it at all. Until then I recommend massages, soaking it in warm water, and when the pain is too great, a cup of wine. I also suggest you have a supportive shoe made. I know a cobbler who can help you with that. His name is Sutorius. You can find him in the forum."

The following day I had my litter bearers carry me to the marketplace on the south side of the forum. Tarus, our male house slave, a tall, sinewy Sardinian, walked alongside. Both Aemilianus and I used Tarus as a bodyguard when out in the streets of Rome. He was a sullen, scary-looking man with a pockmarked face, whose age was difficult to tell. He had been a pirate and had his tongue cut out when he and his comrades were captured by a Roman warship. He could not enunciate at all and communicated with his hands. He was no one's favorite, but he was trustworthy and served a purpose.

The market was crowded and loud. I did not like being there, even in a curtained litter. I held the curtain aside just enough to watch the shops go by. When we reached the part of the market dedicated to cobblers, my litter, the sign of a wealthy woman, drew the attention of all of the shoemakers. I asked the first cobbler we encountered if he knew Sutorius. The man pointed him out. Tarus brought the shoemaker up to the side of the litter. I opened the curtain all the way. Sutorius was a stooped, older man with a kind eye, no beard, deep lines in his face, and a shaggy head of gray hair. His eyes met mine. I liked his confidence right away.

"You were recommended to me by the Greek physician Asclepius. I'm looking for a custom sandal. I will pay extra if you will come to my home to do the fitting."

It was common practice for craftsmen to come to upper-class homes to provide their services. "Yes, of course, madam. What exactly are you looking for?"

I did not want to display my ankle in public, even within the litter. "Come to my house this afternoon, and we can talk about it. I want something very unique, and I don't expect it to be cheap."

That was all it took. Sutorius arrived at the house later that day with a satchel containing his tools and some pieces of leather. I wanted absolute privacy so I took him into the library and told Nadia that I did not want to be disturbed. I sat down in one of the chairs, lifted the edge of my tunic, and removed my sandal so he could see my foot.

Sutorius winced. "You're looking for something that can make the ankle stable. Is that right?"

"Yes, exactly. Something that can give me enough support to walk without a limp or a cane. It can be as tight as necessary and style is unimportant. It just has to work."

He lifted my ankle and placed it gently on his knee. His hands were small and square with large knuckles and thick hair on the backs of his fingers. He turned my ankle slowly to get an idea what kind of flexibility it had and what kind of pain I was in. He looked up at me with eyes of age. "How long has your foot been like this?"

I did not want to reveal that I had been born with it. "In the last year or two it has begun to ache and twist. I turned it several times this past year making it worse."

The man nodded. "I'm thinking of a sandal that straps around your ankle well up the calf. I have done something like this before, but it's very individual."

"Of course. Try whatever you think will work, and if it doesn't, we can try something else."

"That might be what happens, but I'm sure I can help you."

Sutorius made some measurements, then cut a sole for the sandal and matched it to my foot.

"I have what I need to proceed," he said. "I will be back in two days with something to try on. You may pay me then. Three sesterces."

"If it works, I will pay you twice that. Thank you for coming."

I called for Nadia to take the man to the door. For the first time in many months I felt like I had an answer to what had become the focus my life—walking without a limp.

CHAPTER 12

The election of magistrates for the next year took place over several days in December. The first day the Century Assembly, made up entirely of soldiers and arranged by their social order, met at Mars Field to vote for the consuls and the other high-ranking military officers. Aemilianus, one of the sitting consuls, presided. Calpurnius Piso Frugi and Publius Mucius Scaevola, the brother of Gaius' future father-in-law, were chosen as co-consuls. All those associated with Tiberius' plans for land reform felt Scaevola's consulship boded well for the bill should Tiberius be elected to the tribunate.

The People's Assembly met the following morning atop the Capitoline Hill in the field in front of the temple of Jupiter. The Assembly contained in excess of thirty thousand plebeians, divided into thirty-five tribes, which were not equal in their numbers but voted as equal units. The tribes had gathered separately during the previous week and decided who their selections for each office would be. When a tribe was called on to vote, one of the tribe's elders would submit its ballot. In the case of the tribunes, which was the first matter of business, each tribe nominated ten men. The ten men on the most ballots would be the tribunes.

The tribes drew lots for the order of voting. Because of the factor of chance involved, the choosing of lots is believed to be a way for the gods to offer direction. Being first was a great honor, and after the ten men listed on that first ballot were announced to the Assembly, the nominees were given a chance to speak. Although the tribes had already made their decisions, changes were often made based on what these nominees had to say.

One of the current tribunes, Marcus Claudius, the same man who had given the terrella to Aemilianus, presided over the election from an elevated stage or tribunal. After the required religious sacrifices and ceremonies, a flamen was summoned to the tribunal with a ceramic water pitcher and a ceramic bowl. The pitcher was filled with water and contained thirty-five wooden lots—each inscribed with the name of one of the tribes. Marcus Claudius took the pitcher from the flamen and steadied himself to pour the water into the bowl, held outstretched in both hands by the flamen. When the tribune tipped the pitcher, the lot belonging to the Suburana tribe was the first to slosh into the bowl. The Suburana tribe, one of the four urban tribes, and one of the largest in membership, was given the honor of submitting the first nominees. An older man with white hair and a beard came forward with the Suburana ballot. Marcus Claudius read it aloud. Tiberius was the fourth name on the list. The ten nominees then addressed the Assembly in the order they were listed on the ballot.

Tiberius spoke after the third nominee. "Something is gravely amiss with the state of our nation," he announced with clear and resonant conviction. "The stability and security of Rome is dependent on our men in uniform, the men who can use a gladius and help defend the state. But right now too many of our citizens of military age have no land and according to law cannot serve in the army. They are left behind, often in the streets of Rome, poor and destitute, their families on the edge of starvation. This must change.

"I have spent the winter touring Italy to evaluate the situation. What I saw confirmed that our land is in the hands of too few, leaving many citizens without and Rome with a shrinking source of legionnaires."

Tiberius remained calm and mostly still as he spoke. He made few gestures and did no striding from one side of the platform to the other, as was common among Roman orators. Instead he kept his eyes on his audience and used his deliberate, even delivery to ease his ideas into the audience.

"Should I be elected to the tribunate, I will propose a law that grants thirty iugera to any Roman citizen who has no property of his own. The property cannot be sold and must remain in the family, and will require a small annual fee paid to the state. Most of the land will come from the vast amount of undistributed public land that is all over the Italian peninsula, but some will come from large landowners who have surpassed the legal limit of five hundred iugera.

"I propose this as a way to both increase the size and loyalty of our military and to provide a more stable agrarian base for the state. Ownership of land, particularly one's own farmland, and being willing to fight for it, is at the heart of being Roman. I base my campaign on the necessity of putting land in the hands of the common man."

As Appius had told Tiberius, land reform, especially a platform based on a large giveaway, would be very popular. The Assembly responded enthusiastically. This was not the forum where Tiberius had spoken to several hundred people at a time—this was a gathering of tens of thousands. The emotion and energy of their response was overwhelming. Tiberius considered it assurance that what he was doing was right. And in the end, his words generated more than passion in the crowd. He was named on the ballot of every tribe and achieved what he sought—a place on the tribunate of the plebs.

CHAPTER 13

Tiberius invited Blossius, Diophanes, and Appius to his home the day after the election to finalize the language of his land reform bill. He had laid out the basic elements in his speech to the People's Assembly, but the details still needed to be worked out before he took office in two months. Appius arrived with Publius Crassus, whose daughter Gaius would be formally meeting the next day.

Cornelia had come to the house earlier that morning to help Tiberius' wife Claudia with a piece of cloth she was weaving. When the men arrived, Claudia stayed at the loom, but Cornelia joined them in the library to take part in the discussion, which she detailed to me a week later. Blossius sat at a table with a bronze stylus and a wax pad to take notes. Cornelia took a seat at the table opposite Blossius, while the other men stood or paced around the room.

"So far," began Tiberius, "all that's been decided is that each landless citizen will be given thirty iugera. The land can't be sold, will have a small annual rent, and will come from either undistributed public land or from landowners who have exceeded the five hundred iugera limit. What else is needed?"

Appius spoke up. "Our biggest concern is not making too many enemies. There will be several angry senators if this bill passes. We need to include some kind of compensation for those who lose portions of their land."

"We can waive the fine for having exceeded the limit," said Tiberius.

"A fine that hasn't been collected in my lifetime," said Crassus, a middle-aged, somewhat plump man, with graying hair that he combed forward to cover his well-receded hairline. "That's not enough."

"There must be some form of real compensation for anyone who loses land," replied Appius, walking from one side of the room to the other. He was five years older than Crassus, but in better shape and more stately in his presence.

"And that should be for more than the loss of land," added Blossius taking a sip from his cup of wine. He was the only one in the room drinking. "Some of these men have developed their land or passed parts of it on to their children."

"What are you thinking?" asked Tiberius. "Financial compensation? Could we simply pay them half the commercial value of the property?"

"That would be far too costly," said Crassus. "Maybe we allow them to protect blocks of their property, say two hundred and fifty iugera for each of their sons and the same amount to be passed on as part of one daughter's dowry."

"That's good," said Blossius, scratching the ideas into the wax.

"But still not enough," said Diophanes.

Appius stopped pacing. "They will get a title to the land that they retain so there can be no question about their ownership."

"We're getting there," said Tiberius. "What else?"

"Who will determine which land is taken and where it goes?" asked Cornelia. "You'll need someone to oversee the distribution of land."

"How about a commission made up of five men?" said Appius.

"Make it three," said Diophanes. "A smaller number makes agreement easier."

"Will the commission members be paid?" asked Crassus.

"Yes, a small amount, but they will also need money to run the commission," said Cornelia. "They will have to hire teams of surveyors, and those surveyors will have to travel throughout Italy. It will be a long, slow process and a lot of work."

"What kind of authority will the commission have?" asked Crassus. "How will they enforce their actions? I can imagine some very powerful men ignoring the decisions of the commission."

"Should they take input from the landowner himself before cutting up his land?" asked Blossius,

Tiberius stood by quietly as the men talked, trying to take it all in. "A three-man commission that receives nominal pay but also a sum of money each year to do the work itself. Do we agree on that?"

Crassus and Appius both answered. "Yes."

Diophanes stepped up to the table where Blossius wrote. "Would they be elected annually?"

"No, just once, then the commission can choose its own replacements as needed," said Appius, who seemed to have thought much of this through already. "It gives them more control."

"But what about enforcement?" pressed Crassus. "We have to address that somehow. Will there be a squadron of militia that oversees the division of land?"

"That seems too heavy-handed," said Tiberius. "I'm hoping we can convince those who lose land that it's for the public good."

"That sounds like wishful thinking," said Cornelia, ever the realist.

"But that might be the only way it can work," said Diophanes, pulling at his long beard, "if everyone understands that this is for the security of the state."

"Again too much wishful thinking," echoed Crassus.

"But that's where we have to start," said Blossius. "It must be more than confiscation of property."

"Will this only apply to citizens of Rome or to everyone in Italy?" asked Diophanes. "That will make a big difference."

Crassus nodded in agreement. "And if so, will the commission be taking land from non-Roman landowners?"

"Yes, absolutely," said Tiberius. "One thing I discovered during my travels is that some of the land Rome acquired after the war with Hannibal has never been claimed and is being worked by non-Romans as though it were theirs."

"What about cattle and sheep limits?" asked Diophanes.

"I say we leave that alone," said Appius. "Limiting property size will impact the size of the livestock herds. No sense stirring up any more controversy than necessary."

"You sound worried about that, Appius." Cornelia had known the man since childhood. "How much resistance are we going to get?"

Appius looked to Crassus, who tipped his head, then back to Cornelia. "Plenty. The wealthiest men in the Senate will fight this for certain—tooth and nail. That's why it's so necessary to have the unified support of the people." He looked around at everyone in the room. "We're looking for greater balance between senatorial control and popular sovereignty."

"Ah, the elusive Republican ideal." Blossius grinned sardonically and lifted his cup of wine.

"*Senatus Populusque Romanus*," stated Crassus with pride.

After the meeting Cornelia sat down with Tiberius on a bench in the atrium. Tiberius was enthusiastic about the work and could not have been more pleased with the progress so far. "What do you think, Mother? Are we not doing something important?"

Cornelia smiled at her eldest son. He looked a lot like his father and had long displayed the same qualities that had made the elder Tiberius Gracchus so well respected. "I think it is important. Very much so. But I'm sure you noted what Appius said. The most influential men in the Senate will fight land reform with everything they've got. Are you ready for that?"

Tiberius put his hand on his mother's. "I think I am. I mean, what can they do if I muster the votes and pass the bill?"

Cornelia looked into her son's hopeful eyes. "They can make up stories about things you've done. Try to drag you into some kind of scandal. We've seen that before. You'll be asking them to let go of a portion of their wealth. Don't underestimate what that means to a rich man—even if it's cast as patriotic. It's mostly a matter of having thick skin, Tiberius, not overreacting to insults, and staying focused on what you're trying to accomplish." She ran her hand through his hair lovingly. "I think you're up to it."

"I do too, Mother. Besides our family is beyond reproach. If they attack me with lies, the strength of our family name will serve as my defense."

"One might think that, but remember what happened on your return from Numantia. Even saving the lives of twenty thousand legionnaires was considered scandalous. You're young, idealistic," she smiled with the radiance only a son or daughter can see in their mother, "and new to politics. Be prepared for more than you can imagine."

CHAPTER 14

Gaius had not taken part in any of the meetings with Tiberius and his advisors. He was far more interested in his military career than land reform. He had spent the previous summer in Spain, where, much like Tiberius, he had learned the finer point of being a professional soldier under the tutelage of Aemilianus. He had been back a month when he went to meet his future wife Licinia for the first time.

As he walked the few blocks from his mother's home to Publius Crassus' villa with his slave Philocrates, he was thinking about the campaign in Spain. It was not over. Aemilianus had built a wall ten feet tall and eight feet thick around the city of Numantia with the intention of starving the inhabitants into submission. Two legions remained in Spain to manage the siege; two had returned with Aemilianus. Gaius would go back in a few months with Aemilianus to complete the operation. Gaius had loved his time in Spain. At seventeen years of age military glory was his greatest desire. Weddings and marriage were far from his thoughts. Visiting a thirteen-year-old girl seemed like a waste of time when he might be training.

Publius Crassus' home, like Cornelia's, was one of the most spacious and beautiful on the Palatine Hill. Splendor that would have impressed almost any other young man had little or no effect on Gaius as he stood on the doorstep with his slave and glanced around the neighborhood before knocking on the thick plank door.

"What do you think, Philocrates?" The two men had known each other since before they could walk. Philocrates' father, Felix, had been Gaius' father's slave and had been freed upon Tiberius' death. "Is marriage something I should be looking forward to?"

Philocrates smiled. He was extremely loyal and when the two men were alone, Gaius treated him like a friend. When others were around, Philocrates did as all good slaves did; he became invisible. "I have never been married, master. I would guess it depends on the woman.

I've been told that a good wife is essential to a successful career in politics."

"But a wife would be an inconvenience to a soldier."

"Not really, master. She can take care of the home when the soldier is away."

"I suppose so," said Gaius, then he knocked three times firmly.

The housemaid, an elderly, heavyset Thracian by the name of Phyllis, opened the door. The household was expecting Gaius and the woman let him right in. Philocrates stayed outside where he would wait until Gaius was ready to leave.

Licinia's mother, Appius Claudius' sister, and another Claudia, came striding in from the atrium, smiling broadly and looking very excited. She considered Gaius Gracchus the best catch in Rome and had invested a lot of time making the arrangement with Cornelia.

Claudia had dressed for the occasion. Her dress was fine wool, dyed a mallard green, pinned with emerald brooches at the shoulders and belted below her breasts with a matching sash. Overtop she had draped herself in a nearly transparent palla of pale green that wafted in the air as she walked. She had painted her lips red and her face a fashionable pale white. Her hair was dyed black and assembled on top of her head in a cobra-like hood of horizontal rolls and coiled plaits. She could not have been more eager to introduce Gaius to her daughter. The two families had known each other for several generations as leading members of the populuris faction of the Senate. Gaius had seen Licinia only once before, prior to the marriage arrangement, when he was nine and she was five.

Gaius wore a bright white wool toga over a white tunic that reached to just above his knees. A downy brown beard trimmed his jaw line and traced a light shadow above his lip. He bowed to Claudia. "Thank you for inviting me to your home," he said stiffly.

"Gaius, it's such a pleasure to have you here. Licinia is in the peristyle. I'll introduce you."

Gaius followed Claudia through the enormous atrium. The columns that formed the portico were five feet in diameter and three-stories high. Hand-painted flowers and vines wrapped around the columns all the way to the top. Water lilies covered half the surface of the atrium pool. Bronze figurines of satyrs and nymphs were perched on the edge, daring to jump in. Gaius spotted several orange and white carp gliding in and out beneath the lily pads. Fifty imagines, wax masks cast from the faces of one of Rome's oldest families, decorated the atrium walls, adding to the sense of history and tradition in the huge villa.

Gaius saw her from a distance sitting on a limestone bench in the back corner of the garden. The young woman was wearing a sleeveless white silk stola with a nearly transparent marigold yellow palla spun around her shoulders. A matching sash ran just below her breasts that were too small yet to need a breast band. A hint of her budding nipples showed beneath the fine silk. Claudia had dressed Licinia for a specific look, not too alluring, not too innocent, then sprinkled her with attar of roses.

Licinia's hair was auburn and pulled up on top of her head in a tight bun. The loose strands of hair that fell about her neck showed red in the sunlight. She stood as Gaius entered the peristyle with her mother, then lowered her eyes as they approached. Claudia, basking in the thrill of being the matchmaker, introduced them. "Gaius, this is my daughter, Licinia. Licinia, this is Gaius Gracchus, your future husband."

Blushing slightly and fighting a self-conscious smile, Licinia lifted her eyes. "I'm pleased to meet you, Gaius." Somewhat slight of frame, Licinia was a beautiful young girl at the edge of womanhood with large, penetrating green eyes that did not miss a thing.

Gaius appeared to have been struck by a bolt of lightning. A well-spoken youth of tremendous confidence suddenly had no idea what to say or do—except not let his mouth fall open. He managed to mutter, "The pleasure is mine, Licinia."

Claudia watched them like a mother hen. She and Cornelia had been planning this moment since Licinia's seventh year. Together they would track the couple's progress through the yearlong premarriage process.

Licinia had been tutored in Greek tragedy, history, philosophy and astronomy just as Gaius had, even by some of the same men. Until this moment, however, Gaius had focused his last few years on military exercises and physical endurance, not history and literature, but he felt Licinia's intelligence from her first few words. Claudia, the hovering mother, duly noted the impact her daughter had on him.

The three of them walked through the garden. Claudia pointed out her most prized flowers while Licinia and Gaius traded darting looks and finally a few tentative smiles.

"This is one my favorite fragrances." When Claudia bent over to smell the calla lily, Gaius and Licinia dared to gaze into each other's eyes for the first time. It was as much curiosity about this person they would spend the rest of their lives with as something much more visceral. They were both fascinated with each other and felt an immediate attraction.

Claudia lifted her nose from the lily in time to catch them rapt on each other. She had always believed that the first meeting provided an important insight into a marriage. Living together was always easier if it started with some call to the physical in both partners. And that was what she saw. She congratulated herself for making such a good match.

After the three of them had toured the garden, they returned to the limestone bench. This first meeting they sat three across with Licinia's mother in the middle. A house slave came out to the peristyle with a tray containing a bowl of olives and some hardboiled quail eggs. Gaius took two olives. Claudia took an egg. Licinia declined food, but produced a pair of cubed bones from the folds of her sash. "Mother, could we play a game of dice?"

Claudia gasped. "Of course not, Licinia. Put those away."

Gaius chuckled, allowing a bit of himself to show. He knew several dice games that the soldiers played in camp. "What game were you thinking of?"

Licinia revealed an impish grin. "Three toe five."

"No, no," said Claudia. She snatched the dice from her daughter's hand. "There'll be no dice games this afternoon. We'll do as we planned. You'll play the kithara for Gaius."

Licinia gave a glance to Gaius, then said, "Yes, Mother." She got up to retrieve the u-shaped, five-string instrument from the atrium. When she returned, she sat on the bench and played two songs with great finesse and skill. She tended to keep her eyes on the strings, but on several occasions she looked up at Gaius and drew a smile from him. She sang during the second song, and much like her playing, her voice was pleasing and strong. Gaius applauded politely after both performances. Although music was not something he had great interest in, he enjoyed listening to Licinia play.

When the music ended, Claudia asked Gaius what he did for pleasure.

"Soldier," he said. "I just came back from my first campaign. When I have free time, I practice my technique with a sword and a javelin."

"But that's not really something one does for pleasure, Gaius," said Claudia.

"It is for me. Perfection of my skills gives me great pleasure."

"What do you know about your brother's plan for land reform?" asked Licinia, looking directly at him.

The question surprised her mother. "What do you know about that, Licinia?"

"I know that Tiberius is a tribune, and I've overheard Father talking about land redistribution with his friends. It sounds exciting. Are you involved in this work, Gaius?"

Gaius was impressed that Licinia knew about his brother. After growing up in his mother's house, one thing he knew he wanted in a wife was intelligence. "I've been in Spain for eight months, so I haven't taken part," he said, somewhat embarrassed he did not know more than he did. "But I believe my brother is right, and what he hopes to do is for the betterment of Rome."

"I agree," said Licinia. "Would you want to be a tribune like your brother?"

Gaius tilted his head, as though he had never thought about it. "Right now, Licinia, I prefer military life to politics, and I can't imagine that changing. I feel more comfortable with a javelin in my hand than speaking in front of a crowd."

"That might change, Gaius," said Claudia, "as you grow older."

"I can't say," replied Gaius, unused to talking so much about himself.

Claudia smiled at the young man. She didn't blame him for not wanting to get into the ugly business of politics, but she knew the dedication his family, and hers also, had to progressive ideals. Few men in either family had not been part of the effort.

"I almost forgot," said Gaius. He withdrew the iron ring Cornelia had given him from the sinus of his toga, the portion of cloth that draped over his left arm. "I would like you, Licinia," he lowered his eyes, "to be my wife."

"It has been fated," she said to the man she had only just met. She offered him her hand, and he slid the ring over her finger in a symbolic act as old as time. An awkward silence stretched out between them as Claudia watched, trying to keep her joy contained.

Gaius broke the spell. "What do you enjoy most, Licinia?"

Licinia smiled, adding to her radiance. "I enjoy weaving and playing the kithara," she said. "But I like reading most of all—especially the Greek comedies."

"I know a few by Euripides and Aristophanes—but only because my tutors made me read them."

"But you liked them?"

Gaius could not help smiling. He liked this young woman. "Yes, I remember *The Clouds* very well. It's my favorite."

"And very funny!" exclaimed Licinia, thrilled that this handsome young man knew Aristophanes.

The visit was tightly managed by Claudia and mostly superficial. When Gaius got up to leave he was both elated and confused. Licinia was pretty and smart and had a sense of humor. He felt very lucky to have been so fortunately paired. But he knew nothing about courtship, and this woman seemed very clever. He had no idea what to do next, but he agreed to come back before he left again for Spain. The wedding was set for the following spring. They would meet several more times before then.

Philocrates watched Gaius closely as he came out of the villa. As soon as their eyes met, Gaius burst into a big grin.

"That bad?" said the slave, at ease enough with his master to tease him.

Gaius contained his grin, then blushed and smiled in spite of himself. "Yes, absolutely awful," he said with clear sarcasm.

"You're pleased."

Gaius nodded, unable to hide his joy. When he entered his home, he was whistling one of the songs Licinia had played on her kithara. Cornelia heard him come in.

"Gaius," she called out from the atrium. "I didn't know you could whistle."

Gaius suddenly stopped whistling. "I didn't even know I was."

Cornelia nodded to herself. "What did you think of Licinia?"

"Oh, I don't know," Gaius mumbled.

Cornelia came up to him and gave him a brief embrace. "You didn't like her?"

He stared at the floor. "She was a nice girl, I guess."

"Do you look forward to seeing her again?"

Gaius glanced up at his mother. "Yes, I think so." Then he hurried off to the back of the house to polish his armor.

CHAPTER 15

The shoemaker returned to my house during the same week that Gaius met Licinia. He had made a sandal with six long leather straps that crisscrossed around my ankle and halfway up my calf. It worked well, but had to be cinched very tightly and would take some getting used to. I decided to test it by walking to Cornelia's house. The sun was out and the day was warm enough to need only a wool mantle over my stola. Tarus accompanied me and waited outside when I went in.

Cornelia noticed the change right away. "Sempronia, you don't seem to be limping," she said as we walked through the house to the garden. "Is your ankle feeling better?"

I smiled, pleased by the success of my short hike to her home. "I followed Asclepius' advice and had a special sandal made. Take a look."

I sat on a bench in the peristyle and lifted the hem of my stola and the tunic beneath. It may have worked, but even after the brief walk, the pressure of the straps was obvious.

"It looks painful," said Cornelia, reaching down to touch the straps that spiraled up my leg.

"Oh, it's not so bad," I lied, dropping my stola to cover it. "I prefer the tightness to the embarrassment of a limp."

Cornelia's look was a sad one. "Well, I'm not so sure. You might try wearing a sock with it." She bent over and kissed me on the forehead.

I remained seated as Cornelia moved through her rose bushes looking for ripe hips. Coson, Cornelia's lead male slave and a sturdy Macedonian, came out to the peristyle.

"An ornate carriage has pulled up in front of the house, my lady. I believe it's the King of Egypt. Fidelia's at the door with him now."

59

Cornelia straightened up. It had been six months since Physcon's last unannounced visit. She looked at me and shook her head. "Tell Fidelia to bring the pharaoh back to the garden."

We heard the slap of his sandals on the tiles as he strode through the atrium. He entered the peristyle huffing and puffing from the short walk, looking like a blousy purple tent in his long silk robe. He had shaved his head and let his beard grow. It was dyed black, manicured and curled. He smiled immediately upon seeing Cornelia. I doubt he even saw me sitting off to the edge of the garden. Cornelia greeted him as though she were expecting him.

Physcon took her hand. "Cornelia, fortune has it that I'm in Rome again, perhaps all month. There's just time enough for me to show you something I've bought for you."

"My friendship is free, Physcon, but my hand cannot be bought."

"I'm well aware of that, Cornelia." He grinned. "That doesn't mean I can't give you a gift."

Cornelia shook her head at her friend, then smiled. "Yes, and it would be impolite of me not to accept one."

"My carriage is out front. I must take you to it." At this point, he saw me and tilted his head in recognition.

Cornelia bent over a rose bush and delved into one of the blossoms with her fingers. "Take me to it? I'm not really available to leave right now. I have things I've chosen to do today."

Physcon laughed, a laugh as big as he was. "You have time for picking bugs from those flowers but not for me. No, we're going to Misenum. It's a beautiful trip along the coast and the weather is gorgeous."

"I don't think so. That's five days south of here. Besides what kind of gift involves traveling to Misenum?"

"A lovely villa on the cape overlooking the Bay of Naples."

Cornelia actually laughed. "Physcon, you're overdoing it, please. It sounds wonderful. But gifts no matter how large or impressive won't change my mind about marriage. I'm sorry."

"Rome is such a dirty place. The time away would do you good."

"That I won't argue. But you must know that continuing to press me will not get you what you want. Come visit whenever you are in Rome. You are always welcome to join us in our circle. No more gifts though."

Physcon's overwhelming good mood suddenly gave way to disappointment. He took a deep breath. "The house is yours anyway. And there will be a time when I will take you there to see it. Allow me that."

Cornelia sighed. "Perhaps one day. But please respect me on this."

Physcon bowed his head, then looked up at Cornelia. "Only a very strong woman can resist the offers of a man as wealthy as I am. Instead of making me think I've made a mistake, it assures me that I haven't. There is no other woman in the world I could want as much as I want you. I'll trouble you no longer today, but expect me back. I'm sorry to have interrupted." Again he acknowledged me. "Good day." He turned and left the house.

"That was sudden, Mother. Do you think he's angry?"

Cornelia turned to me and shook her head, clearly unsettled by Physcon's persistence.

"At least he only comes to Rome a few times a year."

She nodded. "A villa on the Bay of Naples? Maybe I'm the fool, not him."

"I don't think so. He's a ruthless man who killed his brother and nephew and has married both of his sisters. He's a gentleman here to you, but his life is not something you want to be a part of."

"I'm sure you're right. Besides, Tiberius has just been elected to the tribunate. I'm too worried about him to go anywhere."

CHAPTER 16

Tiberius made his land reform bill public two months after his election. Following the advice of Blossius and Appius, he had passed out copies of the bill in the forum instead of the traditional method of reading it to the Senate. Once this was done, Tiberius had three weeks to promulgate the bill. Contiones, small informal gatherings, were held all over the city and the outlying region to give the voters a chance to read and discuss the bill with the current magistrates. Tiberius acted as the bill's ambassador, attending as many contiones as he could to make sure the people understood all that he was trying to accomplish and why.

During this three-week period Cornelia's nephew and my cousin, Publius Nasica, came to her home. It was in the afternoon. I was there with Cornelia in the atrium when Fidelia announced that the pontiff was there to talk to Cornelia. They were not close, and Cornelia was surprised that he should be there at all.

Fidelia brought Publius Nasica into the atrium where we sat beside a brazier stoked with chunks of oak. His toga was emblazoned with a wide purple stripe, signifying that he was also a senator. The man had known me since childhood, and of course, he knew Aemilianus, but the pontiff was associated with the other political faction, the optimates, not the populares.

"I'm concerned about your son, Cornelia," Publius said, deigning to glance at me. "Tiberius is taking his position as tribune a little too—seriously."

"How so?" asked Cornelia, though she knew very well what he meant.

"I'm sure you're aware of the land reform bill he's written."

Cornelia nodded.

"I think it's a big mistake. It's likely to cause him a lot of trouble."

"And why are you telling me this, Publius?"

"Many important people in the Senate are upset. Many. He didn't even have the courtesy of reading it to the Senate before presenting it to the public. You would save Tiberius a lot of embarrassment if you could convince him to rescind his bill."

"Have you talked to him about it?"

Publius grimaced and pulled at his beard. "We exchanged a few words prior to the election. But my words mean little to him. Yours will have more influence than mine ever will."

"Where do you stand on the issue?"

"Well," he looked around the atrium uncomfortably, "like the majority of the senators, I have a lot of property, property that I have developed over many years. Taking land away from the men who are the foundation of Rome is wrong. It's against the good order of things. I have a lot to lose if this bill goes through."

"Yes, I think I understand what you're saying."

Publius nodded. "Good. I know you're a reasonable woman."

"But I'm afraid I won't be of any use to you."

"What do you mean?"

"I've spoken to Tiberius at length about his proposal already. He's thought it out very carefully and convinced me that it's right for Rome. I even helped him write it."

The pontiff sucked in a lot of air, stomped back and forth, then faced Cornelia. "It's no secret that Appius Claudius and Publius Crassus are part of this. They're using it for their own political gain. They're not thinking of your son at all. Besides, you're at risk to lose a lot of land yourself."

Cornelia looked at me, then back to Publius. "But I don't mind. I believe it's for the betterment of all. I suggest talking to Tiberius yourself."

Publius shook his head, clearly disturbed. "Well then, because I already know he won't listen to me, tell him that he won't get anywhere with it and that it will ruin his career. Tell him the majority of senators are firmly against it, and that they asked me to come here to talk to you—for his sake."

"I believe you would make a better messenger than I, Publius." Even though Cornelia spoke evenly and without obvious emotion, I could tell how angry she was.

"Don't say I didn't warn you." Publius turned abruptly and strode out of the atrium to the front of the house. We heard the front door slam when he left.

"Are you worried, Mother? That sounded like a threat."

Cornelia took a deep breath and let it out. "It was a threat, and I don't like it. I will tell Tiberius he was here and the manner in which he spoke to me. Tiberius needs to be prepared for this. My nephew's resolve will only stiffen."

"Tiberius is a mild, thoughtful man, Mother, but he's stubborn— more stubborn than most people know. He won't back down from these men."

"I know." Cornelia stood up, more upset than she wanted to show. She walked absently across the atrium and stared down into the pool. After a long while, not a word said, I stood, and with some difficulty, even with the new sandal, crossed the room to where she stood. I put my hands on her shoulders and leaned my head next to hers. She was crying, something I had not seen her do since my father's death.

CHAPTER 17

Being the daughter of Publius Cornelius Scipio was enough to assure Cornelia a place in Rome's social elite. Her mother Amelia's dedication to education and the rights of women added yet another layer to Cornelia's almost otherworldly dignitas. But her marriage to Tiberius Gracchus was the perfect fulfillment of the evolution of her early life.

Tiberius, a plebeian with a highly successful military career, including two triumphs, was noted for his virtue and the depth of his character. When my grandfather first arranged Cornelia's wedding to Tiberius, he made the decision on the spur of the moment without first consulting my grandmother. He entered the house that day and announced that he had contracted a husband for Cornelia, who was only six years old at the time. Aemilia, surprised, if not somewhat piqued, that Africanus would make such an important decision without her input, reacted by asking, "Why the haste? Unless your match is Tiberius Gracchus I might ask you to reconsider." When Africanus told her that Tiberius was, in fact, the man he had chosen, she was ecstatic.

In a sense this summed up the early years of my mother's marriage. Despite the number of children lost at birth or early in life and their thirty-year age difference, Tiberius and Cornelia were a match made by the gods. And that was how they were perceived, the ideal Roman couple. But the circumstances surrounding Tiberius' death, eighteen years after the marriage, seemed to foreshadow the difficult times ahead for Cornelia.

Tiberius came home one afternoon to find two rat snakes, a male and a female, curled up together on one of the pillows in the couple's bed. Roman life is deeply interwoven with religious ceremony and rituals. Hardly a thing is done without a sacrifice to the gods or a reading of the auspices. It is not extreme to say that Romans consider everything a reflection of the mood of the gods, and something as unusual as finding snakes in one's bed could not avoid being considered an omen of some kind.

My father, who abided closely with the religious rituals, as did Cornelia, captured the snakes and put them in a sackcloth bag, but he did not dispose of them until seeking the advice of an augur. The augur told Tiberius that the snakes were a sign of mixed meaning and that he had to make a choice. He should neither let both snakes go nor kill them. Instead he must kill one and let the other go. If, however, he killed the male, his own life would be in danger, and if he killed the female, Cornelia's life would be at risk. Tiberius loved Cornelia like life itself. He had lived sixty years; she was in the prime of life. For him, the decision was easy. Without consulting Cornelia, he killed the male and let the female go. Within the month, Tiberius became severely ill.

Only on his deathbed, in his final hours, did he tell Cornelia about the snakes. Of course, this added an extra touch of personal sadness for Cornelia, a kind of double heartbreak, knowing her husband had sacrificed himself for her well-being. After the funeral, Cornelia, though in her early thirties, pledged to never remarry and to live the rest of her life in honor of Tiberius. I would wed Aemilianus the next year, and Cornelia would concentrate on raising her two young sons, educating them with the same effort and energy with which she had educated me, focusing on Greek literature and science, while also assuring they had proper military training. Gaius and Tiberius grew into fine young men, two of Rome's finest, her jewels as Cornelia often referred to them. And she became known as the ideal Roman mother, a matron dedicated to the memory of her husband and the welfare of her children—a dedication that would be challenged in more ways than she could have ever imagined.

CHAPTER 18

During the three weeks that Tiberius was promulgating his land reform bill, Gaius learned that he was returning to Spain at the end of March. He was eager to go. His devotion to his military career, however, had been given a good shaking when he met the young woman who would be his wife. Knowing he could be gone as long as a year, he arranged a second visit to see Licinia before leaving. This was a big change, and everyone was pleased, no one more than Cornelia, who had needed to prod him to visit Licinia the first time.

As far as I knew, Gaius' experience with women up to this point had been entirely innocent. I could only guess what he might have seen or done during his first year in the military, but I knew how he had been raised. He grew up among a group of families where all the women were educated and progressive. Neither Gaius nor Tiberius quite fit the role of a traditional Roman male. The physical side of their life and their military training had been rigorous. Cornelia had insisted on that. They were full-chested, physical specimens and extremely handsome—if you accept a sister's opinion. But they were also of elevated sensitivity and capable of respect for and courtesy to women. Truly a rarity among Roman men.

Licinia certainly felt this when she first met Gaius, and she was as thrilled as he was when they had some time together one afternoon, three days prior to Gaius' return to Spain. They sat out in the garden, all the plants bright green and sprouting anew. The slaves did their work in and around the house. Licinia's mother passed through the peristyle a few times, but the couple was given a modicum of privacy and an opportunity to be alone. It was all part of the introduction process.

Gaius was quite different than his brother. He was generally quiet but capable of passionate outbursts. He sat down next to Licinia on the garden bench and got immediately to the point of his visit. "We are to be married in a year's time," he said very businesslike.

Licinia bowed her head to hide how thrilled she was to see Gaius.

"I will be in Spain much of that time and wanted to see you once more before I left," he hesitated, lowered his eyes, then looked up at her again, "because I truly enjoyed meeting you the first time."

Licinia contained her smile. She was five years younger than Gaius in age but quite possibly his equal in maturity. "I believe we have been fortunate in this arrangement."

"I was hoping that was how you felt."

"It certainly makes things a bit easier." Licinia now bestowed her best smile on him.

With no premeditation, Gaius reached down and put his hand on hers. She looked directly at him and grasped his hand. It passed between them with no words that at some time in the future they would share an even greater intimacy.

Licinia then asked the question she had been thinking about ever since her mother informed her that Gaius was coming to visit. "What is your role in the army?"

"I'm an equestrian in the cavalry. I had very little combat duty last year, but I expect that to increase in this second campaign."

"Is it dangerous?"

Gaius understood what was behind her question. "All campaigns are dangerous. The travel is difficult. The life is hard. But it's something I enjoy. Can you possibly see that I might?" Now it was his turn to offer Licinia his best smile.

Nor did she miss it. She squeezed his hand and looked down at her lap. "I will worry about you." She looked up at him. "After such a grand match, it seems impossible that you won't come back." She compressed her lips to contain her emotion.

"I hope that's true. The campaign will be difficult, and I will be in harm's way. I expect that a significant number of the men who march out of Rome with me won't come back." He was serious and grim.

"Are you more at risk on a horse than a soldier on foot?"

"We're told to think only of duty and dedication to the state. It makes it easier."

"But are you at more risk?"

"Only if my skills are not the best." He looked off momentarily. "The foot soldier, especially those in the front line, the hastati, face the highest likelihood of being killed. But fate chooses her victims without prejudice. I'm as likely to be pierced by an arrow as taken by fever."

Licinia's eyes were welling up, and she lowered her head so Gaius could not see. He squeezed her hand to get her to look at him. "Soldiers are taught not to think about it, and you shouldn't either. Death is invariably an unannounced visitor. Even here in Rome you might fall victim to an illness or the bite of a spider, while I might survive all summer in a valley filled with the dead and wounded."

Licinia embraced Gaius, pressing her face against his shoulder to hide her tears.

"Come now, future wife." He let his head lay against hers, close to her ear. "As you said," he whispered, "we are too well-fated to have any but the best outcomes."

Licinia released him to sit back and look into his face, then smiled. "Yes, that's right." She touched him on the cheek with her finger. "Next time we share time on this bench that will be a kiss."

CHAPTER 19

One month after Tiberius introduced his bill to the public, the tribunate called for a meeting of the People's Assembly to vote on land reform. Shortly before dawn, the day of the Assembly, large clusters of plebeians began the trek to the top the Capitoline Hill where the voting would take place. Tiberius, a man who rarely showed his emotions, could not have been more excited. The bill marked the beginning of his political career, and it was something he believed in deeply. He felt he was doing Rome an important service, and as he climbed the Capitoline Hill that day, he felt exhilarated and filled with pride. He had done the footwork and made the effort to reach as many people as he could. He knew what his constituents thought about the bill and had little doubt it would pass. Then the real work of putting the law into action would begin.

The temple of Jupiter, referred to as the Capitoline Triad because it contained the statues of three gods—Jupiter, Minerva, and Juno, sat on the crest of the hill, facing a large, open field. As the sun broke the horizon in the east, some thirty thousand plebs milled around in the field assembling into their tribes. A tribunal was set up in front of the temple. The tribunes would address the Assembly and supervise the process of voting from this upraised platform. The ten tribunes gathered behind the platform to draw lots to determine who would preside. Blossius and Diophanes stood off to one side of the tribunal to watch. Appius and Crassus were also there but in a less conspicuous location.

The tribune Rubrius Varro drew the proper lot. He was a little older than Tiberius and had experience as an aedile. Unusually tall for a Roman, he wore his black hair long and had a clean-shaven face. He opened the Assembly with a sacrifice to Jupiter and the reading of the entrails. He then called for the poulterer.

The poulterer came forward with a wooden cage containing three chickens. Rubrius accepted a handful of feed from the poulterer and sprinkled it into the cage. The measure of the moment was revealed by how eagerly the chickens consumed the feed. On this occasion they ate but not with great energy. Rubrius interpreted this as an acceptable response and announced that the gods conferred their blessings on the upcoming vote.

The crowd, which had been quiet during the religious ceremonies, now began to talk excitedly among themselves in anticipation of the vote. Despite his confidence that the bill would pass, Tiberius was well aware of Publius Nasica's visit to our mother's home and his cousin's influence in the Senate. He anticipated difficulties down the road, but not today. The vote would be a celebration of populist ideals, another step toward bringing greater balance to the workings of the Republic. And once the bill had become law, only another vote by the Assembly could repeal it.

Before the ballots were collected the entire bill had to be read to the Assembly. A herald climbed onto the tribunal with a scroll in his hand. He stood up to the wooden podium in the center of the platform and placed the scroll in front of him, then lifted his hands for quiet. When the commotion settled down to a low buzz, he unrolled the scroll.

As the herald positioned himself to read the bill, Marcus Octavius, one of the ten tribunes standing behind the herald, stepped forward. "I am vetoing the land reform bill and forbid the herald from reading it."

The entire Assembly was stunned. Although entirely unexpected, Octavius' call to halt the reading was legal. Each of the ten tribunes had the power to impose a veto on any law or magisterial action. Octavius was a longtime friend of Tiberius' and his veto came as a complete surprise to him. He quickly strode across the platform to confront his friend.

"Why are you doing this, Octavius? Have I somehow insulted you or your family? I don't understand."

"It's not a good law."

"What do you mean? This proposal is designed to increase the security of the state. What are your objections?"

When Octavius didn't answer, Tiberius, always a calm and patient man, paced twice across the stage, clearly fighting his emotions. He approached Octavius for a second time. "Is it your own land holdings, Octavius?"

Octavius still didn't respond.

"Is that it? You're protecting your own interests."

Octavius glanced to the far edge of the crowd. Several of the largest landowners, all patricians, were standing in a group to watch the proceedings. Publius Nasica's presence could not be missed.

Tiberius understood right away. Octavius was under the sway of outside forces. He shook his head in dismay. "Octavius, forget these other men. I don't know what influence they have over you, but if it's your own property that you want to protect, I will reimburse you personally for whatever you might lose. This law is too important to be blocked by one man's petty needs."

Tiberius told the herald to go ahead and read the bill, but no sooner did the man pronounce the first words, than Octavius placed his hand on the open scroll to stop him—again imposing his veto.

By this time the Assembly had broken order. The crowd that had been aligned in its thirty-five tribes turned into a mob. Men shouted at the herald to get on with it. Others targeted Octavius with abuse. The rest talked among themselves, trying to make sense of what was happening. They wanted to vote.

Tiberius feared for the life of his bill. He wanted a chance to talk to Octavius in private. He considered him an honorable man who would be open to reason. Tiberius spoke quickly to Rubrius Varro. Rubrius stepped up to the podium and told the increasingly rowdy Assembly that the meeting was over for the day, and that they would reconvene in two days to vote on the bill.

CHAPTER 20

Following the dismissal of the Assembly, Tiberius asked Blossius and Appius to meet him at Cornelia's house at noon the next day. My husband Aemilianus had only recently left for Numantia, as had Gaius. I was with Cornelia in the peristyle when Tiberius arrived. He was clearly out of sorts.

Cornelia met him in the atrium. I could hear them talking. "I heard what happened, Tiberius. Have you talked to Octavius?"

"I've been trying to find him all morning. I finally learned that he has left the city entirely. Apparently he has no interest in conferring with me."

They came into the peristyle. Tiberius looked at me and shook his head sadly.

"Do you think he's been bought off?" I asked.

"That's all I can figure. He's also subject to property losses, but not so grand as some of the senators I saw at the Assembly. Publius Nasica was with them. He appears to be their leader. My own cousin!"

"Do you think they got to Octavius before the election and prompted him to run for the tribunate to represent their interests?"

"That's very possible, Mother. Who could have imagined such a thing?"

"Apparently my nephew," sighed Cornelia.

"How are you, Tiberius?" I asked.

"Not good."

"What do you intend to do?"

"I'm not quite sure. Blossius and Appius should be here soon. I want to talk to them before I make any decisions."

"What kind of support do you have from the other tribunes?"

"Not the best. I think my determination to get this done has them on edge."

We could hear noise coming from the front of the house.

"That must be Blossius and Appius," said Tiberius. "I'm going to take them to the library. Mother, you're welcome to join us. As are you, Sempronia."

We followed Tiberius to the atrium where Blossius and Appius were waiting. The five of us spent most of the afternoon in the library. There were no good ideas. Appius was as angry as anyone about what had happened, but he also knew what had gone on behind the scenes.

"The pontiff and his friends have been working on this since you first made the bill public. Apparently they targeted Octavius from the beginning. I don't know if they bought him off or what. But evidently they're prepared to do anything to stop you."

"And I'm prepared to do anything to put the law in place."

I had never seen Tiberius so worked up. I always imagined him to be one of the most even-tempered people I knew. He was much like Cornelia, reason invariably trumped passion. But he was surely struggling with that now.

"Do you remember what happened six years ago, when one of the tribunes proposed a law that would require the election of magistrates to be conducted by ballot instead of voice?" asked Cornelia. "It was something heavily opposed by the senators. They thought it would interfere with their ability to sway the vote. Much like they have with Octavius, they prompted one of the tribunes to veto the measure."

"Yes, I remember that, Mother," said Tiberius, "Aemilianus stepped in and convinced the tribune to drop his veto. But Octavius won't even talk to me, and Aemilianus is in Spain. I have no idea how to make him change his mind."

"I'm not so sure Aemilianus would be of any help, brother."

Tiberius nodded. "He wasn't too excited about my idea, was he?"

"The central purpose of the tribunate is to represent the view of the people," stated Blossius, who had already filled a cup with my mother's best wine. "Make Octavius defend his veto on those grounds. Everything that this law is trying to do is for the good of the people. Beyond that it's good for the community and the state of Rome. Demand that he explain to the Assembly how plebeians stand to gain from his veto. Ask him to defend his position from the perspective of the common man."

"Blossius is right," said Appius. "Tomorrow, if he throws down his veto, put him on the spot. Ask him how his position benefits the people."

"Or ask him if there are specific parts of the law that particularly offend him," added Cornelia. "Ask him what changes would make the law more acceptable."

"That's giving in, Cornelia." Blossius threw down what was in his cup then refilled it. "Make him defend his veto."

"I agree with Blossius, Mother. I don't see any room for compromise. We are in the right. His motives are transparent to everyone. He represents the optimates."

Appius nodded. "And you would be wise to gather your clients. Bring them to the Assembly tomorrow and make their presence widely known."

Cornelia frowned. "For what reason?"

"To let Octavius know we mean business."

Tiberius looked at his mother, then Appius. "No, I'm against using any kind of intimidation."

"Maybe it's not a bad idea," said Blossius. "For your own protection. You've challenged a powerful group of men."

Cornelia stared at the floor and shook her head. Tiberius put his arm around her shoulder. "I'll make Octavius defend his position. That should be good enough."

CHAPTER 21

Anticipation for the second attempt to vote on land reform could not have been greater. Both the common citizen and the wealthy aristocrat were on edge wondering how Octavius would respond to the building pressure to rescind his veto. Plebeians began gathering on the top of the Capitoline Hill before dawn to assemble into their tribes. It was a typical day in late April, cool with a threat of rain. Nearly everyone wore a woolen cloak over his toga. A large contingent of landowners led by three senators, Publius Nasica, Titus Annius in his orange wig, and Quintus Pompeius, arrived at sunrise and fanned out along the Assembly perimeter to monitor the proceedings. Blossius and Diophanes watched from the right of the tribunal.

The tribune Publius Satureius was chosen by lot to preside. The necessary religious ceremonies were completed without any untoward results. Satureius stepped up to the podium and asked the herald to read the bill. The buzzing Assembly went quiet. The other nine tribunes stood in a line across the rear of the tribunal, Octavius at one end, Tiberius at the other. Octavius did not hesitate. He announced his veto before the herald had a chance to unroll the scroll.

Tiberius stalked across the platform and faced Octavius. "If you are so intent on blocking this bill, Tribune," said Tiberius derisively, "please tell your constituency why you're doing it. Tell them how your veto benefits them."

Octavius said nothing.

Tiberius asked him again. "How does your veto benefit these people? Please tell them. They're anxious to vote."

Several of those standing up close to tribunal shouted at Octavius to answer the question. Others taunted his silence. When Tiberius posed the question a third time, Octavius answered with the same slogans the optimates had been using since the beginning. "This law will disrupt the natural order of our society. Taking land from our wealthiest citizens will weaken the Republic. These are the men that take the most responsibility for our state, leading our legions and doing the work of the Senate. Weakening them impairs their ability to govern."

Tiberius shook his head at Octavius' defense. "So you're saying that these men, who already have great wealth, will be impaired by giving up land they acquired illegally?"

Octavius became incensed. "The ownership of land has always been the standard of responsibility in Roman politics. These men have dedicated their entire lives to the state, something only men of substance can do. Why should we suddenly penalize some of our oldest families for their accumulation of land, something achieved over many generations—and not illegally as you say. It was fair reward for their successful military campaigns and the glory they have won for Rome."

Tiberius had arrived that morning containing a deep anger. He bit onto his words to keep from freeing it. "But can't much the same be said of the ordinary citizen? Won't that man make a better soldier if he has something at stake when he risks his life?"

This brought a great roar of approval from the Assembly. "Yes, yes," they shouted.

Octavius tried to turn away from Tiberius. Tiberius put his hand on Octavius' shoulder, forcing him to face the audience. "Tell the Assembly why your veto is good for them? Not why it's good for the patricians."

Octavius forcefully pushed Tiberius' hand away, glared at Tiberius, then snarled at the crowd. "Why do you seek to punish the greatest men of our time by taking their land? Is it simply to give gifts to those who have not earned it? Have not led armies or sorted through piles of legislative documents for hours on end?"

The crowd responded with a shower of boos and catcalls. Tiberius looked to the heavens, then addressed the Assembly. "This is some tribune we have here." He motioned with his open hand to Octavius. "His heart bleeds for the aristocrats even though he was elected to represent you."

Octavius turned to leave the stage, and for a second time Tiberius stopped him with his hand. "What does this veto do for the common citizen, Octavius? Please tell us before you run off to hide."

Octavius snapped. He pushed Tiberius in the chest. The two men were at each other, wrestling more than throwing fists. The other tribunes rushed forward to pull them apart. Several plebeians rushed the stage as the Assembly edged into chaos.

Two previous consuls, Gaius Fulvius Flaccus and Marcus Manilius, both friends of Tiberius' father, were there to watch. They forced their way onto the stage, and through their personal reputation and prestige, managed to quiet the crowd. Then they asked Publius Satureius to call off the meeting for the day.

Tiberius, held by two tribunes, screamed at Octavius as he hurried off the platform, where he was immediately surrounded by the clients of Publius Nasica and Titus Annius and escorted off the hill.

After the Assembly had dispersed, Fulvius stepped up close to Tiberius, furious at him for losing his composure. "Tiberius, get a hold of yourself. This is not the proper way to stop a veto."

"Then what is?" sneered Tiberius, way out of character.

"Go to the Senate tomorrow. Make your case. Maybe it was a mistake not to do that in the first place. Ask their opinion of the bill. Argue for their support. With the backing of the Senate, these others that are blocking the bill might back off."

Blossius was now on the stage beside Tiberius. He agreed with Fulvius. "Yes, Tiberius, he's right. There's that slim chance the Senate will understand the value of what you're asking for. We don't really know where the majority stands. Surely some of the senators will come to your aid."

Tiberius gradually calmed. He was not convinced, but he told his friends that he would take their advice.

CHAPTER 22

Tiberius lived on the Palatine Hill in Rome's wealthiest neighborhood, but his home was not overly large or ornate. Like his father, Tiberius lived a relatively austere life, reminiscent of Roman life one hundred years earlier.

Tiberius went home after the second failed vote, utterly exasperated. Claudia met him as he came through the front door. Tiberius and his wife were well-suited. Much like her husband, Claudia embraced the simpler life. Her stola was bleached wool. She wore no face paint, and her only jewelry was a pearl pendant on a necklace of gold chain. She saw everything she needed to know in Tiberius' face and immediately embraced him. He allowed her to hold him for only a moment, then turned away, distracted by the fact that he would have to confront the Senate the next day. He also felt bad about arguing with Octavius. The ten tribunes of the plebs were supposed to be of one mind. What had happened was like a family fighting in public

"I'm guessing you didn't talk Octavius out of the veto," said Claudia, following Tiberius into the house, really more concerned about his well-being than his politics. She, like the entire Gracchi family, was well-educated and capable of both speaking and writing in Greek, but she didn't follow politics the way the rest of the family did. Her only real political interest was how it affected her husband.

Tiberius stood in the atrium and stared up at the sky for some time before responding to his wife's question. "It went badly. Octavius imposed his veto for a second time. I'm going to the Senate tomorrow to ask for their support." His tone exposed his skepticism. "I have no idea how that will work out. I just can't believe this is what it's come to—a fight within the tribunate." He shook his head, then suddenly caught himself. He smiled at Claudia and opened his arms to her. "But I should let it rest for the evening."

Claudia nestled into his arms and looked up at him.

He kissed her on the forehead. "Please forgive me for the mood I'm in. All of this is very difficult, but I shouldn't let it into our home. Where are the children?"

Claudia remained in Tiberius' arms, already well aware that his initial coldness had not been directed at her. She knew of no man as caring and thoughtful as her husband. "Tiberius is with Ada in the triclinium. Sempronia's in bed."

Even as simply as my brother and his wife lived, they had four slaves. Ada was an olive-skinned Iberian from the Ilergertes tribe. She had been with them since their son's birth. Despite Tiberius' recent concern over the number of slaves working the land, like many Romans, the couple had become accustomed to the luxury of house slaves, and thought little of it. Claudia touched her husband's cheek. "I'll have Tiberius brought to you when he's finished eating."

"I'm already done," shouted the young boy as he dashed out of the triclinium and ran to his father. "Father, I saw two snakes today."

Tiberius let go of Claudia to catch his five-year-old son in his arms. He swung the little man around once then placed him on a bench beside the pool so he could look him in the eyes.

"Where were they?"

"I found them together in your favorite helmet. They had laid eggs."

"Truly?" Tiberius could not help remembering the story of our father's death. "What did the snakes look like?"

"They were brown with cross hatching on their backs. Ada said they were rat snakes and that they caught rodents."

He thought of the seer's advice to his father. Let one go, kill the other. "And she let them both go?"

"Yes, even though I wanted to keep them, and then she threw out the eggs."

Tiberius touched his son's cheek. "They are better off free, son. And you, I believe, would be better off in bed. It's late."

"But I'm not tired. I don't want to go to bed."

Ada had followed Tiberius out of the triclinium. "I'll take him, sir."

The little boy jumped off the bench and took off at a run, but Claudia caught him and directed him to the housemaid. The boy and slave ascended to the second floor of the atrium, leaving Tiberius standing at the edge of the pool, looking into the water, clearly distracted by what lay ahead, and deeply disturbed that the argument today had nearly come to blows.

Claudia watched her husband stare at his reflection. She had never seen him so upset.

CHAPTER 23

Tiberius went to the Curia before sunrise the next morning. The entire city knew that he would be asking the Senate for an opinion on his land reform bill. The forum and the area around the comitium were already packed with anxious Roman citizens when he arrived with Blossius, Diophanes, and ten of his clients.

The sacrifice prior to convening the Senate took place at dawn. Publius Nasica read the entrails and solemnly reported no abnormalities. Once inside the Curia, which quickly filled with curious citizens, Nasica also served as the aruspex. The chickens ate with vigor, and he announced that the auspices were favorable for that day's session of the Senate. The presiding consul, Mucius Scaevola, took his seat in one of the two ivory chairs that faced the three hundred senators seated in the amphitheater. The other consul, Calpurnius Piso, was in Sicily to put down the slave rebellion.

Tiberius and his advisors huddled to the left of the amphitheater, talking last-minute strategy, trying to make a headcount of the senators for and against the bill. On the opposite side of the room, nearly hidden in the shadows was Octavius, surrounded by his handlers' clients.

The bill had been public for over a month now, and many of the senators had already made their positions known. The co-consuls were split on the subject. Mucius Scaevola, Publius Crassus' brother, supported it; Calpurnius Piso did not. It was fortunate he was absent.

After the ordinary day-to-day business of the Senate was completed and the reports from the Roman provinces were given, Scaevola recognized Appius Claudius. Although everyone present was already well aware of what had happened, Appius described the events that had taken place at the People's Assembly, then requested that Tiberius be given a chance to speak. The request was accepted and

Tiberius, wearing a white toga over a tunic, made his way from the perimeter of the room to the center of the floor.

"By an oversight of mine," he began, talking with his usual calm, "I did not bring my land reform bill to the Senate prior to asking the People's Assembly to vote on it. That was clearly a mistake on my part which I am trying to make amends for today. The tribunate has not been able to come to a consensus on the bill, and I'm hoping to get an advisory statement from the Senate so that we might move forward with the law."

Tiberius went on to review the basic provisions of the law, fully aware that everyone in the Senate had already read the bill. When he finished, Scaevola asked for comments from the senators.

Quintus Pompeius stood up. "Even should this law be passed, I simply can't see how the division of land could be done equitably. The land that I own goes back several generations in my family. We have developed it, built our tombs on it, and even used it as collateral on loans that are still active. Who could possibly decide which part of our land we are to keep and which part we are to lose? Inequity is certain. I consider it a bad bill."

Titus Annius followed Pompeius. "What of compensation? All I see in this bill is that those who have exceeded land limits will not be fined and will get a deed for the land they are allowed to retain." He lifted his arms in exasperation. "Need I remind you, Tiberius, that those land limits you allude to go back two hundred years and haven't been enforced in a hundred? Those regulations are obsolete. Your compensation is worse than an insult. It's a bad joke."

"That's not quite true, Senator," responded Tiberius. "As recently as my father's first consulship those regulations were seen as enforceable. It's just that no one had the courage to do it."

Publius Nasica was given the floor when Annius sat down. He glared at Tiberius then turned to his fellow senators. "It's no wonder the tribunate can't agree on this law—it's a deliberate confiscation of wealth and undermines the efforts of the best men in the commonwealth. This bill is nothing short of treason. In my mind, there is only one possible answer to Tiberius' request. This law should never go to vote."

Appius stood up. "You're exaggerating, Senator. The law is not treason. It's for the betterment of the common man and the security of

Rome. The ownership of land gives the common man a stake in the state and a reason to put his life on the line for Rome."

Many of those standing around the perimeter cheered at Appius' words. Publius Nasica shouted a response without being recognized. "Who needs a reason to fight for the greatest nation in the world? Simply wearing the uniform of a Roman legionnaire is an honor for any man."

A chorus of support sounded from a majority of the senators.

"Then why are we so short of soldiers?" shouted Publius Crassus.

Publius Nasica ignored the question. "I propose the Senate rebuke this bill."

Several of the senators called out for a vote on the pontiff's proposal. Tiberius did not stay around to watch his opponents celebrate their victory. He used his left arm to wrap his toga around his body and strode from the Curia, followed by Blossius, Diophanes, and his ten clients.

Octavius knew that Tiberius was preparing to reconvene the People's Assembly at noon. He conferred with Publius Nasica and then headed to the top of the Capitoline Hill with a small protective body of clients.

CHAPTER 24

Tiberius and his entourage went to Cornelia's house to talk over their strategy before going to the Assembly. His little cluster of clients, led by his close associate Quintus Mummius, waited on the street, acting as guards as much as political allies.

Cornelia was working in the garden when they came in. Claudia was with her. She had been too nervous about the discussion at the Senate to stay home alone. Ada and the children were there also.

Tiberius, Blossius, and Diophanes thundered into the atrium as Cornelia came out of the peristyle wearing a pair of goatskin gloves. She held a small spade in her right hand and a spot of dirt showed on her stola where she had been kneeling. Claudia trailed behind, fearful of what Tiberius' stormy arrival meant.

"It didn't go well, Mother," said Tiberius as he embraced Claudia. "The Senate recommended no vote at all. I'm not sure what we're going to do, but we need to think of something fast. People are assembling in their tribes on the Capitoline Hill as we speak."

Blossius had already gone to find an amphora of wine, though he hardly had time to drink more than a few sips.

"Are you sure it makes sense to force your law through now?" asked Claudia. "What about waiting a few months and trying it again?"

Tiberius shook his head. "I have one year to pass this law and put it into action. If it's not now, it's not at all."

Claudia's eyes reflected *not at all*.

"I've thought of something," said Cornelia as Blossius returned with an amphora in one hand and a cup in the other. They gathered in the atrium beneath a slate gray sky. "Aemilianus established a precedent several years ago for a tribune giving up his position. If I'm not mistaken, it's usually by the tribune's own choosing, but maybe Octavius could be pressured. If the people vote the tribunes in, wouldn't it be possible that they could vote one out?"

The men looked at each other. Blossius spoke. "Yes, Cornelia. I think that could be done."

"On what grounds?" asked Tiberius.

Diophanes put a hand of Tiberius' shoulder. "Dereliction of duty. Octavius is not doing his job. That's what we heard loud and clear two days ago in his defense of the veto. Every reason he offered spoke to the needs of the aristocracy. But his duty is to serve the people. You'd have no trouble getting your assembly to back you on that. You saw how angry they were that the vote didn't take place. Let them vote him out, then proceed with your law."

Cornelia nodded. "But it would be best if he simply rescinded his veto because of the threat of such a move—so that maybe his banishment wouldn't come to a vote. Octavius is not a bad man. I don't know the depth of his relationship with my nephew and his friends, but when you show him that he has no choice, he can salvage some of his respect by accepting what we are all so certain is a promising law."

"I think you've given us some hope, Mother—at least a plan. Thank you. We'll soon find out if it works." Tiberius looked at Blossius and Diophanes. "We should leave." Tiberius gave Claudia a brief embrace, then Cornelia. The three men joined Tiberius' clients on the street and headed directly to the top of the Capitoline Hill.

CHAPTER 25

The scene that had unfolded before repeated itself. The ten tribunes took their place on the tribunal. A very agitated and rowdy thirty thousand plebs were roughly assembled in their tribes, waiting for something to happen. Tiberius asked the herald to read the law. As soon as he opened the scroll, Octavius halted him by enacting his veto. The whole place hushed as Tiberius strode across the platform to confront him. Tiberius' ten clients had collected at the bottom of the tribunal stairs, angrily glaring at Octavius with unstated threats. It was all far beyond the norm.

"Octavius," said Tiberius, only loud enough for those on the tribunal to hear. "I am your friend. We have argued here on this stage twice now. Nothing I have ever done has been harder on me than confronting you on this piece of legislation. Please reconsider."

Octavius heard the sincerity in Tiberius' voice. He hung his head, struggling badly with his conscience, but finally said, "No, Tiberius. I won't allow this bill to be voted on."

Tiberius took a breath to contain his emotions. "I'm going to ask the Assembly to remove you, Octavius. It can be done with a single vote. And you know as well as I do what the outcome will be. The Assembly is not happy with what you're doing. Once you're voted out, we will vote on the law. Your position is hopeless, but you can save us all a lot of trouble, and your own reputation, by lifting your veto."

Octavius simply shook his head no.

"Very well." Tiberius turned to his fellow tribunes. He had already informed them of his intentions. They looked around uneasily, but no one stepped forward to question him. Tiberius went to the podium to address the Assembly. He explained all of the same things that he had to Octavius, emphasizing the position Octavius had defended at the previous meeting. "A tribune's job is to represent the plebeians not the patricians," he concluded. "I propose a vote to dismiss Marcus

Octavius from the tribunate for dereliction of duty. Please discuss this among your tribal members. The question is a simple *yes* or *no*. Octavius is dismissed from the tribunate or not. Draw lots to determine who votes first and then prepare your ballot as soon as you can. We hope to have a second vote—on the land reform bill—pending the outcome of this one."

Tiberius returned to the cluster of tribunes. No one said a word to him. They knew this had never been done before. They were tense and uncomfortable, but also unwilling to confront the man who had taken control.

Publius Nasica, Titus Annis, and Quintus Pompeius were watching from the wings. They had left the Senate confident they had stopped Tiberius. Now they stood there awestruck, visibly angered by Tiberius' tactics. Publius Nasica approached the tribunal with a cluster of his clients and called up to Octavius. "Don't worry. This is illegal. The Senate will annul the vote."

Octavius looked lost. He only nodded.

When the tribes signaled that they were ready, Tiberius instructed the herald to take the vote. The Aemilia tribe had the privilege of voting first. One of their tribal elders stepped forward. "Yes, dismiss the tribune."

There were thirty-five tribes. It took a simple majority of eighteen to carry a vote. The first seventeen tribes voted to dismiss. At this point, Tiberius again came up close to Octavius, and in a soft voice, filled with feeling, begged him to rescind his veto and save himself the embarrassment. Octavius seemed to melt under the pressure. He turned to his handlers, now standing some distance off, as though seeking their permission. No sign was given. Octavius faced Tiberius. The entire Assembly went silent, certain he was going to acquiesce, only to hear Octavius say *no* once more.

Tiberius was now badly shaken. He, like Cornelia, had anticipated that Octavius would yield. He would get no pleasure from removing Octavius, or really any man, from the tribunate. Tears accumulated in his eyes. He embraced Octavius as a friend and whispered in his ear, "Please, Octavius, don't make me do this. I simply don't understand why you must resist."

Octavius pulled away from Tiberius. Tiberius shook his head in frustration, then nodded to the herald. The herald called for the next tribe to vote. It was another yes. Octavius' fate was sealed, but he still refused to leave the stage. Tiberius motioned to the group of his clients beside the platform. Mummius led them up onto the stage. They took hold of Octavius by the arms and forced him off the tribunal. Octavius' slave came out of the crowd to help his master. He was easily pushed aside, but he continued to come at the cluster of clients. In the tumult he was poked in the eye. He fell to the ground, covering the bleeding eye socket with his hands, as Octavius was pushed and shoved past the cluster of senators down the hill away from the Assembly.

Once the eighteenth *yes* was recorded, the vote was over. The other tribes were not asked for their position. The herald announced the result as unanimous. Tiberius then told him to read the bill. No one stopped the herald this time. He read the entire text of Tiberius' land reform bill, then requested a vote. The tribes had discussed this vote weeks before. They needed no time to prepare. The Horatia tribe was called on first. Again the question required either a yes or a no. The first eighteen tribes voted yes. Again a unanimous result. No one had doubted that it would go any other way. Thirty thousand plebeians erupted in celebration. It was a great day for the common man and a great day for Tiberius Gracchus.

Before ending the meeting, Tiberius requested that the Assembly vote on a replacement for Octavius. He suggested Quintus Mummius, and the enthusiastic Assembly quickly accepted Tiberius' nominee. That Mummius was one of Tiberius' clients only further infuriated the senators who were still there to watch. Publius Nasica abruptly swirled his toga around his body and led the others away from the Assembly. Their heated talk was not about the passage of the law, but the power that Tiberius had acquired by legislating such a popular law. "He's a dangerous man," growled the pontifex maximus. "A man who has to be dealt with before he gains any more influence."

After the crowd had dispersed, Tiberius, elated at finally getting the law approved, but exhausted by a day full of turmoil, clomped down the tribunal stairs into the arms of Blossius, then Diophanes, then faced the growing mass of men who wanted to congratulate him. He had done it. Not without pain. Not without tears. But he had done it. Land reform was on the books. There was no way the Senate could annul it. Tiberius turned to the temple behind him, and the statue of the God of

Light inside, sitting on a gilded throne. "Thank you for the strength, Jupiter," he whispered under his breath. "Thank you for the strength."

CHAPTER 26

Tiberius, the unofficial leader of a very reluctant and somewhat divided tribunate, called for the convening of the People's Assembly a week later to elect the three commissioners who would oversee the process of redistributing the land. No one in Rome was more popular among the plebeians by a long measure than Tiberius. When he proposed that he head the commission and that his father-in-law Appius Claudius and his brother Gaius, still in Spain and only eighteen, be his aides, the Assembly quickly voted to accept them all.

The core group of opposing senators watched the proceedings from afar. Already concerned about Tiberius' growing power, they were further outraged by Tiberius' stacking the commission with members of his own family. The ex-consul Titus Annius, standing with Publius Nasica and Quintus Pompeius, and wearing a yellow wig on this occasion, could not restrain himself. He advanced to the front of the tribunal and shouted at Tiberius. "Your vote to remove Octavius was illegal. Expect to be prosecuted when your term as tribune is over."

Those plebeians close enough to hear Annius told him in the roughest way that a patrician was not welcome at a gathering of plebeians, but Tiberius, invigorated by the day's vote, felt compelled to defend his actions. He came to the front of the tribunal to respond to Annius' charge. "I'm afraid your threat is an empty one, Senator. I have done nothing illegal."

Although surrounded by angry plebeians, Annius glared at Tiberius. "Then answer this question," he demanded. "Suppose you propose to disgrace me, and I appeal for protection from one of your colleagues on the tribunate. If he comes to my assistance, and you get angry, will you have him deposed?"

The question quieted the rowdy crowd and caused Tiberius to hesitate before saying anything. It was a trick question, designed to force Tiberius into defending something that was quite different than the action he had pursued—and more like what Appius' daughter had done when the tribune had tried to halt her father's triumph.

Annius stared up at Tiberius, thinking he had him. The plebeians around him seemed confused by the question and looked to Tiberius to provide an answer.

Tiberius paced across the stage several times, collecting his thoughts, knowing if he did not speak accurately, his words could be misconstrued or even used against him. Finally, he stopped and stood at the podium to address Annius, the assembled plebeians, and the senators still standing some distance away.

"Yes, Senator, a tribune does have the authority to protect a citizen from a magistrate, and it would be improper for another tribune to demand that tribune's expulsion for doing so. But that's different than what happened here a week ago. A tribune of the plebs is sacred and inviolable, but only if the tribune does the job he was elected to perform—which is represent the will of the common man. If a tribune's actions lead to measures that oppress the people, abridge their powers, or take away their liberty or their ability to vote, then he no longer deserves the honor bestowed upon him. Octavius was protecting the interests of the aristocracy and working against the interests of the common citizen. He was not providing the service he was elected to perform; so he lost the right to serve."

"But you said it yourself, the tribune is sacrosanct," shouted back Annius. "He cannot be removed from office."

"Untrue, Senator. Are not the Vestal Virgins also sacrosanct? And can they not be executed, nay buried alive, for allowing the sacred flame to go out or breaking their vow of chastity? It's happened several times in our history. The instance of Octavius is no different. He violated his duties, and if the people can vote a man into office, then they can surely vote him out."

The Assembly agreed with Tiberius and responded by chanting his name and peppering Annius with insults. The senator turned away abruptly, causing his wig to twist to the left, then pushed through the crowd back to his associates, who again furious at what they had seen, left the grounds grumbling about Tiberius' demagoguery.

CHAPTER 27

Following the successful though controversial passage of the land reform bill and the equally controversial filling of the three-man commission with members of Tiberius' family, the Roman Senate showed their dissatisfaction by providing an allowance of only one and a half denarii a day for the administration of the law. This was equivalent to the daily pay of a single unskilled laborer. It was a clear insult to Tiberius and his commission. When he asked for extra funds to provide for a tent when the commission traveled through Italy to evaluate the land, he was turned down. The commissioners would, in effect, pay their expenses out of their own pockets and receive no compensation.

Tiberius was infuriated. As far as I could tell my dear brother's entry into politics was changing him from one of the most reasonable and thoughtful people I had ever met into an emotional and reactionary politician. Though his exceptional personal attributes never really changed around me or his family, the pressure he was under was obvious and, though he tried to hide it, painful to watch.

Tiberius' wife Claudia was so distraught she came to talk to Cornelia one afternoon. I happened to be there. Cornelia had her loom set up in the atrium and was weaving, something she loved to do and was very good at.

As I have said, Claudia was the least political of all the women in our family. Part of it was her natural inclination to keep her thoughts to herself, and part of it was that she had a five-year-old son and a two-year-old daughter to care for. Despite her education and wider sense of the world, Claudia was a more typical Roman woman than either Cornelia or I. She was a very pretty woman, and when she came to the house that day with her children, she wore a lovely pale green stola, gathered at the waist with a matching sash, and a similarly matching palla that covered her head. Beneath, her hair was a dark red and held loosely behind her head within a white, knitted hairnet.

Upon entering the house, she dispatched the children with Ava, then joined Cornelia and me in the atrium. She removed the palla from her head, draped it over her shoulders, and began to cry.

Cornelia immediately stood to embrace Claudia. She held her long enough for Claudia to gather herself and sit down on a bench adjacent to mine. Cornelia sat beside her.

"I'm worried about Tiberius," she said—something already very obvious. "I know his intentions are pure, but the political process seems to be taking hold of him. I don't know when you last talked to him, but his latest move, which I believe he's announcing to the Senate as we speak, involves shutting down the treasury until the Senate gives his commission more funds to work with. I think he's going too far."

"I hadn't heard that, Claudia." Cornelia looked at me.

"I hadn't either."

"Blossius and Diophanes were at our home yesterday. One of them made the suggestion. Tiberius didn't sleep at all last night thinking about it. He left the house this morning before dawn. I only had enough time to ask him where he was going. Halfway out the door, he answered, 'To the temple of Saturn to place my seal on the doors.' I shouted back that I didn't think it was right, but he paid me no mind." Claudia heaved with emotion. "I'm more concerned about his safety now than when he was in Spain." Tears were running from her eyes again. "Am I being silly?" she choked out.

"I think military duty is certainly more dangerous than politics, Claudia, but what's going on now," Cornelia sighed, "is unlike anything I've ever seen before. And I agree, Tiberius is changing and I'm not sure if it's helping his cause or not."

I nodded. "We've all seen it, Claudia. I think it was inevitable once he decided to advance on land reform. He knew, we all knew, there would be stiff resistance from certain people."

"Certain people," muttered Claudia. "His own cousin is his staunchest opponent. It's terrible."

Cornelia stood up and paced uneasily across the atrium. The news that Tiberius was sealing the doors to the treasury had upset her. Like Tiberius, she rarely let her emotions show but they were now, and Claudia did not miss it.

"See, Cornelia, even you're distressed. It's bad, very bad. I wish Aemilianus were back. Tiberius might listen to him. I'm afraid my father is leading him on."

Just her saying my husband's name made me cringe. "Aemilianus disagrees with what Tiberius is doing," I said. "They have argued the point several times already."

"I still wish he were back. He provides the high ground. I'm afraid of what these other men might do."

Cornelia sat beside Claudia and put her arm around her. Her face was taut and pale. "Rather than worry, let's put our faith in Tiberius." Her face expressed the opposite. "He's picked a difficult fight. He needs our full support. Nothing good comes easily in Roman politics."

CHAPTER 28

As a tribune, Tiberius did have the power to seal the treasury doors. And that was what he did. He effectively froze government payments and withdrawals, and all but shut down the city. Tiberius' followers, the mass of plebeians, thought it was fantastic. They loved seeing one of their own thumbing his nose at the aristocracy. But the Senate was furious and was forced to meet without its paid staff. Some of the senators who had originally supported Tiberius now backed off, causing an even wider rift between the people and the aristocracy.

According to Cornelia, the city could get by for about a month before the lack of payments would start to impact commerce. Apparently Tiberius was well aware of that and planned to use this timeline to leverage funds for his commission. Two weeks passed with neither side giving in. At the beginning of the third week, a close friend of Tiberius', Decius Pennus, who had fought with him in Africa and then again in Numantia, was found dead in the street.

Rumors that he had been murdered by Tiberius' opponents spread through the populace, but there were no marks on the body or signs of a struggle. Decius was a young man and was not ill in any way. After an unsettling day or two of accusations, the initial fear of political retribution passed. When the body was cremated, however, a dark substance seeped out of the torso extinguishing the funeral pyre. When the priests tried to relight the fire, it would not restart. One of them said he had seen this before with the corpse of a man who had been poisoned. Rumors of foul play again raced through the city and cast even greater darkness over all that was happening.

Tiberius believed Decius had been murdered. Following the funeral, he made a public statement by walking through Rome with Claudia and his two children, all dressed in black. Claudia, who had already been concerned, was now beside herself with worry. But as a good wife, she did not ask Tiberius to change his tactics, nor did Cornelia.

With pressure building every day to open the treasury, Blossius advised Tiberius not to walk the streets alone and to always be surrounded by ten or more of his clients. Not since Rome's last king, Lucius Tarquinius, was physically expelled from the city, some four hundred years earlier, had politics descended into violence. The carrying of a weapon within the city limits was illegal; even soldiers returning from a campaign had to remove their gladii before entering the city. Now when Tiberius walked the streets his clients carried small clubs or daggers concealed in their togas.

Ten days after Decius' death, when the tensions in Rome could not get any greater, short of setting off a civil uprising, I decided to spend the night at Cornelia's home, something I often did when Aemilianus was out of town. A loud pounding on the front door awakened the household shortly after nightfall. Because of the political atmosphere, Cornelia had taken to having her house slave Coson stay up through the night as a precaution. Coson, who had spent nearly half his forty years in the Gracchi household, went to the door. Without opening it, he commanded whoever was there to go away and to come back in the morning. No one answered, but the knocking persisted.

Coson went out the back of the house armed with a club and snuck up the alley to see who was there. When he reached the front of the house, he saw Physcon waiting on the street in his carriage with his full retinue of guards and slaves. One of his guards, who probably did not speak Latin, was on the doorstep, continuing to knock.

Coson retraced his steps down the alley and entered the house through the back to inform Cornelia. Coson found her in the atrium in her robe. He told her who was at the door, and despite the disturbance and the late hour, Cornelia told him to welcome Physcon in. No one in the house was still asleep at this point. I found my robe and had worked my way down the stairs when Physcon entered. He wore a magnificent Tyrian purple cape, pulled around him like a cocoon with the hood over his head. Another man, also rather luxuriously dressed, and holding a scroll in one hand, accompanied Physcon. All was spoken in Greek.

"I hope this is important, Physcon," I heard Cornelia say as I approached. Her voice was thick with sleep, and her hair was undone and lay in waves over her shoulders down to the middle of her back. "It's late, and we all know how dangerous the streets of Rome are after dark." I have no idea how she managed to be so courteous.

Physcon took a moment to catch his breath, then slipped the hood off his head, revealing an ornate gold crown on his shaved head. "My apologies for waking you, Cornelia." He glanced at me as though to say the same. "I would never bother you at this hour if it weren't important." He turned to his companion who had the olive skin of a Persian. "I'd like to introduce you to Eudemus. He comes from Pergamum with the sad news of King Attalus' death."

Cornelia tipped her head toward the man who was tall and thin with a black, pointed beard and keen black eyes. The man bowed. "It's an honor, Cornelia. Your husband was a patron of our nation and is still remembered fondly."

"Thank you for saying that, sir," she replied. "I believe he felt the same way about King Attalus. I give you and your people my deepest sympathies."

The man motioned with his hand and bowed again.

Physcon got right to it. "Eudemus arrived today by ship. He knew I was in Rome and sought me out looking for a place to stay prior to going to the Senate to announce Attalus' death and read his will."

Eudemus nodded and lifted the scroll in his hand.

"Because of the late king's acquaintance with your husband, and the recent position taken by your son, I suggested he might want to talk to Tiberius before going to the Senate. Your son lives close by, I believe. Could you send a slave to get him?"

"Right now?" Cornelia asked in disbelief. I stood a distance off also wondering how this could involve Tiberius.

"Yes," said Physcon. "Attalus, like many of Rome's client kings, has left a generous gift to the people of Rome. Perhaps this is a way to solve Tiberius' current stalemate."

I am not sure if either Cornelia or I were awake enough to understand the implication of what he was offering, but something of Physcon's urgency was compelling. Coson was standing right there. Cornelia sent him to get Tiberius, telling him to emphasize that it was important.

After Coson left, Cornelia invited her guests to wait in the library, where Fidelia had lit a brazier and two oil lamps.

"I'm curious, Physcon," said Cornelia. "I can't say I fully grasp what all of this means, but it appears you're here to help my son. I would think his ideas run counter to yours. No one would ever call you a populist. Am I right?"

The pharaoh nodded then smiled. "Regardless of my beliefs, I'm open to doing anything that will improve my standing with you."

This was not what Cornelia wanted to hear, but she smiled. Despite Physcon's unwanted attention, she did like the man and would ordinarily enjoy his company except for his continuing push to marry her.

Fidelia came into the room with a tray of cups and an amphora of watered wine. She offered the first cup to Physcon and the second to Eudemus, a seemingly reserved and quiet man, yet to say more than a few words.

Tiberius entered the house through the back with Coson and came straight to the library. He wore a white tunic with a plain wool mantle draped over his head and shoulders. He gave an abbreviated bow to Physcon, well aware of his many offers of marriage to Cornelia, and another to the Pergamian envoy. "What is it?" he asked, already under tremendous stress and sleeping little. "The slave said something about King Attalus' death and a will. I'm not sure how this applies to me."

"Thank you for coming, Tiberius." Physcon smiled like a cat. "Eudemus," he motioned to the envoy, "please read the king's will. Then I think everyone will understand."

We all sat down as Eudemus unrolled the scroll and read the entire document. It was long and took some time, but the gist of it was clear. Attalus was leaving everything he owned to "the Roman people," as it was worded in the will. This amounted to a huge piece of land in Asia and a tremendous amount of gold and silver. It was not uncommon for a king in a Roman province to write a will like this. It provided security against assassination from others in his court.

After Eudemus rolled up the scroll, Tiberius looked at Physcon and nodded, then stood, holding back something close to a smirk. He paced across the room several times to gather his thoughts. Cornelia seemed to have some insight, but I had none.

Tiberius stopped pacing, clearly elated. "Pharaoh, I believe I have misjudged you all these years. You have done me a great service. I have one request of the king's envoy." He turned to Eudemus. "Allow me to make the announcement. I will do it as soon as I can gather the

People's Assembly. It may take a couple of days, but if I have understood the will correctly, Attalus has bequeathed his fortune to the Roman people not the Senate."

Eudemus said that was his reading also. And he agreed to give Tiberius the honor of making the announcement to the Assembly.

Tiberius' eyes swung to Cornelia then to me. "This money can be used to fund the commission and help those who are given land to start their lives over again. Nothing could be better. Once the people give me permission to use this money for the commission I can open the treasury and the business of Rome can continue."

CHAPTER 29

Three days after the envoy's arrival, without any notice to the Senate about the will or what he intended to do, Tiberius gathered the tribunate and the People's Assembly at Mars Field. He began the Assembly by having the herald read Attalus' will. When the herald was done, Tiberius explained what the will meant to the assembled tribes. He had already gone through this with the other tribunes, who were both shocked and thrilled by the news. They were also somewhat uneasy about Tiberius' plans for the endowment, but no one stepped up to argue against him, mainly because they believed he had become too popular to obstruct.

Tiberius then had the herald read a bill he had written with Appius and Blossius the day before. It authorized the use of King Attalus' bequest for the implementation of the land reform bill. This was all Tiberius really needed, but he took it a step further. A second part of the bill authorized the People's Assembly to manage the huge windfall of land, something that the Senate would have ordinarily done as part of foreign policy.

The Assembly voted unanimously to support both parts of the bill. When the voting was completed and the tribes had dispersed, Tiberius went to the Senate and told them he had removed his seal from the treasury doors. This was a welcome surprise, but when Tiberius went on to inform them of Attalus' death and the bill that had just been passed, they were furious and shouted him down. When Tiberius stalked out of the Curia, he was immediately surrounded by his clients, now a horde of fifty men. They quickly ushered him across town to his home, where interested citizens were already lining up to talk to him.

One of the most outspoken senators, Quintus Pompeius, took the floor after Tiberius' departure. "Tiberius Gracchus has gone too far. He's used one trick after another to transform the People's Assembly into a weapon to use against the Senate. Twice now he has proposed and passed laws without conferring with us. He clearly sees no need for our advice or our opinions. The man is becoming a demagogue. I believe he's dangerous."

The majority of the Senate applauded Pompeius' angry comments. Appius and Crassus simply sat back and watched, well aware of how powerful their friend and protégé had become.

"I live only a few houses from Tiberius, and not much farther from his mother Cornelia," continued Pompeius. "Four nights ago, I was out late and happened to see Tiberius enter his mother's home. I became curious when I noticed a large carriage parked in front of the house. I had my slave go around to the back of the house to look inside, and though he couldn't hear what was said, he told me that he saw a foreigner, presumably King Attalus' envoy, present Tiberius with a purple robe and a diadem of gold. My slave watched Tiberius try them both on. This man wants more than control of the People's Assembly, he wants to be king."

"Pompeius is right. He seeks a crown," Publius Nasica shouted. "Something must be done to contain this madman."

Quintus Metellus, who had once supported Tiberius but was badly upset by his handling of Attalus' will, stood up and echoed Pompeius' words. "He's determined to run this nation without the Senate. That's tyranny!"

Co-consul Mucius Scaevola, seated before the assembly of senators, stood and raised his hands. He also had been disturbed by Tiberius' latest maneuver. Putting control of a Roman province in the hands of the People's Assembly was a deliberate insult to the Senate and him, but he didn't like what he was hearing. "Let's be cautious in what we say here today, senators. I believe that Pompeius' concerns are legitimate. Tiberius has tremendous popularity among the plebs. This is a man I have assisted, though I won't any longer. Still I'm not convinced his goal is a crown."

"Then you're a fool!" shouted Publius Nasica.

"But what can be done?" cried out a senator in the back. "He's a tribune. He's untouchable."

Pompeius advanced to the center of the floor and scanned the amphitheater with a heavy glower. "He might be untouchable now. But he has broken the law twice—by deposing Marcus Octavius and by usurping Attalus' will. I pledge to the gods that the moment his tribuneship ends I will indict him for these criminal acts. This man must be exiled from Rome before he brings it down around us."

This brought a great standing cheer from the Senate. Appius and Crassus were among the few who remained seated.

CHAPTER 30

Despite all the incriminations against him, Tiberius proceeded through the summer and fall with the work that he believed in so strongly. With Gaius still in Spain, this meant only Tiberius and his father-in-law, now fighting criticism himself, ran the commission. Fortunately the work allowed both men an opportunity to get away. While the Senate stewed in Rome, the two men traveled north to assess the public lands in Eturia and the Po Valley, beginning with tracts that were unclaimed to avoid direct confrontation with some of Tiberius' most rabid detractors. By midsummer they had provided thirty-iugerum plots to nearly a thousand landless Roman citizens. The money from King Attalus was all that made it possible.

One evening during the time when Tiberius was traveling with Appius and Aemilianus was still in Spain, I invited my sister-in-law Claudia, Publius Crassus and his wife Claudia, their daughter Licinia, and Cornelia over for dinner. My cook, an elderly and irritable Etruscan by the name of Vela, roasted quail on the outside hearth and served it with lentil stew and baked apples. Crassus had a cup of mulsum—wine sweetened with honey—and all of the women, except me, had posca. I had half a cup of the mulsum to help with the ache in my ankle.

When the meal was over, we remained in the triclinium to talk. I had specifically invited Crassus hoping he could relieve my sister-in-law's concern for her husband's safety. Up to this point, the evening had been an exchange of pleasantries among family. I introduced the topic of politics, which everyone had been studiously avoiding.

"With Appius and Tiberius due home soon, Crassus, I was wondering if you could give us some insight as to what they might expect from the Senate when they return."

My sister-in-law interrupted before Crassus had a chance to answer. "Will they really indict him once his term as tribune is completed?"

Crassus was not as aggressive politically as Appius. He tended to work at bridging differences in the Senate, and was known more for his capacity to get things accomplished behind the scenes than the delivery of powerful speeches. If anyone held the pulse of the Senate, it was this man.

He answered Claudia's question before getting to mine. "Yes, I think we can count on Pompeius pushing for an indictment. He's repeated this threat at every meeting of the Senate I've attended. "

"Could he be convicted?" continued Claudia.

"I believe there's a good argument supporting Tiberius' expulsion of Octavius from the tribunate. That I'm not so worried about. And his use of King Attalus' money to pay for the business of land reform also stands on firm enough ground. But his decision to circumvent the Senate and place the management of Attalus' land in the hands of the People's Assembly will be very difficult to defend. That worries me. And because of it, Sempronia," he looked at me, "he'll have trouble with the Senate from here on out."

Cornelia spoke up. "Can your brother be of any help?" She was referring to the co-consul Mucius Scaevola.

Crassus took a deep breath. "He was highly supportive of Tiberius until this business of the inheritance. I don't think Mucius will move against him, but I don't expect him to intervene on his behalf."

"I'm afraid the same could be said of Aemilianus," I added.

"What kind of punishment could he face?" asked Crassus' wife.

Crassus tilted his head. "It's hard to say. He's made a lot of enemies. With Pompeius spreading the rumor that Tiberius seeks to be king, it's possible he could be exiled."

"But that's absurd," snapped Cornelia. "Tiberius has absolutely no interest in being king. Pompeius' slave must have seen Physcon in the purple robe and crown, not Tiberius. If there's anything I feel sure of, it's Tiberius' good intentions."

"But you must admit, Mother," I interjected, "he's changing. The move to take over management of Attalus' land was unnecessary—and uncharacteristic. It was like jabbing a viper with a stick. Am I wrong in this, Crassus?"

Crassus took a sip from his cup. He looked at me then Claudia. "I think Tiberius began with pure intentions. I have no doubt about that, but he's discovered the meaning of power. He controls the tribunate through the mere force of his will, and the People's Assembly believes he's their savior. They'll do anything for him, and I agree, his last move was a deliberate show of power, probably prompted by your father, Claudia."

If anything Claudia was now more worried about Tiberius than when she arrived. "Is there any way to use the People's Assembly to protect him from exile?"

Crassus nodded slowly. "He could ask them to grant him a second term as tribune."

"But how would that help?" I asked

"Isn't that just getting in deeper?" followed Claudia.

"He would retain the protection of the office. They couldn't press charges against him."

"Only for another year," said Crassus' wife. "Then it would come up again."

"To my knowledge," said Cornelia, "consecutive terms as a tribune have never happened before. I'm not even sure it's legal."

"Much like the expulsion of Octavius, it's new ground," said Crassus. "It's something Blossius brought up the last time I saw him. He hasn't had a chance to mention it to Tiberius yet. I should run it by my brother—but I think it's a strategy we might want to keep under wraps for now."

The stew was only getting thicker. Claudia hung her head. Cornelia, who sat beside her, put an arm around her.

When the evening drew to a close and I walked my guests to the door, thirteen-year-old Licinia, who had hardly said a word all night, hung back and asked me in a whisper, "When do you expect Aemilianus to return from Spain?"

"At the end of the summer. Maybe early fall. Why?"

She looked at the floor then up at me. "Gaius would be back also."

I smiled. "When's the marriage?"

"The spring."

"Are you excited?"

She blushed. "Yes, I think I have been fortunate."

"I think you both have."

CHAPTER 31

Appius and Tiberius returned in early fall, two months before the next election. Tiberius' tribuneship was nearly over, and his friends reminded him of Pompeius' vow to indict him for overstepping the limits of his office. Blossius told Tiberius to seek a second term. Tiberius resisted the idea at first, then spoke to Crassus to get his opinion. Crassus initially told him that it was impossible, then later, after more thought and research, softened his opinion. Rome's constitution was not written as a single piece. It was based on an oral tradition and the collection of laws that had been passed during the four hundred years of the Republic's existence.

"Nowhere is it explicitly stated," said Crassus, "that a tribune can not serve consecutive terms. But it's never happened. There seems to be an unspoken rule against it, and yet there's no formal law forbidding it. Much like your removal of Octavius, it's a gray area with no clear precedent either way. There's a law against running for a consulship in consecutive years, but that law has been broken several times, as recently as the war with Hannibal. Considering the threats against you, Tiberius, I see no reason not to give it a try."

Tiberius gathered his closest advisors—Blossius, Appius, Diophanes— in the library of my mother's home to make a final decision. Cornelia, of course, joined them. She listened to the entire discussion without saying a word. She tended to give everyone a chance to make their point before offering her opinion.

When the men, including Tiberius, agreed on the strategy of seeking a second term, Cornelia voiced her thoughts. "I'm not so sure about this. The risks are awfully high. Tiberius has already pushed his tribuneship to the edge of legality. Nearly the entire Senate is furious at him. They'll use this attempt for a second tribuneship as more evidence of his will to power and his desire for a crown. Even should he string together a series of tribuneships for his own protection—how long can that go on? I'm worried for his safety. I have never witnessed more ugliness in our political discourse. Never!"

"I don't see the risk," said Blossius. "He already faces exile. What more could they do to him? There is no reason not to test the system."

"Yes, Mother, I agree," said Tiberius. "My travels this summer have inspired ideas for new bills. I want to run. I still have things I want to accomplish."

"And should you be exiled, where would you go? What would you do with your family?"

Tiberius had no answer. He stalked across the room twice then stopped. "I don't think the Senate can stop me. I have the full support of the Assembly. The work this summer went well. The people are pleased. I can make this happen. It's what I want to do—risk or not."

Cornelia paused to think, then asked her son with all the gravitas of her far-reaching wisdom, "For what reason are you doing this, Tiberius? Some have suggested that you have become drunk with power. Who is this for—you or the people?"

Tiberius was taken aback by the question, as though there could be no doubt about his answer. "What, Mother, have you been listening to Pompeius, too?"

"I have heard him," she said. "As has everyone in Rome. But I'm asking you for your own good. I'm asking you to look at yourself in the mirror. Determine your motives. Figure out what it is that inspires you. I believe your intentions are pure and that they follow in the populist tradition of our family. But I also know that power, the kind of power you have already achieved, can test the strongest man's mettle. As the opposition ratchets up, you will be forced to do the same. I just want you to tell me that you know why you're doing it."

Tiberius' hackles rose again, but before he could respond, Blossius interceded. "Cornelia's right, Tiberius. Whatever the reason, for the power, for the people, or simply to avoid being exiled, the reformer must know who he is and why he's doing what he does or it will swallow him up."

Diophanes gave the slightest nod of agreement. Tiberius turned to Appius. The senator grinned. "I think Tiberius knows exactly who he is. Let's write a platform that assures him of election."

"Yes," said Tiberius. "Yes." He went over to Cornelia, who was seated, and put his hand on her shoulder. "I believe in what I'm doing,

Mother. And I know that it's for Rome and its people, not for me. I have seen—no experienced—what pressure can make a man do. I would never have thought to force a tribune from the tribunate, especially Octavius, nor could I have imagined usurping matters of foreign policy from the Senate. You're right. I have significant power, and it's intoxicating. But I must learn to be circumspect in its use, and I believe that I can."

Cornelia put her hand on top of his and looked up at him. "I have every faith in you son. I do."

The rest of the afternoon was used to write a platform tailored to build upon Tiberius' already extensive work. It contained four key proposals. The first would shorten the required length of military service. Long terms in the military, particularly foreign campaigns that might stretch out to two or three years, had been a grievance since the war with Hannibal and made running a farm impossible for a soldier. It was a certain winner among the populace. The second proposal would allow decisions by the high court to be appealed to the People's Assembly, another clear plebeian need, meaning that even if Tiberius were exiled, he could appeal to the people for exoneration. The third addressed the courts. At that time the courts were made up of judges and jurors entirely from the senatorial class. This law would integrate the courts with jurors from the equestrian class, which would appeal to an order of Romans whose needs Tiberius had yet to address. The fourth proposal would extend Roman citizenship to the whole of Italy, not simply the people of Rome and other Latins. Tiberius' land reform had already drawn the support of the rural population, but with this provision it would reach even further, potentially doubling or quadrupling his base of support.

In the weeks prior to the election, Tiberius went to the streets nailing up tracts describing these proposals, then to the forum to announce his candidacy for a second term. The senatorial class, especially the optimates, those who thought of the aristocracy as the chosen, considered Tiberius' proposals blatant pandering to the populace, and his running for a second term even worse. In their minds, Tiberius was positioning himself to take full control of politics in Rome. He wanted a crown. The battle lines were drawn and an outcome would be decided at the People's Assembly on election day.

CHAPTER 32

As the day of the election neared, the optimates became increasingly determined not to allow Tiberius a second tribuneship and thereby escape punishment for the crimes they alleged. A group led by Publius Nasica and Quintus Pompeius used their wealth to prompt several men to run against Tiberius, much as they had done with Octavius the previous year. They also paid plebeians who were or had once been their clients to vote against him.

Knowing this was happening behind the scenes, and fearful he might lose, Tiberius spent the last few days before the election going out into the rural areas, pleading with the farmers to come into Rome to vote. The day before the election, he walked through Subura, one of the poorest parts of Rome, talking personally with as many of Rome's less fortunate as he could, recounting what he intended to do for them as a tribune, and reminding them that he needed the position for protection from indictment.

The plebs began assembling to vote shortly before dawn on the top of the Capitoline Hill. It was early December. Brisk winds swirled across the hilltop, and each tribe huddled together wearing wool cloaks over their togas and tunics. All knew the situation. Tiberius was again challenging the status quo, hoping to be elected to an unprecedented second term as a tribune. Twenty-five men were among the candidates. Ten of them would be chosen. One estimate said that more than half of the candidates were on the payroll of the large landholders.

Rubrius Varro was chosen by lot to preside over the election. He supervised the sacrifice and the feeding of the chickens. No untoward omen was in the forecast. Rubrius reviewed the process of voting and named the twenty-five candidates. The rural tribe Terentina was chosen to make the first ten nominations. When Tiberius' name was read from their ballot, Quintus Pompeius, standing off to the left of the tribunal in anticipation of this moment, and surrounded by ten other senators and their clients, shouted, "The nomination of Tiberius Gracchus is illegal. No man can be tribune in consecutive years."

Quintus Metellus followed. "Tiberius' nomination must be struck from the record."

The Assembly reacted angrily. Tiberius was their favorite. Most of them were there to ensure that he was elected. Rubrius looked around nervously, not certain what to do. The herald waited for instruction. Seeing that Rubrius had been intimidated by the presence of the senators, Quintus Mummius stepped forward, telling the herald to continue with the roll call.

Publius Nasica shouted from the edge of the crowd, "Tribune, you risk angering the gods. The substitute for Rubrius must be chosen by lot."

The entire tribunate knew this was true, and the proceedings began to break down. The tribunes argued among themselves, not only about the choice of who should preside, but also about the legality of Tiberius' second term. Six of them felt that Tiberius should withdraw his candidacy. While they struggled for unity, Publius Nasica and Quintus Pompeius moved up close to the tribunal, threatening criminal charges against all of them for disregard of the religious rituals. At the same time some thirty thousand Roman citizens stomped and shouted. They wanted to vote and get it over with.

In the confusion, the tribunes were unable to make a decision. They decided to adjourn and meet again the next day at dawn. Tiberius was certain the cause was lost. He was so disconsolate he walked through the forum that afternoon dressed in black, holding his son's and daughter's hands, asking people he knew if they would look after his children after his exile.

His clients, of whom there were a growing number, were so concerned for his safety that they went home with him that evening and set up tents around his house to protect him from any threat that might come during the night. That was how tense Rome had become. The issue of the second term was being called illegal by some of the most powerful men in Rome, but neither Appius nor Crassus could find any precedent against it. They advised Tiberius to continue as planned the next morning.

CHAPTER 33

Wearing a hooded, bleached wool cloak, Cornelia slipped out of her house after nightfall accompanied by Coson and followed a little-used alley that led to the rear of Tiberius' home. When she reached the perimeter of tents, she was immediately recognized, even with her hood. One of the clients escorted her and Coson through the back of the property into the peristyle. She continued on alone into the house. Only one room off the atrium was lit. Tiberius sat alone in the library, his elbows on the table, his head in his hands. He looked up with a startled, disjointed expression on his face when Cornelia appeared in the doorway, then he smiled and stood up.

"I'm not quite so downcast as I may appear, Mother. But nothing is better than seeing you. I threw Blossius out an hour ago. He was drunk and I refused to drink with him."

"How's Claudia?"

Tiberius' smile washed away. "Anxious beyond words. She's upstairs trying to sleep." He embraced Cornelia and held on. "She hates this. I know she wants me to give it up. But she won't say it. I admire her for that. The gods graced me when they matched me with Claudia." Tiberius released his mother. "But why are you here?"

Cornelia smiled. "Do I have to tell you?" She leaned into him and kissed him on the cheek. "You are my oldest son. You are the perfect replica of your father. What you are doing is what he would be doing if he were here tonight. I'm here to tell you that I am proud of you."

Tiberius bowed his head.

"That doesn't mean I'm not worried about tomorrow. It means I believe in you and who you are. And I felt I needed to tell you that before you face the Assembly in the morning. You have chosen a good fight, but a hard fight. I've never seen Rome so divided, but like you, I believe all of this is necessary."

Tiberius touched his mother on the shoulder and gazed at her in admiration. "Thank you for saying that, Mother."

"Are you still up, Tiberius?" Claudia stood in the doorway. She wore a nightgown and was barefoot. "Cornelia, what are you doing here?"

"I thought Tiberius might need some reassurance."

Claudia gazed at her husband. "I think I do, too. What's going to happen tomorrow?"

"Tiberius is going to test the law. How that will go? I don't know. Your father likes his chances."

"What about violence? That's what frightens me. Having all these men camped around our house has me on edge. It's as though everyone is expecting something bad. Do you?"

Cornelia looked at Tiberius for a long time before turning to Claudia. "Politics in Rome has never succumbed to violence. I don't know why it would now. Clearly there are no guarantees, but one thing I do know, if Tiberius isn't elected to the tribunate tomorrow, he faces indictment and perhaps charges of treason as soon as his current term ends. The Senate will not be kind to him."

Claudia gazed momentarily at the floor, then up at Cornelia. "So you're saying there's nothing to lose by trying?"

"And everything to lose if I don't," said Tiberius. "It has to be. Mother, go home. Claudia, go back to bed. I'll be up as soon as I think I can sleep."

CHAPTER 34

Tiberius did finally go to bed, but he was up before dawn to make a sacrifice to the lares, then he met briefly in the library with Blossius, Diophanes, and Quintus Mummius, the only tribune who still showed full confidence in what he was doing. A single oil lamp burned in the otherwise dark household while they talked. For once Blossius did not have a cup of wine.

"Large clusters of senatorial landowners and their clients have been at every Assembly," said Diophanes. "I expect the same today. They might try to stop the meeting or intimidate the other tribunes. We'll have to push through that."

Blossius agreed. "Mummius, you will have to help Tiberius with the other tribunes. Prompt whoever presides to go quickly. Once Tiberius has been assured of a position on the tribunate no one can touch him."

Tiberius seemed distracted. Nothing was going as he envisioned. Diophanes came up close to him. "Hide this in your toga." He held out a small dagger. "Just in case."

Tiberius pushed it away. "I want no violence. That's not the way it should be done."

"But it might not be your decision. Just be prepared to protect yourself." Diophanes made him take the dagger and walked away.

The four of them left the library headed to the front of the house. Claudia heard them leaving and rushed from her bedroom and down the stairs in her nightgown. She threw her arms around Tiberius before he could leave. "Don't go, Tiberius. Something's going to happen. I know it is." She began to cry.

Tiberius held her and spoke softly into her ear. "I must go. Don't make this any harder than it already is. Take care of the children."

Claudia felt the dagger in his toga. She looked up at him. "You're carrying a weapon?"

Tiberius turned away from her without a response. When he stepped through the doorway into the street, his sandal caught on the threshold. He stumbled and stubbed his big toe, nearly ripping the toenail off. Tiberius pulled the broken nail free causing the toe to bleed heavily. Claudia came out onto the porch with a cloth to staunch the bleeding. Fifty of Tiberius' most loyal clients stood by watching. They had stayed the night and were now prepared to escort Tiberius to the top of the Capitoline Hill. Their faces reflected the stress of the moment. All expected a showdown of some kind. They muttered among themselves about the need to get going. Claudia ignored them and knelt beside Tiberius taking hold of his arm. "Don't you see the gods are trying to tell you something, Tiberius? Look at your foot." It still bled badly. "The fates are not with you."

Tiberius bid her to leave him and go inside. Only by giving her the dagger could he get her to release his arm. He saw her glance over her shoulder upon reaching the door. He felt a stab of pain in his chest when the door closed, reminding him of how much he loved his wife and his children.

Blossius, Diophanes, Mummius, and his clients were assembled behind Tiberius. He turned to face them. "Above all we don't want violence. I know some of you are carrying clubs or other small weapons. Use all restraint. Remember, what we are doing is legal. We expect the same pack of senators to threaten us with criminal charges. We don't know to what extent they will go to stop the election. If I sense that these men are going to use force, I will raise my right hand to the side of my head." He demonstrated the gesture. "It means be on guard. But again, use all restraint."

Although there had yet to be any violence—other than the unexplained death of Decius—during the entire length of Tiberius' one-year term, the men formed a ring four deep around him, then proceeded to the Capitoline Hill without breaking formation as though Tiberius could be attacked at any moment from any angle.

Just prior to reaching the forum, as they passed down Via Sacra between two four-story tenement buildings, two large ravens pecking at a rat carcass dislodged a roof tile. It slid off the building and landed at Tiberius' foot, narrowly missing the already damaged toe. All of the men saw it. They stopped there in the street hesitant to move, thinking as Claudia had, the gods were making a statement, and their endeavor was ill-advised.

Blossius, a Greek and a non-believer, stepped in front of the group to face Tiberius and the others. "What are you men thinking? Should Tiberius, the son of Gracchus, the grandson of Scipio Africanus, and the most influential man in Rome, be afraid of the actions of a pair of birds? What shame does that cast upon the man? No, we've wasted enough time already. Move on to the Capitol. We have something to accomplish this morning." He headed off at a fast pace not looking back to see if they would follow. Soon they were all behind him in formation, Tiberius in the center.

The plebeians were assembling into their tribes when Tiberius arrived at the top of the Capitoline Hill surrounded by his clients. His arrival prompted a wave of excitement to pass through the Assembly. The lots had already been drawn to establish the order for voting. The ten tribunes had to do the same to determine who would preside over the Assembly. They gathered on the porch of the temple. A flamen came out of the temple with a ceramic pitcher of water containing the ten lots. Publius Satureius stepped in front of the priest, forcing him to stop, then turned to Tiberius. "What you want to do is illegal. I have spoken with the other tribunes. We don't want you to go through with it. We will have the election, but your name must be struck from the list of candidates."

Tiberius knew he might face this kind of resistance. "It's not your choice," he said. "It's for the people to choose. We're here for them, not us."

Satureius cursed. "You're here for yourself, Tiberius. You have used the position of tribune to steadily increase your popularity and influence—and it's gone to your head. We have supported you in this for the last year, but no longer. A single tribuneship is enough for any man, no matter how many bills he proposes to grease the populace."

Mummius stepped up close to the two men. He glared at Satureius. "Is there need to vote out a few more tribunes, Tiberius? Apparently some of these men have forgotten who they represent." He turned to the flamen with the pitcher and the bowl. "Get on with it. Let the fates decide who administers the Assembly."

Satureius cursed again, then swatted the pitcher out of the hands of the flamen. It fell onto the temple porch and with a splash of water broke into pieces. The round wooden lots bounced down the stairs to the ground with the entire Assembly watching.

"That's a sacrilege," shouted one of the tribal elders.

Satureius ignored him. "No, this election is a sacrilege. As far as I'm concerned, this Assembly is over."

The order of the tribes gave way to pushing and shoving to get closer to what was happening. The vast majority of them favored giving Tiberius a second term. Tiberius' proposal to shorten the obligatory term in the military had been almost as well received as land reform. Many were chanting his name and demanding that the tribunes get on with the election. Satureius told the other tribunes he would not take part and stomped down the temple stairs. Rubrius Varro followed him, leaving Tiberius and Mummius with the remaining tribunes, none looking too happy to be there.

Mummius scoured the ground and found the lot with his name on it. He looked up at Tiberius. "I believe I was just chosen to preside over the election."

Tiberius was uncomfortable with what was happening, but the crowd was urging him on. When Mummius announced from the tribunal that the tribes should prepare their ballots, the entire Assembly erupted with loud cheering and more shouts of Tiberius' name. At this point the other six tribunes left the Assembly, something hardly noticed because of the enthusiasm of the crowd.

On this same morning, the co-consul Mucius Scaevola had convened the Senate in the temple of Fides, situated just below the crown of the Capitoline Hill, not more than two stades from the temple of Jupiter. The senators were well aware of what was being voted on at the People's Assembly. Publius Nasica, the first to get the floor, opened the meeting with a long harangue against Tiberius, calling him a demagogue intent on using the People's Assembly to bypass the Senate. "The man is dangerous. He has already broken the law twice and is preparing to do it again as a way to evade punishment. I call for the Senate to stop this man immediately." The pontifex maximus turned to Mucius Scaevola sitting in his curule chair.

"The time to act is now, Consul. We cannot allow the election to take place. We must physically remove Tiberius from the Assembly before any voting occurs." He raised his fist in the air and shook it. "The safety of Rome depends on us."

Scaevola had been disappointed in Tiberius when he had sidestepped the Senate with King Attalus' will, but he did not hate or fear Tiberius the way some of the other senators did. "Such action is not called for, Senator. No law has been broken. Should Tiberius do something illegal, he can be arrested and taken to trial."

Publius Nasica sneered at Scaevola. "And if he is elected to a tribuneship, we must wait another year? No! This man is dangerous. You are ignoring the safety of the commonwealth."

The eight tribunes who had left the People's Assembly suddenly rushed into the temple of Fides. Publius Satureius shouted it out. "Tiberius has dissolved the tribunate and taken over the Assembly. We've come here for your help."

Publius Nasica faced his colleagues, almost all large landowners firmly against land reform. "The state of Rome is in danger. Those who have the courage to defend the commonwealth follow me." He pulled the excess of his toga over his head like a hood and led two hundred senators and the eight tribunes out of the temple, headed to the top of the hill to confront Tiberius. Joining in with the mob were the senators' slaves who were waiting outside the temple of Fides, already warned by the pontiff that something like this might happen.

Marcus Fulvius Flaccus, the younger brother of the ex-consul Gaius Fulvius Flaccus, and one of the few senators still supporting Tiberius, raced out ahead of Publius Nasica and his comrades, who were stopping along the way to gather staves or anything they could use as a weapon. Fulvius reached the Assembly well ahead of the mob and forced his way through the throng shouting Tiberius' name, trying to get his attention.

Mummius stood at the tribunal podium. Four tribes had already voted. All had included Tiberius among their nominees. Tiberius was behind the tribunal, uneasily pacing back and forth on the temple porch when Fulvius rushed up the stairs. He told Tiberius what had happened in the Senate and that Publius Nasica was on his way with a group that intended to break up the Assembly. No sooner had he said the words than the angry mob of senators and their attendants crested the hill. Tiberius understood the danger and put his right hand to the side of his head, signaling to his clients to prepare for trouble. Publius Nasica saw the signal and shouted out to his associates that Tiberius was calling for a crown, enraging them even further.

Seeing that the oncoming mob contained so many esteemed senators, the mass of plebeians, unaware of these men's intentions, parted to let them move through to the front of the Assembly. Publius Nasica rallied the men, now flourishing their clubs and staves, up the temple stairs directly at Tiberius, who was surrounded by his clients. A vicious fight broke out beneath the watchful eyes of Jupiter, sitting stoically on his throne within the temple.

Most of the people at the Assembly simply scattered, but others joined the melee. When his protective ring of clients began to give way, Tiberius pushed through the wall of flailing arms and balled up fists, hoping to gain sanctuary in the temple. But just as he broke free, someone caught hold of his toga and pulled it off him like a sheet. He stumbled and fell down before the temple's gold-plated doors. Publius Satureius saw him go down. He raced up to his fellow tribune, cursed Tiberius to the gods, then bashed him in the back of the head with a leg broken off a chair. The senator Lucius Rufus claimed the second blow. Others quickly seized the opportunity to vent their anger, striking Tiberius over and over, brutally battering him into a bloody, misshapen corpse, while the rest of the mob assailed Tiberius' clients and any other plebeians who tried to stop the attack.

When the crowd finally dispersed and the blood-smeared contingent of senators had disappeared down the hill, three hundred men lay dead on the ground or on the temple porch. One of the aediles, Gaius Lucretius, henceforward known as the undertaker, supervised cleaning up the mess, ordering his aides to throw the bodies, including Tiberius', into the Tiber River.

CHAPTER 35

News of the mass murder spread across Rome like wildfire. Cornelia was at the back of her house in the peristyle picking a bouquet of flowers for the atrium when someone threw a blanket over her head from behind. Someone else pinned her arms to her sides while she was bundled up and carried out the rear of the property. Her screams muffled to nothing by the wool blanket, she was placed with some delicacy in a compartment of some kind, then felt the compartment moving forward. Physcon's voice broke through her terror. "I didn't mean to scare you." He helped her untangle from the blanket. They were sitting opposite each other in a large, luxurious carriage.

"What are you doing?" she snapped in anger. "I don't want to go to Misenum or anywhere else with you." Outside the window she could see Physcon's bodyguards marching beside the carriage.

She started to push the carriage door open, but Physcon caught her by the wrist and looked into her eyes. Although he was, as always, a bit short of breath, his voice was firm. "There's been a tragedy."

Cornelia gasped. "Tiberius!"

"He's been murdered."

Cornelia burst into tears, then caught herself. "I must see him."

Physcon shook his head. "It's too late for that. The city is verging on riot. I'm getting you out of Rome."

"No, no, I must see my son," she wailed, "and what of his wife and children?"

Physcon still held her. Again he forced her to look into his face. "You can't see Tiberius, Cornelia. It's impossible. His body's in the river. We're on our way to his home to get his family. You will talk them into coming with us to Misenum. No one knows about the house on the cape. The turmoil is far from over. Rome will be an ugly place for some time to come. Don't worry, I'll bring you back when things quiet down." He exuded confidence and calm. "There's a second carriage carrying Fidelia and Coson. Trust me. This is not another marriage proposal. I'm here to save you and your family."

Cornelia gasped and kind of deflated, finally giving in to the necessity of the moment. She looked out the window again. People were running through the streets waving sticks and shouting. It was clear something awful had happened. She would have to trust Physcon. "We must get Sempronia also," she exclaimed. "With her husband gone, she's at risk, too."

Physcon nodded. "We can get her, but it will have to be quick. We need to get out of the city as soon as possible."

Cornelia began to sob. Physcon, breathing heavily, slipped over to her side of the carriage and held her. They pulled up in front of Tiberius' home just as Helios, Tiberius' slave, ran up to the house bruised and beaten. "Tiberius is dead," he shouted.

Cornelia climbed from the carriage, and with a shaking voice told the slave that she already knew. She then gathered herself enough to go inside to face her daughter-in-law and do what had to be done.

I remember the trip to Misenum. It took five days. Claudia was hysterical. I felt so badly about my brother I wished it had been me not him who had been murdered. Cornelia rose to the occasion. Yes, she was devastated. Tiberius had meant everything to her. She had been so proud of him and the task he had taken on. She had even encouraged him. So yes, her heart was shattered into tiny pieces. But she could mourn later. Claudia and the children needed her now.

The view along the coast to Misenum was gorgeous, nearly equal in beauty to what we felt in loss. Claudia broke into periods of wailing and pulling at her hair. The children were too young to understand anything but the agony. It made for a very wearing trip.

We had no plan when we arrived at the massive villa on the tip of the Cape of Misenum, but Physcon had taken care of everything. There was a complete staff of house slaves and attendants, including a chef and a kitchen full of food. The villa sprawled across the top of a rocky promontory that extended out into sea and overlooked the Bay of Naples to the south. The vast atrium opened onto an expansive garden populated with rose bushes, apple trees, and olive trees. An arbor covered in grape vines provided shade. A long stone stairway wound down the side of the promontory to the rocky shoreline. It was as lovely a place as I had ever seen.

We decided to stay there until Aemilianus returned from Spain. We all needed it. I believe Cornelia was at her strongest during this time. Though distraught, she endured. Over time, she even seemed to gain a greater strength, the kind acquired by those who have suffered a terrible tragedy—like the loss of their eldest son.

PART II

AEMILIANUS

"So perished on the Capitol, and while still tribune, Tiberius, the son of that Gracchus who was twice consul, and of Cornelia, daughter of that Scipio who robbed Carthage of her supremacy. He lost his life in consequence of a most excellent design too violently pursued; and this abominable crime, the first that was perpetrated in a public assembly, would also open the door for others to occur."

-Appian of Alexandria, Civil Wars

CHAPTER 36

The Republic had been changed forever. Never before had political disagreements in Rome resulted in physical violence. The people had lost one of their strongest advocates. Tiberius' blood at the doors to the temple of Jupiter would leave a permanent stain on the soul of Rome. The split in the populace, which had been evident but mostly submerged before Tiberius' death, widened and became more divisive. What had begun as an effort to strengthen the military base of the Republic through land reform degenerated into a vicious crime of hate against one of the most gifted, brilliant, and eloquent young nobles in Rome. For several days afterward bands of plebeians roamed the streets shouting slogans and engaging in random acts of vandalism, inspiring only more anger in the city and seemingly justifying the actions of the ruling class.

In the elections that took place that week, Publius Popilius and Publius Rupilius were chosen as the co-consuls. The Senate urged them to quickly conduct an inquiry into the incident. Rather than seek out the cause or the perpetrators of the violence, the consuls, under pressure from those who had carried out the crime, conducted a purge. Anyone associated with Tiberius or his movement was sought out, tried, and in many cases executed. Tiberius' clients were at the top of the list. Diophanes, the great rhetorician, was one of the victims. Quintus Mummius was placed in a wine cask filled with vipers. Blossius was specifically called to the Senate floor by Publius Nasica. When Popilius asked him about his part in the movement, he replied that he would do anything that Tiberius asked of him.

"What?" screamed Publius Nasica. "If he had told you to burn down the Capitol, would you have done that too?"

"He would never have made such a request," replied Blossius calmly.

"But what if he had?" demanded Rupilius.

"If Tiberius had commanded it, it would have been right for me to do it, but he would never have given an order that did not benefit the people."

Blossius' gall probably kept him from being executed. Instead he was exiled. He left for Asia within the week.

Word of the purge and the executions spread down the coast like the red tide. When the news reached us in Misenum, we were grateful for Physcon's quick decision to get us out of Rome.

Cornelia suffered more than any of us, even more than Tiberius' wife. Claudia grieved in the Roman fashion, expressing her pain by throwing herself on the ground and wailing. It was horrible to witness, but at least she was able to relieve her grief somewhat. Cornelia kept it all in, maintaining a great silence, like the Egyptian Sphinx, trying to serve as an example of stoicism to the rest of us. Only in the late hours of the night, when I was alone with her, did some of her anguish spill out. She blamed herself for not doing more to address the changes in Tiberius that we had all witnessed as his political career unfolded.

"Tiberius was always such a sound individual," she said in tears. "He maintained a reasoned calm through everything he encountered. I should have recognized the danger when I saw his passion rising."

Aemilianus was in Spain the entire time. All of us—yes even I—felt that his presence was needed to calm the political waters. Never before had I wished so deeply for him to return to Rome. But that was before we learned of Aemilianus' response to Tiberius' death. He received the news while outside the walls of Numantia. He quoted Homer from the *Iliad*, repeating the line used after Orestes had murdered Aegisthus: "And so will perish any other man whose crimes be like his."

Although thoroughly disappointed, I was not surprised by his comment. He had been against Tiberius' land reform from the beginning. Cornelia was furious. Her relationship with Aemilianus would never be the same.

Curiously enough, the Senate made no move to annul land reform. Publius Crassus was chosen to take Tiberius' position on the commission, and with Gaius still in Spain, the two elder statesman, Crassus and Appius, continued with the work, verifying what many people thought—the attack on Tiberius had been a personal vendetta led by his cousin Publius Nasica, not a political reprisal.

CHAPTER 37

Aemilianus returned from Spain in the spring, four months after Tiberius' death. The siege of Numantia had been a tremendous success, even though the Numantians chose to starve to death within their city rather than surrender to a life of slavery. Publius Scipio's grandson, now fifty-three years of age, had gained yet another significant military victory and was praised as the most important Roman of the era. He was immediately granted a triumph and entered the city four days after his return in a gilded chariot pulled by four white horses, leading a three-mile long procession of plunder, battle trophies, and jubilant Roman soldiers.

Gaius did not take part. Instead he rode on horseback to Misenum to see Cornelia, making the trip in just three days. Physcon had returned to Egypt during the winter, and Cornelia, unable to stomach the new political atmosphere in Rome, had chosen to remain at the villa indefinitely with Claudia and her children. I was there the day Gaius arrived but was leaving for Rome the next day in a carriage Physcon had left for our use.

Gaius appeared dumbstruck when he entered the house. He had learned a great deal more about his brother's murder since returning to Rome. "How could such a thing happen?" he muttered when he embraced Cornelia in the entry hall, prior to them both breaking into tears.

Claudia and I, standing helplessly a few feet away, added more tears to the difficult reunion. In some ways, only in Gaius' return did the full impact of the tragedy hit our family. He was nearly twenty years old now. His beard had thickened and he looked more like his brother than when he had left. Seeing him made the stark absence of Tiberius more real, more painful, and more appalling. The four of us went out to the garden. Claudia and I sat on a bench while Cornelia recounted the whole terrible story.

When she was done, Gaius shook his head, stunned by an act no one believed could ever happen in Rome. He said very little that day, as though he were struggling to process what seemed so impossible.

The following morning, just before taking the carriage to Rome, I found Gaius in the atrium sitting at the edge of the pool, beneath a clear, azure sky. I was old enough to be his mother and had stayed up many nights with him when he was an infant. I sat down beside him hoping to somehow relieve his despair.

"What are you thinking, Gaius?"

He looked up at me, his big sister. "I want nothing to do with politics," he said sullenly.

"No one could blame you for that."

"War makes more sense," he said, looking down at the surface of the water for a long time before speaking again. "What is your assessment, Sempronia? Where did Tiberius go wrong?"

Gaius, like Tiberius twelve years earlier, had grown close to my husband during their time together in the military. I wondered what Aemilianus had already said to Gaius about Tiberius' actions. "What he hoped to do," I said, "and what he did partly accomplish, was not wrong at all. I believe wholeheartedly that he was acting on behalf of the state's best interests. But the pressure from his opponents was hard on him. He wasn't fully prepared for the amount of resistance he got, particularly the anger that his land reform bill generated in specific senators."

"Publius Nasica," he said.

I nodded. "And others. Because of the vitriol, Tiberius did things that were out of character. The ousting of Octavius was extremely hard on him. It changed him. He became more determined, and it became difficult to tell if he were fighting for his bill or his prestige."

"Do you think he overdid it?"

I shook my head sadly. "I'm not sure he could have done anything differently, Gaius. It snowballed on him. As though it were all predestined, a tragedy composed by the gods."

"Aemilianus said he brought it down on himself."

I took a little breath and tipped my head.

"He said Tiberius had been stung when the Senate annulled his treaty with the Numantians. His land reform bill was retribution. Could that be true?"

I stood up, my ankle cinched tightly, and paced off a few steps, then returned. "No, Aemilianus is dead wrong about that. Tiberius felt he had a genuine insight. His vision was for the betterment of the common man, not an angry reaction to a slight. The anger came later, after he waded all the way into the morass of Roman politics."

Gaius seemed to weigh my opinion against Aemilianus'. After a moment, he reached out and took my hand. "I believe you're right, Sempronia. That seems more like our brother. I returned to Rome thinking he had done something to be ashamed of. That it would reflect badly on my career." He looked down at the ground. "Now it doesn't seem that way at all."

"Our brother was a good man, Gaius. A brother to be proud of."

Gaius looked up at me hopefully.

I squeezed his hand. "What has happened with your wedding?"

Gaius actually smiled. I knew how he felt about Licinia. "It should have been last month. We were in Spain longer than expected. I believe it's set for later this summer."

"Are you excited?"

Gaius blushed. "Yes. And I haven't even seen Licinia yet. I came here as soon as I could. I'll leave for Rome within the week. Seeing Licinia is my highest priority."

I tousled his hair. "I'm glad we had a chance to talk."

"Me too."

CHAPTER 38

Gaius remained at the villa in Misenum for a week. Unfortunately Cornelia thought of Tiberius every time she looked at her youngest son. As she would tell me later, she knew that she had changed. Tiberius' murder had made her cynical, and she had tried to hide that from Gaius when he first arrived. His fourth day there, in the hour before sunset, she sat down with Gaius on a bench in the garden to make what she felt was a necessary confession.

The view from the garden was directly south over the Bay of Naples. The sun sat three diameters above the horizon in the west, just low enough to cut the glare and turn the bay's three islands, Aenaria, Procida, and Capri, into silhouettes against a sky the color of pale red wine. Mount Vesuvius, the long inactive volcano, squatted open-mouthed twenty miles off to the east like some ominous hint of the underworld's power. The mother and son sat for a long time with nothing said, absently watching the sea's slow moving swells roll into the bay.

Cornelia had described the events surrounding Tiberius' death to Gaius the day he arrived, but she had not shared her grief with him. Now it was time.

"The wedding will be in two months, Gaius. Your future mother-in-law and I have carefully chosen a day that bodes well for you and Licinia. Because I've decided to stay here for the time being, I'm giving my house in Rome to you and your bride."

"That's wonderful, Mother, but you'll be so far away."

"Rome has changed for me, Gaius." She looked down at her lap, then up into her son's eyes. "It will be hard for me to go back even for those few days of the wedding festivities. You missed the initial backlash against your brother and those who supported him. All concern for civil discourse vanished. Diophanes was executed. Blossius exiled. Had you been here you might have been part of the purge as well."

"Diophanes dead?" Gaius shook his head slowly in disbelief. "Was he given a trial?"

"Some might call what happened a trial. I don't. I hate Rome right now. If it wouldn't make things so difficult, I'd request to have the wedding here. But you need a house of your own and everyone who's invited lives in Rome. It would be a great inconvenience."

Gaius stood up and walked away, then came back. "Diophanes dead. Blossius exiled. Was Tiberius given a proper funeral?"

"His body was thrown into the Tiber." Her anger showed in her eyes, then melted into sadness. "It was more than I could do to protest. I left Rome shortly after it happened and came here."

Gaius stared out at the bay, still trying to sort it out in his mind.

"Be wary when you're in Rome, Gaius. There may yet be recriminations against our family."

"What am I to do, Mother?" He was crying. "Run away or seek revenge?"

"We all have to let it go. Stay away from politics. Enjoy your time with Licinia. In the end, reason must prevail over anger."

Tiberius' son came out into the garden with his sister. They were both too young to understand. Gaius watched them prance around like nothing had happened. He took a deep breath then turned to Cornelia.

She nodded. "The world has changed."

CHAPTER 39

Gaius' response to Tiberius' death was not what I expected. Quite different than his brother, Gaius tended to be passionate, and when angered, outspoken and emotional. I worried that he would seek revenge, but he went the other way. He said almost nothing. Either he was hiding what was inside of him or he had turned cynical and found the whole thing too insulting to acknowledge.

Upon returning to Rome, he secluded himself in Cornelia's home for five days then arranged a visit with Licinia. It had been a year since he had seen her. He confided to his slave as they walked the few blocks to Crassus' home.

"I struggle to forgive Rome for killing my brother, Philocrates."

The slave bobbed his head in understanding as they proceeded.

"I have even wondered if Rome still embodies principles for which I wish to fight."

"Gaius, that can't be true."

Gaius shook his head. "You're right. It's treachery to even consider such a thought. But it's the way I feel."

"Can you go on in good faith, master?"

"I have no choice. I must. The battlefield is my only escape from the black undercurrents in Rome."

The mood in Publius Crassus' home was subdued. Claudia met Gaius in the entryway after the housemaid Phyllis had let him in. Although it had been several months since Tiberius' death, Claudia knew Gaius had just spent a week with Cornelia and took great pains to be especially considerate to the young man, uncertain how he had reacted to what had happened while he was in Spain. Instead of being her gregarious matchmaker self, she led Gaius out to the garden with only a few soft words of welcome.

It was midspring and the day was quite warm. Licinia, now fourteen, sat in the shade of an apple tree, wearing a plain white, sleeveless stola, tied with an aqua sash beneath her breasts. Her head and shoulders were bare. She could not have looked lovelier. Licinia tried to read Gaius' face as he approached. With the couple due to be married in two months, Claudia spent only a short time in their company before going off to another part of the house so they could be alone.

"Does my safe return verify the gods' decision that we should marry?" said Gaius.

Licinia, who had tried to contain herself, stood to embrace him. "Oh yes, Gaius, it does. I know you will go off again in the years to come, but not before we're married."

Gaius welcomed her embrace. "Seeing you again was all I thought about while I was gone."

Licinia kissed him on the cheek, causing Gaius to blush and lower his eyes.

"Am I being too forward?" she asked, suddenly realizing this was only the third time they had been together.

Gaius laughed. "I think you promised me that kiss. I would have been disappointed without it."

Now Licinia blushed, then became serious and looked into his eyes. "I don't want to bring up something untoward, but I must say what I'm feeling." She looked down at the ground. "I am so sorry about your brother. Are you all right?"

Gaius took her hand. "Thank you for saying something. It has been difficult, but I will be fine by our wedding day. Seeing you helps." His smile was restrained. "You must know that I have seen many dead in my short time in the army. Many friends, many good men I knew well, did not come back from Spain and never will. Tiberius' death is different, yes, but he is also gone." Gaius looked away. He was not as settled with the issue as his words suggested.

Licinia squeezed his hand and drew him down beside her on one of the garden benches. "Will you pursue his politics?"

Gaius faced her and sighed. "I'm part of the land commission so I must, but I won't enter into politics on my own. I would be a marked man. Although it will mean more time away from you, I plan to make a career in the military."

"After what happened, I must wonder which is more dangerous."

"I would prefer an enemy's sword to the club of a fellow Roman."

A long silence hung between them, an understood recognition of the tragedy of Tiberius' death. Licinia broke the spell.

"Can you tell me anything about your campaign? I know that it was highly successful."

"It became quite brutal at the end. Aemilianus had us build a wall around Numantia. Then he diverted a nearby river to flood the area between our walls and theirs. When their envoys rejected Aemilianus' terms of surrender, they committed themselves to starvation. In the final weeks they began to eat their dead."

Licinia turned away. "I think you've told me more than I wanted to know."

"The last day they set fire to the city to limit our plunder. It was awful, but our tactics worked. It's what war is."

"Maybe you should be a farmer?"

Gaius laughed, then hugged her again.

Claudia came through the garden and stopped when she saw them. "You're not married yet, Gaius! You'll have plenty of time for that after the wedding."

"Mother, please, he's just returned from the war. How else should a man greet his future wife?"

"With an accent on the word *future*. Please sit a little farther apart."

After Claudia had gone to another part of the house, Licinia took Gaius' hand in both of hers. "Are you as excited as I am about the wedding? Please tell me you are."

Gaius squeezed her hands. "A better question is *are you as excited as I am?*"

Before Licinia could answer Gaius broke into laugher and she joined in. They were both very excited to be married.

CHAPTER 40

With Cornelia in Misenum and Aemilianus back in Rome, I felt as though I had been returned to prison. Aemilianus' success in Numantia gave him even greater prestige, which meant I only saw him in the evenings. We rarely talked, and with my ankle seemingly worse each day, I did my best to stay out of his sight. But even with his overbearing presence and his constant criticism of me, which I could bear as well as any woman, nothing galled me more than his comments about Tiberius, whose failed efforts in politics he considered, like everything it seemed, a reflection upon his honor.

All of this worked to erode anything resembling confidence in myself. I could not have said this then, but in reviewing those times to write this narrative, I can see that it was during this period that I grew increasingly bitter. The religious rituals that Aemilianus felt were so important grew meaningless to me. If Aemilianus was away, I simply skipped the day-to-day ceremonies so common in a Roman household as a deliberate insult to him. The lares, the little figurines that were moved about the house like good luck charms, remained on a shelf in the atrium like sad little dolls for a family that never materialized. The penates sat above the hearth, never getting their portion of the meal—a piece of bread or meat thrown into the fire—except when Aemilianus was there to enforce those long-held Roman traditions.

Having spent so much time with Cornelia and Claudia in the months after Tiberius' murder, I had built up a lot of anger about what had happened. From the perspective of these many years later, I realize that Tiberius did make a serious mistake by allowing himself to be caught up in Publius Nasica's ugly game of politics. But even with that said, Aemilianus' steady flow of off-hand comments about Tiberius only added to my loathing of him.

One evening, when Aemilianus came home from a dinner he had attended without the embarrassing company of his crippled wife, I decided to confront him. Drinking, as Asclepius had suggested, was one way to ease the pain in my ankle, and I had two cups of mulsum while he was out.

The night was pleasant and I was lying on a couch in the atrium with my sandals off, starring up at the stars, when Aemilianus strode into the courtyard. He appeared to have had a drink or two himself.

"I'm curious," I said. "What are they saying in the Senate? Have we entered some new age in Rome where senators can freely murder their opposition?"

We had hardly said anything to each other since his return from Spain, and I rarely asked his opinion about anything other than what he might like for the evening meal, but my sarcasm grabbed his attention. He came up close to the couch and looked down at me in his usual condescending way, deciding whether he would answer me or not. "What happened to your brother was of his own making, not Rome moving into some new era of political violence. I told him pushing land reform was a serious mistake. And it was." He turned away and started out of the room as though the discussion were over.

"So serious that he should be beaten to death at the doors to the temple of Jupiter?" I said to his back. "Did his actions truly justify that?"

He stopped and faced me. "He sought a second tribuneship. He was out for unprecedented power. Had I been here I would have taken a club to him myself."

"You don't know that he sought power," I snapped back at him. "You weren't here. You rely too much on what your friends have told you. Have you thought to ask Publius Crassus or Appius Claudius for their opinions?"

Aemilianus came back toward me. "Those men led him into it. Would you prefer that I had coaxed him into such a foolish confrontation with the optimates? In my opinion his confidants had as much to do with his murder as any of the others."

"And you're satisfied with the so-called trial that took place afterward?"

"What is good for the state is all that matters," he said, coming up close to me, displeased that I had continued to question him. "Tiberius' actions were threatening the state. That's all that needs to be said."

"What of the unchecked power and excessive land holdings of the senators? Are they not also a threat to the state?"

Aemilianus slapped me across the face. "Don't challenge my words, woman." He glared at me as though I were a dog to be beaten.

I dared to growl back at him, "I'll say what I like."

He slapped me again, then spun on his heels to leave. "I'm not finished," I said trying to stand up. My ankle gave way and I fell to the floor.

Aemilianus laughed derisively, then stood over me, watching as I rose to my hands and knees. Fearful that I could not regain my feet without embarrassing myself further, I tried to crawl over to one of the atrium columns for support. He trailed after me then took hold of the edge of my stola, making it impossible for me to go any farther. Again he laughed at me, but the laughter was without humor. He pulled my stola and tunic up over my head so that I could not see and my backside was uncovered. As I struggled to push the dress out of my face, he grabbed me by the waist, lifted his tunic, and mounted me from behind. His thrusts drove me to floor as he pounded at me until his rage was fulfilled. Then he simply stood, rearranged his tunic, and stalked away to his bedroom.

I screamed at him from the floor. "I thought you didn't want to waste your seed on the likes of me?"

"What have I to worry?" he called back from some higher plane. "Only should we produce offspring would there be a problem—and we know that's an impossibility with you."

Drawn by the loud voices, Nadia came into the atrium after Aemilianus had left. She quickly came to my side and helped me back onto the couch. She was a woman who had experienced the ravages of a conquering army during Rome's third war with Carthage. She had lost her family and at very young age her virginity. Aemilianus brought her back to Rome as a gift to me. "It's a man's world, my lady. You must not be disrespectful to your husband."

I looked at her knowing it was what she had lived. "No, Nadia, the fault is his. He disrespected me."

"Please remember, my lady, you are only a wife." Her reply did not match what I saw in her eyes. "Your respect is measured by your husband's."

CHAPTER 41

The upcoming wedding was a saving grace. It was no secret that Gaius and Licinia had taken to each other and were as excited about the marriage as the parents. The enthusiasm around the festivities, the preparation and the planning, served to push the darkness surrounding Tiberius' death further into the past. Cornelia showed her strongest side. Claudia had a harder time. Her grief for Tiberius would prove slow to heal. I did my best to help her work through it.

The night before the wedding Licinia sacrificed the toys of her childhood to the lares. This marked the first step of freeing a woman from her father and her family. The wedding began the next day at Publius Crassus' home when Gaius arrived with the rest of our family. We were escorted to the peristyle where the ceremony would take place. Aemilianus and I, Appius, Claudia and her children, Cornelia, Publius Crassus and his wife Claudia, and just a few others, including Polybius and the satirist Lucilius, were there. The attendance would have been somewhat larger if not for Tiberius' death. Publius Nasica and Mucius Scaevola, both relatives, were not invited.

Claudia, Tiberius' widow, as a once married matron, was given the honor of administering the wedding. Licinia wore a plain white dress with a sash below her breasts, saffron slippers, and a transparent flame-colored veil over her face and head. Her hair was separated into six braids that were wound up to form a cone-shaped bun at the back of her head, held in place by a wreath made of marjoram and aromatic herbs. Gaius wore a plain, white linen tunic.

The ceremony began with Licinia and Gaius sacrificing a calf to Juno, Queen of the Gods. They both sprinkled a handful of wheat on the ground for the chickens. The birds ate with vigor—having not been fed in two days—promising a good marriage. Claudia then took Gaius' left hand and placed it in Licinia's right. Claudia lifted Licinia's veil. The couple exchanged a whispered vow, which I was not able to hear, then kissed. With the ceremony completed, the wedding papers were signed, officially making Licinia Gaius' property. As defined by the institution of manus, which was part of all upper-class marriages, he now had the same authority over her that her father once had.

A huge feast followed. The main course was the calf that had been sacrificed. Several amphorae of wine were drained. I had more than one cup. The mood was celebratory. Cornelia seemed to transcend her dread of Rome for the day and spoke cheerfully with everyone, even Aemilianus. There was no talk of Tiberius or land reform or anything to do with politics.

Following the meal, Gaius returned to Cornelia's house, now his home, to wait for his bride. Shortly after he left, Claudia escorted Licinia, followed by a procession of all the guests, to the newlyweds' home. Claudia's children, six-year-old Tiberius and three-year-old Sempronia, led the joyous group that sang nuptial songs and told ribald jokes as they walked. Little Tiberius carried a torch lit from the hearth in Licinia's parent's home. His sister carried a pitcher of water.

When the wedding entourage reached Gaius' house, the threshold was smeared with lard and covered with strands of wool. Licinia approached the door and called into the house. "Where are you, Gaius?"

As was the custom, he responded by asking her name.

"Shall I be Gaia?" she answered.

Gaius came to the door and carried her over the threshold. Claudia followed them into the house and escorted them to their bedroom, which had been decorated with hundreds of flowers. Little Tiberius came in with Cornelia to light the hearth with his torch, while Claudia made a sacrifice to the goddess Hymen and helped Gaius untie the sash around Licinia's waist. At that point Claudia left the bedroom, and along with Cornelia and Tiberius, returned to the bride's home with all the other guests.

Finally alone, the couple consummated the marriage with hopes of conceiving their first child. The next day a second feast was held at the couple's new home. In many ways, it seemed the horrible spell cast eighteen months earlier had finally been broken. It was time to move on.

CHAPTER 42

Cornelia and Claudia and her two children returned to Misenum two days after the wedding. Cornelia would continue to spend almost all of her time at the villa, only coming to Rome if necessary. She would never quite recover her faith in the process of Roman government.

To fill her time Cornelia formed a literary circle much like Aemilianus'. It began with just women. I would go to Misenum every other month to take part. When Gaius was off on military duty, I would bring Licinia with me. The first meetings were just the four women in our immediate family. But gradually word got out, and visitors from all over Italy and beyond began to join in. Polybius came on occasion, as did Lucilius and Physcon, though he used it as an excuse to see Cornelia.

The Senate's effort to purge Roman politics of Tiberius' influence lasted less than a year, but the populace had lost one of its strongest advocates and still carried a grudge. Publius Nasica, though occupying the revered position of pontifex maximus, became the target of abuse whenever he was in public. The situation only got worse with time. Crowds would gather outside the Curia calling for the pontiff to be tried for Tiberius' murder. Instead of trying the man, the Senate decided to send him to Asia to act as a legate in Ephesus. He died six months later. Surprisingly, Publius Crassus, one of the few senators to remain loyal to Tiberius throughout the ordeal, was chosen to replace him as pontifex maximus.

The elections for the following year further supported this change in the political atmosphere. Crassus was elected to his first consulship at the age of forty-nine. As consul and pontifex maximus he was now one of the most powerful people in the city, rivaled only by Aemilianus, who had fallen short in his bid for a third consulship.

In the same election, Gaius Papirius Carbo, one of a handful of Tiberius' clients who had not been eliminated in the purge, was elected to the tribunate. Carbo followed Tiberius' lead as a tribune, pushing legislation that would build his constituency in the People's Assembly. Early in his term, he proposed two bills, one to allow a tribune to serve consecutive terms and one to extend the use of secret ballots, which were already in use for the election of officials, to votes on legislation.

The first bill got the most attention. It was seen as a deliberate attempt to retroactively clear Tiberius of the alleged crime of seeking a second tribuneship and immediately became a topic of intense debate. The Senate came out strongly against it. The issue brought Gaius to the forum to speak for the first time. Although he had stayed out of the fray for almost eighteen months, half of that on military duty, he had used his free time to improve his oratorical skills.

Gaius had said he would not engage in politics, but after spending time in Rome listening to the discourse, he began to change. He was twenty-one, and at the urging of Tiberius' friend Marcus Fulvius Flaccus, he spoke out in favor of Carbo's bill, expressing for the first time in public his as yet unvented rage against his brother's murderers.

"Why was my brother not allowed a second term?" he shouted to a large audience in the forum. "A lie was spread that he sought power, that he wanted a crown. No, that was not who my brother was. The work of a tribune, like the siege of a city, can be a task that takes more than one year. Land reform was an enormous undertaking that he was just beginning to make progress with. Another year was not a selfish request. It was dedication to duty. And yet, some people in high places had such fear of Tiberius, and his popularity, that they killed him for seeking to complete what he had begun."

This was powerful rhetoric coming from Gaius, and the people saw a young Tiberius in him, which added force to his words and sent a quiver of anxiety through the senatorial class.

Two days before the vote, Aemilianus spoke strongly against the bill to a completely filled comitium. He was a near mythic military figure. He had celebrated two triumphs, served as consul twice, and with his huge private library and extensive friendships with international scholars was widely regarded as one of the most intelligent and highly educated men in Rome. Although a known popularis, from a family of populists, he spoke from above the political fray, or so he would have everyone believe.

"You know that I have spent my entire life, exerted my every effort, into securing the well-being of Rome. I believe that is what all citizens should strive to do. To contribute to the perfection of the state is what it means to be Roman, whether as a politician, a military officer, or a legionnaire." Aemilianus was in his mid-fifties, strong of body and spirit. He was proud and arrogant in the way he felt a man from a noted and wealthy family should be.

"The tradition of Rome has remained constant," he continued. "Our forefathers were well aware that the greatest crime against the state was the tyranny of a demagogue, and specifically built barriers within our system of laws to contain the power of any single individual. When officials are elected to a position, it is for one year. That has been true for every public office, except that of censor, for four hundred years, with particular emphasis on the positions of tribune and consul. One might even argue that within the city limits, the tribune is more powerful than a consul; and yet now, the tribunate seeks to expand upon its powers by opening the position to consecutive terms. What would it mean if a tribune became so popular that he proceeded to three then four consecutive terms? Is that not a step in the direction we Romans fear most—a tyrant in Rome?"

Carbo stood up in the audience, and calling out Aemilianus' name, asked him, "Are you alluding to Tiberius? Are you trying to justify the acts of his murderers?"

Aemilianus stood his ground, repeating the view he had expressed when he had first learned of Tiberius' death. "If Gracchus had the intention of seizing the administration of the state, he was justly slain."

In the year and a half since his death, Tiberius had become both a hero and a martyr to the plebeians. Anything said against him inspired outrage. To them, the vast majority in the audience that day, Aemilianus was suggesting that Tiberius sought a crown. In their minds this was a terrible exaggeration, if not an absolute lie. The audience became restless. Several people demanded Aemilianus rescind his words. Others called out threats against him.

This infuriated Aemilianus. A man accustomed to almost god-like worship in Rome, he glared at the unruly crowd and shouted back at them, "I have never been frightened by the clamor of an enemy in arms, nor shall I be alarmed by the cries of the stepsons of Italy."

The stepsons allusion was a deliberate insult to the lower class. They were not from as pure a Roman bloodline as his. The statement only aroused greater protest in the crowd and a barrage of catcalls and insults. Aemilianus answered by mocking them further. "I brought many of you to Rome in chains. Now that you are freedmen, do you believe that you are truly Romans? Or only half-breeds?"

The crowd erupted with increased anger and coarser insults, accompanied by a hail of ripe fruit. A soggy plum splattered on Aemilianus' shoulder, staining his immaculate white toga. He abruptly turned away from the rostra and stormed off across the forum, cursing to himself about ungrateful hooligans.

Aemilianus entered our house later that afternoon like a hurricane. He slammed the door and stomped through the atrium and back again. Wondering what could have happened, I entered the house from the peristyle. Aemilianus let go with long string of insults against both Tiberius and Gaius, calling them instigators of a revolt against Roman tradition.

I did not bother to ask him about the wet mark on his toga. I backed away from his rage and returned to the peristyle, fearful he might turn his anger on me.

CHAPTER 43

Despite the reaction to Aemilianus in the comitium, Papirius Carbo's bill did not pass. A tribune's term remained limited to one year. The age-old fear of a single despotic ruler, which Aemilianus had harped on so heavily, carried a close vote at the People's Assembly. The bill for a secret ballot when voting on legislation also surprisingly failed.

Appius Claudius died in the months following the vote. He was in his midfifties and seemingly in good health when he suddenly became ill and died. This added to Claudia's continuing grief. She was now without a husband or a father. Appius was replaced on the land reform commission by the progressive tribune Papirius Carbo, thus joining Gaius and Crassus.

Licinia gave birth to a son that spring, two weeks before Gaius left on a military campaign with his father-in-law. A renegade Syrian king by the name of Aristonicus had assembled a mercenary army that was running wild in the Roman provinces in Asia, and Crassus, as a newly elected consul, was determined to stop him.

Despite her aversion to Rome, Cornelia could not resist visiting the new mother and child. She left Claudia and her two children in Misenum and came to Rome to stay at her old home with Licinia and the baby Gaius. (All first-born males received their father's name, and all the female children received the feminine version of the clan name, Sempronia in this case, just like Tiberius' daughter. *Yes, it can get confusing.*)

I went to Gaius' home several times while Cornelia was in Rome. Seeing young children was invariably bittersweet for me. I loved to hold little Gaius, but it always left me feeling inadequate and especially vulnerable to the caustic remarks of my husband.

On one occasion when I was there, after Licinia had been up all night with the baby, she took the opportunity of my visit to take a nap.

She went to her bedroom and I held Gaius, while sitting beside Cornelia in the garden—once her garden—which was like visiting an old friend for her, especially on a pleasant afternoon in late spring when all the flowers were beginning to bloom.

I had become lost in my own life. Living with Aemilianus was like being beaten down emotionally a little bit each day. I sought solace by writing in a journal, but my ankle and the steady abuse had me wondering why I was even alive. Out of sheer desperation, I opened up to Cornelia that day. She was well aware of the difficulties I had with Aemilianus, and after his latest public statement about Tiberius' murder, Cornelia wanted nothing to do with him. And to be sure, Aemilianus wanted nothing to do with her. It was in this atmosphere of mutual distaste for my husband that I finally felt I could reveal the anguish I was feeling.

"Mother," I said, holding the swaddled infant in my arms, and gaining some unnamable strength from the little package of life. "Why did you nurture me as a child?"

Cornelia knew what this question meant. I had asked her more than once over the years, invariably when my womb seemed to be moving about inside of me. "To have a daughter who can talk openly to me like you are now." Her smile was forlorn.

"Would you have done so if you'd known I would be barren?"

"Oh, Sempronia, why would I even try to answer such a question?"

I bowed my head to hide my tears. "Since his lost popularity, Aemilianus takes me at random, in any part of the house, with force and no thought of producing children. I've become little more than a depository for his anger."

Cornelia wrapped an arm around my shoulder and laid her head next to mine. "A husband is a woman's burden, Sempronia. That doesn't answer your question, but just know that you are not alone. I was fortunate to marry the man I did. I tried to raise Gaius—and Tiberius—to have a deeper understanding of the sacred nature of a lifetime partner. But I never told you about the darker side of matrimony. Maybe that was a mistake on my part. Has he hurt you?"

I looked up at her. "In no serious physical way. But I hate myself—and feel I deserve his abuse." My tears were flowing now. "Mother, I'm sorry, I'm sorry, forgive my weakness, but why did you do this to me?"

"I thought if I nurtured your mind, Sempronia," she said as she stroked my hair, "that I was giving you an internal sanctuary. I felt that opening your mind to aesthetic truths would give you strength—and because of your ankle, I feared you might need it."

"But it hasn't been enough. In some ways it only deepens my troubles. Maybe if I had never learned to read Greek or understand philosophy, I wouldn't be so badly frustrated by who I've become."

Tears formed in Cornelia's eyes.

"Do other women bear it, Mother, because they think so little of themselves?"

"They bear their life in the same way a slave who works in a mine does. Because they believe it's their fate and that there's nothing more."

I looked into the puffy face of the infant in my arms, who at that moment looked more like a funny old man than a child.

"Would you like to come to Misenum to live? Claudia and I have a good life there. You're welcome any time. I can even send a carriage for you."

I looked at her. "I don't know, Mother. I'll have to think about it. Perhaps Aemilianus will divorce me and I'll have to."

"Maybe that wouldn't be so bad."

I shook my head dejectedly. "I don't know. I just don't know."

CHAPTER 44

Crassus died in Asia six months after arriving. In one of his many clashes with Aristonicus, he was captured. While riding to his imprisonment with an escort of four soldiers, he used his riding crop to stab one of his guards in the eye. When he tried to ride off, he was chased down and killed. This meant both of Cornelia's daughters-in-law had lost their fathers in a year's time.

Marcus Fulvius Flaccus was chosen to replace Crassus on the land reform commission. The three commissioners were now Fulvius, Carbo, and my brother. Gaius had been gone every summer since being elected to the commission, but now with Crassus' death, he returned to Rome to take a year off from military service to help Fulvius and Carbo with the work.

Despite all that had occurred, the commission had been going about its work for nearly three years. For the most part the process had gone smoothly. The commission had wisely concentrated on the distribution of unclaimed public land. No one's property had been confiscated, and none of the senators or large landowners had yet to feel the pinch. Under the guidance of Appius and Crassus more than five thousand Roman citizens had been granted thirty-iugerum parcels, with no interference from the Senate. The large sum of money gained through Attalus' gift to the Roman people—thank you, Physcon—had made it all possible.

However, as more and more unclaimed public land was distributed over the next year, the work of the commission became increasingly difficult. The commission had to address the complication of distributing land that "belonged" to men who had more than the legal limit of five hundred iugera. Rather than going after land owned by influential men in Rome, the commission chose to seek out large landowners in Rome's allied Latin and Italian states. This involved land that had been requisitioned by Rome at the end of the war with

Hannibal. The division of this land had been done hastily and with no consideration for what would happen in the years to come. Over the course of the intervening seventy years, the land was steadily absorbed by wealthy Latin and Italian farm owners whose land was adjacent to unclaimed public property. Some of this land now belonged to families going back nearly three generations. Some of the property had even been sold, sometimes more than once. When the commission began to cut this property into thirty-iugerum parcels for Roman citizens, the difficulty of the task greatly multiplied. Sorting out ownership alone was difficult. If the landowner had no contract for his property, it was taken. Others with contracts were given land of less agricultural value in exchange for land that had been developed with farm buildings or planted with fruit trees. A series of lawsuits sprang up due to unclear property lines and poorly written contracts. The work of the commission got bogged down in the courts, and progress slowed to a crawl.

But it was more than arguments over property lines and previous investments in the land. The leaders of these Italian and Latin city-states, many of whom had property at stake, were as powerful and wealthy as the Roman aristocrats, and they complained to the Roman Senate about the process—not just with individual suits, but with an attack on the entire concept of redistribution and the legality of the commission's work in general. In an effort to get more influence in Rome, a collection of these aristocrats sought the assistance of Aemilianus, who had made his career building legions from these allied states. Aemilianus, who would have been better served to leave the whole thing alone, had been against land reform from the beginning. Now extremely bitter about how Tiberius' actions reflected on him, he chose to get involved, more out of spite than legal principle.

When Aemilianus was prompted to address the Senate on behalf of the Italian and Latin allies, he spent an evening with his childhood tutor and long-time friend Polybius, who had recently reached his seventieth year. Aemilianus wanted the history scholar's advice before he drafted his speech to the Senate.

Polybius had been my tutor and was someone I greatly admired. He acknowledged me that evening when he arrived. We exchanged pleasantries, mostly his teasing me about incidents that had occurred when I was his student. All of it was good-natured and caused me to laugh more than I had in an awfully long time.

The two men spoke over a dinner of roast pork, fresh bread, and Vela's excellent vegetable soup. Both men had cups of wine. I had none at the table, but two afterward. Aemilianus opened the conversation with a description of the problem. "I need to be careful with what I say, Polybius. I was recently dogged by Papirius Carbo for my criticism of Tiberius. I let my arrogance get the better of me and said some things that angered the plebeians."

Polybius' hair, what little he had, was snow white. He was completely bald on the top with a clean-shaven face. "If you already have a problem with the plebeians, why have you decided to represent the Latins and Italians? You're only asking for more trouble."

"They've been a sure source of soldiers throughout my career. Troops are easier to raise in the south than in Rome. I feel I owe them something."

"Still I suggest letting this one go, my friend. Your military career is over. You'll never need to draft another army."

"But I've already promised to help them. What can I do?"

Polybius looked off as though thinking, then took a sip from his cup of wine. "In some ways, these disputes are similar to those that have existed for years between Roman commercial interests and outside proprietors. Think about it. Contracts for public construction projects all over Italy are let out by the censors to both Roman and non-Roman contractors. Repairs to our harbors are the same. So are the surety contracts for these projects. If there are problems, the contractors or lenders come to the Senate with their complaints. Some of these men are Romans, some are not. In the end, everything comes back to the Senate for adjudication. In all fiscal matters the Senate's had the final word. This instance should be no different."

"You think these suits would be best administered by the Senate?"

"Yes. They're matters of foreign policy and should be considered beyond the authority of the reform commission."

Aemilianus nodded. "And most should see the sense of that."

"I would think so. It will take some of the power from the commission. But didn't the Senate react so strongly to Tiberius because they felt he'd overreached? This is one example of it."

"Yes, yes, Polybius." Aemilianus lifted his cup to his friend. "Few are so lucky to have such clear-thinking advisors."

Polybius reluctantly lifted his cup. "My advice might be helpful, but you've ignored my initial comment. You'd be better served letting others handle this."

"No, it will be fine if I choose my words carefully."

Aemilianus had long been associated with the popularis faction of the Senate, and had even been considered the plebeians staunchest advocate prior to Tiberius' rise and fall. When he spoke to the Senate the next day, he wisely decided to stick to detailing his solution to the lawsuits and did not veer off into denigration of his cousin's land reform bill.

"The land commission was never set up to act as a court," he began, "especially for legal issues that relate to our allies, who in some cases do not believe they can get a just hearing from the same people who are making the demands. This is a fair grievance. It makes more sense to leave the settlement of these suits to the Senate, which has always adjudicated disputes with our allies and other foreign nations. This way the decisions will have greater standing in the eyes of those pressing suits." Aemilianus looked at his fellow senators. "I propose the Senate vote on establishing a special court to settle these disputes."

The co-consuls for the year were Marcus Aquillius and Gaius Sempronius Tuditanus. Aquillius was in Spain on military duty. Tuditanus presided over the meeting.

Aemilianus faced him. "And I suggest that our current consul, Sempronius Tuditanus, act as the supervising judge for this new court."

Tuditanus spoke in favor of the measure, and the proposal passed easily.

The land commissioners initially welcomed Aemilianus' proposal as a reasonable idea and as something that would lessen their work load in the long run. Over the next month Tuditanus set up the proposed court and began to adjudicate law suits. But he had not looked at the situation carefully prior to agreeing to the job, and soon understood the size and difficulty of the task he had accepted. Barely five weeks into the work, he threw up his hands in frustration. He drummed up a military campaign in Illyria and left Rome with two legions, more interested in accumulating plunder than untying legal knots that stretched back seventy years into the past.

Rather than solving the problem, the situation became worse. Tuditanus was gone, and the commission no longer had the power to settle disputes. The entire land reform effort stagnated. The commission, which had been distributing property to as many as fifty landless plebeians a week, could only manage to complete a few transactions a month. And in the uproar that followed, Aemilianus became the target of plebeian frustration. They accused him of trying to undermine the land reform bill and further condemned him for taking the side of Rome's Italian and Latin allies over them.

Three years earlier Aemilianus had ridden into Rome in a gilded chariot, a historic Roman hero. Now he could not go anywhere in public without hearing shouts against his name and his reputation. He was even called a traitor for his allegiance to Rome's allies. In one such instance, when Tarus was accompanying him for protection, three men attacked Aemilianus. Tarus intervened with all the savagery of a one-time pirate. Aemilianus was never touched, but Tarus received a serious blow to his head that left him slow and listless the rest of his life.

Sadly, the worse things got for my husband, the more he seemed intent on taking it out on me. He began to drink in excess, and then come to my bed, or anywhere I might be, to vent his anger in violent bursts of sexual passion. My already dismal life took yet another downturn.

CHAPTER 45

With Cornelia in Misenum I had no one to talk to. I became increasingly despondent. I began to entertain taking my life. I had little insight how I would do it, but hoped to find some potion that could quickly solve my problems and yet not be so horrible a death. I suppose I was the coward in the family.

One morning I strapped on my supportive sandal and borrowed Nadia's hooded, raw wool cloak. I added some face paint, something I never wore, and used a cane to venture out into the city unaccompanied, hoping to find some kind of poison. I was not entirely certain where I needed to go but knew I did not want to be recognized. I had no money of my own, so I had rifled Tiberius' bedroom to obtain a silver denarius, two sesterces, and four asses. I dared not take more fearing he might notice it was missing.

I went to the Subura district to begin my search. It was the poorest part of Rome and not far from my house. I had never been there before, much less alone. Even with the supportive sandal, my ankle became troublesome almost immediately. Without the cane, it would have been impossible.

The streets in Subura were more like muddy alleys, very narrow and filled with trash and chickens and dogs and rats. Any progress I made was a struggle. Bent over the cane, and wearing the hood over my head, I blended in well, and though the language used in the street was coarse, I was mostly left alone. I saw more women selling themselves than I care to mention. Legionnaires whose military service had left them badly crippled or with missing limbs seemed to sit on every doorstep or limp down the street with the same trouble I had.

Little shops, if you could call them that, were tucked in between the poorly built tenement buildings like dark caves. The first one I dared to enter contained two young women sitting on stools. Behind them a third woman was servicing a soldier. I quickly backed out, realizing that I had no idea what I was doing. A little farther down the street I noticed a man selling snakes. He held a long black snake in his hands and let it wind around one arm then the other. He had several others in wooden cages stacked on the ground behind him. When I hesitated for a moment in passing him, his eyes fastened on mine, and he held the black snake out to me. "No better pet than a snake, lady. Got a problem with rodents? This beauty will clean your house out in a week. She's yours for three asses."

"Are any of your snakes poisonous?" I asked, surprised that I responded to the man at all.

He grinned, making his eyes small. "For a lover you would like to surprise?" He winked, then holding the black snake with one hand, lifted one of the cages so I could look inside. A rather large brown snake was coiled into the cage like a length of braided hair. "You might like this Sicilian viper. One little bite will do. No more horrible death can I imagine—except maybe burning." He winked at me. "Yours for two sesterces."

"I'm looking for something a little less dramatic?"

He came up close to me, wagging the black snake in my face. "What have you got in mind? A child or an adult?"

"N-n-neither," I stammered backing away. "I have dog with a bad temper. It bit my child. I wanted a humane way to get rid of it."

"My snakes are too dangerous with a child in the house. What you need is some hemlock. With the right dose, the dog will simply go to sleep and never wake up."

I nodded, recalling the story of Socrates' death. "Where might I get hemlock?"

"I know a woman who deals in such herbs. For two asses, I'll tell you where to find her."

I was not accustomed to dealing with street people. I was almost afraid to show him that I had any money at all, but I fished into my cloak and retrieved two of the four asses I had with me. He snatched them out of my hand before I had a chance to give them to him, then he laughed at me in a hideous way.

"Where's this woman?" I hesitated, wondering if he would bother to answer.

He squinched one eye and leaned in close to me. "You're not regularly in these parts are you?"

"Well, I don't go out much, no."

He laughed again. "Go to the top of the Aventine Hill. Behind the temple of Minerva there's an alley. It leads into a little community of," he grinned, "Rome's finest thieves and con artists. She's an ugly old woman. She has no shop, just wanders around with her entire inventory hidden beneath her cloak."

"How will I recognize her?"

"Have another as?"

This was the sort of situation I had hoped to avoid. I was just too naive to be bargaining for poison in the street. I drew a third as from my cloak, but gripped it tightly in my hand and pressed my fist up against my chest. "Tell me how I can recognize her?" I asked again.

"She wears a striped bandana around her head, and she has a pet cat that sits on her shoulder. You can't miss her. This time of day she'll be there."

I gave him the as and limped away, wondering how I would ever climb to the top of the Aventine Hill. I had not gone very far when a rough-looking man pushed up close to me. "I've got a room," he muttered under his breath. "How much?"

I ignored the man and struggled ahead in the muddy street.

He stayed with me as I lurched ahead with my cane trying to get away. "How much?" he asked again.

I could not maintain the pace. I had to stop. I leaned up against the nearest wall. "I'm not for sale," I said, out of breath, more frightened than angry. "Leave me alone."

The man stared at me. "Too bad," he snapped, "I like cripples," then walked away.

I remained against the wall for a long time wondering if I should return home or dare the climb to the temple of Minerva. The immediate area stunk of human waste. The street might as well have been a long, thin pigsty. And there I was, splattered with the stuff, my ankle killing me, contemplating buying poison to take my life. I decided to find the woman with the cat on her shoulder.

The climb was not so difficult or steep. Most could climb to the top without breaking stride or losing breath. But for me it was torture. I gritted my teeth with every step. At times I felt that I would need to crawl, all the more intensifying my purpose. *What value was I?*

Upon reaching the crest of the hill, I rested on a bench in front of the temple of Minerva, built to the Goddess of Art and Wisdom. They should have called her Cornelia. The temple was white limestone, built in the traditional style with a red tile, peaked roof and surrounded on all four sides by a portico of fluted columns. The painted statue of the goddess inside was powerful—a lovely young woman posed dramatically in a long flowing gown and wearing a soldier's helmet. An owl perched on her outstretched left arm. A large serpent stood erect beside her. A shield was at her feet.

I gave my ankle a good rest, then hobbled down the length of the temple looking for the alley I had been told about. I found a narrow and not so obvious passageway between two buildings and followed it into a courtyard surrounded by dilapidated three- and four-story tenement apartments. Much like the Subura neighborhood, the courtyard contained piles of refuse and an excess of loose chickens and dogs, but there were also jugglers and minstrels mixed in with clusters of beggars, all milling around as though it were some kind of festival for the poor. Well-disguised with my crutch and Nadia's cloak, I meandered through the motley crowd looking for a woman with a cat on her shoulder. It did not take long even with all the activity that was going on. I spotted her standing alone at the edge of a makeshift theater stage where two drunken mimes were failing to draw an audience.

I approached the woman cautiously. She had several knobby growths on her face and looked the part of someone selling herbs in the street, the uncomfortable mix of a homeless woman and a witch. Her hair was dark, streaked with gray and wiry. It stuck out in all directions from her striped bandana like a frizzy halo. She wore a long, multicolored, patchwork cloak with holes at the elbows and a frayed hem. I edged up close to her. The black cat on her shoulder noticed me before she did. "I was told you sell herbs."

The woman appraised me with small dark eyes. "Who might have said that?"

"A man selling snakes in Subura."

She assessed me as a mark. "Do you have any money?"

"If you have what I'm looking for."

She looked around as though the mere mention of money would draw others, then ushered me away to a corner of the courtyard where there weren't so many people. "What do you need?" she hissed.

"I have a dog that bit my child. The dog is close to me, but I want to be rid of it. Rather than loosing him on the street, I thought I might poison him. Do you have something that will be a quick and painless death?" The cat was watching me the entire time.

"Poison, hmmm?" She stared into my face as though she did not believe a word I had said. A little smile curled at the corners of her mouth. "That will cost you more than a copper or two. Can you manage that?"

"I can pay as much as a denarius."

Her grin widened. She opened her cloak, forcing the cat to move behind her head. Thirty or more small cloth bundles hung from cords on the inside of her cloak. "Something deadly but not too painful, you say?" Again she peered into my eyes like she was reading my mind. "For your dog?"

I nodded, knowing she did not believe me.

She touched one of the little parcels. "Wolf bane, perhaps?" She touched a second. "Hemlock is a favorite for loved ones."

"Which would you suggest for the most mercy?"

"Hemlock mixed with honey." She lifted the cloth bundle and looked inside. "You can have all of this for a denarius. Half of it will make for a very pleasant death."

I swallowed at the mention of it. "I'll take it."

"For her dog," she said to the cat.

I withdrew the silver denarius from my cloak. "For my dog."

The old woman took the coin, tried to bend it with her teeth, then handed me the hemlock. "You're not fooling me. You're planning to kill your husband aren't you?"

"No, no," I muttered, "my dog." I tucked the cloth bundle into my cloak, glanced up at her, then limped off into the crowd. The ankle hurt more than ever. I had to stop three times on the way back to my house to cope with the pain. When I finally entered the door, I dropped Nadia's cloak on the floor and hobbled into the atrium before collapsing on a bench beside the pool.

Nadia heard me come in and was at my side almost immediately. "My lady, are you all right?"

I shook my head no. "Please get me some warm water to soak my foot—and a cup of mulsum. I turned my ankle again."

She did not believe me any more than Aemilianus did. She returned with a bucket of hot water, a linen cloth, and a small cup of mulsum. She unwrapped the cords that bound my ankle while I sipped from the cup. My entire foot had turned purple with the swelling and was twisted so badly it appeared to be attached sideways to my ankle. Nadia lifted my leg at the calf and eased my foot in the water. I was so exhausted I just stretched out on the bench. She dipped the cloth in the water and used it to clean the paint off my face without asking why I was wearing it.

"Thank you, Nadia."

She looked at me full of questions. Clearly she wanted to know where I had been but was too gracious to ask.

When the water cooled and my cup was empty, I used the crutch to hike up to my bedroom. I hid the bundle of hemlock beneath my straw-filled mattress, then lay down hoping to go to sleep, but even with the mulsum, the throbbing in my ankle would not allow it. I was simply thankful to be off my feet. The trip down the Aventine Hill had been worse than going up. I had fallen twice. Something about having the hemlock seemed comforting. Maybe I would never use it, but at least now I had an option.

CHAPTER 46

During this period of rancor regarding land reform, Aemilianus invited a few of his friends to dinner to discuss Tuditanus' failure to accept the responsibility of presiding over the land settlement court. After the meal, Aemilianus, Gaius Laelius, Spurius Mummius—Quintus Mummius' older brother—and Quintus Tubero, Aemilianus' nephew, a man a few years older than Gaius, lounged on couches around the table in the triclinium. The table was cleared of everything but an amphora of chian wine and the men's drinking cups.

I had eaten alone much earlier. I had Nadia set up my spinning wheel in the atrium. Curious about what the men might say, I sat close enough to the triclinium to see in through the doorway and overhear some of what they talked about.

The men came to no solution for running the settlement court, which seemed to be an impossible task, but with more drinking the conversation turned to unabashed criticism of Tiberius. Gaius Laelius, the grandson of the same Gaius Laelius who had fought with my grandfather in Africa, and who was known for having first suggested land reform twenty years earlier, seemed to be the most offended by Tiberius' efforts. I had not taken heed of their talk with much interest or anger—I already knew what these men thought about my brother—until I heard Laelius say something that got my blood boiling. "Why, I wonder," he said to the other men, "have we not erected a statue to Publius Nasica? Should he not get credit for ridding Rome of Tiberius? I mean, isn't the man a true Roman patriot?"

"Whether proper or not, I don't think that would be very popular," said Mummius. "Tiberius' name still resounds in certain quarters of Rome."

"What difference does it make what the lower orders think?" said Tubero, an unattractive man with red blotchy skin, greasy black hair, and over-sized ears. He took a swallow from his cup. "Had Publius

Nascia not taken the initiative, who knows where Rome would be today. A statue is more than called for. I say it's demanded."

Aemilianus, as troubled as anyone by the measures Tiberius had passed as a tribune, had a completely different angle on the subject. "I think too much is made of statues," he said with a little grin, something rare for him unless he had several cups of wine.

"How so?" asked Laelius. "What's a better way to remember our ancestors?"

Mummius and Tubero echoed the same sentiments.

Aemilianus, who had stretched out on the couch, sat up, and drawing in close to the table, spoke softly to project the seriousness of what he would say. "Although the memory of great deeds alone is considered ample reward for virtue, one's divine nature needs a more stable reward than statues fixed in lead or triumphs with withering laurels."

"To what are you referring, Aemilianus?" asked Laelius.

"Not some unearthly rewards?" queried Tubero.

"I believe he must be," said Mummius, lifting his cup to take a drink.

Aemilianus' eyes sparkled and he nodded. "Do you recall Plato's story about the Pamphylian soldier who appeared to die in battle, then twelve days later, as he was about to be placed on his funeral pyre, sat up fully alive, saying that he had come back from the dead."

"No, but it seems quite far-fetched," said Tubero.

"Go on, Aemilianus," said Laelius. "I recall the story. What's your point?"

"The man spoke of having spent time in the heavens and offered it as proof of the existence of something beyond life on Earth."

"A fine story," said Mummius, "but nothing more."

"Perhaps that's all it is," said Aemilianus, "but I had a dream many years ago that I never told to anyone—because it touched on these ideas of divinity. It was during my time in Africa, shortly after I arrived, when I was a tribune under Manilius and had yet to initiate the siege of Carthage. I made a deliberate effort to find the aged Numidian king Masinissa, then past his eightieth year, who had been such a fond friend of my grandfather's." Aemilianus took a sip of wine.

"On seeing me, Masinissa was overcome with emotion, saying, 'Oh I thank the supreme Sun and the other celestial beings, that before I have departed from this life I can behold in my kingdom, and in my palace, Publius Cornelius Scipio, by whose mere name I feel so thrilled.'

"This opening led to a pleasant evening where I explained to him the issues of our commonwealth, and he talked about the affairs of his kingdom, then went on, as an old man will, about his time with Africanus and the battles they fought together. It was a night I will never forget. The great king died less than a year later and it was the only time I ever saw him."

"How does that figure into these rewards you mentioned?" asked Laelius.

"That night, after our talk, when we had retired to our chambers, I had the dream I have kept to myself for so long."

"And how much longer will you keep it from us?" Laelius raised his cup, chuckling. "Get on with it, my friend."

"As so often happens after a large meal and good talk, the conversation of the night returns in some haphazard way to your dreams."

"Yes, yes," said Mummius.

"Africanus, looking just like the bust here in my library, came to me in a dream that night, though I thought I was awake sitting up in bed. Seeing that his appearance frightened me, he spoke comfortingly. 'Take courage, Aemilianus, be not afraid, and carefully remember what I say to you.'"

The other three men leaned forward to listen as the story drew them in.

"'The city of Carthage,' he said, 'once brought under the Roman yoke by me, is now renewing former wars and cannot live in peace. Although you are only a tribune today, before two years have elapsed, you shall be a consul and complete the overthrow of this city, and obtain by your own merit the surname Africanus, just as I have. And when you have destroyed Carthage, and received the honor of a triumph, and have been made censor, and as an ambassador visited Egypt, Syria, Asia, and Greece, you shall be elected consul again and win a dangerous war with Numantia. Then when you have entered Rome for a second time in your triumphal chariot, you will find the Roman Commonwealth all in a ferment through the intrigues of my great-grandson Tiberius Gracchus.'"

"In other words, Aemilianus," said Laelius, "this ghost told you twenty years ago all the things that would make your career?"

"Yes."

"And you never said anything—even as these things happened?" asked Tubero.

"Impossible," sneered Mummius.

"Let me finish my story before you judge it." Aemilianus grinned. "'It will be on this occasion,' continued Africanus, 'that you will show your country, all good citizens, the allies, and all the people of Latium, the greatness of your understanding and prudence by calming the uncertain times. When your age shall have accomplished seven times eight revolutions of the sun, and your fatal hours shall be marked by the natural product of these two numbers, then the whole city will take recourse in you alone and will place its hopes in your auspicious name, and the preservation of the state will depend on you. In other words, if you escape the impious machinations of your relatives, you will, in the way of a dictator, establish order and tranquility in the commonwealth.'"

"Oh, so you're telling us because of all the great things you've done," groaned Laelius, "that you have every confidence you can solve these legal problems?"

Aemilianus shook his head in a playful way. "Don't wake me from this dream so soon, Laelius. I have more to tell. Africanus is still imparting his advice. Be quiet and listen, so he may continue. 'Now, in order to encourage you to defend the state with the greatest cheerfulness,'—he said to me—'be assured that, for all those who have in any way applied themselves to the preservation, defense, and enlargement of their native country, there is a certain place in heaven where they shall enjoy an eternity of happiness. For nothing on Earth is more agreeable to God, the Supreme Governor of the Universe, than the assemblies and societies of men united together by laws and called states. It is from heaven their rulers and preservers came and to there do they return.'"

Scipio took a moment to wet his lips with wine, then went on. "Of all Africanus' predictions, the suggested perfidy of my own relatives troubled me most. And yet I pushed this aside, and collected myself enough to inquire whether my father, Aemilius Paullus, and others whom we look upon as dead were really still living?

"'Yes,' Africanus replied, 'they all enjoy life, and have escaped from the chains of the body as though it were a prison. What you call life on

Earth is no more than one form of death. See, here comes your father now!'

"And as soon as I saw him I burst into a flood of tears, but he took me in his arms and embraced me and bade me not to weep. 'Men are likewise endowed with a soul,' said Africanus, 'which is a portion of the eternal fires that you call the stars, and which being round, spherical bodies, animated by divine intelligence, perform their cycles and revolutions with the perfection of the music of the spheres. And he, who does live that life which seeks perfection in the sphere of men, to him entirely is this heaven.'

"The dream ended on this uplifting note, and from that moment on, I saw the universe as something beautiful and admirable and that those whose deeds merit this heaven have the highest recognition of all—and in comparison to this, statues of stone or writing on papyrus is nothing. So I would say, even should there never be a statue to memorialize Publius Nasica—and because of the feelings of the common man, there may never be—it matters not, for there is only one judgment that matters, and it's made by the gods that inhabit the heavens."

The other three men sat back, impressed by the story and the seriousness with which Aemilianus had related it, and yet uncertain what to think because they were not already believers in such a place as the infinite heavens. After a short time, Tubero, perhaps because of his youth, asked a question. "And because of a dream, Uncle, you believe in a life after what we call death?"

Aemilianus nodded. "Yes, because after all my years, I have begun to believe that dreams are the imperfect way those who we believe are dead are able to communicate with us."

"And what of Africanus' prediction? How many years are you now?" asked Tubero, still incredulous that this great man whom he so admired could make these statements with such conviction.

"I am seven times eight."

"Then this is the predicted year of your death."

"And will be the ultimate test of my dream, Quintus—if this is, in fact, the year I die."

"But are you not afraid?" asked Laelius.

"Why should I be? If the dream reveals a truth, then death will take me to a greater place to be. And if I'm only deluding myself by such beliefs, then the dream is false and the prophecy of my death is also."

I remember hearing these words and wishing I were so confident in the meaning of my life. Aemilianus was a great but haughty man. And his dream, whether made up or something that really occurred, portrayed my grandfather, Africanus, as making a negative judgment upon Tiberius, which in my heart I knew could not be true. Should Publius Nasica ever be judged at the gates of this wonderful heaven, he would be summarily rejected.

CHAPTER 47

Aemilianus came home in a foul mood one evening a few days after revealing his dream to his friends. The lack of movement on the land reform settlements had caused a lot of tension in the populace, and it was directed at him. He knew he needed to address the problem and was planning to deliver a speech from the rostra the next day. I went up to my bedroom to get off my feet and stay out of his way. He came upstairs a little while later to change his clothes. In passing my room he noticed me lying on the bed. My ankle was propped up on a pillow. My crutch was lying on the floor beside the bed. Aemilianus stood in the doorway, little more than a shadow. I could not see his eyes, but I could see his head turn to stare at my ankle, and then the crutch.

He shook his head, then said it again. "Thank the gods you were made barren." He turned and continued on to his room.

The continuing insults were more than I could take. The words of the old woman selling herbs repeated in my head—*You're planning to kill your husband aren't you?* Suddenly I found myself wondering if the hemlock I had bought was not meant for me. Cornelia had hoped my education would give me sanctuary from the shackles of my marriage. And maybe it would. But not in the way she thought. I had a mind of my own. I was capable of difficult and extended logic. I could poison Aemilianus, who had already been targeted by plebeian threats, and cover my tracks in such a way that no one would ever know. He would be gone. I would own his house, his library, his land, and all his wealth. I would be like Cornelia, wealthy enough to live alone in my own home and pursue my education within the circle of women I enjoyed so much. My ankle would never heal but my heart might.

I did not go down for dinner that night. I told Aemilianus I could not manage the stairs. After he had eaten, Nadia brought me a tray containing sliced apples, a piece of rye bread, a dollop of honey, a wedge of goat cheese, and a cup of mulsum. I could see down to the ground floor of the atrium from my bed. Light projected from the library doorway. Aemilianus had a difficult speech to prepare. I knew him. He would stay up late to finish it. He would nurse a cup of mulsum and at intervals go out to the peristyle and practice his speech beneath the stars.

Nadia and two of the other slaves had seen my ankle. So had Aemilianus. No one expected me to go downstairs that night. I doubt anyone even believed that I could. What could be better?

I stirred some honey and half the parcel of hemlock into my cup of mulsum. I left the rest of the hemlock for myself in case my plan went awry. I rewrapped my ankle as tightly as I could and lay in bed watching the doorway to the library. After a while I saw Aemilianus leave the library and go to the back of the house. He was a man of strict routine. He would be in the garden reciting his speech for at least a quarter hour. I gathered up my strength, and trying not to spill what was in the cup, limped to the stairs using my crutch. I crept down the stairs backwards on my hands and knees then slid down the wall to the library doorway. Only one of the oil lamps was lit. A cup of mulsum sat beside Aemilianus' wax pad. A bronze stylus lay beside that. I crept into the library and emptied my potion into his cup.

I had to hurry, but I also had to be as quiet as possible. I slipped down the wall to the stairway. Just as I knelt on the first stair to climb upward on my hands and knees, I heard Aemilianus coming from the peristyle. The only light came from the library doorway and a quarter moon. I was in the shadows, visible, but only upon close inspection. Aemilianus did not even look at the stairs and strode into the library.

The house was completely silent. There was no way I could get up the stairs and into my room quietly enough not to be heard. I decided to stay as still as I could and wait until he took another break in the garden or drank the mulsum. If he tasted the poison and did not drink it, he would find me helpless on the stairs when he went to bed. Why I was there would be impossible to explain. If he drank all of it, he would die and I could return to my room with no hurry.

I was very close to the library doorway. I could hear everything he did. I heard his chair scoot across the floor when he sat down. I heard him slide the wax pad on the table to begin writing. I heard him pick up his cup and take a drink. I waited to hear if he would spit it out. I held my breath. He replaced the cup on the table. More time passed.

He took another drink, then two more. I'm not sure how long it was before I heard him struggling to breathe. I hoped the sounds would not wake the slaves in their quarters at the back of the house. I heard him fall out of his chair, but he was still sucking and snorting trying to breathe. He choked out a few indistinguishable words. It was horrible. I pushed myself up on my hands and knees, and as quietly as I could, crawled up the stairs to my room. I collapsed on the bed thinking the awful deed was done.

As I lay in bed wide awake, I realized I could still hear him struggling to breath and issuing weak chirps for help. I began to wonder if I had given him enough hemlock. I had no idea what to do. I could not go back down the stairs, finish the job, and climb back up to my room again. I simply did not have the strength. Instead I lay in bed thinking what a failure I was. Not only could I not bring new life into the world, but I was also incapable of assisting existing life out.

It seemed impossible that the slaves could not hear Aemilianus as he continued to fight for his life, but no one came to his aid. Some amount of time passed during which I closed my eyes and tried to sleep. I suddenly became aware of a great silence. I could not see far enough into the library from my bed to see Aemilianus, but I was certain he had finally died.

I tossed and turned the rest of the night, wavering between relief that he was dead and fear of being found out. I thought about taking the remaining dose of hemlock, now hidden beneath my bed. *Only a crazy woman would kill her husband* repeated in my head until I did not know if I were dreaming or awake.

CHAPTER 48

Shortly after the sun came up, someone knocked heavily on the front door. Nadia answered it. I heard Polybius' voice. Apparently Aemilianus had asked him to come over to review his speech. Nadia said she had not seen her master yet that morning and told Polybius to wait in the library while she looked for him. I held my breath knowing what Polybius would find.

Nadia came up the stairs and passed down the hall to look for Aemilianus in his bedroom. She peeked into my room before going back down the stairs. I pretended to be asleep.

I heard her say, "I can't find my master, sir."

"His body is in the library," answered Polybius. "He appears to have died last night."

Nadia gasped.

"Please get Sempronia," said Polybius calmly.

Nadia ran up the stairs to my room. She knelt beside the bed. "Please wake up, my lady."

I blinked my eyes and sat up slowly, as though I had been asleep and had no idea what had happened.

"Aemilianus died during the night," she whispered tensely.

"What?" I mumbled loud enough for Polybius to hear.

"Polybius found his body in the library. Can you go downstairs? He's requested to see you."

"Yes, yes, how could Aemilianus be dead? He was fine last night." I swung my legs off the bed. "Give me a hand. I'm not sure if I can stand."

Nadia retrieved my robe and helped me slip it over my gown. With me leaning heavily on Nadia, the two of us crept down the hall to the stairs. Polybius watched us descend one stair at a time. My ankle was not wrapped and was visible at the hem of my gown.

"Sempronia, what have you done to your ankle?" asked Polybius, giving us a hand at the bottom of the stairs.

"I turned it badly yesterday. But what about Aemilianus?" I am no actress, but I put as much dismay in my voice as possible. "How could he be dead?"

The aged historian sighed as he shook his head. "It must have happened while he was writing his speech. I found him lying on the floor."

Polybius and Nadia helped me into the library. The oil lamp had burnt out. The morning sun illuminated the room with long bright streaks of light. Aemilianus' body was sprawled on the floor beside his chair. I fell to the floor beside him and touched his face in a way that I never had while he was alive. I embraced his corpse and sobbed and wailed until Nadia lifted me off his body and into a chair.

Polybius looked around the room suspiciously. He knew that Aemilianus had fallen from his high standing and had many enemies among the plebeians. While I watched, he knelt down to inspect Aemilianus' corpse.

Polybius was a man of great experience both in war and politics. He had been a Greek cavalry officer when he was young and had seen plenty of dead men. During Rome's war with King Perseus of Macedonia, he was taken as a hostage and held in Rome for seventeen years. During that time he gained a reputation as a brilliant man with an extensive education. Aemilianus' natural father, Aemilius Paullus, befriended Polybius and paid him to tutor his two sons, thus spawning my husband's friendship with Polybius. Polybius had accompanied Aemilianus during parts of all of his campaigns. He was there when Carthage was burned to the ground. He witnessed the successful siege of Numantia. And now he was there to pronounce his friend dead.

Polybius looked closely into Aemilianus' eyes, then closed the eyelids. He put his nose up to Aemilianus' mouth to smell what was exhausted when he pushed down on the corpse's chest. He turned Aemilianus' head from side to side inspecting his neck.

Polybius looked up at me. "Sempronia, would you ask your slave to leave the room?"

Nadia was more upset than I pretended to be. She hurried out of the room to tell the rest of the slaves.

Polybius turned Aemilianus' head. "Look here. There are marks on his neck as though he's been strangled."

I leaned over to get a closer look. And yes, there was bruising in the shape of fingers on both sides of his neck. I no longer needed to pretend surprise.

"He's been murdered, Sempronia. This happened sometime last night." He stood up. "I smelled something bitter on his breath. It could be poison." He lifted the empty cup off the table and sniffed the rim. "Did you hear anything last night?"

"Nothing out of the ordinary. Aemilianus often paces through the house when he's working on a speech."

I could see the gears turning in Polybius' head. Mine were turning as well. Someone had come in after I had poisoned Aemilianus and finished him off while I dozed. I felt myself beginning to sweat.

Polybius took a deep breath and let out a long sigh. Aemilianus had been one of his closest friends. Although he contained his emotions, I could see the sadness in his eyes. "I want to keep this secret, Sempronia," he said softly, just above a whisper. "The way a man dies or the way history says a man dies is critical to the way he is remembered. Being murdered like this is a strong mark against a man's legacy. Aemilianus doesn't deserve this. Have your slaves lay his body out on his bed covered with a sheet. I'm not sure what happened, but any kind of official investigation will lead to ugly gossip about this great man."

I nodded. "What will we say?"

"We found him dead on the floor. He died during the night of natural causes. I know he wasn't ill. I saw him yesterday. But in the long run this will be better for all."

"But someone will get away with murder?"

He looked at me. "I will conduct my own investigation and keep it to myself."

"And if you find the murderer?"

"I'm not sure. It depends who it is. If it's an angry pleb or several of them, maybe I'll say nothing. If it's someone of note—like Papirius Carbo or," his eyes met mine, "your brother, I'll demand that they exile themselves—with no mention of the crime to the public. The man will simply have to leave Rome."

"You think Gaius had something to do with this?"

Polybius frowned. "He and Carbo had a motive. Fulvius, too. There was widespread belief that Aemilianus wanted to break up the commission. I never heard him say that, but the people had begun to distrust him. He was going to address that today in his speech. It's sad. He stood up for the common man his whole life and now this." He looked down on Aemilianus' corpse and shook his head.

"How can you possibly find out who it was?"

"Maybe I can't, but I'd like to talk to your slaves. I won't let on that I'm looking for a murderer. I'll say it's something I need for my histories. I'll be subtle. Do you mind?"

"Not at all. Do what you must. Just let me know if you stumble onto something."

"Of course. But no mention of what I've said or what I plan to do. Aemilianus died of natural causes. That's all we know."

"Yes, certainly. I understand."

After Polybius left I asked Tarus to wrap Aemilianus' body in a sheet. Tarus who had admired Aemilianus showed no grief at all. The hit on the head he had received to protect his master had taken a huge toll on him. He carried the corpse up to Aemilianus' bedroom where Nadia would prepare the body for cremation.

I sat in the library a long time after Tarus took the body away. I tried to imagine someone finding Aemilianus on the floor and then strangling him. I could not imagine my brother doing it. What about Carbo? Or our slaves? Could one of them have done it as an act of mercy?

As I stood up to leave, I saw a piece of thread caught by a splinter on the edge of the table. I did not think much about it, but I did slip it off the splinter. I took it into the atrium and looked at it in the sunlight. It was three very fine strands—red, yellow, and green— wound together, surely something pulled off a piece of clothing. I wound it into a ball and put it in my jewelry box as a curiosity.

CHAPTER 49

By the end of the day all of Rome knew that Aemilianus had died. As Polybius had requested, the cause was reported as natural. This did not stop the rumors. By standing up for the Italians and non-citizen Latins, Aemilianus had made himself a target. There was good reason to assume foul play, especially in the wake of Tiberius' murder and the new wave of thuggery that had invaded Roman politics. Papirius Carbo, Fulvius Flaccus, and my brother were mentioned as suspects.

As the truest measure of Aemilianus' fall from grace, he was not given a public funeral. Even I, the perpetrator, felt this insult against my husband. He had served as a consul twice. He had commandeered the destruction of Carthage. He had righted Roman standing in Numantia. He had spent twenty years in the Senate as the most outspoken proponent of the populares. He had been the leading advocate of Greek literature and art in Rome. His character was considered the highest example of the Roman ideal. He lived for the state and served with strength and courage. But it had all run out on him at the end. Such was the fickle nature of the Roman populace. One day a hero, the next day forgotten.

I knew deep in my heart that what I had done was simply an act of survival. I did not second-guess myself on that. But someone else had strangled him. There had been an accomplice and I wanted to know who that was. But how could I find out without also raising questions about Aemilianus' death? And more importantly, did this other person know about the poison or me?

I was not a natural-born killer. I was not prepared for the emotional aftermath. I suffered with bouts of guilt and vulnerability. On top of that, Polybius, one of the smartest men I had ever met, with uncommon understanding of logic and human frailty, was set on finding the murderer—or murderers. This was unsettling to say the least. I did not think he suspected me. He saw my ankle that morning.

I was incapable of going up and down the stairs alone without a superhuman effort, of which no one felt I was capable. But the inclusion of another murderer was deeply unsettling. Maybe Polybius would discover who that was. Would that person then give me away? I thought about this constantly. I struggled to sleep at night. When I gazed into the eyes of anyone I encountered, I wondered what they might be seeing in mine.

We held a private funeral for Aemilianus. The whole family took part. Cornelia came up from Misenum with Claudia and her children. Polybius was there, as were other circle members, Lucilius and Panaetius. We walked in a procession four miles east on Via Tusculana to the Scipionic tomb, one of the most impressive tombs along a road lined by hundreds of memorial sepulchers and mausoleums. I rode in a two-wheel carriage pulled by a mule. I deposited Aemilianus' ashes in the tomb. Because the public had so shunned Aemilianus at the end, the funeral was an especially sad and somber event, one of almost suffocating guilt for me.

There was a sacrifice and a feast. Then we reformed our procession for the walk back to Rome. Once inside the city walls, Gaius rode with me in the carriage back to my house. He was not aware of the oppression I felt in my marriage, but he knew that Aemilianus had been extremely critical of Tiberius and that some of that had bled onto him when he had spoken in favor of consecutive terms for a tribune.

"There are rumors that I had something to do with Aemilianus' death, Sempronia. Quintus Tubero confronted me in the street the other day. He said Aemilianus had worried that his relatives—meaning me—were plotting against him. I nearly knocked him down." We sat side by side on the carriage seat. Gaius held the reins. "I want to assure you that there's nothing to this gossip."

"Don't worry, Gaius. I don't believe he was murdered." Although I had never spoken openly to Aemilianus about my ankle, and in many ways that had been a lifelong deception, I was not practiced as an outright liar. Now I would forever be saying things that were not true to cover up my guilt. I did believe Gaius, however. He was not the accomplice.

"Could he have taken his own life?" Gaius asked. "He was under tremendous pressure at the end—after a life of unbounded glory."

"It's possible. I try not to think about it. Polybius suggested giving him the grace of a natural passing. You and I have both read Herodotus' *Histories* and know Solon's answer to Croesus when he asked about the judgment of a man's life."

Gaius nodded. "No matter what a man has done in his life or what treasure he has accumulated, it matters little if he doesn't finish his life with honor."

"And to Polybius murder or even suicide would be a stain upon Aemilianus' honor."

"I spoke to Polybius at the funeral today," said Gaius. "He asked several leading questions about Aemilianus. I thought it was strange. I hope he doesn't think I had anything to do with his death. He and I spent many nights talking with Aemilianus in his tent outside Numantia during the siege. He had to have seen how much respect I had for the man." He wagged his head. "Yes, I have been disturbed by Aemilianus' comments about Tiberius—and me—but I still maintained a high opinion of the man."

"Polybius was his best friend. He puts up a stoic front to disguise his deeper feelings. He might have been the person most gravely affected by Aemilianus' death."

"More than you?"

I looked down at my lap. "My marriage was not a pleasant one, Gaius. Our lack of children and my bad ankle didn't help. When Aemilianus was criticized by those he had fought for all his life, he became less tolerant of my shortcomings." I bit my lip. "For me, his death was bittersweet." I lifted my eyes to his.

Gaius nodded slowly. "I didn't know that. There's a sadness there that is almost worse than his dying."

Gaius was a remarkable young man. His empathy brought tears to my eyes. He put his arm around me as we rode the rest of the way to my house in silence.

CHAPTER 50

My mother remained in Rome after the funeral to spend time with Gaius and his family. Little Gaius was one year old, and Licinia was about to have a second child. Cornelia came to my home one morning in her litter, and after much cajoling, convinced me to go with her to one of the private baths. We had not spoken in several months, other than incidentally at the funeral. The baths would be a good place to soak and talk. The warm water would soothe my ankle, the rest of my leg, and my hip. I loved going to the baths, but rarely did for fear of revealing my ankle in public.

The bathhouse close to our home was brand new and exquisite. There were separate baths for men and women. Black and white Cyrenian tile laid out in geometric designs covered the floor and walls. There were three baths—one cold, one warm, and one hot. The pools were also fully tiled and adorned with mosaic images of dolphins, turtles, and seahorses. Cornelia walked beside me to help disguise my disfigurement. All the women bathed in light gowns. Full nudity, so common in the Greek culture, was not the tradition in Rome.

I suggested we go to the hot bath immediately. I slid into the steaming water and felt all the tightness in my right side relax. I imagined myself conjoining with the water. Cornelia and I shared a corner. Three other women lounged in the water on the opposite side of the pool. I closed my eyes and tried to forget about everything, but could not help wondering if Cornelia would ask me about Aemilianus' death. Other than Nadia, only she knew how difficult the marriage had become.

I opened my eyes briefly. Cornelia lay stretched out in the water, eyes closed, her head against the apron, where she had placed a towel. Her gown had become transparent with wetness. I had not seen her in the bath in years. She was nearly sixty years old. Her body had changed. Although not apparent when wearing clothing, her once sleek figure had gained some curves. I considered her the most beautiful woman I had ever seen.

She opened her eyes and looked directly at me. "Do you miss him?"

I lowered my eyes. "No. It's as though he's on a permanent military campaign. All the tension has left the house. I wouldn't say this to anyone else, but I feel terribly relieved." And then I started silently crying. I was terribly wound up from poisoning Aemilianus. Having held it inside for more than two weeks, I just melted into the warm water.

Cornelia did not understand the depth of my angst at first, but she certainly understood how much I needed to talk about whatever it was. She knelt beside me in the shallow water and put her hand on my shoulder. "It's all right, Sempronia. I breathed a sign of relief for you when I heard." She wiped my tears away with her finger. "Are you all right being alone in your home?"

"I think so. Seeing you helps. The library is now mine." I think I actually glimmered a smile. "The best collection in all of Rome—in all of Italy. That's comforting—in a way."

"Maybe we should put more time into our circle. We can meet here in Rome at your house or in Misenum at mine."

"I would love that, Mother. More than that, I need it."

Her eyes softened and she smiled. I put my hand on hers.

"What's Polybius up to, Sempronia? He came over to Gaius' home and sought me out right after I arrived in Rome. He seemed to be paying his condolences for my nephew's death, but he asked a lot of questions, too. He was polite, and I love the man, but I couldn't help thinking he had some kind of agenda—connected to Aemilianus. Am I reading too much into this?"

I did not know what to say. The whole thing welled up in me again, Aemilianus' choking sounds, the unknown accomplice, and the guilt. She saw it in my face when I did not say anything.

"He asked about you. And your relationship with Aemilianus."

A tremor passed through my body. I pulled my legs beneath me and moved away from the edge of the pool. "What did he ask about?"

"Some unpleasant things."

"My being barren?"

"Yes."

"And what did you say?" As soon as I asked, I saw it in her eyes. She had heard the guilt in my voice.

"I said nothing, Sempronia. I said I didn't feel it was his business to ask. That's when I began to wonder what he was up to."

I surveyed the steamy room to see if anyone might hear us. I faced Cornelia and whispered, "He thinks Aemilianus was murdered."

"And he's not saying that."

"Except to me."

Cornelia's look was a question.

"Polybius found him that morning. He came to discuss Aemilianus' upcoming speech. Polybius immediately suspected a murder, but didn't want to make it public. He was afraid some angry pleb had done it, and it would sully Aemilianus' legacy."

"An angry pleb? Really?"

I lifted my eyes. "Or Carbo? Or Gaius? He saw some bruises on Aemilianus' neck. Someone strangled him—and possibly poisoned him also."

Cornelia was flabbergasted. Something that almost never happened to her. "He thinks Gaius could have poisoned him? There is so much hatred in the air. Oh my. And that's why he's been asking questions?"

I nodded. "He wants to find the murderer."

"What do you know about it? You were there that night."

I looked down at the water. I had to tell her, but I could not say it. Cornelia suddenly embraced me. "Oh, Sempronia, oh my baby."

"I put the poison in his cup," I whispered. "But someone else strangled him."

"Who?"

"I'm afraid to guess. But whoever it was might also know about me."

Cornelia was stunned. "What can you do now?"

"I don't know. Try to figure out who the other person was—and talk to them."

"What if Polybius finds them first?"

"I will be found out."

CHAPTER 51

Three weeks after the funeral, Licinia gave birth to her second child, another boy, this one named Publius after my grandfather. Cornelia had remained in Rome for the birth and to help Licinia with the children. Gaius was in south Italy with the land commission. We held a circle at my home one afternoon. Along with Cornelia and myself, we invited three other women from our family—Claudia, Licinia, and Licinia's mother, the other Claudia. When Licinia's mother said she could not make it, Licinia invited another woman, Laelia, the daughter of Aemilianus' friend Gaius Laelius. She had married Mucius Scaevola's son Quintus and given him three sons. Only Licinia had met her before. She was a lovely woman, twenty-five, with wavy, jet black hair and an ivory complexion. Her eyes were dark and blazing. She had been educated in Greek literature and art and was thrilled to talk with other educated women, especially Cornelia, whom she had heard about since childhood.

Laelia's clear hunger for knowledge added enthusiasm to our group—though things got off to a rocky start that first meeting. Licinia had invited Laelia without asking Cornelia. Her father Gaius had been severely critical of Tiberius, and her father-in-law, who had been consul at the time of Tiberius' murder, had not stepped in to halt the violence when he had the chance. Cornelia, Claudia, and myself were extremely disappointed by his lack of action. Cornelia still held a grudge against him. We all became uncomfortable when Licinia introduced Laelia to the group.

Four years had passed since Tiberius' death. Now a murderer myself, I did not dare judge another person. But I certainly understood what Claudia and Cornelia were feeling, though neither Licinia nor Laelia, it seemed, were aware of the abiding rancor.

Laelia was an uncommonly forthright woman and broke right through the tension. "I've been counseling legal cases in the forum," she said as an opening. "Not advocating for a client—yet—but advising. I've been tutored well at home." We all knew her father-in-law was one of the top legal minds in Rome.

All of Cornelia's resistance to Laelia melted away when she heard the confidence in the young woman's voice. "You want to be an advocate?" Only during extreme circumstances had women even spoken in the forum, much less as advocates in a court of law.

"Yes, and I know that having the opportunity—the honor—of spending time with all of you will be of tremendous value." She looked at each of us to emphasize what she was saying. "I'm particularly interested in history. It provides precedent for just about everything in law. But I'm also happy to listen to whatever you want to talk about."

Cornelia loved nothing more than a young woman with an inquisitive mind, and so did I. "Laelia, are you familiar with the demonstrations against Lex Oppia sixty-five years ago?"

"Oh, yes, Cornelia. It could be called the most successful organization of women in our history. Your mother, Aemilia, was one of the leaders."

"She was, primarily because she had the support of my father. He was really the originator of these intellectual discussions. It was initially all men, but he had the foresight to include my mother. She became a strong advocate for the education of women and formed a circle of her own. Her circle was responsible for bringing the cult of the Great Mother to Rome during the war with Hannibal. She was a modern woman before there were modern women."

"But there were other incidents of women's protests before Lex Oppia," I said.

"That's right, but this one was the most tightly organized," said Cornelia. "The most well-conceived."

"And it worked," added Laelia.

"Can you tell us more about this protest?" asked Licinia, glancing at Claudia, who also appeared to know little about it.

"Let's have Laelia do that," said Cornelia.

Laelia had a classically round face. When she smiled she beamed—and she did now. "If I have it correctly, Lex Oppia was put in place by a tribune of the plebs by the name of Gaius Oppius. It was during the war with Hannibal, following the disastrous Roman defeat at Cannae. The treasury was running dry, and there was a movement to eliminate excess in Roman society, starting with wealthy women. The law forbade a woman to own more than an ounce of gold, wear the color purple, or ride in a carriage anywhere within a mile of Rome. It made sense at the time. Rome needed money for the war. Everyone had to sacrifice. But five years after the war was over, Lex Oppia was still in place. Two of the tribunes at that time—I think they were prompted by your father, Cornelia—proposed a bill to repeal the law, but two other tribunes threatened to veto the proposal if it were brought up at the Assembly. The women of Rome, mustered by Cornelia's mother, decided to protest the veto."

"And what happened?" asked Claudia.

I spoke up. "The day before the vote the Assembly held a debate. One of the tribunes, Lucius Valerius, I believe, spoke in favor of repeal, emphasizing that the war was over and that the law was unnecessary because a husband already had the authority to control his wife's actions in any way he wanted. The outspoken conservative Porcius Cato spoke vehemently against it, claiming it would only lead to more decadence and an excess of Greek influence in our society— something he hated. The day of the vote women came out early and in number to block all access to the assembly grounds. When their disruption caused the meeting to be put off, they came in greater numbers the next day. Although no woman spoke, the two tribunes rescinded their threat to veto and the law was repealed."

Cornelia looked at each of us. "Was this a victory for women?"

"Yes," answered Laelia, "but not a great one. The repeal of the law only meant that things went back to the way they were—full control of a woman by her husband through the marriage institution of manus. But the huge number of women acting together demonstrated the power of such a protest. It's the sort of thing that gives me hope for serving as an advocate and speaking in the forum one day."

"Would you consider advancing changes to the laws of marriage?" Cornelia asked.

When Laelia hesitated, Cornelia looked to Licinia and Claudia. With Gaius and Tiberius as husbands, they had not witnessed the dark side of marriage that I had, but my convictions were so bound up in guilt I kept my thoughts to myself.

"It's an important question," said Cornelia, "but a bigger part of it is having the words and ideas of women included in the political discourse. Many women have difficult marriages, but they have been taught to stay at home and say nothing. We might be the only women in Rome who would even think to bring marriage up as a political issue. If these circles do nothing else, I hope that each of you acts as an ambassador for women's education as I have. Things may not change for women for several generations, but my mother always felt that learning how to speak intelligently and in public was the path to greater rights for women."

After that first meeting I told Laelia that she was welcome at all of our circles and that she could use the library any time she wanted. She interested me for a couple of reasons. Like Cornelia, I wanted to see the rights of women defended, and who could do that better than a woman trained in law? But I was also worried that Polybius might eventually confront me about Aemilianus' death. While suicide was the obvious option, knowing a woman who knew the law seemed like a good backup plan.

CHAPTER 52

No one had more to do with shaping Cornelia's character and intellect than her mother Aemilia Tertia. The third daughter of Lucius Aemilius Paullus, Aemilia came from one of Rome's greatest families. She openly basked in her patrician heritage and dressed as eloquently as any woman in Rome, especially after my grandfather's success in Africa and the increased wealth that came with it. She indulged in the purchase of works of art and made a show of her trips across the city, traveling in an elaborate carriage with a train of slaves. Though Cornelia was not ostentatious like Aemilia, she was proud of her bloodline and always presented herself at home and in public in the manner of an aristocrat.

While Africanus was the preeminent ambassador of Greek learning of his time, Aemilia was nearly an equal part of it, advocating for the education of women and leading her own lesser-known intellectual circle. After Africanus' death, she had provided the best tutors for Cornelia and was responsible for Cornelia's love of literature and art.

Aemilia was gentle and mild-mannered, but also fiercely loyal to her husband. When she was pregnant with Cornelia, Africanus was unfaithful to her with one of their housemaids, something that ran counter to all that he had boasted of earlier in his life. Aemilia chose not to make the matter public, either to protect her husband's image or to save herself the embarrassment.

Cornelia spoke about this to me and my brothers many years later. She emphasized the importance of fidelity for both partners in a marriage, though Roman custom typically condemned the wife for such indiscretions and overlooked the husband's. Cornelia made sure all of us understood the hypocrisy of this kind of social inequity.

Aemilia died when I was a child, but I did know her, and though my memory of her is limited, I do remember thinking she was a grand woman, but a little intimidating. I was always on my best behavior when my grandmother came to our house.

More importantly, though, Aemilia maintained the progressive politics of her husband, even after his death. While he was alive, she organized and led the resistance to Lex Oppia. Cornelia spoke of this proudly, and yet there might have been a bit of hypocrisy there as well. Yes, Aemilia organized the women of Rome in a way that had never happened before, but I have wondered if it was because of the law's oppression of women's rights or my grandmother's love of extravagance. One way or the other, she wanted to ride in a carriage and wear her jewelry and purple clothing.

Regardless of her motivation, Aemilia was a fine woman. Some might argue that she was the most notable woman in Roman history to that point. I give her credit, but would argue in favor of her daughter's superiority, in part because of the sons she raised and their impact on the course of Roman politics.

CHAPTER 53

A week after Cornelia returned to Misenum with Claudia and her children, I was called on to be a witness in a trial at the forum. Fortunately it had nothing to do with Aemilianus or his death.

Appuleius Saturninus, a man associated with the populares, put forth a candidate for one of the tribune positions, a Lucius Equitius, who claimed to be the illegitimate son of my brother Tiberius. Saturninus felt that the Gracchi connection would help Equitius get elected. The censor at that time, Metellus Numidicus, intervened saying there was no evidence that Equitius was even a citizen, much less the offspring of Tiberius Gracchus.

I knew nothing of this until Saturninus charged Metellus with dereliction of duty, claiming that he had not done enough research to prove or disprove Equitius' identity. "The censor," he said, "is simply acting on his hatred of me and the issues I stand for." This led to a trial, and the day before, Metellus sent a subordinate to my house requesting that I appear as a witness to verify if Equitius was my brother's son or not.

One of Metellus' slaves came to my home the next morning with a litter and four bearers. I was taken to Metellus who stood at the edge of the forum, a short distance from the Basilica Porcia where the trial would take place. Metellus, a man I had never met, described the situation in greater detail than his messenger had the day before, adding that he was certain the man was an imposter. "I have told no one, Sempronia," he confided, "that you will be a witness. Everyone knows that your brother and mother are not in Rome. No one will expect you to be here. That you are a woman will also cause some controversy. I hope you are up to it."

"I am a capable speaker," I said, though I had no public experience, "and I will do everything I can to defend my brother's name."

"Perfect. Stay here with my slaves. I will motion to you when the time comes for you to testify."

The trial began with Saturninus making his accusation against Metellus. From where I stood, I could see the proceedings but hear little of what was said. A senator, whom I did not recognize, acted as the judge. He sat at a table with a number of documents laid out before him. A jury of fifty-one men sat to his right. Because there was quite a lot at stake in the trial, a good number of onlookers, perhaps two hundred, some senators, fanned out around the periphery of the covered court.

I watched Saturninus bring forward a man I assumed was Lucius Equitius. The judge asked him a few questions. All I could see was that the senator seemed to be nodding and agreeing with what was said. Equitius remained before the judge while Metellus made his argument. It was not long before he turned and motioned to me.

It was late fall and brisk. A layer of low gray clouds covered the sky. I had tried to dress as simply as possible. I wore a pale blue stola over a tunic, with a pale blue sash tied at my waist. I also had a hooded wool cape, dyed black, on my shoulders. My hair was braided and coiled on each side of my head and covered with a transparent blue palla.

I had decided not to use my crutch and instead relied entirely on my new supportive shoe, a second made by the same cobbler. It was more like a boot than a sandal and worked better than the first, but I could only wear it for short periods of time because of its stiffness. It was already beginning to bother me when I crossed the forum into the realm of men. I forced myself not to limp or show any sign of weakness.

Everyone turned as I approached. Muttered comments spread through the audience as I advanced to the front of the court. The judge frowned at me, then looked at Metellus. "You have a woman for a witness? I've never seen this before, nor am I happy to now."

Saturninus said something considerably more offensive under his breath. Many of the men present laughed. I remained stiff and upright, gritting my teeth to bear the pain in my ankle.

Metellus did not back off. "This woman is Sempronia Gracchus, Tiberius' sister. I believe she is the most qualified person in Rome to make a judgment on this man Equitius."

"I object," snapped Saturninus. "The words of a woman can't hold up in court. I demand you dismiss this witness immediately." Several other men in the audience called out in approval.

The judge seemed to consider the objection, then shook his head. "The woman is a family member. If anyone would know, she would. I'd like to hear what she has to say."

Metellus, an older, heavyset man, turned to me. "You've had a look at this man, Sempronia. Could this man be your nephew?"

Grim, angry men surrounded me. I was out of place and frightened. I gathered myself and tried to imagine that I was Tiberius speaking at the forum. "My brother did not live loosely. As everyone knows he was a man of honor and pride. He had no illegitimate children and this man is an imposter."

Saturninus came up close to me, playing to the crowd. "How could a sister know what her brother did when she was not around? Didn't Tiberius serve twelve campaigns in the military? What soldier comes back from a conquest without a taste of the spoils?" Several voices in the audience expressed the clear sense of this statement. "No matter what Tiberius' life was like here in Rome, a man is a man when at war, and it serves no strike against his honor." A chorus of *that's right* and *how could it be otherwise?* sounded from the onlookers.

One man shouted, "Kiss your nephew for us! That will prove his blood."

I stared the man down. "You may kiss him if you like, sir, but he is no kin of mine. Look at his short forehead and the closeness of his eyes. If my family is known for anything, it's a countenance expressing intelligence."

A few men laughed at my critique of Equitius, but *kiss your nephew* was repeated by many others. The judge called for quiet. "Does the witness have anything else to say?"

"Yes. I'd like to know how old this man is. Shouldn't he be at least twenty-five to run for the tribunate?"

"Yes, that's correct," said the judge. "How old are you, Equitius? Tell the court."

"Twenty-five. Just this year."

"If this man is twenty-five, my brother, who would be thirty-five were he alive, would have been ten years old at the time of this imposter's birth. I lived with Tiberius when he was ten. I was his older sister. He bathed in my presence as a child. I can attest that he had not achieved the hair of a man at age ten nor did he show the slightest interest in women."

As soon as I said what should have been so obvious, the entire crowd groaned. My argument was more than sound. Saturninus took a deep breath and looked at Equitius, a look that exposed how foolish he felt. Metellus hid his grin. The judge stood. "I dismiss the charge against Metellus Numidicus. This man is not the offspring of Tiberius Gracchus. He is not a citizen, and he cannot run for the position of tribune."

After Saturninus and Equitius and their friends slumped away in a group, the judge addressed me. "Thank you, Sempronia. I should have known the granddaughter of Africanus would make a just witness. My apologies for the comments of the others."

I thanked the judge for his kind words, then confessed to Metellus that my ankle was bothering me. He was more than happy to help me back to the litter, repeating his thanks over and over again. "How odd no one had the forethought to find out your brother's exact age. You made a difficult case easy."

CHAPTER 54

Polybius was at my house when I returned from the forum. He was pacing in the atrium waiting for me. He had caught me at a bad time. The trial had angered me, but also emboldened me. And my ankle was screaming with pain. Polybius immediately saw how badly I was limping, and though an old man, an old man in good health, he came to the door to help me before Nadia had the chance. He assisted me into the atrium and onto a bench, then sat beside me.

I asked Nadia to bring me a bucket of warm water.

"You don't look well, Sempronia." He said it with genuine feeling.

"It's this ankle, Polybius. I just can't be on it for long periods of time."

He nodded, fully understanding. "I've been here a while. I spoke with the slaves. I'm still trying to put together what happened that night Aemilianus was murdered."

"Were the slaves of any help?"

"Not really. It was difficult to ask the questions without giving away my purpose. Both Veda and Tarus were asleep and heard nothing. Nadia said she heard what she assumed was Aemilianus moving around in the house after dark, but nothing more. If someone else was here, no one saw them. And yet, there were marks on Aemilianus' neck. He was definitely strangled." He looked directly at me. "And he was poisoned."

"You're sure of that?"

"I could smell the hemlock on his breath and in his cup. I went out into the city looking for it, but had no luck. It's my only lead. Have you any idea where someone might get hemlock?"

"No, not at all. I don't get out that much. Today was a rarity."

"You were a witness at a trial?" He was well aware of the nature of the trial.

I nodded. "I did a lot of standing around. It's why my ankle aches so badly now."

"How did it go?"

"It was belittling," I said. "But I convinced them the man was not Tiberius' son."

"Even during the pillaging of Carthage, Tiberius didn't go after the women. It's not who he was." Polybius glanced round the atrium finally fixing on the stairs. "Did you come down from your bedroom the night Aemilianus was murdered?"

"No."

"When did you last see him alive?"

"The day before you found him—in the afternoon when he returned from the Senate. I went upstairs shortly afterwards. I didn't even eat with him that night." Now Polybius was quizzing me! I wanted to make a point. I lifted the hem of my stola and began to uncinch my boot. "I can't go anywhere near those stairs alone." I opened the boot and peeled back the leather to release the pressure on my ankle. I usually had Nadia help me, but by doing it myself I was able to add a touch of drama when I slipped my foot from the shoe.

It had never looked worse. Polybius sat back at the sight of it. Nadia arrived with the bucket. I dipped my foot into the warm water and immediately felt relief. I waved Nadia from the room and tried to get comfortable on the bench.

Polybius gave me a moment to get situated. "Sempronia, is there anyone that you suspect—even the slightest?"

"I know my brother has been mentioned, but I've spoken to him. I would stake my life that it wasn't him. I can only imagine it was an angry pleb or a few of them. You know how the populace had turned on Aemilianus. At the end he hated them as much as they hated him. If you recall, he was attacked in the street not that long before he was murdered."

"Yes, that was when Tarus was struck on the head." Polybius got up and walked over to the library. He stared into the room as though thinking what might have happened that night.

"And you've ruled out suicide?" I asked. "He was under a lot of pressure."

"It wouldn't have been like him. And with the marks on his throat, it seems impossible. Just to make sure I took the liberty of searching the kitchen and his bedroom while you were out."

My heart rose into my throat. "You didn't find anything did you? None of the slaves could have done it. I'm confident of their loyalty."

"I think you're right about that. It was always my opinion that the house slaves liked Aemilianus despite his stiff manner."

He had evaded my question about finding anything. "So what are you thinking?"

Polybius came back to the bench and stood beside me. "It's confusing. I'm sure he was poisoned. And those marks on his neck were real. I've been wondering if the person who poisoned him didn't give him enough, then strangled him when he was weakened. Otherwise I just don't see how anyone could have killed him without a fight or without the aid of several other people. He was too strong. And yet from everything I've heard from you and the slaves, there was no commotion." He peered down at me. "I'm thinking it was someone he knew—maybe very well."

"Are you still thinking Carbo or Fulvius?"

"They had motive, but I've yet to find any other connection."

"Maybe someone came by to help him with the speech that night. And no one noticed."

Polybius nodded slowly. "That's possible. But who would that be? It could only be a friend. Like me. That's why I came by in the morning." He stared at the stairs again. "Locating a source of hemlock is probably my best chance of finding out something more. Are you sure? You've no idea where I might find some?"

Why did he ask this again? Had he found the hemlock beneath my bed? "No, it's not something I would ever need."

"Who would? But a murderer." He smiled, then touched me on the shoulder. "I should get going. I can see you want a chance to lie down."

"I do." I stared down at my foot in the bucket.

"I'll be back. I'm sure you're as interested in finding the killer as I am."

I could barely look him in the eye. I muttered, "Yes, of course." Then glanced to the back of the house. "Nadia? Please come out here. I need your help."

"Another day," he said politely and walked out of the atrium.

By the time he was gone, Nadia was there with a towel. She dried my foot then helped me climb to the second floor and get into bed. I was tempted to ask her about Polybius' questions, but feared it would only raise suspicions about something I wanted to keep quiet just as much as Polybius did.

After Nadia had gone downstairs, I slipped out of the bed and looked underneath to see if the hemlock were still there. It was—but had it been moved? I was not sure. Something seemed different—or was it my memory? Or my guilt? *Did Polybius know?* Had he been trying to get me to confess so he would not have to accuse me to my face? That was all I could figure. How many sources of hemlock existed in Rome? There had to be more than one. Many more. But if he found that same woman, she would remember the woman with the limp and a crutch. *Maybe I should just confess—or take the rest of the hemlock?*

CHAPTER 55

I expected Polybius to return any day with news that he had found the source of the poison. If he did, I would confess. I could not play this game any longer. He was too wise, too insightful. I had made mistakes and he would discover them.

I woke up one morning before sunrise with Aemilianus sitting at the end of my bed. Somehow I did not scream. He spoke to me as Africanus had to him. "Why did you poison me?" he asked, little more than a shadow in the dimly lit room.

I was too frightened to answer.

He lifted this head and rubbed the side of his neck. "I know you didn't do this." He almost smiled.

Fighting my fear, I asked, "Who did?"

"Your brother."

"No, Aemilianus, he didn't. I'm sure of that."

He grinned now in a way he never had. "He may as well have."

"What's that mean?"

"Follow the thread," whispered the fading vapor.

I lay beneath the sheets until dawn thinking about the strange visitation, then climbed out of bed and went to my jewelry box. Even in the poor light, I could see the piece of thread and took it out of the box.

After I had dressed and worked my way down the stairs, I crossed the atrium to the sewing room. The room contained two frames for weaving and three spinning wheels. The slaves used them to make our clothing. I enjoyed spinning and weaving and often used them myself.

A wooden box in the corner of the room contained spools of thread, big ones, little ones, all colors. I dug into the box, looking at every spool. I found a small spool with not many turns of thread around it. I took it out into the sunlight and saw that it was the same as the thread I had found in the library.

I called for Nadia and asked her if she had ever used it.

"Yes, my lady, on the clothing for the slave's children."

"Oh yes, of course." Slaves often had children. They lived in the slaves' quarters with their mothers, and because they became the property of the master, were generally welcomed. One of the children was Nadia's. Seven years earlier Nadia and Philocrates had become close and had a son, Aesop. As marriage among slaves, especially of different owners, was frowned upon, their relationship did not sustain, but they did remain friends and Aesop lived with Nadia. Philocrates would visit him when Gaius came to my house.

"I embroider with it, my lady. Would you like me to do the same for you?"

"No, thank you. I just saw it and thought it was pretty. How long have we had it?"

"Years. I spun it myself. Maybe I should make some more."

"If you like."

"Anything else, my lady?"

"No, I was just curious."

When I returned to the atrium, I thought about it. It seemed unlikely that the thread was a clue to the murder. It could have been caught on the splinter days, weeks, or even months before Aemilianus' death. The only thing that made me think otherwise were the words spoken by whatever it was I had seen or dreamed that morning.

CHAPTER 56

Two weeks passed without any word from Polybius. I got a letter from my mother. Physcon had returned. There was a civil war going on in Egypt. Over the last year he had lost control of Alexandria where his sister Cleopatra had secluded herself for safety. The stress of besieging the fabled city had worn him down. He came to Misenum seeking sanctuary. Cornelia's letter ended with a request that I come to Misenum to help her with the Egyptian pharaoh. She would organize a circle, include him, and afterward politely send him back to Egypt. There was nothing I wanted more than to get out of Rome. After Aemilianus' death I had a four-wheel carriage built for myself. I knew I would travel to Misenum several times a year. Why not have a nice carriage? The trip to Misenum would be its first time out of the city.

When I arrived I could see that my mother was already fed up with Physcon. He had asked her to marry him again. She threatened to move out of the villa. "I'm not here to be besieged by him," was how she said it to me.

To distract Physcon, Cornelia had invited Lucilius, Lucius Accius, the son of a freedman who had made a name for himself translating Greek poetry into Latin, and the stoic philosopher Panaetius. Aemilianus' death had affected Panaetius so badly that he had decided to leave Rome and move to Athens. This would be his last circle in Italy. Cornelia decided to make it a celebration of his work.

There were two surprises while I was there. The first surprise came the day I arrived. Cornelia gave me a present for my fortieth birthday. It was a hand carved chair with two large wooden wheels on either side. I could propel it by turning the wheels with my hands. It allowed me to move around the villa without having to use my ankle or walk at all. It felt a little funny to have my own little cart, but it kept me off my feet and helped with the swelling and even allowed my ankle to strengthen somewhat.

The second surprise came the morning of the second day of the circle. Polybius arrived. Lucilius had invited him. He had declined at first then changed his mind.

As unsettled as I was by his arrival, I still needed to socialize with him as though it were nothing. With the excitable Lucilius and the celebrating Panaetius dominating the talk in both circles that day—one in the morning over a buffet lunch and one late in the afternoon—it was easy to be quiet. I had very little interaction with Polybius without appearing to avoid him.

Physcon's chef prepared the evening meal—flamingo tongues sprinkled with paprika, peacock eggs poached in beer, sturgeon steaks, and wine from Sicily. Afterward the men gathered around the edge of the pool in the atrium and drank more wine. Claudia took her children to bed, and I slipped off to the edge of the garden with Cornelia. The sun was down. A yellow, nearly full moon sat above Vesuvius in the east. It was a pleasant evening with just a whisper of breeze. Cornelia stood gazing out at the heaving surf. I sat in my wonderful wheeled chair watching her.

"Physcon just got word from Egypt," she said turning to face me. "His sister has hired the Seleucid king Demetrius II to break the siege. He's leaving tomorrow."

"You must be relieved."

She smiled at the obvious. "I love the man, but I don't want a husband or any of the things that go with living with Physcon."

My stomach sank with the mere mention of the word *husband*. I was about to ask her if she had spoken to Polybius when he came out to the garden from the rear of the villa. "Lovely view you've got here, Cornelia."

My mother smiled. "Good evening, Polybius. Did you enjoy the conversation today?"

"Very much. I hope you didn't mind my arriving late."

"Of course not."

"Part of my reason for coming was to get some time alone with you and Sempronia. Do you have a few moments?" He looked at me with all the graciousness that was the man, but he appeared sad.

"What's on your mind?" said Cornelia, perhaps feeling what was coming.

"I wanted to tell you about my investigation into Aemilianus' death. Sempronia is already aware of it, but I've said nothing to you."

Cornelia lifted her head.

"I believe Aemilianus was murdered—actually poisoned and strangled."

Cornelia pretended to be surprised. "Why didn't you say something earlier?"

"I didn't want your nephew's legacy sullied by an ugly ending. Can you forgive me for that?"

"Of course, Polybius. It was for the better I'm sure. But why do you believe he was murdered and why are you telling me now?"

"I was the first to find his body. I think you already knew that. There were bruises on his neck. Marks left by the pressure of hands. I also smelled hemlock on his breath and in his empty cup." He looked at the ground, then at me. "I recently found a source of hemlock in Rome."

I looked to my mother. We both knew what was coming.

"It was an old woman. I found her in some little beggars' community at the top of the Aventine Hill. She said she had sold some six weeks earlier to a woman with a bad limp."

Tears were running down my cheeks. I gripped the wheels of my chair to keep my hands from shaking. I stuttered out a few sounds but Cornelia cut me off.

"I've known all along, Polybius, that you've been looking into Aemilianus' murder. After the funeral, when you spent an afternoon talking with me, seemingly about Aemilianus and his life, you were probing me. It seems that you are about to tell Sempronia and me the result of your work."

Polybius tried to respond, but Cornelia continued. "For fear that you might have made a mistake, I would like to save you the trouble of pointing a finger. It was I who chose to kill Aemilianus. I know he was your friend. I know he was a great man. But he denigrated my son politically and my daughter physically. I hired a man to poison him. The dose was too small and he had to strangle Aemilianus to end his life. I was sorry it came to that. I sent the man to Egypt and paid him to never speak of it."

Polybius looked at me then back to Cornelia. The obvious question was *who was the woman with the limp who bought the hemlock?* For all I knew Polybius had searched my house while I was in Misenum and found the pouch beneath my bed. But Polybius did not ask the question. Instead he bowed to Cornelia and then to me and walked away.

At the time I was not certain if Polybius was sufficiently satisfied with what he had heard to stop his investigation. It was more likely he knew Cornelia was shielding me and had too much respect for her to say anything more about it, leaving one important question still up in the air—who strangled Aemilianus? Even if Polybius believed Cornelia's story and felt he no longer needed to find that out, I did.

When I returned to Rome a week later, I went to my room and looked under the bed. The parcel of hemlock was gone. My first thought was Polybius, then I noticed a piece of one-folded papyrus beneath the mattress. I opened it up. It was a note in sloppily written Greek: *Your secret is safe. However, when the time is right, a small favor will be requested.* Polybius' handwriting was immaculate. This was not from him. And none of my slaves could speak much less write Greek. I shuddered. My accomplice wanted something for his silence—probably money. Despite the confrontation in Misenum, Aemilianus' death still trailed me like a shadow.

PART III

GAIUS

"Even after these events, problems in the court postponed the division of land for a very long time. Fulvius Flaccus proposed that all the Italian allies, who made the greatest resistance to redistribution, should be admitted to Roman citizenship so that, out of gratitude for the greater favor, they might no longer quarrel about the land. The Italians were ready to accept this, because they preferred Roman citizenship to possession of additional property, but the populace of Rome resisted."

-Appian of Alexandria, *Foreign Wars of Rome*

CHAPTER 57

Nothing happened. Days, weeks, months, then a year went by with no word from whoever had written the note. For all I knew the perpetrator had left Rome or died. I never told anyone else about the note, and though the mystery ran through my thoughts every day, I hoped that the whole horrible episode had slipped into the past.

Another year went by. Lucius Aurelius Orestes and Marcus Aemilius Lepidus were elected co-consuls. Gaius, at twenty-six, was chosen to be Orestes' quaestor. Not counting his placement on Tiberius' land reform commission, quaestor was Gaius' first elected position. Although the duties were primarily military, it marked a hesitant initial step into politics. That spring Gaius sailed with Orestes and two Roman legions to the island province of Sardinia to put down a revolt of the highland tribes. As quaestor, Gaius served as the consul's top aide and managed all the documents associated with the campaign.

What Orestes had hoped would be a quick campaign did not turn out that way. The army was forced to stay the entire year in Sardinia through an exceptionally severe and difficult winter, something they had not prepared for, leading to a shortage of warm blankets and winter capes for the soldiers. Orestes sent envoys to the local villages requesting help. Already inconvenienced by the presence of the Roman army, the Sardinians said they had no extra blankets or cloaks to spare. When Orestes continued to pressure them for assistance, a Sardinian envoy went to the Roman Senate asking that his people be excused from the burden. In response, the Senate castigated Orestes for not being prepared. Despite this rebuke, Gaius took it upon himself to go back to the small towns and villages to personally ask for help.

Through his own intense training Gaius had become a skilled orator. Rather than demanding winter clothing, he appealed to the Sardinians' compassion by describing the conditions in the Roman camp and how little it would take to improve them. When given a choice instead of an order, the Sardinians responded with enough gifts to cover the army's needs.

The following spring, with the campaign still incomplete, Orestes was prorogued for a second year in Sardinia. Gaius remained as his quaestor. The second summer went no better than the first, and the army was forced to stay yet another winter in Sardinia. This was one of the greatest drawbacks to military service. It could extend over several consecutive years in distant lands. Gaius did not see Licinia or his two young sons the entire time. Never anticipating that they would stay on the island that long, the army ran short of provisions, particularly wheat.

Gaius again felt this was a problem he could solve. He went to the Numidian king Micipsa requesting assistance. Micipsa, who had been a friend of our father's, responded by sending several shipments of wheat to Sardinia at no cost. For a second time, Gaius saved Orestes' army from a humiliating disaster through intelligent diplomacy and his gift for articulate expression.

Unfortunately, much like his brother's treaty with the Numantians ten years earlier, Gaius' actions were called inappropriate. He was covering for Orestes' lack of preparation by appealing for gifts from others. An angry Senate recalled Orestes' two legions and sent two more to replace them. Orestes, however, as punishment, was ordered to stay a third year in Sardinia. This meant his quaestor would do the same. No small part of this was the Senate's lingering hatred of Tiberius, and the fear that Gaius would follow in his brother's footsteps. They simply did not want another Gracchi in Rome because of the political issues then at play.

Gaius' friend and fellow member of the land commission Marcus Fulvius Flaccus was halfway through his term as co-consul with Marcus Plautius Hypsaeus. In an effort to break the legal logjam surrounding land reform, Fulvius offered citizenship to all Italians and non-Roman Latins in exchange for giving up their objections to land reform, something they were completely willing to do. But the measure had to pass through the People's Assembly, and the plebeians, much as they had when Aemilianus represented the non-citizen allies, felt threatened by the potential of so many new Roman citizens. The Senate also wanted no part of Fulvius' citizenship plan for fear that a greater number of citizens would dilute their senatorial powers. The optimates were worried that Fulvius, aided by Gaius, could actually convince the People's Assembly to pass the measure.

While in Sardinia, Gaius had received communication from both Papirius Carbo and Fulvius. He knew exactly what was happening and why he had been ordered to stay in Sardinia. The Senate was trying to shut him out of the work that his brother had begun. Rather than stay in Sardinia, he immediately left for Rome to protect his name and rejoin the land commission.

CHAPTER 58

Gaius returned to Rome in early fall just as Fulvius Flaccus' plan for universal citizenship began to fall apart. The Senate had advised against it, and in the week prior to Gaius' unannounced arrival, the People's Assembly voted it down. Any concern that Gaius could turn the tide was put aside. The issue, however, was still of interest to Gaius, and on his third night in Rome, he invited Fulvius and Carbo to his home for dinner. I was not there that night, but Licinia sat quietly through the meal and filled me in on what was said.

Gaius, who still had little or no desire to enter into politics, was intrigued by the idea of citizenship for all of Italy. Carbo and Fulvius spent the evening recounting recent events, in what amounted to a convening of the land reform commission, from which Gaius had been absent for over two years.

"So Fulvius," said Gaius, "you hoped to relieve pressure on the commission by giving our allies citizenship in exchange for recognizing our authority to redistribute land. Is that correct?"

"That's only part of it," answered Fulvius. "We believe that universal citizenship will eventually have to happen and that it would only strengthen Rome in the long run. It will increase the loyalty of our allies and relieve the ongoing shortage of citizen soldiers."

"It's failed for the time being," added Carbo, "but we would like to readdress it at some time in the future. The key is convincing the People's Assembly." Carbo looked at Fulvius.

Fulvius was a powerfully built man with thick, curly brown hair and a full, untrimmed beard. He had been elected to the consulship because of his strong record in the military. He tended to use force as opposed to subtlety to get things done. It worked on the battlefield, but not as well in politics, and was probably the reason his citizenship bill had failed. Fulvius turned to Gaius. "We're hoping to convince you to run for a position on the tribunate this winter. Your way with words is far superior to mine."

"Or mine," chimed in Carbo.

Gaius shook his head. "That's not something I want to do. My position on the commission is more than enough politics for me."

"It's not politics at all," said Carbo, "if the work is tied up in a court that no consul has the nerve to administer."

"And never will," said Fulvius. "I had a chance, but when I reviewed the cases, they made my head swim. There are too many suits and no easy solutions. Aemilianus might have thought he was solving the problem, but instead he effectively stopped all efforts to redistribute property. Land reform is not happening at all right now."

"And with the vote last week, the Italian and Latin cities are angry. They want citizenship more than they want land. We started something that will have to come to a resolution one way or the other."

Gaius looked at the two men. "What do you mean?"

"Fregellae is contemplating dropping out of the Latin Federation," said Fulvius.

"They were one of our most loyal allies against Hannibal. How can that be?"

"The denial of citizenship was a slap in the face."

"Yes, I imagine it was," said Gaius.

"And you're exactly what we need," exclaimed Fulvius.

Gaius stared down at his empty plate, then looked to Licinia. "No more politics. I simply don't want to get involved."

"You might not want to run for a tribuneship, Gaius," said Carbo, "but you're already up to your neck in politics."

"How so?"

"I heard it today. The censor's going to accuse you of leaving your post without permission."

Fulvius nodded slowly. "You're still Orestes' quaestor. And you're here in Rome not Sardinia."

"Even the populace, who see you as another Tiberius, were shocked to learn that you had returned to Rome without permission."

Gaius looked at his wife and shook his head.

"You might not be seeking a magisterial position, but everything is politics in Rome these days. Everything," said Fulvius. "Expect to be in court sometime this week."

CHAPTER 59

Gaius was called to the forum to stand trial five days later. Two of his friends, Pomponius Atticus, whom he had known since childhood, and Laetorius Antonius, whom he had met in the military, went with him. Gaius' personal slave Philocrates accompanied them. I had heard about the trial and wanted to watch. I went to the forum that morning in my litter. Because of her knowledge of the courts, I asked Laelia to come with me.

Everyone in Rome knew about the trial, and because of the huge turnout, the hearing was moved from the forum to the well of the comitium. I had my bearers get as close to the proceedings as possible without Laelia and me being noticed.

It was November. The sun was out, but the day was cool. Large fluffy white clouds moved slowly across the sky. A senator Laelia identified as Popilius Laenus presided. He read the charges. "You, Gaius Sempronius Gracchus, left your position in Sardinia as quaestor to Lucius Aurelius Orestes without permission. You are accused of dereliction of duty. If you are found guilty the punishment is exile from Rome. I have been informed that you will represent yourself. You have this opportunity to defend your actions prior to my asking the jury for a judgment."

Gaius wore a white toga over a belted white tunic. He had grown a full beard while in Sardinia but had trimmed it short for the trial. I doubt there was a more handsome man in Rome. The audience was primarily plebs, but a significant part of the Senate stood along the upper edge of the amphitheater as interested in the outcome as any faction in Rome.

"Friends, citizens of Rome, and honored members of the Senate," Gaius began, scanning the huge audience, "many here believe that I should be in Sardinia today, not standing before you in the comitium, and in many ways I wish I were, but not because I feel the charges against me are true, but because what I must say to defend myself will call into question the actions of several men of significance, including a number of the praetors currently serving in Rome's foreign provinces."

Gaius' opening surprised everyone there, including myself. How could these others he mentioned have any bearing on his leaving Sardinia?

"The law requires a citizen to serve ten years in the military. I'm not yet thirty and have already served twelve in regions as far flung as Asia, Spain, Africa, and Gaul. What I have witnessed in those twelve years makes a joke of the charges I currently face."

Gaius did not possess the same composure his brother had when speaking. He stalked back and forth and gestured with his hands in a way Tiberius never had.

"The censor has leveled a charge of dereliction of duty against me—a charge I consider as dishonorable as murder and an insult to me and my name. I was elected to the position of quaestor two years ago. After serving in that position for one year, I was ordered to serve a second. I fulfilled that duty without hesitation. However, with the campaign in Sardinia still unfinished after two years, Orestes was ordered by the Senate to stay another year. At the same time his legions were recalled to Rome and replaced with fresh troops. I returned with those men who were recalled, as did several other officers—though many did choose to stay. Some might say that I should have stayed in Sardinia out of loyalty to my superior officer. And I would agree except that I had learned the land reform commission was under pressure here in Rome, putting all my late brother's efforts in jeopardy. Being both a member of that commission and a military officer, I had two responsibilities, one in Rome and one in Sardinia. After two years in Sardinia, twice my elected term, I felt my duties in Rome were more urgent."

Even from my perspective inside the litter, it was clear that Gaius had caught the attention of his audience. What he was saying was making sense to the collection of plebs and causing nervous tremors in the string of bright white togas along the top edge of the amphitheater.

"So, to verify just how insulting I consider these allegations, I only need to compare my actions to those I have encountered during my twelve years of service—and kept quiet about until today. Duty abroad is widely looked upon by those in power as a way to riches. When I left for Sardinia, I carried a full purse." He withdrew a leather pouch from the sinus of his toga and held it out. "Now that I am back, it is empty." He tipped it upside down and shook it. Two bronze asses tinkled across the stone floor of the comitium. "Not so for the praetors of Rome's foreign provinces. I've been there. I've seen their sumptuous living accommodations. I've seen the exotic meals they serve. I've seen the lascivious women and pretty boys who surround these magistrates chosen to represent Rome. These same men took jugs filled with wine to their provinces." Gaius, whose passion had steadily risen throughout his speech, tore his toga from his shoulder dramatically. "Only to return with those same jugs filled with silver and gold! While our legionnaires return to farms two years gone to seed and not an as to their name. Something somewhere is terribly wrong."

The plebeian audience loved it and erupted with cheers. Any question of his leaving Sardinia early was chicken feed compared to scandal among Rome's rich and famous. Laelia turned to me and placed her hand on my thigh affectionately. "This is what I must learn. To draw the audience along as Gaius has done."

We watched as he brought his speech to a highly emotional conclusion.

"While I was gone, Fulvius Flaccus sought to clear the courts of land reform suits with a bill that offered Roman citizenship to Italians and non-Roman Latins. Four days before the vote Junius Pennus passed an alien expulsion act to cast non-Romans from the city—an obvious move to undermine the citizenship vote and maintain the land reform logjam. That's why I came back. I had a higher calling—protecting the work of my brother. A man you all saw murdered," Gaius pointed to the top of the Capitoline Hill and shouted, "at the doors to Jupiter's temple. What greater insult can there be?"

It was a scene no one had forgotten. Several people in the crowd shouted Tiberius' name.

"Now you tell me," continued Gaius, "was it a mistake for me to leave Sardinia? Or would you rather have me here?"

The crowd stood as one and shouted over and over again, "Here in Rome! Here in Rome!" Popilius, a stiff, self-righteous aristocrat, unimpressed by Gaius' passionate speech, turned to the jury with a frown I could see from two hundred feet away. The vote was quick. A split jury, populated entirely by senators, decided to drop the charges. Afterward scores of plebs came to Gaius and apologized for doubting him.

I had no intention of staying around to talk to Gaius. Laelia knew about my ankle and suggested we go to a bath. I never went to a bathhouse alone, but nothing I did was more relaxing than sitting in the warm water. Going with Laelia, whom I greatly enjoyed, would be like going with Cornelia. I readily agreed.

As my bearers carried the litter past the comitium, I saw clusters of senators forming around the edge of the amphitheater, talking among themselves, all gravely upset by Gaius' speech. Not only had Gaius stated in public what every aristocrat knew in private—assignments in foreign lands were driven by the allure of riches—but his oratorical ability also appeared to be even greater, and more dangerous, than his brother's.

We went to the same private bath I had gone to with Cornelia. Laelia surprised me by removing all of her clothing to enter the pool. No one did that. She was quite casual about it and seemed to flaunt that she had not removed her body hair, as almost all upper-class Roman women did.

"The water feels so much nicer without the weight of the clothing," she said, standing in the bath, sparkling with a thin veneer of water.

While I stretched out from the side of the pool, letting my legs and hips float in the water within the wet folds of my gown, Laelia splashed about without the slightest restraint or modesty. She came up along side of me. She was a beautiful woman with pale, nearly white skin and striking black hair. I found myself gazing at her breasts. They were small and stood out rather than sagged. The nipples were pink and tight, so different than mine I must have stared. Laelia took my hand and pressed it to her breast. "See how smooth the wet skin feels without the encumbrance of cloth?"

My entire body must have blushed. Laelia slipped beneath the water. I watched her push off with her legs and streak under water to the other side of the pool. Her immodesty was something foreign to me. I had spent my entire life hiding my ankle beneath my clothing. I did not expect to change who I was, but I could not help admiring Laelia's freedom.

CHAPTER 60

Gaius had pledged not to get into politics, but as Carbo had said, he was in already. His experience on the floor of the comitium had also affected him more than he wanted to admit. Afterward Fulvius, fifteen years his senior, had pressed him to reconsider running for the position of tribune. Gaius turned him down again, but not as emphatically.

Three days after the trial he came to my home in the morning, something he rarely if ever did. He was agitated and wanted to talk to me in private. He pushed my wheelchair out to the peristyle. The morning was cold. It had rained during the night and threatened to rain again. We both wore wool cloaks.

"Tiberius came to me in a dream last night," he said as soon as he was certain no one else could hear him. He knelt down in front of my chair and looked up at me.

"He spoke to me," he gasped, clearly shaken by the dream. "It was as though he were standing beside my bed. 'Why do you tarry?' he asked. 'There is no escape; one life and one death is appointed to each of us, to spend the one and to meet the other in the service of the people.'" Gaius looked over his shoulder, then back to me. "Can there be any doubt? He was telling me to run for a tribuneship."

I did not want to say yes, but that was what I thought. I had seen his passion in the comitium. He was headed down the same path that Tiberius had taken. He was chosen for it from birth. But I feared what had happened to Tiberius would also happen to him. "Perhaps," was my weak answer.

"I've been troubling over this since returning from Sardinia. I even thought about it there. When Carbo and Fulvius confronted me with the possibility, I immediately said no. But I didn't stop thinking about it." Gaius shook his head in confusion. "And now this dream."

"Talk to Cornelia. See what she thinks."

208

His eyes darted with thought. "No, I must decide for myself."

"But you asked me?"

"I asked you because you won't try to force your opinion on me."

"Mother would be the same."

"No, there's no need. Revealing the dream to you has convinced me of its meaning. I will file the necessary papers tomorrow."

CHAPTER 61

Gaius did as he said. He added his name to the list of candidates for the position of tribune. The election was a month and a half away. During that time the Latin colony of Fregellae, angered by the rejection of Fulvius' citizenship proposal, forced the Roman magistrates from their city, dropped out of the Latin Federation, and denied all allegiance to Rome.

The Senate reacted by sending two legions under the command of Lucius Opimius to Fregellae to put down the rebellion. Opimius gained entry to the gates through treachery, then burned the city to the ground as an example to other Latin colonies that might have similar plans. In the aftermath of the rebellion, several of the senators placed the blame on Fulvius' promise of citizenship. They claimed that his proposal was insincere and that he had used it to gain popularity and expand his following. The same accusations were leveled at Gaius, even though he had not been in Italy at the time of Fulvius' political campaign. All of this was strictly backlash against Gaius. It was common knowledge he was running for the tribunate. The smear of his name and character was already under way.

Even worse, however, was Cornelia's response when I told her of Gaius' intentions. She sent Gaius a letter which he later showed to me:

> *You will say, Gaius, that it is a beautiful thing to take vengeance on our enemies by running for the position of tribune. To no one does this seem either greater or more beautiful than it does to me, but only if it is possible to pursue these aims without harming the state. But seeing as that cannot be done, and that our enemies will not perish for a long time nor will they change, pushing them to do so will do nothing good for our Rome.*
>
> *I would take a solemn oath, swearing that, except for those who murdered Tiberius, no enemy has foisted so much difficulty*

and so much distress upon me as you have because of this matter. You should desist immediately to ensure that I might have the least anxiety possible in my old age; and that, whatever you do, you should answer to me rather than your anger; and that you would consider it sacrilegious to do anything of great significance contrary to my feelings, especially as I am someone with only a short portion of my life left. Cannot even that time span, as brief as it is, be of help in keeping you from opposing me and destroying our country? Because, in the final analysis, that's what you'll do. When will our family stop behaving insanely? When will we cease insisting on troubles, both suffering and causing them? When will we begin to feel shame about disrupting and disturbing our country? But if you are unable to resist this temptation, seek the office of tribune after I am gone. Then do what you please, when I cannot perceive what you are doing. May Jupiter not for a single instant allow you to continue in these actions nor permit such madness to come into your mind. And if you persist, I fear that, by your own fault, you may incur such trouble for your entire life that at no time would you be able to make yourself happy.

Although I also believed that Gaius should stay out of politics, Cornelia's tone upset me and revealed how much Tiberius' death had affected her. She had supported Tiberius, even helped him. Now she almost sounded like Aemilianus. She wanted nothing that might disrupt Rome, even when the issues that Gaius would pursue would be for the benefit of the people, which she had to know.

When I returned the letter to Gaius, there were tears in his eyes. The letter hurt him badly, and as the youngest of Cornelia's children, the last thing he wanted to do was hurt her.

"But I'm already committed, Sempronia," he said, wiping the tears from his cheeks. "I must honor the spirit of Tiberius more than the wishes of our mother. Can you find it in yourself to support me in this?"

I was old enough to be his mother. I had carried out many of the duties of a nursemaid when he was an infant. He was dearer to me than Tiberius had been, though such a judgment seems silly in retrospect. But even more touching to me was that he sought my approval when Cornelia refused it. "Gaius, I must admit to some of the same fears that haunt our mother, but I have seen your passion and I know that your motives are mostly pure. Yes, mostly, as Cornelia foresees, revenge is clearly part of it. But only part of it." I embraced him. "How can I say no? You have my blessing."

He thanked me, then held me at arm's length and looked into my eyes. "Can you possibly talk to Mother? I would be afraid to now for the malice it could create between us. Maybe you can make her see that I have no other choice."

"Tell her about your dream. That will help."

Gaius nodded absently. "I will certainly have to talk to her at some point. And I will tell her I'm following Tiberius' wishes. Maybe she will accept this as my destiny—to complete what he began. But you must talk to her first, please. Get some measure of her displeasure beyond this letter. Perhaps it was written in haste, in a moment of anger."

"Yes, that's very possible. I'll talk to her."

He embraced me this time.

CHAPTER 62

Prior to the election I went to Misenum to see Cornelia and take part in a circle she had organized. Licinia had also read Cornelia's letter. Worried that she might have lost favor with the great woman, she remained in Rome. Laelia, however, joined me, and we rode south together in my carriage to spend a week in Misenum. It was not a safe trip without an escort so I hired guards to travel with us.

This was the first time I had spent more than an afternoon with Laelia. The trip was five days in good weather. It took us six. The first few days alone in the carriage, Laelia asked me which Greek plays I had read and what I knew about geometry. That was my attraction for her. I had a much broader education. She was hungry for it, and I found it flattering.

The fourth day presented unusually good weather for late fall. The sun was out and there were no clouds at all. We followed Via Appia along the coast, and not far from Fregellae, we skirted a beautiful beach outside the little town of Formiea. Laelia begged me to stop so she could walk along the seashore.

Laelia had already completely charmed me, asking me questions about things no one asked me about, making me feel smart and needed. Of course, I said yes.

The beach was empty for as far as we could see. I traveled with my wheelchair and had Tarus, who drove the carriage, carry it down to the beach so I could sit and take in the sea breeze. Laelia walked along the water's edge barefoot, daring to get the edge of her tunic wet. When a wave splashed her to the hips, she suddenly shed her clothes and dove into the waves. The water was cold and she did not stay in long. I watched her stalk from the surf onto the beach, her wet hair hanging over her shoulders in thick black ribbons. She picked up her clothing and hiked up the beach to where I was.

213

She had an athletic body. She was proud of it and walked that way. I had never seen a woman with such confidence in her appearance. She did not put her tunic and stola on right away, but instead wrapped her palla around her shoulders, hardly covering herself at all.

"Don't be embarrassed, Sempronia," she said standing beside me. "Just like a tiger is a stunning animal to look at, so is a human." She laughed gaily. "I must have been a Greek in a previous lifetime," she joked, then lifted her palla over her head and did a slow turn showing herself off.

"Well, you certainly are beautiful, Laelia." I lowered my eyes, then glanced to where the carriage was parked. "But the guards have seen you also."

"They're too far away to tell if I'm wearing clothes or not. But I can see I'm making you uncomfortable."

Laelia dressed and we returned to the carriage. We sat across from each other. As soon as the movement of the carriage ensured that Tarus could not overhear our conversation, she leaned toward me.

"How was your marriage?" she asked. "Did you enjoy living with Aemilianus?"

Just the mention of his name sent a chill through me. Four years had passed since the murder, and it still felt like it had happened yesterday. I had heard nothing from my accomplice and hoped I never would. "Aemilianus was gone a lot," I said. "Our time together was limited, but even then tense." I looked down at my lap. "I couldn't give him a child."

"I'm sure that was pressure you didn't need. I was fortunate to have three of five survive—so far." She looked out the window at the sea. "But my husband is a dullard and drinks too much. He thinks my study of law is a waste of time." She shook her head at the insult of it. "I'd just as soon kill him as allow him between my legs—for what little pleasure *that* might give me."

I had no idea what to say. Her language was not what I was accustomed to. I must have blushed—even though she expressed what I had already felt and done.

"I've embarrassed you again, Sempronia. I'm sorry if I'm too crude. I can mind my mouth."

"It's fine, Laelia. Your honesty is refreshing." I shifted my legs to get the pressure off my ankle.

Laelia reached out to lift my leg. "May I?"

I did not understand her question.

"This might help." She placed my foot on her lap and removed my supportive boot. "My, this is quite bad."

"One gets used to things," I sighed.

She began to gently massage my ankle and talk. "I'm sure that Aemilianus was a kinder man than Quintus. My husband is twenty years older than I am. He rides me like dog and has no idea how to give me pleasure. The man's a brute. What about Aemilianus? Did you enjoy sex with him?"

My stomach tightened. I had never been asked this question before. It was not something proper Roman women talked about. "Maybe at times," I lied, trying not to give myself away. "I thought of it as a duty."

"It's more than that. More than producing children, sex can be pleasurable, even ecstatic."

"I wanted a child too badly. I didn't think of it as pleasure."

"That's sad, Sempronia." She continued to work on my ankle. "Do you ever touch yourself?"

"Touch myself?"

She pointed to her groin.

"Well, uh, you mean?"

She allowed a little grin. "Yes. The lower class talk about it—men and women—like it's a common practice for everyone."

I looked out the window not knowing what to say.

"I know, you're thinking what kind of witch is this woman? Is it so strange though? It's your body. Your sexuality." She shrugged like it was nothing. "Did you ever hear of the cult of Bacchus that became the fashion in Rome shortly after the war with Hannibal? It was so un-Roman," she laughed. "I wish I had lived then. I would have wanted to take part in a drunken orgy."

"But it was illegal and—and..."

"Uncouth? I'll bet it was exciting. I wonder what Cornelia would say about it. Dare I ask?"

I was both fascinated and disturbed. "I'm not sure. She might appreciate it as a part of our history."

Laelia stopped her massage, but allowed my leg to rest on her thigh.

"Thank you, Laelia. You don't know how good that feels."

"My pleasure. Who will be joining us in the circle this week?"

"My sister-in-law Claudia and two other women. One is the guest speaker. She's from Athens, a poet and midwife. Her name is Elephantis. The other woman is King Ptolemy's daughter Tryphaena. She just turned sixteen, and the king wants her to have the experience of participating in one of Cornelia's circles."

"Is he the one who keeps asking Cornelia to marry him?"

"Yes. He's too fat. I just hope his daughter comes alone."

CHAPTER 63

Laelia and I arrived in Misenum in the afternoon. The other two guests were due the next day. I had come to take part in the circle, but I was more interested in talking to Cornelia about Gaius. I understood her position all too well, but I was worried that Gaius' decision would cause a permanent rift in the family. My mother had already lost Tiberius. Losing Gaius to a disagreement seemed almost as tragic.

Prior to the evening meal I spent some time with Claudia and her two children Tiberius and Sempronia. Tiberius was now fourteen years old and Sempronia was eleven. Cornelia supervised their education just as she had with her own children, and they were terribly precocious and quite fun to be around.

After the evening meal I managed to get some time alone with Cornelia. We sat in the atrium beside a brazier, wrapped in thick wool mantles. She was on a bench. I was in my wheelchair. I had not seen her in several months. She was sixty-four now, and for the first time, possibly because of what she had written in her letter to Gaius, I thought of her as a woman approaching the end of her life. She asked me about my ankle and life alone. She never mentioned Aemilianus, or the situation with Gaius—until I brought it up.

"Gaius showed me the letter you wrote him."

"I got no letter back. I assume it didn't change his mind."

"No and nothing will. That's why I'm here."

"To argue for him?"

"No. I feel the same way you do, but I haven't taken so hard a line. And I wish you hadn't." I rarely gave her advice, but I felt I was someone she might listen to.

Cornelia's eyes narrowed. "It's how I feel, Sempronia. I wrote what I had to. What Tiberius did, despite his intentions, damaged the Republic and what it stands for."

"But it wasn't his fault."

"No, it was mine. I encouraged him. And I haven't forgiven myself. And I suppose you're about to tell me I'm going to lose my youngest son—not to brutal thugs but to my own obstinance."

"I just don't want to see it create a divide in our family."

Cornelia looked upward to the stars. "In this case, I'm afraid, I agree with Aemilianus. The good of a man, or a woman, is judged by how his or her actions benefit the state. All other actions must be subordinate to that."

"You're becoming a conservative, Mother. That's not how you raised us. What Tiberius did was purposely designed to benefit the people in a way that would be good for the state. Gaius' intentions are the same."

"No matter what he hopes to do, the senatorial class will use their money and influence to stop him—maybe in the same way they stopped Tiberius. That will not be good for anyone."

"But hasn't our family always embraced the plebeian cause—win or lose? Only through a sustained effort can there be hope for any kind of balance between the plebeian and the senatorial orders."

"You speak like a true Gracchi." Her smile was in her eyes.

"I am a Gracchi. And so are you."

She knew I was right. She bowed her head, then looked up at me. "I was hard on Gaius in my letter. I was angry when I wrote it. I won't deny that. It's what happens when we get older. We try to hold on to our children because we know there will soon be a time when we can't."

"It's time to let go, Mother. I'm not his mother, but as his sister, I have. I just don't want you to lose him at a time when you don't have to."

She looked off into the shadows of the atrium.

"Tiberius spoke to him in a dream."

She faced me.

"It was before Gaius made his decision. Tiberius told him that he was trying to avoid his fate. That he had one life and one death to give. And as the son of Tiberius Gracchus, both must be in the service of the people of Rome. It's what you told both my brothers and me all of our lives."

"But not to the detriment of the state."

"Tiberius did what he thought was good for the state. He could never have known what forces he might unleash. One never does."

"I should have known. And I do now. It's not worth it."

I shook my head. "You and I are afraid of what could happen. Gaius, like all good Roman men, does not know fear. He believes the tribuneship is his fate. And I'm here asking you to accept it as I have."

"I don't want a second son killed by a mob." She stood up, paused a moment, as though she might have one more thing to say, then walked away.

The abrupt end to the conversation felt cold. But I was confident that I had made a fair case for Gaius and that she would rethink her position—maybe not change it, but rethink it. It was a good talk. She just needed some time. And it was a sign that our relationship was changing. I was advising her, not the reverse.

The villa was huge. It had twenty bedrooms. I had never visited when they were all in use. I had not slept well at the inns we had stopped at during the trip south. Because of my ankle, Cornelia gave me a ground-floor bedroom. I went to my bedroom after my talk with her. I removed my supportive shoe and instead of soaking my foot like I usually did, I put on a gown and fell asleep.

I was awakened in the middle of the night by Laelia sliding in bed beside me. She whispered that she had been cold and snuggled up close to me. I welcomed her into my arms as I would a sister. She kissed me on the cheek and settled in against me.

I had not been touched in a comforting way since the first year of my marriage to Aemilianus. Laelia, in her sleep, gently held my body and entwined her legs with mine—and it felt good. Like something I needed.

Laelia was gone when I woke up. I wondered if her visit had been a dream.

CHAPTER 64

Our guests arrived in a train of carriages, slaves, and bodyguards. It was still morning when we heard them coming up the road to the villa. Cornelia visibly wilted when she saw that Physcon was part of the entourage. It was rare to have women come from beyond Italy, and she was looking forward to spending time with these women she had never met. But she had planned for a circle entirely of women, and she had not invited Physcon. His oversized ego would stifle conversation, especially with Elephantis there to talk about women's health.

Cornelia greeted everyone warmly. Physcon had gained even more weight since I had last seen him. Huffing and puffing from simply getting out of the carriage, he embraced Cornelia and kissed her on both cheeks. He then turned to his daughter who was being helped from the carriage. Tryphaena was a frail little thing, with large eyes lined with stibium and a peculiar fluid way of moving, like a dancer. She was a princess and wore a gold-threaded white silk robe with a diadem of white silk holding her straight black hair in place. She lifted her head proudly when her father said her name, and we all bowed to her. Physcon told us she had been promised to King Antiochus VIII and would wed within the year.

The last to exit the carriage was Elephantis. She was my age and quite tall, with long dark hair, free of braids or ribbons. I noticed her eyes right away. They were green, alive and observant. Cornelia, speaking in Greek, introduced herself, then me in my wheelchair, Claudia, and Laelia. The circle would similarly be conducted in Greek.

"It's a great pleasure," replied Elephantis, gazing into each of our faces. She was a tawny Greek with the pleasant open countenance of a thoughtful woman. A thin scar ran vertically up the right side of her face from her jaw to her eye. She must have been very beautiful prior to the injury, but the scar added something to her presence. Not something I could name; something I could feel. I was immediately interested in getting to know her.

We went into the house, with Laelia pushing my wheelchair, and settled down in the atrium around the pool. Although the sun shone brightly and provided for a pleasant day, four braziers were lit for additional warmth. Fidelia, who had moved to Misenum with Cornelia, brought out two trays of food—olives from the garden, boiled pigeon eggs sprinkled with cardamom, and a large plate of cheese and bread. A pitcher of fresh squeezed apple juice might have been the biggest treat.

While everyone else ate, Cornelia took Physcon aside in the library. I could see them from where I was sitting. Cornelia filled me in on the conversation later that day.

"We're going to have a circle this afternoon," she told the pharaoh. "Only women will take part."

Physcon smiled like someone who always got what he wanted. His size alone provided a certain presumption. "What am I to do, Cornelia? Walk on the beach alone? I love these discussions. I think they show you at your best."

Cornelia could not help smiling. Physcon's capacity for flattery seemed unbounded. "Not this time. One thing that I overlooked as a mother was educating my daughter on the nature of marriage—the deeper nature."

"I love it when you talk like that."

Cornelia shook her head and continued. "It was a terrible oversight. Your daughter is about to marry a man much older than she is. We have women here from the ages of twenty-five to sixty-four to help inform her about married life. It's something I have never talked about in my circles, and I don't want any men here to complicate things when we do. So you can't stay."

"If that's the case, my dear, I'll leave right away," said Physcon with surprising grace. "I know another house nearby where I can stay. My carriage will return in a week to get the women. But I've come a long way." He smiled. "If this is my one chance to talk to you, then I have one request before I leave."

"No, I will not marry you."

Physcon laughed. "I want one kiss—given like it's the last kiss you'll ever give me."

Cornelia smiled at first, then tipped her head. "Are you ill?"

"Although the weight I carry is not the best way to grow old, no, I'm not ill. But who knows, with the war going on at home, it's possible I will not be back again. So in exchange for my early departure, kiss me like it's the last."

"You won't be picking up your daughter?"

"I'll simply send my carriage."

"Then sit down. I can't properly reach your face because of your girth."

He laughed again, then sat in a chair he barely fit in. Cornelia came up close to him and smiled. "I have loved you all of these years, Physcon, but I never wanted a second husband. I hope you have understood that through all of your proposals and all of my refusals. I never had any intention of hurting you." She leaned into him and pressed her lips against his. She stroked his temples and ran her fingers through his beard, extending the kiss with real sentiment. Then she stood back.

There were tears in Physcon's eyes. He did love her and still did want to marry her. Instead of asking her yet again, he called for his slaves. Cornelia escorted him to the door. He turned to her as he walked out. "Thank you, Cornelia. If I never see you again, that kiss is how I want to remember you. Take good care of Tryphaena."

"I wish all women had the opportunity Tryphaena has being here."

"I'll have her picked up in one week's time."

"Travel safely."

Midafternoon we all went into the library. Cornelia's library in Misenum was nearly as extensive as the one in my house. Using chairs and my wheelchair, Claudia, Laelia, Cornelia, Tryphaena, Elephantis, and I formed a circle in the center of the room. With two braziers it was warm enough to discard my heavy mantle. Each of us got a chance to describe ourselves to the group. Tryphaena said only that she was a Ptolemy and soon to be a queen

Elephantis spoke last. "I grew up outside Athens. My father was a physician. When my mother died, I assisted my father in his work. Much of it was delivering babies and helping women who were pregnant. By the time I was twenty I was delivering babies by myself. I have now delivered several thousand babies in all manner of circumstances and know the physical anatomy of a woman as well as anyone I've ever met.

"I'm also a writer," she said looking directly at me. "I have written a book about women's health, another about abortive herbs, two short collections of poems, and I'm currently working on a book about sexual intercourse."

All of our eyes widened—even Tryphaena's already very wide eyes. Cornelia, who had invited Elephantis to speak, might have been the most surprised by this last statement. Cornelia rarely spoke openly of sex and invariably shunned common sexual terms. Claudia and I were much like Cornelia, and Laelia had already proven she was not.

"We've never really talked about these more intimate things," said Cornelia looking around at the other women. "But we've touched upon the nature of marriage. I, personally, had a fine husband, but I worry about the treatment of other wives and the clear iniquity of the Roman institution of manus—which is essentially ownership of the wife."

"It's much the same in Greece," said Elephantis, "but because of my work with pregnant women, I've tried to include the act of procreation in the conversation. Our hesitance to speak about it, except in the most private way, prevents women from making progress in other realms."

Cornelia turned to Claudia, Laelia, and me. "I think we all accept that a woman's duty to the state is to produce children."

"But there's more to it than that, Cornelia," said Elephantis. "Sex can enhance the relationship and also offer mutual pleasure. In my book I describe a variety of sexual positions. Several of which are not male dominant."

Claudia seemed the furthest behind on the topic. "But isn't that what a prostitute does? The things that married women don't."

Elephantis smiled gently. "To me, that's archaic thinking. I've seen too much violence, too much forced sex, too many women injured simply because they did not speak up about their husband's practices. Do they want to be lubricated before the man enters them? Are there positions that are more comfortable for them or that facilitate getting pregnant? Are there specific acts that enable orgasms for women who struggle to climax? These are the issues I want to address, and I think they get at the root of equality in marriage."

Our little group of upper-class women was not entirely prepared for these kinds of insights. All of us who had been married knew a form of sex that was traditionally enacted in the dark. Certainly we had heard of or experienced more than one position for pleasing our husbands, but that was the man's choice and we accepted that. Cornelia had read too much Greek literature not to know more than the rest of us, but at sixty-four, her discomfort with the topic showed. As did mine, I'm sure, and Claudia's, but Laelia thirsted for this kind of openness, and Tryphaena, a virgin who had lived a cloistered life, was all ears.

Cornelia tried to change the subject. "What about your books of poetry? Did you bring any copies?"

But Laelia's interest had been piqued and she pushed past Cornelia's question. "Elephantis, are you familiar with the cult of Bacchus that spread through Rome sixty years ago? I'm curious what you think of that."

Cornelia stiffened. She had been a child when some seven thousand men and women were arrested for immoral behavior. Her mother had spoken out against the cult.

"It's called the cult of Dionysius in Greece and the cult of Isis in Egypt." Elephantis glanced at Tryphaena, then at Cornelia. "They bring groups of men and women together to drink freely of wine and explore sexuality. It's an orgiastic cult. I have seen it in Athens, but I'm a midwife. I tend to focus on the production of children and the health of the mother and her newborn."

"What can you tell a woman like myself?" asked Tryphaena, engaging for the first time. "I have no experience at all, and my husband will be thirty years older than I am. Does intercourse hurt?"

"Tryphaena, you and I should find some time to talk alone. I often advise women about to be married."

"What about masturbation?" asked Laelia, barely able to contain herself. "There's no harm in it. Is that right?"

"That's correct, Laelia. In fact, it's one way for a woman to learn about her body and what positions will enable her to climax. But let's slow down. Cornelia asked about my poems, and she is my host." She turned to Cornelia. "We have several days together. Let me read a few poems right now. We can return to this other material as we have the opportunity."

"Yes, I think that makes a lot of sense," said Cornelia. "I'm fascinated by your work with women"—her voice did not convey that—"but let's take our time getting there."

Claudia came to me after the evening meal and told me she had something to show me. She got behind my chair and pushed me across the atrium to the room where she kept her loom. She had learned to cope with her grief by spending more time spinning and weaving. "This is cotton," she said proudly, as she positioned my chair before her two-beam loom. "What do you think of the design?"

"It's beautiful," I said, totally captured by the intricate pattern she had woven and its bright colors.

"It's for you, Sempronia. It's a tube dress. It will be all of one piece with no seam. I hope to have it done later this year."

"I can hardly wait. Thank you. You've gotten imaginative with your weaving. I'm impressed."

Claudia glimmered a smile. "Cornelia's been helping. She makes a good teacher."

Claudia rolled me out to the garden to enjoy the last of the daylight. The sun had sunken below the horizon. The ocean was a deep green; the sky a brilliant orange, bleeding upward from the edge of the sea.

"What did you think of Elephantis?" I asked.

"She seems quite remarkable," said Claudia, bringing the chair to a stop before a bench. She sat down facing me. "Were you aware of what she would be talking about?"

"No, I don't think Cornelia was either."

Claudia laughed. "Are you shocked?"

"Yes, but I try to think of it as science. I don't think sexual positions will be that useful to me." I gave her a forlorn smile. "But it is interesting."

Claudia looked over her shoulder, back toward the atrium.

"Is someone coming?"

"No." She faced me. "I want to talk to you in private."

"You mean about something other than Elephantis?" I asked, trying to be funny.

Her answer was a leaden, "Yes." She looked at her lap then up at me. "You're a good one to talk to, Sempronia."

"I try to be. Is something wrong?"

"I want to remarry."

"Has someone proposed?"

"No. And I have no one in mind. But I'm only thirty years old. If I return to Rome, I will have my father's villa. I'll be considered wealthy and will attract suitors." She looked away from me then back. "I don't know. I'm just thinking about it. What do you think? Do I sound silly?"

"Was this prompted by Elephantis?"

"No, not at all. I've been thinking about it for a while."

"Cornelia would be disappointed."

She nodded knowingly.

"But you might not want to live the rest of your life with her. You'll never free yourself from Tiberius' memory living here."

Claudia hung her head.

"Cornelia might distance herself from you. Be prepared for that."

She looked up at me. "If she ever mentions it to you, for any reason, help her see it my way."

"Is that why you're making me a dress?" I asked trying to lighten things up.

"Of course not," she said seriously, then realizing I had been teasing her, laughed. "But maybe it will help inspire you."

"I'm happy to say whatever I can to help, Claudia. Perhaps Elephantis is going to open all of our minds to new things before the week is over. Even Cornelia's."

Claudia's smile was hopeful.

I lay in bed that night wondering if Laelia would come to my room again. I had mixed feelings about it, but the more time that passed, the more I wanted her to be there. It was warm and cozy beneath the covers with her. I had no such thing in my life. I had no child to nurse, no man to hold.

I was asleep when Laelia slipped into my bed. I accepted her embrace and thought how nice it was. But Laelia did not want to sleep. She allowed her gown to rise above her waist, then took my hand and pressed it into her maidenhair. She held my finger and used it to rub the top of her vagina. I was barely part of the act, but she grew very excited. She gripped my hand tightly and pushed my finger into her vagina. I found her moaning pleasure embarrassing at first, then it began to arouse me.

When she finally let go of my hand, she asked me if I would like her to do the same to me. Even though my body called for it, I was a deeply introverted person. With my ankle I was damaged goods and not quite ready to allow that kind of intimacy. "No, that was enough."

"Did I do something wrong? You saw how it transported me."
"No, no. It was fine. But a little new for me."
When I awoke in the morning, she was gone.

CHAPTER 65

There was a large heated bath at Cornelia's villa. The fourth day of the gathering Elephantis convened her talk in the bath. Of course Cornelia, Claudia, and I entered the water clothed in light gowns. Tryphaena was even more modest. She wore a linen tunic. Laelia wore nothing, and Elephantis did the same.

We arranged ourselves in a small circle, all of us squatting so that the water came up to our shoulders. After we had been in the water awhile, and had a chance to allow its warmth to relax us, Elephantis asked those of us wearing clothing to take it off. "If you are modest, stay below the water. But remember. If there's one thing I want to communicate to you this week, *it's know your body*. Most women don't."

She continued to talk as we reluctantly removed our gowns.

"Doesn't it feel better?" asked Elephantis when all of us were naked, squatting beneath the water so that only our heads were visible. "But don't just crouch there. Feel the water. Extend your arms and legs. It's hard to imagine a feeling nicer than this warm water, warm like a womb, warm like a memory we all retain but have forgotten."

Elephantis stood up in the water. From the navel down she was underwater. Her breasts were long and narrow with especially wide areolas around the nipples. She put her hands on her breasts. "Learn to feel your breasts." She looked around the circle. "Do what I'm doing. Get used to the feeling."

Laelia did this immediately. The rest of us were hesitant.

"Come now, ladies," said Elephantis. "There is no shame in touching yourself." She gave us a moment to get comfortable with this, then said, "Now use your fingertips to feel for lumps in the soft tissue. Often there are tumors that become cancerous. Though I don't know the technique, I have learned that they can be removed."

Except for Laelia, all of us were doing this below the water line. Elephantis pressed us for more. "All of you, stand up. Let me watch how you use your hands. Forget your modesty. This is not a sexual exercise. It's for your health."

It was awkward at first. Tryphaena seemed even more uncomfortable than Cornelia as Elephantis led us all over our bodies, leaving no nook or cranny unexplored. Our ages spanned fifty years. All the various shapes of a woman's body, other than overly fat, were there to be seen. Tryphaena had few curves at all. Small breasts with tiny nipples and no hips. Cornelia's body had been lovely as a younger woman, but now it sagged in all the obvious places. With my limited mobility I had lost my muscle tone. All the firmness in my body was gone. Laelia was beautiful without clothing. Her body was lithe and athletic like a Greek statue. I thought of her in my bed that second night and wondered if she felt I had rejected her. It was more complicated than that for me, but the experience in the bath helped, and I hoped she would visit me again before the week was over.

The six-day circle with Elephantis stood out as perhaps the most educational of all that I had ever attended. But only Laelia seemed ready for the sexual openness the midwife promoted. Cornelia struggled with it the most. She saw that it was correct intellectually, but she was too settled in her ways to completely let go.

No one benefited from the circle more than Tryphaena. One afternoon she took a long walk with Elephantis down the garden's stone stairway to the edge of the bay, where they talked as they strolled along the shore. She would not go into marriage the way I had, frightened of the act of intercourse and unsure how to touch a penis—or how it acted when you did.

I spoke once with the young queen to be. I asked her about her home in Egypt. "I have lived almost all my life in Alexandria, Sempronia, until last year. Everything is political." Her voice was soft and small, like a bird. But her Greek was sharp and so was her mind. "My marriage is no different. It's my royal duty and will provide troops for my father—troops that might bring an end to the war. Or so my father hopes.

"I have never met my husband," she confided. "I'm frightened. He's known as fierce warrior, and I don't know if I'm capable of what Elephantis has been teaching us. But I certainly feel less apprehensive than I did before this circle."

The last night of the gathering I was feeling badly about Laelia. She had not come back to my bed. Superficially it was fine. Nothing had changed. We spoke, but about other things, and I felt that I needed to explain myself to her somehow. I decided to go to her bedroom. It was on the ground floor of another wing of the villa. I was not really certain if I would let her touch me or if I just wanted to talk.

Only a sliver of the moon lit the night, but the stars were aplenty. Using my crutch, I quietly crept across the atrium to the adjoining wing. I heard them before I got there. The light limited what I could see. Elephantis and Laelia were lying side by side in bed with the face of one in the groin of the other. The tangle of arms and legs wound in and out in the shadowy darkness like a nest of restless snakes. Their inverted position and wet slurping sounds unsettled me. I stared in spite of myself as they chirped and moaned in clear ecstatic pleasure. It seemed like a graphic demonstration of what the entire week had been—both alluring and uncomfortable.

When I returned to my room, I wondered if they had been together other nights. I had been too slow and reluctant. Laelia wanted a more sophisticated partner. Now I was the one with hurt feelings—over something I was not even sure I wanted.

CHAPTER 66

Physcon's entourage came as scheduled on the morning of the seventh day to pick up Tryphaena. Physcon was not part of it. I know Cornelia was relieved that he had kept his promise, but the truth was she did like the man.

Tryphaena expressed her gratitude to Cornelia before climbing into the carriage. "Thank you for allowing me to take part in your circle, Cornelia. I feel like a different woman than the one who arrived seven days ago. I'm ready to be a queen and a wife."

Cornelia wrapped the little woman in her arms. "Please stay in contact. You are welcome to attend any circle I hold."

Elephantis also thanked Cornelia for inviting her. "I know that I tested you, Cornelia," said the poet and midwife. "I hope you realize that all I sought to do was introduce openness to matters of the female body."

"Had I known what you were going to talk about, I would not have invited you, but I would have been wrong." Cornelia smiled, then embraced Elephantis with warmth. "I'm an older women, well set in my ways, but I know that all women, of any age, could benefit from your teachings. As I said to Tryphaena, please come back any time."

"Perhaps next time we should include men. It will make the topic a little more difficult, but they need this information as well."

Elephantis embraced each of us before climbing into the carriage. She included a kiss with Laelia, adding to my turmoil. Elephantis was an elegant and engaging woman. I was damaged goods. Whether I sought intimacy with a man or a woman, I would always be disadvantaged.

I found a few moments alone with Cornelia prior to leaving. Despite all that had gone on, my main purpose for visiting had been to talk to Cornelia about her letter to Gaius. Neither of us had mentioned it since our talk the day I arrived. We were in the garden the morning of my last day. The sky was gray with winter clouds. The usually blue bay was a turgid green. Vesuvius' crater, an open mouth to the sky, stood out with a white collar of snow.

"What did you think of the circle, Sempronia?" Cornelia stood. I sat in my wheelchair.

"It was difficult, Mother. Much of what Elephantis spoke about I needed to know quite a while ago."

She nodded. "And for all my regrets about not giving you a better idea of what to expect in marriage, I could not have told you what she did. I'm sure you saw how uncomfortable some of the discussions were for me."

"You did well, Mother. I was impressed by your composure when she described the various sexual positions to us."

She smiled hesitantly. "It wasn't easy. And you did well yourself, especially when she noted how some of those positions might enhance the chance of getting pregnant."

"It was good for the other women, but to think that I might have been able to do something differently was painful."

She knelt beside me and stroked my hair. "Do you forgive me for the life I gave you?"

I took her hand in both of mine. "There's nothing to forgive. My life has been full. Difficult times make us stronger."

She squeezed my hands. "We've known some difficult times, Sempronia. Thank you for being my daughter."

"Do you have a message I might pass on to Gaius?"

She bowed her head then looked up at me. "I'm still against his running for the tribunate. I cry every time I think about it. I cannot give him my support."

"Can you accept it though? Can you distance yourself enough from his decision to not take it personally? To understand that he's doing it to honor Tiberius, not hurt you or our family's name or the state?"

"I need more time."

"But can I tell him that you know he's not doing this to hurt you?"

She let go of my hands and stood. She gazed out at the bay for a long time before facing me. "If you can say it in a way that doesn't give him any sense that I support his decision."

"Yes, I can do that. Thank you."

CHAPTER 67

This second conversation with Cornelia brought back the memory of an even more difficult conversation from our past. To some extent it foreshadowed the candor of all the ensuing discussions she and I would have. I was twenty-two. After one miscarriage and a stillborn, I delivered a tiny baby girl. Aemilianus and I named her Cornelia, and though not a son, she did bring a measure of joy to our generally joyless household for a while.

Cornelia was very skinny and small. Almost any infant's first year is a delicate time, and I held her to my breast each day hoping the milk from my body would help her put on weight. I remember thinking how much I wanted a daughter to educate, who would look up to me the way I did to Cornelia. But it was not to be. Cornelia remained little and weak. Before six months had passed she caught the fever that was running through Rome that fall. I found her little body one morning completely still in her crib.

As much as Tiberius' murder had grieved me, losing my baby daughter was worse. I fell into a deep depression. Already a woman uncertain of her value, I struggled badly for many months with no support from Aemilianus.

Cornelia got me through it. Living close by, she came to my house every day for weeks on end. Some days we would talk. Some days she simply sat beside me and held me. Of course, her central piece of wisdom was that I was young and would have other children. Had I known then that this would not be so, I suspect I might have sought out hemlock long before I did.

Maybe six months after the infant's passing, Cornelia came to visit. We sat in the peristyle, as was our custom, on a warm spring morning. The garden had broken free of winter with brilliant green shoots and swelling blossoms. Instead of lifting me with its natural beauty, I was filled with the perversion that everything was coming to life, except that which I brought into the world. This idea had settled down on me like a huge animal, and I confessed to Cornelia that I felt little reason to go on. I asked her what I had asked her before and would ask her again. "Why did you decide to nurture a child who you knew could only have a difficult life?"

Cornelia had always answered this dreadful question with the compassion of a mother for her child, repeating her desire to educate me in the same way that she had been. On this occasion, I got a different answer.

"You must know, Sempronia, how much it hurts me to hear you ask this question. I know it's a way of revealing how badly you're hurting. I appreciate that. But please remember, Cornelia was also my grandchild, my first lovely granddaughter." She was crying now, when before she had hidden her tears from me. "Although I have tried to share my strength with you, I am also suffering. And it's extremely difficult when you express your frustration in a way that feels like an attack on me. This is a time when we both need each other, when we both need to trust each other."

She wiped her eyes with the edge of her palla. "I once said that I nurtured you so that I could have a daughter to educate. I imagine you hoped to do the same with little Cornelia. I also commented on how much I wanted to be able to talk with you about art and literature. Which we have, and which I believe is, in itself, enough to warrant my decision to preserve your life. I do. But there's something in an education that is more than high art and subtle turns of a phrase. It's in this conversation we're having now—one of utmost gravity, not airy aesthetics—when sad events have left us both exposed and sensitive— you to the point that even the fragrances of spring"—she breathed in—"cause you to avoid the light and dwell in darkness. This is when our ability to articulate our thoughts is the most important, allowing us an opportunity to heal each other by exchanging our deepest emotions with conviction and feeling. We often praise the man who can capture an audience in the forum with his words, but this one-on-one exchange is where life is deepest and the most meaningful, where this thing that animates us can be shared with words."

She dabbed at her cheeks again. "Maybe I don't truly know why I did what I did when you were an infant, but I believe now that it was for this very moment, when you and I must share something in life that is terribly sad, but also profound." She reached out and touched her palla to my wet cheeks.

I embraced her and whispered hoarsely. "Forgive me, Mother. I have overlooked what my child might have meant to you. And I see now, understand now, that asking you to defend my life, in the way that I have, is unfair to you. If I share my pain in this way again, please know, it's weakness, not a conscious effort to hurt you. I apologize in advance because what you've just said tells me that you have already forgiven me."

She whispered back. "We're getting there, Sempronia. We're getting there."

And we were. In the days that followed my depression eased, and I could once again look at a flower and not feel the anguish of my loss. But the ultimate meaning of that conversation was more than just lifting me out of my depression. It was an awareness that we, she and I, could talk about any difficult issue—and make it better. Our two discussions of Gaius that week in Misenum were example of this, and for once, I was helping her.

CHAPTER 68

The trip back to Rome with Laelia was not easy. She remained her confident self. She massaged my ankle at least once each day. She spoke freely about how much she enjoyed the circle and how surprised she was that Cornelia had chosen Elephantis as a speaker. But she made no comment about her visits to my bed or to Elephantis'. We stopped at four inns during the five-day trip. Our rooms were separate but invariably contained a connecting door. I imagined her visiting me in the night, but it never happened. On the last night, I found myself so wanting her intimacy, just someone beside me to hold, that I lay in bed all night thinking I should take the initiative, but I could not make myself do it for fear of rejection. Only on the last day of the trip, less than five miles from Rome, did I finally open up to her.

"I believe I must have disappointed you in some way, Laelia," I said to break an extended silence. The trip had been long and wearing. I am sure she was as anxious to be home as I was.

She looked at me and tilted her head. "How so?"

"I think I disappointed you the second night you came to my bed. I feel that I let you down in some way. Is that why you never came back?"

"I had never been in bed with woman before, Sempronia. After what Elephantis had said that day, I wanted to show you that masturbation was pleasurable. Later I realized that I had been too forward. I decided not to bother you again."

I nodded ever so slightly. "After Aemilianus' death I felt that the sexual part of my life was over. I had not been with a woman in any way other than as a sister, and masturbation was not something I did. But," I hesitated for fear of revealing the extent of my loneliness, "I needed to be held. When you didn't come back I missed you."

She nodded her understanding. "Tell me more about Aemilianus. You must miss him badly."

The night I poisoned him replayed in my memory. "No, Laelia, I don't miss him at all. I was barren and had no value to him. He was cold and his touch infrequent. And when he did touch me, he was rough, with no consideration for my needs." My emotions began to rise as I spoke. "He mocked my ankle. He disparaged Tiberius who had once so admired him. He cut off communication with Cornelia. He distanced himself from Gaius and everything our family stood for. I became afraid of him because of his anger." Tears were now running down my cheeks.

Laelia slid over next to me. She wrapped her arm around my shoulder and held me.

"He became so unbearable I wished he were gone. I was only comfortable when he was off on a military campaign. I grew to despise him." I looked into her eyes and blurted it out. "It got so bad I poisoned him."

"You poisoned Aemilianus?" Laelia asked in disbelief. "And that was what killed him?"

"Yes," I hissed through gritted teeth, continuing to sob. "He deserved it."

"But it was said he died of natural causes."

"That was a lie."

Laelia was stunned. "Not only did you do it; you got away with it!" She laughed and hugged me tighter, not so much comforting as congratulating me.

"I shouldn't have told you."

"I won't say a word, Sempronia. I'm impressed."

"Don't be. It comes back to me with all its horror every time his name is mentioned. I can't talk about him without it bubbling up out of me. His ghost appears. I see him in my dreams. It's awful."

"I'll be your advocate if it ever goes to court. We'll use it as a way to challenge the law of manus. An abused woman must have the right to divorce her husband. It beats murder." Her eyes were wild. "I would divorce Quintus right now, but as it is, only he has that choice."

"It can never go to court! You cannot tell anyone—anyone!"

"Don't worry, Sempronia. It happened four years ago. I don't believe anyone cares any more."

"Well, let's not find out. I apologize for saying anything about it."

CHAPTER 69

In the aftermath of my confession to Laelia, I realized that I was struggling to know who I was. I had little confidence in myself, and I believe, in retrospect, that I told Laelia about my poisoning Aemilianus to get closer to her, hoping that by revealing my darkest secret it would act as a bond between us. It was impulsive and risky, but her response was more than I could have anticipated. Her respect for me, beyond my education, increased. I was no longer just a smart woman. I was a renegade like her. Despite my crippling ankle, I had revealed an inner strength, and it rekindled our friendship. However, I had not told her that Aemilianus had also been strangled—or about the note I had found beneath my bed. Though there had yet to be a follow-up of any kind, neither the accomplice nor the note were ever far from my mind.

While these personal issues dominated my life, my youngest brother, not yet thirty years old, was taking on the optimates with a courage equal to, perhaps surpassing, Tiberius'. While I was in Misenum, he had been speaking daily in the forum and steadily gathering a small army of clients.

The election took place three weeks after my return to Rome. It was one of the most memorable elections in recent memory because of the turnout. Gaius had become extremely popular. The people saw him as another Tiberius. Plebeians from all over the region came to Rome to vote. It was like a massive pilgrimage. All available lodging quickly sold out, forcing the travelers to pitch tents or huddle in any vacant corner of the city they could find.

Because of the crowds, the election was moved from the top of the Capitoline Hill to Mars Field, and even then the entire exercise grounds filled to overflowing, preventing some people from voting at all. Many of the pilgrims were so excited to be there, they climbed to the top of the nearby hills or stood on the roofs of houses, happy just to watch.

Throughout the lead-up to the actual process of voting, however, a contingent of senators had conspired to prevent Gaius from obtaining a position on the tribunate. All of these senators had voting blocks of clients built up over years. Many of their clients were plebeians, some whose fathers or grandfathers had been clients for these same senators or their fathers. They had voted as instructed for two or three generations as a way to incur favor with this senator or that. Even with the large turnout of plebeians who had come to Rome specifically because of Gaius, the senators' countering action had an effect. Many anticipated that Gaius would be the highest-ranking candidate by vote. To do so was a special honor that came with the understood leadership of the tribunate. But the backroom plotting and the money spent to sway voters were enough to drop his vote total to fourth in the final list of ten.

It was a minor setback. With the agenda he had been preparing and his captivating oratorical style, Gaius was soon the leading tribune regardless of the vote, bringing new laws to the People's Assembly at an astounding rate, and making the entire senatorial class cringe. Every month it seemed he had something new to present to the Assembly, with each proposal focused on bringing greater balance to our system of government. I wrote to Cornelia through it all, hoping to convince her that Gaius was not the threat to the state that she feared.

Gaius' first bill addressed his brother's murder. In the aftermath of the brutal slaying, the consuls Publius Rupilius and Popilius Laenus had led an angry Senate through a heavy-handed purge of Tiberius' remaining clients. Some thirty men had been executed or exiled with no real trial. In an effort to prevent such purges from happening again, Gaius proposed a law that would make it a crime for the Senate to authorize capital punishment against a Roman citizen without a vote from the People's Assembly. It was a variation of a bill Tiberius had hoped to pass had he achieved a second tribuneship.

When the law came to a vote, Gaius used the memory of our brother to stir the Assembly's emotions. "In all our prior history a tribune of the plebs was sacrosanct. There was a time when we declared war on the Faliscans for using crude language to address the tribune Genucius. Caius Veturius was sentenced to death for merely standing in the way of a tribune as he crossed the forum. And yet when my brother, while still serving as a tribune, attempted to run for a second term, he may as well have been a beggar in the street.

"They beat Tiberius to death with cudgels at the doors to Jupiter's temple, then dragged his corpse from the Capitoline Hill and cast it into the river. Those of his friends who were not killed that day were rounded up and put to death untried. And yet our constitution is intended to guard against those things and serve as a legal buffer for a citizen's life. If a man is accused of a capital crime and does not immediately obey the summons, it is ordained that a herald must come at dawn to his door and summon him by trumpet. So carefully did our ancestors regulate the course of justice that no decision could be pronounced against a litigant until this was done. None of my brother's followers were given that courtesy. They were simply rounded up and executed.

"The law I propose states that no man can be executed or exiled without the authorization of this assembly." The huge crowd roared with approval. "And it will be the people who determine the punishment, not the avenging senators." Again the crowd erupted with enthusiastic support. "This law will not only protect the common man, but also punish anyone attempting to pass such a sentence without the Assembly's permission."

The entire Capitoline Hill shook with the Assembly's wild reaction. The people loved Gaius. He was Tiberius all over again but with greater passion. The law passed unanimously, a law that was specifically retroactive and aimed at Popilius Laenus and Publius Rupilius. Rather than face trial, both ex-consuls left Rome the next day, going separate ways into voluntary exile.

Much of what Gaius did was driven by what had happened to his brother. Cornelia, it seemed, had come to terms with Tiberius' murder through stoicism. I had become a cynic, and Gaius had let his anger build up in him over many years then managed to channel it into effective populist action. However, his anger was not always contained. He was a different kind of orator than Tiberius. Tiberius relied on logic, common sense, and his calm demeanor to get his message across. Gaius relied on his passion. In many ways he was a more effective speaker than Tiberius, but on occasion, especially when he spoke about our brother's murder, he could become so incensed that the clarity of his words was obscured by his anger and dramatic gesticulations.

Following one of his more passionate speeches, Fulvius confronted Gaius as he walked away from the rostra trailed by Philocrates.

"Gaius, you are an excellent speaker, but you've acquired a habit of getting carried away with your words. At the end today, it seemed you lost track of what you were saying. It was all furious passion. It doesn't always help our cause."

Gaius knew this was true. He apologized to Fulvius for not having better control. "I will do what I can to change. It's just that I believe strongly in what I'm saying and passion is critical to engaging the audience."

"Yes, I understand that. Just try to be more aware of yourself. It's your only real flaw as a speaker."

After Fulvius had walked away, Philocrates approached Gaius. "Master, I couldn't help overhearing your conversation with Fulvius. I have a suggestion."

Gaius was as close to Philocrates as Philocrates was loyal. Gaius put a hand on his slave's shoulder. "What is your idea, my friend? I'm afraid my passion is something I might never be able to control."

Philocrates carried a small wooden flute on a leather cord around his neck. He withdrew the flute from beneath his tunic. Gaius had seen it many times before. "What if I were to play a few notes on my flute," Philocrates put the flute to his mouth and played a little ditty, "when I think you are beginning to lose the focus of your speech?"

Gaius tilted his head as in thought and paused long enough for Philocrates to wonder if he had insulted his master. Then Gaius smiled. "That might work, Philocrates. That might work. Try it the next time you hear me getting too worked up. I just hope I'm capable of regaining my composure once my passion has risen."

"I'm sure you can, master. Thank you for not taking offense."

Gaius shook his head. "It's just a shame that someone needed to tell me this. We'll work on it."

CHAPTER 70

Gaius' next law, like the first, contained a measure of revenge. The bill had two parts. It gave the People's Assembly the power to vote out a magistrate, as had happened to Marcus Octavius during Tiberius' term as tribune, and it forbade any magistrate who had been ousted from office from ever running for an elected position again. Ostensibly it was aimed at forcing officials who had been caught in bribery schemes or other forms of corruption out of government permanently. It was a good law, but Gaius had aimed it specifically at Octavius, and he made the law retroactive so that the vetoing tribune would be banned from government for life.

The common practice was for a tribune who proposed a law to make it public by introducing it to the Senate. Tiberius had broken with this tradition. It had been a mistake, and Gaius had learned from it. He convened the Senate in the comitium, as he had for his first bill, and read his latest bill to the senators. He stood at the rostra facing the senators in the sunken amphitheater. To his left, in the forum, were hundreds of his constituents, there to show their support. After reading the bill, he described why he felt it was needed. Toward the end of the speech, he touched on the topic of Octavius and his veto. As he recounted the events, Gaius' passion steadily rose and he began to ramble on angrily.

Philocrates, standing behind the rostra, lifted his flute to his lips and played a five-note line. It worked perfectly. Gaius caught himself, then deliberately slowed his delivery to gather his concentration and bring the speech to a proper conclusion. Afterward, when the crowds had cleared, Gaius approached Philocrates.

Philocrates looked at the ground, then up at Gaius. "Did I react too soon, master?"

Gaius wagged his head and wrapped his arm around his slave. "No, not at all, Philocrates. You did just fine. Thank you. This is something we should continue to do."

The next three weeks were set aside for promulgating the bill. Contiones were held in all parts of the city, while proponents and opponents of the bill were given an opportunity to express their opinions in the forum.

Gaius kept me advised of his work throughout his tribuneship, and I kept Cornelia up to date from afar. A hired rider could deliver a letter to Misenum in three days. When I sent Cornelia a description of this latest bill, she responded with a long letter detailing why Gaius should rescind the proposal and not put it up for a vote. She felt that issuing a law so clearly aimed at a single man was beneath Gaius and the tradition of our family. As requested, I passed the letter on to my brother.

Gaius became furious upon reading it. "What is Cornelia trying to do? Her first letter was difficult enough, but now she wants to manage my law making."

I did not argue one way or the other. He came to my house the next day. "Can Cornelia stay here? I'm inviting her to Rome. I want to talk to her, face to face. No more letters or passed on information. And I want you present."

I agreed.

CHAPTER 71

Licinia knew about Cornelia's letters and how they affected Gaius. From the day she had met my brother she had encouraged him to enter into politics. She had followed the topic of land reform from the beginning and felt it was right. But after Cornelia's first letter, she began to have doubts about Gaius' tribuneship, which she kept to herself—until she revealed them to me one afternoon after the arrival of the second letter.

We were in her atrium. The weather had turned mild. There had been rain in the morning, but the sun had come out and the day felt like a harbinger of summer. The boys, Gaius and Publius, now eight and seven, played in the peristyle with wooden swords, while Licinia and I sat on a stone bench beside the pool. Gaius had left the house in the morning to visit the various contiones and promote his bill, so we were alone except for the slaves who were busy in some other part of the house.

"Gaius told me he has invited Cornelia to Rome," said Licinia. "How soon will she be here?"

"In a couple of days. I hope the meeting goes well."

"What do you anticipate? I know that Cornelia has distanced herself from Gaius' political ambitions."

"They've had a disagreement. I think Gaius wants to talk to her rather than exchange letters. Has he mentioned anything to you?"

"No, he's been unusually quiet since her second letter. What do you think? Not just about this second law, but his career in politics?"

"I've tried not to be judgmental, Licinia. He seems to be far better prepared than Tiberius was and has several more bills that he plans to promote."

"Do you worry about—about what could happen?"

I knew immediately what she meant. She had never mentioned it before. "Could Gaius be victimized like his brother? Yes, I do worry about that, and so does Cornelia, but it seems unlikely. I think Rome has made progress since then. Besides, the first law Gaius passed should prevent it."

"But there were laws before, Sempronia. A tribune was deemed untouchable."

"Well, yes, some men felt that they were above the law."

Licinia bowed her head. When she looked up at me, her eyes glistened with forming tears. "I want him to quit," she said haltingly. "When we first married I was surprised how little he cared about politics. I even hoped that would change. But I'm scared now that he's a tribune and fully immersed in it."

"And doing remarkably well."

Licinia shook her head sadly. "So well a faction against Gaius is gaining influence in the Senate. Some of these men still have blood on their hands from nine years ago." She wiped her eyes. "Is there any chance Cornelia could talk him out of what he's doing?"

"And quit the tribunate? No. Even should she try, Gaius would certainly finish what he's started."

"But he's got ten more months," she gasped.

"And six or seven more laws to pass." I took her hand. "I'm frightened too, Licinia. I try not to think about it. Cornelia has made a stand and it troubles Gaius. I just don't want to make things any harder on him than they already are."

"I'm afraid he will lecture her, and it will only make things worse."

"I have thought the same thing. But he asked me to be there when he speaks to her. I think that's a good thing. I think it shows that he's concerned about his own reaction to her."

"Maybe both of you can talk him out of it."

"Have you said anything to Gaius about your fears?"

"Absolutely not. He has enough on his plate already. I keep it all to myself." She looked into my eyes. "And now I've told you."

I embraced her.

"You are a good sister, Sempronia. Both Gaius and I know that. Thank you for listening to his weak wife." Then she sat back. "How is Claudia? Didn't you just see her?"

"Yes, two months ago." The whole experience at the circle arose in my memory. I pushed it aside. "Claudia is having a hard time also. She wants to remarry and is worried it will upset Cornelia."

"I can see how she might think that. Did she tell you this?"

I nodded.

"Has she met a man?"

"No. It's something she's just begun to think about."

The two boys suddenly ran into the atrium, the older chasing the younger. Publius was crying. "Tell Gaius to stop stabbing me."

"He needs to learn to defend himself, Mother," followed Gaius right behind his brother.

Licinia wagged her head like a mother. "You must be careful, Gaius. He's not as big or as strong as you."

"But fighting me will make him better. One always encounters someone bigger and stronger in battle."

"That's no reason to bully Publius. We'd like him to live through his childhood."

"Yeah," said Publius.

"Then how will I get any better if I can't really practice my skills?"

"Find another boy to joust with. I'm sure there's a bigger boy out there somewhere to give you a fair test."

Gaius raised his wooden sword in the air. "I doubt it, Mother. I'll be as good as Father. You watch." Then he dashed off. Publius ran after him.

Licinia looked at me. "Please don't mention our conversation to anyone."

"I won't. Just have faith in Gaius."

CHAPTER 72

Cornelia arrived in Rome three days after I spoke to Licinia. She stayed at my house. Gaius came over the next morning. He embraced Cornelia upon seeing her, but she was stiff and resistant. Gaius pushed my wheelchair into the library and Cornelia followed. After Nadia brought us cups of posca, I gave her some chores to keep her busy while we talked in private. Cornelia sat at the table. Gaius stood in the corner beside Archimedes' terrella. Both were visibly uneasy. Cornelia had led the family since our father's death. The current clash with Gaius marked the first time there had been any real challenge to her authority. But she was getting older and Gaius had become an individual with a powerful presence.

"I'm glad you've come, Mother. I was worried that you might not want to see me at all."

Cornelia met Gaius' gaze. "It wasn't easy for me to come here. We've never disagreed, and it doesn't settle well with me now."

Gaius nodded, then paced across the room. "But we need to talk. Shutting off communication gets us nowhere. Isolated letters feel like ultimatums. We've never had that in our family."

"No, and you're right, Gaius, that's not how we should proceed. Despite my reluctance, I appreciate your inviting me to Rome."

Gaius took a deep breath. "As you know, Mother, I was elected to the tribunate. That was not what you wanted. And you made that clear. I went ahead anyway, but not because I wanted to add pain to your life, but because I felt obligated to fulfill Tiberius' dream. Giving my loyalty to his memory doesn't diminish my loyalty to you. It was simply a decision that I had to make for myself, as a man."

Cornelia went straight to her point. "And it includes revenge?"

"In this case, yes—but the law is also right. It keeps corrupt officials out of government."

"If you must be a politician, Gaius, then please learn to take the high road." Anger spiked behind her words. "It was when your brother began to waver from his highest ideals that he ran into difficulties. And that's what I see in this second bill of yours. You're targeting one man, and it's unbecoming of a Gracchi."

Gaius strode back across the library to where he had stood before. "But what about the first bill? It was aimed specifically at two individuals. One might argue it was more vengeful than my current proposal. Are you going to ask me to repeal it also?"

I had never heard them speak to each other this way. It made me feel small.

"I saw that first law differently," Cornelia answered, fully as firm in her stance as Gaius was in his. "It was a necessary law, far more necessary than this second, and it addressed a crime far more vicious than Orestes' being bought out. Those two consuls executed some thirty men without a trial. That was flagrant disrespect for the rights of citizenship and the meaning of the Republic. The crime was against the people, not specifically against you or our family. And that's why I care so much. Everything you do reflects upon my name and the Gracchi name. We take the high road. That's what the name of Tiberius Gracchus stands for. That's what I stand for."

Gaius stalked back across the room. "But the high road also means standing up for the people. My father and my brother were both tribunes for that reason. My becoming a tribune is fulfillment of my family duty."

"But I don't want you dead for it."

"You're exaggerating the risk. I'm pursuing my fate. It's what I must do. Regardless of what you might think of this one law, can you at least see that? How do we proceed if you can't?"

"Remove the bull's-eye from Octavius' chest. Concede the portion of the law that makes it retroactive," I said, surprised that I was speaking at all. "And in exchange, Mother, allow that what Gaius has said is true. Neither you nor I want him risking his life in the underworld that is Roman politics, and yet our own family tradition, which he seeks to honor, demands that he engage, that he promote change."

Gaius glanced at me.

Cornelia did not miss it. "Are you both conspiring against me?" she snapped.

"No. I'm conspiring to bring you both together. Consider what I asked. Gaius, you too."

"I'm not sure if I can do that," said Gaius, standing beside the bust of his grandfather. "Not at this stage in the process. We're two weeks into the review of the law. The vote is next week. It's going to pass. How could I possibly change it now?"

"And I can't condone Gaius' presence in Roman politics," countered Cornelia. "For all the good he might hope to do, in the end his actions will weaken the Republic. The Senate needs to have its power, Gaius, and I fear you will not be content until you have taken it all away."

It was the most conservative thing I had ever heard her say. It exposed her frustration and restated the optimates' fundamental principle—the people with the longest lineages and the best blood were also, in fact, the best men; their leadership was imperative to the advancement of Rome.

Gaius did not back down. Cornelia's statement angered him. He strode back across the room to the terrella. "I have already written a preliminary schedule for the introduction of several new bills. None of them can be considered vengeful in the slightest. I want to lower the price of wheat for the common citizen. I want to build roads, and I want to build granaries along those roads so the wheat is easily available. I will forgo the confiscation and redistribution of land in the way that Tiberius proposed. Instead I will concentrate on using the public land to build colonies, with the intent of avoiding the legal problems that have plagued the land commission. I can achieve the same or better results without having to take land away from our hallowed senators. It can be done."

"But you can't change your current proposal?"

"Without loss of prestige, Sempronia? No!"

"What if you told the populace that your mother made the request? That might protect your prestige."

"I haven't agreed to anything yet," said Cornelia.

"Think about it, Gaius." I rolled my chair closer to him. "What you fear would be a loss of prestige might result in a gain of respect. By openly crediting the removal of the retroactive portion of your bill to Cornelia, whom everyone admires, you regain the high ground and Mother's support."

Gaius tilted his head, then used his hand to spin the terrella as he puzzled over my proposition.

I turned my chair to face my mother. "Can you agree to this, Mother?" I could see it in her eyes. She had finally been tempted enough by my offer to think about it.

Cornelia pursed her lips, fighting her emotions. "Gaius, if you pull the offending portion of the second law, I will accept that you have chosen a career in politics."

Gaius was not quite sure. After a moment he realized he had to make a concession of some kind. "I'll do it then. Yes, absolutely, I'll do it." He actually laughed. He came over to me and placed his hand on my shoulder. "I'll turn the whole thing into something positive as well as regain my mother."

"In some limited way," she said, giving in as little as possible.

"Good enough." Gaius leaned over and kissed Cornelia on the forehead. She dabbed two tears from her eyes. Despite all appearances, it meant more to her than to Gaius.

Gaius paced across the room twice, then suddenly stopped. "Now it's time to eat some crow," he muttered. "I've got to go out and revise my bill."

CHAPTER 73

Gaius rewrote the bill without the retroactive clause, explaining the change by saying that Cornelia had requested it. The populace responded just as I had predicted. Because of her husband, and because of her son Tiberius, and because of her own actions, Cornelia's reputation for dignity and intelligence was the highest of any woman's in Rome, and rivaled any man's. To deny the need for revenge against a man who had caused so much trouble for her son seemed perfectly in character. The populace praised her with eyes full of tears. The revised bill passed easily.

Two weeks later, Gaius had another bill, his most popular yet. It called for a discounted price on wheat for every Roman citizen. The wheat market was subject to great fluctuation and for the most part depended on foreign dealers. Stabilizing and cutting the price of grain through a government buying program was a sure winner with the People's Assembly.

Gaius introduced his wheat bill by reading it to the Senate. He spoke from the rostra to three hundred senators seated in the comitium. As he read the bill, the group of senators grew agitated and began to talk among themselves. They did not like the idea of state-funded grain. They felt that Gaius was using the bill to make himself more popular and were infuriated.

Gaius anticipated this kind of reaction, and when he saw the senators muttering and whispering as he read, he turned away from the comitium and faced the forum to his left, reading, as it were, to the plebeians who had gathered there, not the senators. No one had ever done this before, but it was a clear demonstration of Gaius' courage, and the people in the forum loved it just as much as the Senate hated it. Some of the senators walked out, but Gaius continued, clearly drawing a line in the sand. He was the people's spokesman, and from that day on, whenever he called the Senate to the comitium to read a bill, he faced the forum and read to his constituency, not his detractors.

I accepted that Gaius was doing what he was meant to do. And he was doing it well. Like his brother, he had become a public hero. But what was I meant to do? This had become a much more complicated question due to my continuing friendship with Laelia. We had gone to the bath once a week since our return from Misenum. I had not conquered my self-consciousness enough to bathe in the nude. Laelia always did. Some days we would return to my house so that Laelia could use the library.

On two of these occasions we had left the library and gone to my bed to slip beneath the sheets. As I had told her in the carriage on the way back from Misenum, I enjoyed being held and physically comforted, but I really wanted nothing more. It was not something sexual for me. It was something deeper, an unanswered loneliness and a need to be touched. She was different and enjoyed masturbating while in bed with me. It was an odd form of intimacy, but I wanted her as a friend.

Several days after Cornelia had returned to her villa in Misenum, Laelia and I took our weekly trip to the bath. After a long soak, I had my bearers carry us back to my house. While we drank cups of watered wine in the library, Laelia came up close to me and whispered in my ear like a kiss, "Let's slip off to your bedroom."

I gave Nadia some chores to keep her and the other slaves busy, then cautiously, with Laelia's assistance, climbed the stairs. We stripped down to just our tunics and slipped into my bed. Laelia always tried to push my limits. On this occasion, once we were beneath the sheets, she allowed her tunic to slip up above her waist and in time had coaxed mine upward also. I lay in the bed wrapped in her arms while she entwined her bare legs with mine. I liked the feel of her skin on mine, and it seemed innocent enough not to resist, but she gradually engaged her hands and I became more and more aroused. I had never allowed her hands between my legs. But as her own excitement grew, she became more aggressive, whispering in my ear, telling me how much she wanted to bring me to climax. I had avoided this in all of our previous encounters, but with my tunic up and the contact of our thighs and stomachs, I became too heated to resist and opened my legs for her. I rarely had orgasms with Aemilianus and did not crave sex the way Laelia did. She seemed to climax whenever she wanted. She massaged me with her fingers until I became sore, but she could not bring me to orgasm. This frustrated her, and without warning, she slid beneath the sheet to use her tongue. It was more than I felt was proper, but I was under her spell and gave in fully. I moaned and whimpered in pleasure, which only drove Laelia on, as though she were determine to melt me into a puddle.

I lost awareness of how loud I had become, and Laelia seemed to relish my ecstasy. Then from outside the room I heard a gasp. Nadia had heard the sounds and come upstairs thinking that something was wrong. She stood in the doorway. "Are you all right, my lady?" she whispered into the shadowy room. When I stiffened, Laelia came out from beneath the covers.

Nadia uttered a muted cry. "I'm sorry, my lady." She quickly turned away and ran down the stairs.

I got out of the bed upset and told Laelia that she must go.

"It was only your housemaid, Sempronia. Why worry?"

"It's not something I want known."

"Are you embarrassed to be with me?"

"No, it's not that. It's just more than I ever imagined. And if people know, it's only more trouble."

"Command your slave to keep to it to herself."

"But I won't be able to look her in the eye."

Laelia used the sheet to wipe her mouth, then climbed from the bed. "Why should it matter? Didn't you like it?"

I lowered my head. "Yes." I remembered what I had seen when we were in Misenum. I had to ask. "Have you done that before?"

"This was the first time," she said slipping her stola over her tunic.

"And I'm the only woman you've known intimately?"

She did not like the question. "Would you be jealous if you weren't?"

"I don't know," I said, though the answer was decidedly *yes*. "Let's go downstairs. You should leave. I need to talk to Nadia."

"Would you do it to me?"

"No."

"Why not?"

"It reminds me of when Aemilianus would force me to use my mouth on him. It's unclean."

"Except when I do it to you?"

"Please, Laelia."

She was already headed down the stairs. I heard her go out the front door and slam it before I got to the stairs. I just stood there and began to cry. What was I doing? I felt so confused I had no idea what I would say to Nadia. I submerged beneath another layer of guilt and said nothing.

CHAPTER 74

Gaius' wheat bill was nearly as popular as Tiberius' land reform bill. After three weeks of discussion, it passed unanimously. Gaius had become another Tiberius, creating a new wave of fear in the senatorial class.

Gaius made a point of being at Mars Field for the first distribution of the discounted wheat. The process began early in the morning with four long lines of plebeians stretched across the exercise field. Toward noon, after the greater part of the populace had been served and the lines were almost gone, Calpurnius Piso, Mucius Scaevola's co-consul the year of Tiberius' death, came to Mars Field. He was a plebeian but also a senator, and very wealthy. He had spoken out vehemently against the grain "giveaway" when Gaius had first presented it to the Senate for review. Because there was no financial restriction for those receiving the grain, Piso, clearly seeking to put Gaius on the spot, wanted his allowance of wheat.

Gaius stood a short distance away when the senator and his slave stepped up to the table where an aedile was weighing out portions of wheat for dispersal. Piso saw Gaius and glared at him. "I do not care for this fancy of yours, Gracchus. As far as I can tell you're dividing up goods that belong to me and giving them to the riffraff of Rome. But if you're determined to waste my money," he said with a grin, "I might as well claim my share."

The insult was not missed by anyone within hearing range. Gaius came up close to Piso. "If you had read the bill in its entirety, Senator, you would have noticed that I added new public revenues to help offset the expenditure. There will be no draw on the treasury to provide for those who need help putting food on their table." He emphasized the last phrase.

"So you may think, Tribune. But when did Rome indulge their citizens with luxuries such as this?" He let a handful of the wheat pass through his fingers and fall on the ground.

"You might do well to spend a few nights in Subura, Senator, and visit a family that isn't as fortunate as yours. There will be no pheasant eggs or imported oysters on the dinner table. Wheat might be all they have."

"Only because they are too lazy to put in a day's work or take responsibility for the infants that spring from their women's loins. This godless giveaway can only inspire a growing class of never-do-wells."

Gaius noted the angry looks of the others who were standing in line. "Be careful, Senator, whom you disparage. While you may worry that I'm undermining initiative, I would argue that assuring our citizens are well fed makes good stock for legionnaires."

When several others close by voiced approval for Gaius' response, Piso ordered his slave to take the bag of wheat, then abruptly turned and walked away to a shower of crude suggestions for what he should do with his allowance.

CHAPTER 75

While my brother fed the poor, I wrestled with sexual demons. Not only had Nadia seen something I hoped to keep secret, but my friendship with Laelia had also come into doubt. She had seduced me—for better or worse. Then she had lied to me, and I had not immediately confronted her. She had known other women, at least one, Elephantis. She was not the novice she claimed to be, and the whole thing left me feeling used.

For the Roman male, sex with a man was not considered a strike against his masculinity as long as he maintained the position of dominance. Only the dominated was considered to be weak and effeminate. Domination defined virility and was fulfilled through the marriage contract of manus.

Little was ever said about a woman with another woman, though I had heard of men using it as a reason to divorce their wives. Intimacy between women surely had parallels to that of men with men. There was often a dominator and a dominated. Laelia seemed to seek that dominant role with me. Despite my need to be touched and held, I had no desire to be dominated. Yes, Laelia was a remarkably strong and alluring personality. She was brilliant and exciting and as beautiful as any woman I knew. But I had enough of dominance with Aemilianus. If killing him had taught me anything about myself, I knew I wanted something more than to be manipulated by the people close to me. With Laelia I felt that could only be achieved through friendship, not a clandestine physical relationship that she controlled. If Laelia had not already cast me aside, I knew I would have to confront her on this if I wanted to know her at all.

When Laelia did not come by on our usual day to go to the bath, I decided to go alone, something that was very difficult for me. Without a friend to assist me, I brought Nadia. As she helped me limp across the steamy pool area, I noticed that Laelia was in the middle pool—not hot, not cold. I continued on to the hot pool, which provided so much relief for me. I struggled to a sitting position on the side of the pool, then slid in. I did what I always did at the bath. I leaned back against the side, and with legs extended, let my body float in the water. I closed my eyes and tried to forget that Laelia was forty feet away in the other pool.

Every now and then, however, I could not resist a glance at Laelia. On one occasion she looked up. Neither of us acknowledged the other except by the steadying of our eyes. She climbed from the pool and sauntered across to where I was. Many of the women watched her because of her complete nudity. Some of the women stripped down to breast wraps and a loincloth, but most wore a light gown like I did, which the water made all but transparent. Laelia sat down on the edge of the pool with her legs in the water. Even as a regular at the bath, she knew she created a sensation. Everyone knew that she was a consul's daughter-in-law, and that she was as brilliant as she was lovely in the nude. I am sure she made everyone uncomfortable with her lack of modesty, but I would bet they all wished they were confident enough to do the same.

Although Laelia always attracted attention in the bathing area, no one dared to stare at us. But what could be more interesting than the most daring woman in Rome sitting beside the wallflower with the twisted ankle?

"I was hoping to see you today," I said, deciding that part of my plan would be taking the initiative in the conversation.

"Yes, I guess I didn't come by your house today."

"I wondered about that." I looked out across the pool, then to her. "I thought there might be something we needed to talk about."

She slid into the water next to me. "You mean since I last saw you." She extended her legs the way I had so that our heads were side by side resting against the pool apron.

"I don't want to lose you as a friend, Laelia, and I'm worried about that."

"Do you think that I might have shown you something nice?"

"Well—yes." This was not where I wanted to go.

She smiled contentedly and closed her eyes.

I had no intention of confronting her at the pool. I just wanted her to know I needed to talk to her, perhaps later, in private. I closed my eyes and wondered how many of the women might be furtively watching us.

Then I felt Laelia's hand on my hip beneath the water. My eyes popped open. Her eyes were closed. I did not want to react too suddenly and cause a scene. I took a breath and tried to relax, but her hand slid from my hip to a full caress of the right cheek of my rear. When her forefinger edged down lower, I stood up and lifted myself onto the side of the pool. Laelia did not even open her eyes. I was furious. I had let it happen. I had allowed myself to be manipulated when I had wanted to talk to her specifically about that issue.

Laelia spoke to me without opening her eyes. "We'll find a time to talk." She said it like nothing had happened.

"Yes, come by one day," I said, biting onto my anger.

Then, as the center of attention for about twenty women, I struggled to my feet, and Nadia helped me cross the bath area to my dry clothes.

CHAPTER 76

Gaius was proving to be an even more dynamic politician than Tiberius. Tiberius went at it without a clear understanding of his impact or the resistance he would face. Gaius went at it entirely prepared and fueled by the passion of a barely submerged anger. By the time the wheat bill had passed, he had two more bills lined up to push through the People's Assembly. He announced them both on the same day by reading them to the Senate from the comitium rostra while facing the crowd assembled in the forum.

The first included three provisions regarding the military: 1) All soldier's clothing and equipment would be provided by the state, instead of being supplied by the soldier himself, 2) the lower age limit for service, seventeen, was to be strictly enforced, and 3) the tribunes for the first four legions were to be elected by the People's Assembly instead of chosen by the current consuls—this was an attempt to minimize the abuse of enlisted men by officers known for their excessive severity. All three provisions were positives for the common man. Calpurnius Piso criticized the added cost to the state. Another senator blasted Gaius for seeking to weaken discipline in the army, and the growing number of senators worried about Gaius' seeming thirst for power grumbled that it was a needless bill designed to increase his popularity.

The second bill was really an addendum to the wheat bill. It called for building long-term grain storage in the region around Rome as a way to ensure that the government could weather fluctuations in the price of wheat while providing grain to citizens at essentially half the market price. Again the resistance came from Piso. "Who will pay for these buildings?" he shouted at Gaius.

Gaius' answer was simple and straightforward. "The savings the government will make by buying in quantity will more than make up for any losses incurred by building storage facilities."

Both laws were passed unanimously by the People's Assembly, and despite senatorial resistance, caused little political stir other than increased fear of Gaius' political acumen and his growing ability to control the direction of the state through the People's Assembly.

Following the vote, Gaius had a modest celebratory dinner at his home. I was invited as were his friend from the army Laetorius Antonius and his wife, Fulvia, and his friend since childhood Pomponius Atticus and his wife, Marcia. We ate in the triclinium. Two oil lamps provided light. The women sat in chairs, and the men lounged on the couches. Licinia's Sicilian cook Catalda filled the table with a small feast—roast lamb, blood pudding, boiled cabbage, three types of cheese, and two loaves of bread—one rye, one whole wheat. Gaius opened a cask of Falerian red for the occasion; an amphora sat at each end of the table. The men drank with vigor; Marcia, Fulvia, and Licinia sipped from a single cup all night. I had two.

Pomponius, a short man with cropped blonde hair, raised his glass to Gaius. "To the success of your next bill!"

Licinia half-heartedly lifted her cup. Laetorius, known for his sense of humor, laughed as he raised his. "What else do you have in mind, Gaius? I know you won't rest with the two passed today."

Pomponius joined in the laughter. Gaius took a sip from his cup and then became serious. "I have four more bills planned for the remainder of my term. I'm still working out the order I will present them, but if I can trust that none of what I say goes beyond this room, I would be interested in your response."

"I think you can trust us," said Laetorius with a chuckle before taking a sip from his cup. The others agreed, but I noticed Licinia lower her eyes. She accepted what her husband did, but as she had confessed to me, Gaius' involvement in politics worried her.

"I want to build some new roads. Rome is verging on becoming all of Italy. Easier travel will benefit everyone."

"And bring more of our constituents to the elections," added Pomponius.

"As well as enabling the building of my granaries and the distribution of wheat," said Gaius. "Another bill will address the method of granting provinces to the consuls."

"How's that?" I asked.

"Right now," said Gaius, "the consuls are chosen, and then they pick their province of operation based on the potential for plunder and added wealth. I will propose that the provinces be determined by the Senate prior to the election so that each consul is elected for a specific province and duty. This puts the business of Rome ahead of the personal desires of the consuls."

"I like it," piped in Laetorius.

"But I doubt ambitious senators will," said Pomponius.

"Of course they won't, but it will mean they'll be doing the work of the state rather than simply going out and enriching themselves."

Pomponius' wife, a woman I had never met before, followed. "What else, Gaius?"

"I want to readdress land reform. It's stagnated since Aemilianus put adjudication in the hands of the Senate."

Just hearing my husband's name, though dead five years now, made me cringe. And for the ten thousandth time I wondered about the unanswered mystery—who had left the note beneath my bed?

"I will propose six new colonies to avoid the legal clutter of redistribution that has bogged down the commission."

Everyone agreed this was a better way to go and toasted the idea.

"Lastly, and most importantly," Gaius grinned, "I want to address an issue my brother hoped to confront but never got the chance to. I want to change the makeup of the courts. Right now the courts are adjudicated by senators before a jury of senators. I want half the jurors to be equestrians." The equestrians were the class just below the senatorial class, wealthy businessmen who did not pursue political careers.

All of us knew this was a completely sensible step in the direction Gaius was taking Rome, but it was also a direct abridgement of the Senate's powers. It would get a lot of resistance. Pomponius nodded at Gaius. "Brilliant, my friend. Daring, but brilliant."

Laetorius lifted his cup to Gaius. "And it would bring the equestrians into our camp."

"No mention of this. Any of it. To anyone." Gaius made eye contact with everyone around the table but Licinia, whose head was bowed. "It will be one step at a time. Pomponius and Laetorius, you'll both be needed. Expect a busy summer and fall."

After the meal Licinia led the other women out to the peristyle. It was lit with torches on a pleasant summer evening. A light breeze blew in from the south. We all wore our pallas wrapped around our shoulders with our heads left bare. I propelled my wheelchair with my hands as Licinia, Fulvia, and Marcia, the only woman wearing face paint, strolled through the moon shadows cast by the colonnade. Without anyone saying a word, we all knew that Licinia was struggling.

Fulvia was the first to comment. She was a large, forceful woman with long blonde hair, plaited and wound around her head, held in place by a blue filet to match her eyes. "It's no time to be weak, Licinia. Your husband has become the most important man in Rome. We all know it. The gods have blessed him—and you. You have no choice. As a good Roman wife you must bear the responsibility of power with him."

It was what I thought also. But Gaius was my brother and I had already given in to the idea of our family's fate.

We heard the men raise their voices then burst into laughter. Tears began to run down Licinia's cheeks. "I know that," she blubbered, "but I keep imagining him dead and me alone with the two children."

Marcia came from a family with a long legacy of losses on the battlefield. "Widows with children are a tradition in Rome. My mother, your mother."

"My sister-in-law," muttered Licinia. She looked at me, then pulled her palla up over her head, and walked back to the house.

CHAPTER 77

I wrote Cornelia once a week describing Gaius' work. Cornelia commented little in her return letters. She had retreated from her initial position, but she was as frightened as Licinia for her son's life. I imagined that she was holding her breath waiting for the end of Gaius' year as tribune. Maybe I was too.

A week after the dinner at Gaius' house, I saw Laelia at the bath. She asked me if she could come to my house and use the library.

"Certainly. Perhaps we could find some time to talk."

Laelia arrived in her litter not long after I had returned from the bath. Nadia met her at the door. Laelia held a wax pad and a cloth sack and swept past my housemaid, headed straight to the atrium where I was sitting in my wheelchair. Nadia followed behind watching Laelia closely.

Laelia leaned over to embrace me and whispered in my ear. "Could we go into the library for some privacy? I have some exciting news that I don't want getting out quite yet."

"Nadia," I said, "would you get us something to drink? We'll be in the library."

Laelia pushed me into the library, peeked out into the atrium to make sure no other slaves were nearby, then faced me. "I'm going to file for a divorce from Quintus."

"How can you do that? Manus doesn't allow it." Like all of the upper-class women in Rome, her marriage had been arranged through manus, which gave the wife little or no rights, and expressly no avenue for seeking a divorce.

"That's why I wanted to use your library. It has several scrolls on Roman law. I'm looking for any angle I can get—and I can't exactly ask my father-in-law for help. Once I've prepared a case, I will act as my own advocate and take my husband to court." She came close to me and lowered her voice. "It's a safer bet than murder."

264

I had no answer for that, and she turned away from me to thumb through the shelves of scrolls. She looked over her shoulder. "I don't even know what I'm looking for. But there's got to be something."

Nadia came into the room with a tray containing two cups of posca. She placed the cups on the table, and with one dark look at Laelia, whose back was to her, quickly left the room.

Laelia never touched her posca. I sipped mine as she worked her way through one scroll after another.

"On what grounds will you base your request for divorce?"

"Anything I can find precedent for. Physical abuse is a possibility, or I could claim that I'm not attracted to men."

"Is that how you feel?"

"Not really." She looked at me with a sly grin. "I enjoy men and women, but I could lie."

"You wouldn't mention me would you?"

"Only if necessary."

"Please don't, Laelia. It could lead back to Aemilianus," I whispered.

Laelia did not respond. She just kept opening one scroll after another, checking the contents, and moving on.

"This touches on something I need to talk to you about, Laelia. Do you mind?"

"Go ahead," she said over her shoulder. "I'm listening."

I wanted her to sit down and face me, but rather than ask her to do that, I spoke to her back. "You lied to me."

She continued to the next niche of scrolls without even a glance over her shoulder. "Oh, and when was that?"

"You've known other women."

She turned to me as though surprised. "Does that matter?"

"You told me otherwise."

"I do what I want, Sempronia. And now I want to be divorced."

"Then you *have* been with other women?"

I finally had her attention. She came over to me and knelt in front of my wheelchair. "Have you?" She placed her hand on my thigh.

"No, of course, not. I—I—I..."

"I wouldn't mind." She stroked my thigh and looked into my eyes. "Too much."

"But I do. So can you please answer my question?"

"Yes," she hissed, then leaned into me and kissed me on the mouth.

I pulled back from her. "And you've done the same things?"

"More than that," she whispered, then stood up to retrieve the cloth bag she had come into the house with. "But here's something I haven't used with anyone—*yet*." Laelia was doing it again, using her aggressive nature to dominate the situation. She opened the bag and withdrew a phallus sculpted in polished oak. It was attached to a belt so that it could be worn.

The thing horrified me. I quickly put my hands on the wheels of my chair and propelled myself out of the library.

Laelia remained in the library while I hid in the peristyle. After Nadia informed me that Laelia had left, I retired to my bedroom to cry. Laelia was different than I was. The sex did not matter to me. I just wanted to be held. And if it was by a woman, I wanted it kept private. Because, whether it was a sign of weakness or not, I did care how I was perceived and how I was talked about.

CHAPTER 78

While I nursed my wounds, uncertain if I wanted to see Laelia ever again, Gaius proceeded with the work he had planned. He began with his least controversial proposal, a bill to build several long roads across the Italian interior. His enemies in the Senate immediately labeled it as a way for Gaius to increase the voter turnout in Rome. It did have that potential, but it also enabled business operations to expand, particularly the transport of heavy products like timber and grain. And it also looked forward to Rome's future. It seemed inevitable that all of Italy would one day be a unified Roman state. Working roads would be necessary for everything from troop movements to travel plans for the individual.

Gaius did more than propose and pass the bill. He went out into the countryside with a work crew and supervised the construction of several hundred miles of straight, level stone roads. His experience in the military building bridges and transporting huge stores of supplies and men was directly applicable. When the road encountered a valley or a deep watercourse, Gaius would either fill the valley or bridge the water in order to keep the road straight and easily navigable. He placed mile-markers along the road and erected stone pillars noting the distances to various destinations. Smaller, flat-topped stones were placed periodically on both sides of the thoroughfares for travelers to sit on or to mount a horse from without the assistance of a groom. The quality and efficiency of his work only added to the Gaius' appeal to the populace.

While he did this work, he returned to Rome for a few days to introduce his next bill, a law that would require naming the consular provinces prior to electing the consuls who would serve there. The bill was aimed at the profligate use of the consular position. Not all, but many of the consuls of recent years had leveraged the position to increase their individual wealth, not govern. It was a very sensible law from any perspective but that of a senator—especially one who intended to add consul to his résumé. "Who is this demagogue?" shouted Calpurnius Piso from the floor of the Senate. "Will we even need a Senate when this man is through?"

After making his initial presentation to the Senate, Gaius left town to continue his work on the roads. Pomponius and Laetorius would supervise the contiones and educate the populace. Gaius had become very confident. The Assembly had yet to turn down any of his proposals. Nearly every one had been carried unanimously. He did not even need to be in Rome to assure their passage. Gaius did the necessary paperwork and left the rest to the other tribunes and his clients.

Gaius did, however, make it a point on this occasion to be in Rome the day of the vote so he could speak to the People's Assembly. "Too many states throughout history have come to ruin through the greed and shortsightedness of their leaders," he announced in his loud, powerful voice to some thirty thousand plebeians. "And that is exactly what I'm seeing in Rome. A recently elected consul chooses his province not because of necessary foreign policy, but because this king or that king told him of an opportunity to enrich himself there—either through bribes or illegal transactions.

"When my post took me to a foreign province, I comported myself in a way I judged to be to the advantage of all Romans, not to enable my own interests. I kept no extravagant table. I didn't accepted gifts from those who might try to sway my opinion. If ever a prostitute or somebody's pretty serving boy was solicited on my behalf, I told them to go away. I resisted every temptation and stuck to my duties. And that is how all Roman magistrates should conduct themselves. But that's not what I've seen.

"Beware of the self-seekers," he shouted gaining passion with every word. "If you use your intelligence and your common sense, you will realized there is not one politician who climbs onto this tribunal who doesn't have an ulterior motive. All of us who address you are looking for something. No one stands here without expecting some personal gain. Even that so-called honorable man seeking a consulship—in the province of his choice—is to be doubted.

"As for myself, like these other men, I'm not here for nothing. But what I seek from you is not money but your good esteem and honor. Those who seek to persuade you to reject this bill are not after honor, but money from King Nicomedes or some such potentate." This was a reference to a recent scandal in Asia. "Those who seek to persuade you to reject this bill are not after your good esteem, but a rich reward to put in their pockets. You might even believe that these men are above such things. But in truth, they are no more than agents for King Nicomedes or King Mithridates." Gaius began to stalk back and forth on the tribunal, waving his hands and tugging at his toga theatrically. "When they leave for foreign lands, they are paid to further the interests of the local ruler, not Rome's. Money, not honor, moves these men. Money, not esteem, is what these men seek."

Somewhere behind the tribunal a gentle flute played. Gaius lifted his head on hearing it, then took a moment to gather himself. He took a great breath and lowered his voice and his intensity.

"There is a story of a Greek dramatist who bragged that he had been paid the fantastic sum of one golden talent for a play that he had written, but Demades, the finest public speaker in all of Greece at the time, replied, 'So you think it's wonderful that your words have earned you a talent? I have been paid ten talents by a king to keep my mouth shut.' And that's just how it is now, fellow Romans," stated Gaius. "If I wanted money, there are scores of men in Rome who would pay me to be quiet—to keep all of this hidden away." He extended his arms as a gesture of openness, then grinned. "You can see how much I love money by how much I have to say."

As always Gaius spoke with both common sense and the power of his commitment. The people loved it. And so did he. His work became, as it had been for Tiberius, all encompassing. It sucked him in. As far as I could tell, he was born for it, far surpassing his brother in oratorical power and administrative facility. And everyone saw it, including the quivering optimates. The bill passed that afternoon.

I went to Misenum shortly after the vote. I wanted to give Cornelia more than a letter describing what Gaius had achieved. I wanted to impress her that she must have faith in Gaius and that what he was doing was strengthening Rome. I had also been badly hurt by Laelia, and I needed to talk to Cornelia about that. I felt as though I had been taken advantage of and that I had been weak. And worst of all, I was afraid of losing my friendship with Laelia. That was how enchanting she was. Her sexual games were beyond me. But her beauty was disarming and her courage admirable. I wanted to see her take on the institution of manus. I wanted to give her use of my library. But mostly, I wanted her as a friend, not a sexual partner. And with Laelia I was not sure if that were possible.

I arrived at Cornelia's villa three days after she received the letter saying I was on my way. "I was pleased to learn that you were coming," she said upon embracing me. My chair was taken off its rack on the back of the carriage, and Cornelia pushed me into the house and through the expansive atrium to her garden where it was secluded and private.

We both knew that I was there to talk. She had become my most trusted friend and I hers. She sat on a bench that faced the bay. She loved to look out at the sea. She was approaching seventy years old. It showed in her face in the sunlight. She was aging, still clear of mind, but frail of body. A staunch populist all of her life, she had grown conservative in the years since Tiberius' death. She fretted that Gaius was upsetting the natural order of things and that he would fall victim to the same forces that had taken his brother.

"You have to see what's he done, Mother. I understand the position he's put himself in could be dangerous. It shouldn't be that way, but we know that it is. Still, all considered, Gaius is fulfilling himself with what is truly remarkable work." I recounted the numerous bills I had already detailed in my letters. "He was born for this work. That's all I can say, and there has never been another Roman like him. Your fear of the forces against him is not equal to what he brings to the people."

"But you have also said that he's being swept away by it, Sempronia. We have seen that before. Politics can become a fever, especially for a young man who feels as strong a sense of duty as Gaius does." She shook her head. "For him to have done so much work in so short a time is clear evidence that the fever is already upon him. I have read your letters. His bills are all issues I would champion were they separate from my personal feelings. I thank the gods that his term is nearly up. I recall thinking that Carbo's bill to open the tribuneship to multiple terms was a good idea. Now I am thankful it failed."

"I would disagree with that, Cornelia. Truly. I see Gaius as a visionary. He sees a unified Italy in Rome's future, and if he got the chance, he would make it happen."

Cornelia looked into my face for an extended moment, measuring my words. "I would rather have your strong conviction than my fears, Sempronia. Yes, I dwell on his achievements when you write about them—and my pride swells. But he is my last remaining jewel." She looked down at her hands, one on top of the other in her lap. "I will be glad when his term is done. That's all I can say. How is Licinia?"

"She struggles with the pressure. Like you, she's afraid of losing Gaius. But she says nothing, not a single complaint."

"As is her duty."

"And she knows that, but maybe a letter from you would help."

"And what would I say? That I feel the same way."

"No, remind her of her duty and that in many ways you are in the same position. Say whatever you can to give her support. She needs reassurance from someone other than me. Invite her to come here when Gaius is away from Rome."

Cornelia nodded, then stared out at the bay as though thinking about my suggestion. Neither of us said anything for a long time.

"Laelia is planning to challenge manus," I said suddenly. "She's going to seek a divorce."

"That's brave of her, but she's asking for trouble. I'll be interested to hear what comes of it. What's her reason for requesting the divorce?"

"She has no specific complaint except she can't stand living with Quintus. She just wants to be rid of him. She's been scouring Aemilianus' library looking for any precedent she might use."

"Who will get the children?"

"She hasn't mentioned it."

"Possession of the children. That figures in anything that happens. They are considered the father's property."

"She's a different woman, Cornelia. I'm not sure how much she cares."

Cornelia turned to face me. "What do you mean?"

"She's very promiscuous."

"After the circle with Elephantis, I guess I shouldn't be surprised."

"She's made advances at me."

"At you? I don't understand."

"When we were here for the circle, she came to my bedroom in the middle of the night."

"What did you do?"

"I let her into my bed."

Cornelia stiffened.

"She held me and I needed it."

Cornelia stood up and walked off to the edge of the garden.

"Part of the reason I'm here was to tell this. I haven't felt good about what happened."

Cornelia was clearly unsettled by my admission.

"It happened in a fit of loneliness. And happened again when we returned to Rome. But it's left me confused about who I am, and I needed someone to talk to."

Cornelia allowed a little sigh, then came over to me and knelt before my wheelchair. "I have known women who became intimate with other women, Sempronia. With husbands often gone long periods of time, wives can want other men or, perhaps feeling it's not so great a transgression, seek comfort with another woman. It's something I have struggled with myself. Not seeking another women, but accepting this practice among women of high birth. I made some progress with this during Elephantis' visit, but I still don't think it's proper. Laelia is a lovely woman, and her freedom was apparent the day Elephantis asked us to undress in the bath. I imagine Laelia can be quite alluring if she wants to be."

I bowed my head.

"Is this related to her wanting a divorce?"

"I don't think so. She has spoken to me about the cult of Bacchus. She calls herself a hedonist and favors neither men nor women."

"And will you see her again?"

"Intimately, no. But I want to keep her as a friend. I like her courage and have given her use of the library for her research."

Cornelia stood, then bent over to embrace me. "My poor girl. I'm sorry life has been so hard for you."

While still in her arms, I whispered. "And she knows about Aemilianus."

Cornelia stood back. "Everything?"

"Just my part. It came out in a moment of weakness—but she understood and has promised to secrecy."

"With every additional person who knows, the likelihood of it getting out increases many fold. Even with what?—nearly five years passed. Be wary, Sempronia. Please."

"I never told you. I got an anonymous note from whoever strangled him."

"When?"

"Right after Polybius confronted us."

"What did it say? Was it a threat?'

"No. Not exactly. It requested a favor."

"Like what? Money?"

"It didn't say. It's been an awfully long time—years—and I haven't heard anything since. That's the only reason I'm telling you now. I think it's over."

"Let's hope so. Whoever it was would want money, I'm sure.

I shook my head sadly. "Yes, probably. I'm just glad there's been no follow-up."

Cornelia sighed. "Now I must worry about Gaius and you. What's a mother to do?"

"Let her children do what they must."

CHAPTER 79

My conversation with Cornelia about Laelia relieved some of my guilt. Cornelia, who had a very conservative and upright approach to her personal bearing, could have responded quite differently. The process of getting older had pushed her political views to the center, but her personal views had softened. Tiberius' death, it seemed, had made her more tolerant of the choices of others.

The next morning Claudia presented me with the dress she had been weaving. "It's all done, except for the final fitting," she said, holding it up for me.

"It's beautiful, Claudia. I've never seen anything like it." She had created an intricate design of zigzagging horizontal stripes of purple, yellow, and green. The cotton dress was considerably lighter than any of my wool dresses and perfect for the summer.

As she said, it was a tube dress, and we retired to the weaving room so that I could take off my stola and try it on. It was mostly shapeless, as most women's dresses are. Sashes and brooches are invariably part of all women's attires. Claudia fussed and fidgeted with it, pulling it up to my armpits, where I held it as she pinned on the purple straps that went over my shoulders to hold it up.

"I spoke to Cornelia about seeking a husband," she said as she moved around me, making sure it fit just right.

"What did she say?"

"It was clear she wasn't pleased. She might have felt it was an insult to Tiberius, but she didn't say that. She told me it was my decision and that she understood."

Cornelia must have felt she was giving in, but I saw it as fundamental growth in a woman who had devoted her life to understanding the complexities of life, the world, and her children. "Nothing more?"

Claudia stood back and looked at me with a bone pin pinched between her lips. "Turn around," she said through clenched teeth. "Oh my, it looks great on you, Sempronia. It really does."

"And it's so light and comfortable." I stroked the front of the dress smoothing it out on my torso. "But what else did she say?"

Claudia removed the pin from her mouth to smile. "She said she would miss me and the children, but that perhaps a father would be good for Tiberius."

"No criticism at all?"

She shook her head. "She told me you had mentioned it to her. Giving her some time to think about it before I confronted her surely had a lot to do with her response. Thank you." She came up close and embraced me.

"Well, thank you, Claudia, for this lovely dress," I said as she released me. "Let's find a mirror. I want to see how it looks on me."

"You'll have plenty of time for admiring yourself later. Slip it off. I have to sew those bands on. Then you can show it to Cornelia. She knows how much time I've put into it and will be just as anxious to see it on you as you are."

When I left Misenum, Claudia and her two children traveled with me. They would move into her father's vacant villa. Cornelia would certainly miss Claudia's company and tutoring the two children, but for Claudia the prospect of finding a new husband was considerably greater in Rome. During the trip back Claudia continually praised Cornelia for her open mind and her care and support when things had been so awful after Tiberius' murder. All I could say was that my feelings were the same.

CHAPTER 80

Back in Rome, Gaius was preparing what would be his last two bills of his term as tribune. The first of these was a revision—or, as one might say, a complete rewriting—of Tiberius' land reform bill. It included two key provisions. One gave the commission full authority to administer the redistribution of land in allied regions, essentially reversing Aemilianus' intervention five years earlier. The other changed the focus of land reform from the distribution of individual plots to the creation of colonies. This was considerably less controversial than Tiberius' plan and served much the same purpose—providing farmland to landless Roman citizens.

The Senate's response was predictable. There were no real objections. They even welcomed relief from the duty of resolving the suits filed against the land commission. But they were afraid of Gaius and felt that every accomplishment, every bill he passed, only made him that much stronger. A core of ultra-aristocratic senators constantly grumbled about the danger of a second ambitious Gracchi trying to strip power from the Senate. The bill passed unanimously in the People's Assembly.

The second bill was Gaius' most ambitious and most unexpected. It called for integrating members of the equestrian class, Rome's upper middle class, into the Roman courts. As Gaius had said at the dinner party following the passage of his granary bill, the courts were entirely controlled and populated by senators—judge and jury. Meaning senators were often called on to pass judgment on other senators, their friends and peers—with predictable results. Gaius sought to make the reservoir of possible jurors a mix of the senatorial class and the equestrian class. This accomplished two things: A senator accused of a crime would not be judged by an entirely incestuous jury, and it added a measure of power to the equestrian class, which would potentially bring a new faction of Romans into Gaius' camp.

One of Tiberius' mistakes during his tribuneship was disregarding the opinions of the other tribunes. When Tiberius attempted to run for a second tribuneship, eight of the ten tribunes were against him. This played no small part in his downfall. Well aware of this shortsightedness, Gaius deliberately engaged the other tribunes in all of his work. In some cases their names were put on bills that he wrote. They would argue for the bill and take the lead role in the three weeks of contiones. With jury reform, however, Gaius did all the work himself.

He introduced the law in the traditional manner by reading it to the Senate from the rostra above the comitium. As had become his custom, however, he faced the forum as he read, not the senators. The Senate received the bill with greater indignity than they had for either his grain bill or his bill to reform the selection of consular provinces.

Aemilius Lepidus, a consul two years earlier, stood up in the middle of Gaius' speech and shouted, "What? First the tribune wants to run Rome through the People's Assembly; now he plans to place the equites in a position to judge the senators. This is topsy-turvy government at its worst! The man is set on destroying a system that has worked smoothly for four hundred years."

Gaius responded with his usual fire. "No, Senator, it has worked for four hundred years, but hardly smoothly or equitably. What we've seen recently demonstrates that the Senate cannot fairly judge its own kind. Aurelius Cotta, Gaius Livius Salinator, and Manius Aquilius, all known to have taken bribes in foreign provinces, were acquitted by senatorial juries despite reports sent from their provinces that verified their abysmal conduct. It's time for a change."

No one had forgotten these men. The senators knew Gaius' comments were true and had no way to respond to his accusations. Whether right or not, they still wanted nothing to do with equestrian juries. They advised him not to put the bill up for a vote.

Of course, Gaius ignored the Senate's advice. He was trying to do much more than bring social diversity to the court system—he was completely overhauling it. His bill identified the magistrate who would preside over each court, included definitions for each criminal offense, named who was liable in these offenses, defined the penalties and punishments, established a method for a citizen to bring about a charge against a magistrate or another citizen, arranged for representatives to assist the plaintiff, and detailed the qualifications for a jury member and how they would be selected from a pool of four hundred and fifty potential jurors—of which three hundred were equites and one hundred and fifty were senators. Gaius also established guidelines for protecting witnesses, provisions if the man charged died before the trial, and an oath that all judges and jurors had to take prior to a trial.

All of this went back to Gaius' first major public speech when he defended his leaving Sardinia by attacking the excesses of Roman magistrates in foreign provinces. Although an increasingly frightening man to those who milked military expansion for their own enrichment, Gaius was making a serious attempt at bringing equitable justice to all. It was a noble and absolutely necessary part of the evolution of the Roman state. My brother had become more than I could imagine. If Tiberius were watching from the invisible heavens, he would have been impressed with his younger brother. I wrote as much in a letter to Cornelia.

CHAPTER 81

At a time when most of Gaius' bills passed unanimously or nearly so, the bill to reform the judicial system passed by the narrowest of margins. Thirty-two tribes had voted before it had the necessary majority of eighteen. It was clearly a bill written to gain support from the equestrians, and offered little to the plebeians except, hopefully, less corruption in the courts. Two days later Gaius invited his closest advisors to his home to celebrate the passage of the law and the conclusion of his term as tribune. I attended. Fulvius Flaccus and Papirius Carbo came with their wives, as did Laetorius and Pomponius. A supportive senator, Gaius Fannius, someone I had never met, came alone. Licinia was the hostess and Catalda put out a magnificent spread. A plump baked tuna stuffed with bread pudding, sitting in a bed of steamed oysters, occupied the center of the table. A bowl of mulberries sat at one end of the table, a cutting board with bread and cheese at the other. Wine from Apulia added to the festive evening.

Licinia, who had maintained her poise throughout Gaius' tribuneship, helped me with my wheelchair when I arrived. She seemed relieved.

"I thought this day would never come," she whispered as she pushed my chair toward the triclinium. "I have no idea what Gaius plans to do now that his term is over, but nothing could be as stressful as the position of tribune."

"He hasn't said a word to me. I imagine he'll remain on the land commission and somehow enter into the planning of the colonies he's proposed."

Licinia nodded. "I hope that's all. Obstacles still exist for the commission, but they are not direct confrontations with the Senate, and he won't be speaking so often in public. It's his popularity that creates all the jealousy and acrimony."

"I don't know this man Fannius, Licinia. Do you know anything about him?"

"According to Gaius he's running for consul in the next election."

I made a face. "Really? Prepare yourself. We might have more politics than celebrating tonight."

Licinia groaned as she pushed me into the triclinium where everyone else was already seated.

The dinner conversation did not get deep into politics. There were several toasts to the passage of the bill and Gaius' year as tribune. Then Gaius introduced Fannius to Licinia and the other women, describing him as a wealthy equestrian who had been maneuvering for the last three years for an opportunity to run for a consulship. The elections were a month away and Fannius had put his name into the mix.

Gaius called for his sons to make an appearance at the table. They were tall and smart, now nine and eight years old. When Marcia, Fulvius' wife, asked young Gaius if he wanted to be in politics, he frowned. "My life is meant for war." Licinia then shooed them out of the room with Catalda.

After the meal the men moved into the library with two amphorae of wine. The women chatted in the atrium. This had been Cornelia's home. She had never really let go of her sense of privilege and had decorated the villa in an understated sumptuousness. The atrium was large for a residence within the city limits and contained many important pieces of Greek art. It was a fall evening, so juniper burned in four braziers and torches on bronze stanchions provided light.

Catalda and another slave brought in a tray of sweets for the six women—Licinia, Pomponius' wife Marcia, Laetorius' wife Fulvia, Fulvius' wife Lavinia, Carbo's wife Messalina, and myself. Messalina had not seen my chair before and that was where our conversation started. Fulvia's perfume was next, then everyone's children. I eased to the edge of the group and eavesdropped on the men whose voices had grown serious and had attracted my attention.

They had deliberately steered away from politics at the table, but that was why they were really there—to plot a strategy for the upcoming election. Fannius came because of Gaius' influence on the plebeian vote, and of late, the equestrian vote. The People's Assembly, where Gaius had his largest constituency, was restricted to plebeians. The Century Assembly, however, which voted for the consuls, was entirely made up of soldiers and was a mix of all classes, meaning Gaius had influence there also. Fannius felt Gaius' backing was essential to winning a consulship.

"So, Gaius," I heard him say, "I have made my needs very clear. But I don't know what you want. What ambitions drive you now that your tribuneship is over? How could I return your favor should I get elected?"

Fulvius Flaccus, two years removed from his consulship, had just celebrated a triumph for defending the city of Massilia from the Salluvii, a mix of Gaulish and Ligurian barbarians from between the Rhone River and the Alps. Fulvius, who hoped to ride that success to a tribuneship, something rare for an ex-consul, answered for Gaius. "He wants a second tribuneship."

My heart rose in my throat. I immediately thought of Cornelia and Licinia.

"But he hasn't campaigned," said Fannius, clearly as surprised as I was.

"And I'm not going to," said Gaius. "It would create an undercurrent in some parts of Rome that I would like to avoid."

Fulvius filled in the details. "Carbo's bill to allow consecutive terms for a tribune failed six years ago, but there is a way for a tribune to serve consecutive terms that was never mentioned when Tiberius tried. The man can't openly run for the position, but if his name is listed as a write-in on a majority of the ballots on the first roll call, and at the same time less than ten of the registered candidates receive the necessary eighteen tribal votes, the write-in becomes a legal candidate in the second round of voting. I don't believe it's ever happened, but it's an option, and Gaius wants to give it a try. But he will need help to make it work."

Fannius looked at Gaius. "Why two terms?"

"I've put a lot of bills into law this year. I want to remain on the tribunate so those bills are implemented properly. Another year would be invaluable. Especially if Fulvius is also elected to the tribunate. In return for my support of you, I want you to talk to any tribal elders you have sway with. Ask them to write in my name on their ballots."

Fannius had not expected this, but he did want a consulship. He was in a tough battle with Lucius Opimius who had just put down the rebellion in Fregellae and was a strong proponent of the aristocracy.

Fannius, on the other hand, was seen as a moderate. "What new issues would you promote should you be elected, Gaius?"

Carbo stepped into the conversation. Clearly Gaius and his associates had already discussed a strategy. "We're interested in returning to Fulvius' effort to unify Italy."

"What do you mean?"

"Full citizenship and voting rights for all Latins and partial citizenship with voting rights for all Italians," said Fulvius.

"With the hope of eventually giving full citizenship to them both," said Gaius.

"It's the future of Rome," added Carbo. "If it doesn't happen now, it will happen later."

This was exactly what I had said to Cornelia, but I had not known how far Gaius had advanced on this agenda. It was not surprising, and yet his desire for a second tribuneship was.

Fannius was not overly excited by the idea. "What else might you do?"

Gaius nodded to Pomponius. "The collection of taxes and other fees in Roman provinces abroad brings in large sums of money. Right now the province governors sell the rights to collect taxes as a way to make money on the side or bribe local officials. It's an entirely corrupt system. We've drafted a bill that would require open bidding for all tax farming in Roman provinces."

"The bidding would take place here in Rome under the supervision of the tribunate," added Gaius. "Senators would not be allowed to place bids, so the only class wealthy enough to take part would be equestrians."

Fannius nodded slowly. This measure would appeal to his strongest constituency. "So not only would your bill curb corruption, but it would also be another incentive for the equestrians to vote with your constituents."

"That's one way of looking at it," said Gaius.

I did not have a good angle into the room, but I could see Fannius stalking back and forth in the library, pondering the offer. He stopped somewhere in the library where I could not see him. His voice was loud with drink. "What happens if you give me your support and you don't get the tribuneship?"

"As long as you do your part and talk to the tribal elders, we will accept the loss without a word."

"And what exactly will you do for me?" asked Fannius.

"I will be complimentary of you whenever I'm out lobbying for myself," said Fulvius, "as will my clients."

"I'll stay out of the discussion completely until the day of the election," said Gaius. "But on that day, I will come to Mars Field with you and make it obvious that you are my choice for the consulate. Just my presence beside you will be enough to serve your purpose."

"Very good," I heard Fannius say. "Let's do it."

All the men I could see raised their cups. "To our next consul," announced Fulvius.

I did not say anything to Licinia or Cornelia. I understood what Gaius was doing. It made sense at one level, but it seemed awfully risky at another. I admired Gaius for his courage and his vision. His ambition, however, was growing. The same thing had happened to Tiberius. The momentum of the work and the thrill of success had taken over. But trying for a second tribuneship had gotten Tiberius murdered. My feelings at this point were mixed to say the least. Gaius was doing great work that did need follow-up, but I hoped his attempt for a second tribuneship would fail. If ten tribunes received a majority on the first ballot, it would all be over. If Fulvius were elected to the tribunate, he could carry the mantle instead of Gaius.

CHAPTER 82

Despite our last confrontation, Laelia continued to come to the house once a week to use the library. I did what I could to help with her research, but I no longer went to the bathhouse or to my bedroom with her. Although she was always kind to me, embraced me and kissed me like a sister, we maintained an uneasy non-sexual friendship without ever discussing it again.

Laelia loved politics and identified with the populares. She followed Gaius' work and considered my brother a genius and an inspiration. He came by the house one day to use the library just as Laelia was leaving.

Gaius had the kind of face that demanded immediacy and attention. His features were large and expressive. His eyes blazed. He was handsome through his intensity and his powerful physical presence. He was a soldier called to politics.

He came into the house with no announcement and entered the library where Laelia was assembling her notes to leave. She was as room-filling as Gaius, and always dressed to display her beauty. She wore a peach-colored, one-shouldered gown of coan silk that hugged her body like a second layer of skin and a matching transparent palla that wrapped around her torso and shoulders, barely veiling the revealing nature of her gown.

When I rolled into the library, they were staring at each other. "Laelia," I said, "this is my brother Gaius. I don't believe you've met."

Laelia pretended modesty. "I follow politics closely," she said, flashing her loveliest smile, "and your work with the tribunate has been admirable. Truly. I am honored." She bowed to him.

"I knew your father," said Gaius. Laelia's father, Gaius Laelius, Aemilianus' friend, had died a year earlier.

"She's our cousin once removed," I said. "She's married to Quintus Scaevola."

"What are your researching?"

Laelia gave him a wry grin. "Divorce."

"I don't understand," said Gaius.

"And you don't want to," I said. "Laelia was just leaving."

Laelia laughed. "She's probably right, Gaius. I want to test manus in the courts."

"For what reason?"

"I think you have to be a woman to understand."

When this left Gaius speechless, Laelia bid us goodbye. She walked out with her wax pad and stylus just as Nadia came from the back of the house with some posca for Gaius. I noted how both Gaius and Nadia watched Laelia walk across the atrium to leave. Her slave, who was waiting outside the door, stepped into the entry to place a wool mantle on her shoulders.

Gaius stayed in the library all afternoon. He seemed to be writing something so I left him alone. Philocrates had gone to the back of the villa. I saw him beside the slaves' quarters talking to a few of my slaves' children. One was his son Aesop, now twelve years old.

Philocrates had been one of these slave children when Gaius was a child. The two boys played together for several years before Philocrates became Gaius' slave. He had accompanied Gaius on all of his military campaigns and traveled with the construction crew when Gaius had been building roads. They were surprisingly close, but Philocrates was a slave and always deferred when anyone else was present.

A short time later I went to the peristyle to cut some flowers. Philocrates was kneeling beside one of the flower beds. He looked up at me as I approached, then stood with a handful of dandelions in his fist. "I hope you don't mind me picking at your garden, my lady. I was waiting for Gaius."

"Of course not, there are never enough hands to keep up with the weeds. Do as you please." Then I noticed it. His tunic, clearly an old one, was embroidered at the hem and neckline with red, green, and yellow thread. When he knelt down again, I saw that the embroidery had a short break in it on the back hem—as though it had been torn out. I immediately thought of Aemilianus' visitation: *Follow the thread.*

"How long have you had that tunic, Philocrates?" I asked. "It looks like you need a new one."

"Yes, perhaps, my lady," he said turning to face me. "Nadia made it for me when we were closer."

"That's quite a while ago. Maybe you should get her to make you another."

"I have others. This is just the one I picked out for today."

"There's a break in the embroidery. When did that happen?"

He had to twist around to see the gap. "Years ago, I suppose. I never noticed it before."

"Too bad, it's a nice touch," I said, then walked away thinking about the murder. Was there any chance Philocrates came to the house that night? Could Gaius have sent him? The questions I had long buried began to bubble up in me. I thought about the note I had found. Philocrates knew Greek. Could he be the answer to the mystery? He was so loyal to Gaius he could easily have strangled Ameilianus on an order or on his own, but it seemed impossible that he would pressure me for money for any reason. I could ask him outright, but if it were not him, I would be giving myself away. Too much time had passed. The thread proved nothing. I decided to let it go.

CHAPTER 83

Gaius accompanied Fannius to Mars Field when the Century Assembly gathered to elect the consuls, praetors, and other high-ranking military officials. The sight of Gaius and Fannius crossing the exercise field west of Rome created a huge sensation. The one hundred and ninety-three centuries, that voted as groups in the same way the tribes did, quickly assembled and reviewed their lists of nominees. The vote was a close one, but Fannius was chosen to share the consulship with the patrician Gnaeus Domitius Ahenobarbus. Lucius Opimius was a close third. No one doubted that Gaius' appearance with Fannius was the difference.

The following day the plebeians assembled in their tribes at the top of the Capitoline Hill to elect the tribunes. Gaius was not listed as a candidate. He stood with the Cornelia tribe, and as part of the tribal discussion, expressed his opinion on the nominees and made a statement on behalf of Fulvius Flaccus.

The Papiria tribe was given the honor of naming the first ten nominees. To be selected, a candidate had to be named on at least eighteen ballots, meaning a majority of the thirty-five tribes. If more than ten achieved such a majority, the ten men named on the most ballots were given positions on the tribunate.

After all thirty-five tribes had voted, a tribune from the current year, a tall, fair-haired man by the name of Servilius Rullus, stood up to the podium on the speakers' platform to announce the results. "Only eight men were named on a majority of the ballots," he shouted to the Assembly. "All tribes should reconvene to revise their ballot for a second vote."

This caused some mumbling among the tribes and some outbursts of frustration. No one wanted to go through the process for a second time.

Rullus continued. "There were several names written on the ballots that were not on the register. One, in particular, Gaius Sempronius Gracchus," the entire place went quiet, "was on twenty ballots. Because of this he should be considered one of the eligible candidates." The Assembly roared with approval, and surely any of the senators there to watch were stunned. They had universally believed that Gaius could not possibly receive a second year on the tribunate.

Rullus conducted the second ballot. The Voturia tribe was selected to vote first. When the results were tallied, Gaius was on every ballot and nine other men, including Fulvius Flaccus, appeared on a majority of them. The vote was over. Gaius had achieved his second consecutive term as a tribune, something never before achieved. The reaction of the Assembly was so loud it could be heard all over Rome. Even those who were not there might have guessed what it meant.

Also named to the tribunate was a Lucius Drusus. Much like Marcus Octavius, the tribune who repeatedly vetoed Tiberius' land reform bill, Drusus had been backed heavily by the optimates as an agent to undo several of Gaius' measures from the previous year. Both Gaius and Fulvius understood this as soon as the results were announced.

CHAPTER 84

I was at Gaius' home when he came back from the Assembly with Fulvius, Laetorius, and Pomponius, all trailed by loyal Philocrates. Licinia and I were in the garden. I sat in my wheelchair. She stood. We had heard the uproar and knew it must have been related to the election. As far as Licinia knew, the biggest issue was Fulvius getting a position on the tribunate. We came out of the garden, her pushing me, and met the men as they filled up the atrium with their excited talk. Licinia understood what had happened even before Gaius told her. She ran out of the atrium in tears. Only I saw her go.

I listened to the men long enough to learn what had happened, including the election of Lucius Drusus, then rolled off to find Licinia. I found her hiding in the shadows in the far corner of the garden.

When she heard me coming, she faced me, wiping tears from her eyes. "I can't do another year of this."

I knew fear, and I knew crying alone.

"I know he's your brother, but—but it's just too much." She slammed it at me angrily.

"I'm frightened also, Licinia. For Cornelia, it will be even worse. But I have gradually learned to accept what Gaius does. I'm beginning to believe he can't help himself. It's bigger than he is. It's our family's fate. That's the only way I can live with it. And I don't see how any of us, my mother included, have any other choice. Go live in Misenum for the year. Take the children. Cornelia wouldn't mind. You are best off leaving him be."

Gaius came out to the garden. The other men were talking loudly in the atrium. Gaius saw Licinia and joined us in the shadows. He watched Licinia dry her cheeks with her palla. "I guess you're the only one not celebrating."

She hung her head. Gaius came up close to her. He touched her cheek to get her to look at him. "I've got to do this. You know that." He glanced at me with the message I already understood.

"No, Gaius. You might have to do this. But I can't. I see your dead body on the forum floor. I see it every night in my dreams. You're trying to defeat a force that always wins." She was crying again.

Gaius hung his head. He knew that the thing that frightened her empowered him. Like his brother, he was a thoughtful man, but he was considerably more intense and often given to overreaction. But not on this day. He embraced Licinia because he really did love her and his children. He had loved her since the first time he had seen her and that feeling had never left him.

He whispered something into Licinia's ear. I could not hear him. He held her a long time. Knowing this was their moment, I rolled myself back to the atrium.

Fulvius greeted me when I reached the other men. "Sempronia, I see you're gotten quite good with that device." A huge, powerfully built man, he invariably seemed more eager to wrestle and fight than wrangle with government policy. He grinned at me. "I know a good many soldiers who could use a chair like that."

He teased people as a way of communicating. I never felt his comments to be anything but playful. "How much trouble could this man Drusus cause?" I asked the group of men.

Pomponius, a man I had known since Gaius' childhood, shook his head. "At lot. While we were thinking we might surprise them, they slipped in their own little trick."

Laetorius was equally upset. "I don't like the man, but maybe we can work with him. Maybe even change his mind. At least if he crosses us with a veto we'll be expecting it this time."

This was bad news. I rolled away from the men thinking Gaius' second year as a tribune was sure to be harder than the first.

CHAPTER 85

I sent a letter to Cornelia with the latest news. I got a reply two weeks later. She had decided to come back to Rome for the duration of Gaius' second tribuneship, which would not begin for two more months. She wanted to stay at my home and act as an advisor to Gaius. I was not certain how good an idea this was, but I wrote back saying she was welcome whenever she arrived.

Soon after I received Cornelia's letter, Licinia added to the drama by announcing that she was pregnant. Gaius was, of course, excited, but Licinia only pretended to be. Her fears were obvious: What was another child if she lost her husband? Licinia, once such a radiant young woman, had become a different person. Gaius' involvement in politics hung over her like a dark cloud. She said nothing, kept her complaints to herself, and soldiered on like any good Roman wife should, but she was not the same.

While all these family tensions were coming to a boil, Laelia was on a mission of her own, perhaps in some ways even more important than the planning of Roman colonies or the voting rights of the Italians. She wanted to make a breakthrough for the rights of women. Despite what she owed to her father-in-law, who had made a special effort to introduce her to Roman law, she had grown to hate the man's son. She registered a petition of divorce with the court and signed it with her husband's name, Quintus Scaevola. She would act as her own advocate and was likely to create a considerable sensation even if she were denied.

Laelia told me the date of her appearance in court. I decided to go to the forum to watch. I had my bearers carry my litter to the edge of the forum with Tarus accompanying us. We got close enough to see and partly hear the proceedings. Despite the difficulties I had experienced knowing Laelia, I was terribly worried about how she would be received by the all-male court.

Laelia arrived at the forum carrying a parasol and looking beautiful, if not entirely prepossessing, in a bright white linen toga over a white linen tunic worn off her left shoulder. She left her wavy black hair free, except for a red ribbon holding it all together behind her head in a loose ponytail. She stopped by my litter and thanked me for coming, then made her way across the forum to the Basilica Aemilia where the day's trials would take place. Manius Manilius, a friend of my husband's, was there to preside. He was not a progressive in the Scipionic sense, but he was also not an ultra-conservative. I felt he might actually give Laelia an opportunity to make her point.

I heard the herald call out, "Quintus Mucius Scaevola, come forward to present your case."

Manilius was sitting at a table with several open scrolls when Laelia approached him. He eyed her up and down and gave her a lascivious grin. "What may I do for you, young lady? You do know this is a court of law?"

She closed her parasol and placed the divorce documents on the table. "I'm here to petition for a divorce."

Manilius scowled and reappraised her. "Who are you? What do you want?" he asked roughly.

"I'm Laelia Sapiens," she said without the slightest give. "As I said, I'm here to petition for a divorce. All the documents are here and in order."

Manilius gave a glance to the fifty-one jurors to his left. "I'm sorry, madam, but there's no platform for a woman to request a divorce." He handed her documents back to her, then turned to the herald beside him. "Call for the first case."

The herald repeated his call. "Quintus Mucius Scaevola, come forward to present your case."

Laelia laid her documents back on the table. "I seek a divorce from Quintus Mucius Scaevola."

Manilius addressed the herald. "Please have this woman removed from the court."

When the herald came toward her, she held out her parasol to stop him, then spoke directly to Manilius. "There is no law, Senator, that says a woman cannot present a case. It's just never been done. Please hear me out," she said, turning to the seated jurors. "I have been trained by one of the best legal minds in Rome and have offered advice on nearly a hundred cases."

This got the jurors talking among themselves, but Manilius had already made up his mind. "I will not hear a case from a woman. If you desire a divorce against the wishes of your husband, your father must present the case."

"My father can't be here. He died a year ago. I'm completely capable of presenting the case myself."

Manilius shook his head to the contrary. "I'm sorry, madam, the court demands that you leave."

"On what grounds, Senator? I'm fully prepared to make a case."

Laelia's confrontation with Manilius had already begun to attract attention. Her appearance did not hurt. Several men in the growing crowd of onlookers shouted out support. *Give the woman her due!*

Manilius' face darkened. He stood and leaned up close to Laelia. "A woman married through the institution of manus has no legal right to divorce her husband—no matter who or what she knows. Leave now or I will have you physically removed."

This invoked more comments from the growing crowd.

One of the jurors came over to Manilius and whispered something in his ear. Manilius frowned at the man, then reluctantly read through Laelia's brief. When he was done, he glared at her. "You registered this case in your husband's name. He's the defendant. Where is he?"

"I issued him a summons to be here today. He ignored it."

Manilius nodded. "Your documentation is otherwise in order. You may make one short statement to the court and be done."

"Thank you, Senator," said Laelia. She made a slight bow to the supportive onlookers, who responded with a combination of suggestive remarks and encouragement, then she turned to the jurors. "As the senator has just said, there is no provision in the institution of manus for a woman to seek a divorce from her husband. That's one reason why I'm here." She glanced briefly at Manilius. "Currently manus is an extension of patria potestas, the power of the head of a family to exercise complete control over his wife, children, and slaves, including the right to punish them. A father transfers this authority to the man he chooses to marry his daughter. This includes exclusive rights to divorce."

Manilius rolled his eyes. All she had done was repeat what everyone already knew and accepted as law.

Laelia continued. "The authority of a husband also comes with a responsibility—the responsibility to treat the members of his family—his wife, children, and slaves—with a certain level of respect and dignity to ensure a proper upbringing. That is part of the job of being head of a family. This means that a husband has the legal authority to control all that his wife does, but that does not give him permission to abuse that right. This is common sense and one of the pillars of a good and just society."

Laelia paused to scan those around her, allowing them a moment to absorb the logic she was using. Then she continued. "I have been married to Quintus Mucius Scaevola since I was fourteen, a total of twelve years. I have given him three sons. I make no judgment on his position in Roman society, but I can no longer live with this man because he has not lived up to the responsibility of his authority." Laelia lifted her toga from her left shoulder, revealing a large purple bruise that seeped in yellows and blues down her arm. Many in the crowd uttered sympathetic groans. A few of the jurors whispered to each other.

"My husband has used his physical strength to subjugate me during fits of drunkenness or rage." Laelia lifted the edge of her tunic up to her thigh. I nearly choked at her daring. It froze every man in the place, including Manilius who was sitting just a few feet from her. The thigh looked much like her shoulder; a long bruise ran down her leg from an ugly contusion. She dropped her tunic. "I contend that a husband can be determined unfit for marriage when he uses his authority for no other reason than the fact that he can. Because of my husband's physical attacks, I can no longer conceive a child. He might soon claim that I am unfit to be a wife. I ask the court to grant me a divorce because my husband has abused me and his legal rights."

The entire court and its audience were stunned by Laelia's performance. Manilius sat there with his mouth open for uncounted moments before regaining his senses. He looked wide-eyed at Laelia and nodded his approval. "The court accepts your case. But we must wait for a statement from the defendant before making a ruling. The court will issue an order for Quintus Scaevola's appearance in three weeks. You, Laelia Sapiens, will also be required to be here."

Laelia acknowledged the judge's decision and strode from the court, parasol held high, followed by the eyes of nearly everyone present. It was a huge, though only partial, victory. She stopped by my litter on her way out of the forum. She slipped into the curtained chamber and lay beside me. When the curtain fell closed behind her, she beamed with pride.

"Congratulations, Laelia, you put on quite a show."

Laelia pulled her tunic up and showed me the bruise on her leg. She wet her handkerchief and wiped part of it away.

"You painted that on yourself? And the other one too?"

"It was either that or slam myself with a board."

"Quintus never hit you?"

"Not in the last two weeks, but I had to show the jury something."

"And your statement that you couldn't conceive?"

She grinned. "It could be true."

"But what if Quintus comes to the court? He'll simply deny it all, and by then your bruises will have washed away."

"Not if I know him. When I tell him he's been called to the court, he's sure to hit me. I'll have a new bruise and a story he can't deny."

She leaned over and kissed me, then slipped out of the litter. "Thank you for coming. Only you of all the audience today have any idea what I'm trying to achieve."

CHAPTER 86

Gaius arrived at my home unannounced two days after Laelia's appearance in court. He stormed into the house when Nadia opened the door and immediately asked to see me. Nadia found me in the peristyle and wheeled me into the atrium where Gaius was waiting. He dismissed Nadia, as though she were his slave, and rolled me into the library to talk to "in private."

Gaius, who was always so kind to me, stalked back and forth in the library before finally turning on me angrily. "I've heard some disturbing things about you, Sempronia. I'm hoping they're not true, but I'm not sure how you can convince me otherwise."

"What are you saying, Gaius? What things?"

"It's that woman I met here in your library, Mucius Scaevola's daughter-in-law."

"Laelia. Yes, what about her? She still comes here to use the library."

"And climb in bed with you?"

I was dumbstruck.

"So it's true. Is that why she wants to file for a divorce?"

"Who have you been talking to?"

"Your housemaid told Philocrates that she found you in bed with the woman—both in a state of undress."

"It happened. Yes. But it's not what you think."

"What do I think?"

Gaius had never attacked me like this before. I struggled for composure. "I did have a short relationship with the woman. I confess to being lonely, and on a few occasions she held me in bed and comforted me. Yes, that happened. And the last time—Nadia found us at an inopportune moment. But it's something that has passed."

Gaius glared at me. "How can you do this kind of thing when I'm actively engaged as a tribune? Every little scandal gets magnified. Your reputation becomes mine."

He crossed the room twice then faced me again. "I have done some checking. The woman has a reputation for promiscuousness with men and women. I saw how she was dressed that day and how she looked at me. What are you doing with her? Do you want to become like her?"

"No, Gaius, please. I understand that distractions can interfere with your work, but what I did is in the past. I was responding to needs that I had at the time. And yes, now, I do regret it, but not because it was wrong, but because Laelia is—is difficult."

"Difficult?" He shook his head. "Immoral is the word I would use. And she plans to divorce her husband. What does that mean? Does this woman think she's a man?"

"It's about equality, Gaius. A man can divorce a woman, but not the reverse. Much as you have made a stand against the authority of the Senate, she intends to make a stand against the institution of manus."

"By engaging with other women?"

"Some marriages are bad, Gaius. Women can be trapped in a life where their husbands beat them or regularly denigrate them—treating them as little more than slaves. A woman deserves more than that or at least a way to escape from it."

For all Gaius' upbringing and his real respect for the intelligence of women, he did not understand. "Escape? As though the marriage bond is a prison?"

"Yes," I said, gaining my own sense of indignation. "I experienced it in my marriage. Aemilianus belittled me for my ankle and my—my infertility. Life with him was like living in a prison."

His face was more incomprehension. "Did Aemilianus beat you?"

"He didn't beat me, but he struck me several times and was rough and always verbally abusive."

Gaius shook his head and turned away from me as though it were all beneath him—in the same way Aemilianus had done—further infuriating me. He took a step toward the doorway.

"It was so bad I killed him," I said to his back.

He spun around. "What?"

"There's a story that might upend your political career!"

He came up close to me and spoke in a low voice. "You killed Aemilianus."

"I poisoned him. He deserved it."

Now it was Gaius who was stunned.

"I had to, Gaius. He treated me like dirt. He would throw me on the atrium floor and—and force himself on me like I was plunder. And if that's not enough, he constantly criticized Tiberius' work. Little comments. Everyday venom. Drip, drip, drip. In my mind he was as guilty as anyone in the Senate for what happened. I heard his good friend Laelius recommend that a statue of Publius Nasica be built— and Aemilianus didn't even wince. And what was your experience with the man? He all but shackled your land commission! He had become a monster."

Gaius just stared at me.

"You know something of revenge, Gaius. Aemilianus' constant attack on me and our family demanded it."

Gaius shook his head, shocked by my outburst, then hushed, "Who else knows?"

"Cornelia."

Again he was dumbfounded.

"And she didn't condemn me."

He had no response.

"And Polybius found out."

"And said nothing?"

"He didn't want Aemilianus' legacy spoiled. He knew right away it was murder. He smelled the poison. But it was many months before he confronted me. Cornelia defended me. I think his silence was to protect Cornelia's reputation."

Gaius paced around room utterly confounded by my revelation.

"Please, Gaius, don't hate me."

He kneeled before me. "Dear sister, you are more than I imagined. I accept your revenge against Aemilianus. He had changed. He became a different man. He attacked the legacy of our brother and me. I shed no tears when I learned of his death." Gaius put his hand on my shoulder. "You are a Gracchi, Sempronia—like all of us, with more courage than might be wise."

"There's more."

He visibly wilted.

"I poisoned Aemilianus, but the dose was too small. Someone found him after the poison had weakened him—and strangled him."

"Who was that?"

"Polybius thought it might have been you or someone else on the land commission."

He swung his head sideways in disbelief. "But you still don't know?"

I thought of telling him about the note, but instead said, "No."

Even with me in the chair, Gaius embraced me. "None of this can come out. None of it."

After Gaius left the house, I called Nadia into the library. She stood before me with her head down. She clearly knew why Gaius had been there.

"A few weeks ago you saw me in bed with my friend Laelia."

She nodded.

"Then you told Philocrates and he told my brother."

She continued to stare at the floor.

"I can't have that, Nadia. You are my personal attendant. You know everything about me. I can't have an attendant who gossips about my private life. I can't. Can you give me any reason why I should trust you?"

Nadia knew that she had made a mistake and that I might very well decide to sell her—an absolutely terrible thing for a slave of her age who lived as well as she did. She got down on her knees in front of my chair. "I'm so sorry, my lady," she said with tears in her eyes. "It was a terrible intrusion on your privacy. It will never happen again. Please know there is no other woman I would want as my master."

"I'm sure you mean that, Nadia, but you have hurt me. I'm just not sure I can trust you any more." She put her head on my knees and sobbed. Then I thought of it—where I needed her loyalty most. "Did you know that Aemilianus was murdered?"

Nadia sat up on her haunches, her tears suddenly gone. I could see it in her eyes.

"Did you?" I asked again. "Polybius said you heard something that night. What was it?"

Nadia looked around uncomfortably, then took a deep breath. "I heard Aemilianus gasping for breath. It frightened me. I knew something was wrong. Everyone else was asleep. Tarus was the wrong one to wake up, so I ran to Gaius' home to get Philocrates."

I thought of the thread.

"We both went into the library. Aemilianus was barely alive. He sputtered out that he had been poisoned. I knew how badly he treated you. I thought it might have been you. I coaxed Philocrates to finish him off. He had no love for the man, nor did I. Philocrates strangled him for Gaius. I asked him to do it for you."

I sat back in my chair. "Who else knows this?"

"Only Philocrates."

"And the poisoning?"

She bowed her head. "Polybius came by during one of your trips to Misenum. He began to search the house. I knew what he was after." She looked up at me. "I got to the poison before he did—so he couldn't find it—and you wouldn't use it on yourself."

"Who put the note beneath my bed?"

"I did. Philocrates wrote it."

"What's the favor he wants from me?"

"It's something we both want."

I sat back and took a deep breath. "What is it? Gold?"

"No, of course not, my lady. We are not that sort." She sighed heavily. "We want you to free Aesop when he reaches his seventeenth year. We weren't going to ask until he was nearly that age."

How could I have been so wrong? I leaned forward and took her hands. "Yes, I will free Aesop when he's seventeen." I drew her up to her feet as I awkwardly stood and wrapped my arms around her. "I think we have found a new level of honesty between us. I can trust you if you can trust me."

She wept openly on my shoulder. I knew the fear I had put in her heart. I had scared her—and she had scared me.

I saw Gaius two days later. I told him about Philocrates and Nadia and the note. For a second time Gaius repeated what I already knew. This could not get out. People would say that he had instructed his slave to kill Aemilianus. All the work he planned to do in the next year was at risk.

We both met with Philocrates and Nadia. We told them if anyone should find out, it meant trouble for all of us. Philocrates would be executed for his part. Nadia would likely be sold. A solemn pact was made between the four of us to never talk about it again. Even Cornelia would be left in the dark.

CHAPTER 87

Gaius never brought up Laelia again. Instead of hating me, he had gained respect for me. Cornelia's arrival in Rome one week later, however, complicated things. Gaius did his best to ease the tensions. He stopped by once a week to brief both Cornelia and me on what he was doing. Licinia had accepted her fate and sunk into a defensive shell. Cornelia went the other way. She loved Gaius more than life itself. We all did. But Cornelia, in a stiff and sometimes unpleasant way, criticized and chided Gaius on every issue she did not agree with. He listened. Sometimes he made changes or adjustments in the language of a bill. Sometimes he did not. When I was alone with her, she wore me out venting her frustration. In the end, though, all of us soldiered on as Gaius continued on his visionary path of reform.

When Gaius was elected to a second tribuneship, backed by a following that contained both the plebeian and equestrian classes, he had become without question the most powerful man in Rome. The Senate was little more than an advisory committee to which he would air his proposals before taking them to the People's Assembly. He began the term with what he hoped would be a noncontroversial proposal to create three new Roman colonies—one in Capua, one outside Tarentum called Neptonia, and one on the Bruttian coast named Scylacium. It was land reform, but without the confiscation of property. For a modest rental fee, three thousand landless Roman citizens would be given the opportunity to restart their lives in a location with clear potential for growth—prime farmland in the case of Capua and excellent harbors in the cases of Neptonia and Scylacium.

During the three-week period of public discussion, Livius Drusus made an alternative proposal calling for twelve colonies of three thousand colonist each, with no rental fee. This was essentially a much bigger and better deal than what Gaius had proposed. Drusus' bill came with the open support of the Senate; Gaius' did not. The People's Assembly chose Drusus' twelve colonies over Gaius' three.

This was the Senate's latest strategy to diminish Gaius' influence. For every proposal that Gaius brought to the People's Assembly, their man Drusus would make an even more generous offer. And in each case, Drusus' bill came with the Senate's blessing. If it were not such an ugly and disingenuous political strategy, one might have laughed at the extremes the Senate was going to undercut Gaius. Unfortunately it was succeeding. Gaius was in a position similar to what Tiberius had faced. He was part of a tribunate that had been compromised. Drusus was playing the part of Octavius but with a bigger box of political tools.

Gaius countered by having a fellow tribune, Gnaeus Rubrius, propose a colony, to be called Junonia, in the location once occupied by the city of Carthage. Each colonist would get a two hundred-iugerum plot of Africa's rich farmland with no rental fee. And with Rubrius' name on the bill, it passed. This was what Gaius was up against—a complete attack on his name that had little to do with the bills he offered.

One aspect of Drusus' work that added to his popularity was that he never put himself in a position to administer his own bills or profit from them. His laws were for the people, not any advantage he might gain. Tiberius had put himself, his father-in-law, and his brother on the land reform commission, and Gaius had contracted and supervised the work crews that built the roads and granaries his bills put into law. Both brothers had been knee deep in everything they did. Though neither Gaius nor Tiberius sought personal gain from their projects, their altruism was not as obvious as Drusus' complete separation from his proposals. Despite Gaius' tremendous popularity, Drusus' actions began to steadily erode his influence.

Gaius' most ambitious project for his second tribuneship was to create a path to Roman citizenship for everyone in Italy. In many ways, this proposal was the reason he had risked seeking a second term. Shortly after Rubrius' colony in Africa was accepted, Gaius rolled out his bill. It would give all Latins who lived south of the Po River full Roman citizenship. Latins already had some limited voting privileges, but this would include full voting rights and all the legal protections a Roman citizen enjoyed. The bill would also give suffrage to all Italians south of the Po River, as a first step toward full citizenship. Roman citizenship was highly valued and gave one the right to a fair trial in any Roman province, and a certain level of dignitas in any part of the Mediterranean world. Both the Italians and the Latins were excited about the bill, but Roman citizens had already rejected a similar bill two years earlier. And with Drusus on the tribunate, passing this one would be considerably more difficult.

Many of the bills Gaius had passed in his first term included obvious benefits to the common man—a reduced price of wheat, checks and balances on the magistrates, and less required military duty. But universal citizenship was not so clearly advantageous to the plebeian, and in the eyes of the senatorial class, it was a calculated move by Gaius to increase his voting constituency.

"Let all these Latins in," declared Fannius, once Gaius' political partner, but now an outspoken adversary, "and real Romans will find that they are crowded out at the games and gladiatorial exhibitions. Why would any citizen possibly want to expand the privileges of a Roman to the rest of Italy? It will only result in less for us!"

Two days after Gaius read his proposal to the Senate, Drusus countered with a bill that made it a crime for a Roman officer to scourge an allied levy. It was a political smoke screen meant as a distraction. While the allies were of course thrilled by Drusus' proposal, it was a nonsensical bill from the perspective of the Senate. How could a Roman officer possibly maintain the regimen of an allied company without strict and decisive corporal discipline? But the Senate did not care. They feared Gaius' leadership skills and were intent on showing him up through any means possible.

Gaius countered with a furious three-week campaign to promote universal citizenship. He attended every contio he could and spoke at the forum daily. "Try to imagine a Rome of the future," Gaius shouted to a gathering at the forum. "It can't possibly remain a walled city with a narrow apron of land around it. Roman conquests currently reach from Spain to Syria, from Transalpine Gaul to Africa. Our vision of ourselves must change with Rome's expansion. We must dare to think big. We must dare to become a unified Italy. When it comes to building our armies, when it comes to managing our farmland, when it comes to building roads and enabling commerce, everything functions more smoothly if we are one.

"Our goal must be that all residents of Italy live under the same laws that Romans do. As it is now, a Roman magistrate can appear in a

Latin or Italian town and impose his will on those who live there. We have all heard the stories. The local magistrate in Teanum who was flogged by the order of a Roman consul because the public baths had not been cleaned quickly enough for his wife to use them. Or what about the young Roman staff officer who had a Venusian ploughman flailed to death for making a comic remark when the officer passed him on the street? The common Italian, the common Latin, hovers in fear when a Roman of any rank comes into their town. Who can possibly know what minor incident will inflame them? This makes no sense. You may be Romans, but you must recognize that you and all of Italy would be better off if everyone lived under the same laws."

But no matter how Gaius might beseech the Roman populace, those who stood the most to gain, the Latins and Italians, would have little or no impact on the vote. And his appeal to the Roman citizens' higher sense of justice and the inevitability of a unified Italy fell short when compared to the short-term material loses that Fannius emphasized would come with extended citizenship.

"Would you want to share the spoils our generals bring home from Asia and Africa with the rest of Italy? Would you want to share the wonderful fortune of being born Roman with any of these lesser people? Would that not detract from what it means to be a Roman? Why would anyone want to change our great Republic from what it is already? Why venture into some new order when what we have works so well? There is absolutely no reason for this kind of change."

CHAPTER 88

The tribes assembled on the top of the Capitoline Hill before dawn to prepare for the referendum on universal citizenship. It was early summer. It would be a long hot day, but the morning was alive with anticipation for an outcome on this viciously contested issue. I remember that Gaius got a rough head count the day before. At least fifteen of the tribes would support the bill.

After the religious ceremonies were completed, the ten tribunes lined up across the speaking platform with Livius Drusus in the center and Gaius on the far left. His second tribuneship had proven to be a tough one. He had passed no bills written under his name, while Drusus, guided by a large faction of senators, had outmaneuvered him at every turn and passed several bills. This vote could not have been more critical to Gaius' reputation. He told the herald to read the bill to the Assembly.

The herald stood up to the podium, opened the scroll, and Livius Drusus stepped forward and stopped the herald from reading. He was vetoing the bill. It was a repeat of what had happened to Tiberius' initial attempt at land reform. Gaius had not anticipated a veto because there was such a strong chance the bill would be defeated anyway. But no, the opposition was not taking any chances. There would be no vote at all.

After the Assembly was dismissed, Gaius retired to his home with his closest advisors, Fulvius, Carbo, Pomponius, and Laetorius. "It would have been nice to have the vote just to see how close it was," said Fulvius as the group barged into the house and sought out the shaded side of the atrium.

Laetorius went to the pantry and returned with an amphora of wine and a handful of cups. He offered a cup to Gaius, but he pushed it away. Licinia came into the atrium from the peristyle, looked around, then returned to where she had been. Gaius watched her the entire time.

"Dare we try it again tomorrow, Gaius?" asked Pomponius

"It's the same thing they did to your brother," said Carbo. "Maybe we should just vote egg-sucking Drusus out!"

Gaius was agitated. He paced around, shaking his head. "That won't work. He has too strong a following in the Assembly. The vote today would have told us how strong."

"Let's give it some time," said Laetorius. "We should focus on revealing who Drusus really works for. Undermine his influence. Then try the vote again in a couple of months."

Gaius looked up from his gloom.

Fulvius, always upbeat and confident, laughed. "You need a break, Gaius. Go to Junonia. Start the colony. Get out of Rome for a few months. Prove that mixing Italians and Romans can work. Make it an example of what enfranchisement of Italy could mean. I'll manage things here in Rome."

"There's too much to do in Rome for me to leave."

"No, you should go," said Carbo. "The rest of us can continue to push the bill. And with you gone, the Senate won't pay such close attention. Then we'll try another vote when you get back."

"But what if Drusus vetoes it again? What do we do then?"

"We'll make sure we have the votes before doing anything," said Fulvius. "If we have the numbers and he vetoes it, we vote him out."

"And if we don't have the votes," said Carbo, "we wait until next year."

Gaius shook his head. It had been a dismal day. What was he to do? Leaving Rome seemed like quitting, but maybe a break was what he needed.

CHAPTER 89

Gaius decided to talk to Cornelia before making a decision. The summer had been hot and this afternoon was no different. I sat with Gaius and Cornelia in the peristyle in the shade of a large willow. I was in my wheelchair, Cornelia on a bench. Gaius, wearing a tunic and no toga because of the heat, sat beside Cornelia.

Cornelia began the conversation by asking Gaius the same question Pomponius had asked. "How will you counter the veto?" Drusus' veto had disturbed her more than it had Gaius. It brought back memories of Tiberius' death. Her worries became mine and were further magnified in Licinia.

"I'm contemplating leaving Rome for two months to supervise the building of Junonia—which means leaving Fulvius in control."

Cornelia understood the trip to Africa would involve its own dangers, but she immediately supported the idea, probably because it would get Gaius out of Rome and two months closer to the end of his term when he came back.

"When I return," he said, "we will try the citizenship bill one more time."

"Is there any reason to think it would not be vetoed?"

"Not really. We're simply hoping Fulvius and the others can rally the other tribunes to put pressure of Drusus."

"Fulvius is nowhere near the strategist you are, Gaius," replied Cornelia. "I'm not sure he can accomplish what you want."

"He's still quite a favorite since his success in Massilia, Mother. He held a triumph less than a year ago. He should have no trouble managing things here for two months."

"And what if you come back and citizenship fails again. What will you do then?"

Gaius stood from the bench and began to pace. "I'm not certain. It will depend on how things go in Africa. I'm hoping to use Junonia's success as a means of gaining an edge on Drusus."

"Would you try another term as tribune to get the citizenship bill passed?" The tone of Cornelia's voice expressed her opinion on the idea.

Gaius looked at me before answering. "I've considered it."

Cornelia took a deep breath. "Then let's hope Fulvius can do some good work while you're gone."

"Gaius," I said, "truly, you would try again?"

"What else would I do?" Anger flashed behind his words. He did not like being challenged. "It's the most important thing I've tried to accomplish. I believe it's as important to me as land reform was to Tiberius."

"And could get your body thrown in the Tiber," snapped Cornelia.

Gaius replied evenly. "I have one life to live and one death to give. They belong to the people of Rome. Nothing is more worthy than this work."

CHAPTER 90

Gaius decided to go to Africa to do the work of colonization instead of trying to outmaneuver Drusus. Three thousand Roman citizens were initially slated to settle Junonia. Gaius added three thousand Italians to bolster his chances for success and to demonstrate the promise of a united Italy.

When Aemilianus besieged and destroyed Carthage, he placed a curse on the ground where the city had stood, pledging that no man should tread the ground that had once been Carthage. Because of Carthage's excellent harbor, which still existed in a skeletal form, Gaius ignored his uncle's curse. He decided to build homes and infrastructure on both the elevated area on the coast that had been the city proper and the prime farmland that extended well inland.

The process began, as did all Roman events, with a series of ritualized customs. The six thousand settlers marched in military style to the site of the colony's inauguration, where the isthmus that was Carthage met the mainland. At the lead was an ensign held high on a staff. During the march, the colonists encountered strong winds, and the staff was blown from the bearer's grip and fell to the ground, breaking the ensign into several pieces. The next day when the altars were raised and three sheep were sacrificed to Juno, again a furious wind dispersed the ceremony and blew the sheep carcasses from the altar onto the ground. Although these ominous signs frightened some colonists, Gaius kept at the work with the same effort and efficiency that he brought to everything he did.

CHAPTER 91

Three weeks after Gaius left for Africa, Laelia got her second day in court—after two delays for no apparent reason. Laelia arrived early. Her case was second on the docket. She watched the first case, constantly on the lookout for her husband, who had been issued a summons to be there.

I came to the forum to observe. I saw Laelia watching the first trial and ordered my slaves to carry my litter to where she was waiting. When I opened the litter curtains to give her a few words of support, she was intent on the trial in progress. A man was accusing his neighbor of stealing his goat. I said her name and she turned to face me. An ugly bruise blackened her right eye—and was clearly not something she had painted on her face.

Her smile was a hesitant wince. "It went just as I said, Sempronia. When I asked him if he would honor the summons, he tore it up then hit me in the face. My first piece of evidence." She grinned. "It doesn't hurt that much any more."

"Will Quintus actually come to the trial?"

Laelia looked around. "He's not here yet. If he doesn't, the court has the authority to bring him here by force. As you can see, the judge is Manilius again. I can't imagine him giving me this second day in court without fairly judging my complaint."

"What about the jury? They're not the same group that was here the first time. They might be less sympathetic."

Laelia shrugged, suggesting it was out of her control, then noticed that the first trial had ended. She reached into the litter and touched my hand. "Let's see what happens."

"May all the goddesses be with you."

The herald stepped forward and called for the second case, this time using Laelia's name to identify it. She walked the short distance to

311

the table where Manilius held court. She placed her petition on the table and looked directly at Manilius.

The judge made no acknowledgment of the condition of her face. "Where is the defendant?"

"I have no idea, Senator. I can verify that he did receive the summons." She turned to the jurors. "At which point he struck me."

The jurors did not react the way the previous jury had, perhaps because they had not witnessed Laelia's display of her thigh and shoulder.

"We'll give the defendant a little more time," said Manilius. "Herald, call for the third case on the docket."

"Sir, I'm concerned my husband won't come at all. I request that you send a representative of the court to get him."

Manilius ignored her and told the herald to move on to the next case. I remained in the litter watching and waiting, as Laelia, now growing anxious, paced through what turned out to be four more trials without any sign of Quintus. A long hot day grew longer. Laelia approached Manilius after the herald called for the next case.

"Sir, did you send anyone after my husband? We're wasting time. I don't think he'll come without some kind of action from the court."

Manilius waved her away as the advocate for the next case placed his documents on the table.

Even from a distance I could see how angry Laelia had become. She stalked over to my litter. "I'm not sure what's going on, Sempronia. Manilius is making no effort to get Quintus here. I'm beginning to worry."

I took her hand to comfort her, but she pulled away and returned to pacing and looking for her husband. After six more cases, the sun was behind the city walls to the west. Manilius motioned to the herald. The herald stood out before the gallery of jurors and announced that the court had closed for the day. The jurors stood to leave. Manilius gathered the scrolls on his table, stuck them under his arm, and took two steps right into a determined Laelia.

"What about my petition, Senator? How do we proceed?"

Manilius barely looked at her. "A wife has no right to petition for a divorce. Only your husband does. He's not here. Your petition is denied." He walked away from her.

Laelia cursed him to his back. Manilius spun on her. "Watch your mouth, woman. I'll hold you in contempt of court." Then he shook his head and sneered, "I'm actually quite surprised your husband didn't come. Who would want to be married to a witch like you?"

Laelia spat at his feet. Manilius puffed up his chest and continued off across the forum.

Laelia came to my litter steaming. She let loose with a long rant against Manilius, then concluded by saying, "I'm not done with this."

"But what can you do? To whom can you appeal?"

"I'm not sure. If I only wanted to be rid of Quintus, I'd follow your lead and buy some hemlock. But I want some kind of precedent set here. My motives are not simply for myself, they're for all women."

CHAPTER 92

During the time that Gaius was gone, Fulvius, who tended to be brusque and outspoken and had none of Gaius' personal grace, lost more ground to Drusus, who had launched an attack on Gaius' efforts in Africa. Reports about the inauspicious signs witnessed in the first few days of colonization reached Rome. Drusus fabricated a third incident, saying that the boundary stones used to mark Junonia's perimeter had been carried off in the mouths of wolves. He called the omens a clear consequence of Gaius' ignoring the curse Aemilianus had placed on Carthage. Rather than praise for Gaius' work, the conversation in Rome turned to repealing Rubrius' bill and canceling the colonization effort entirely.

This is what confronted Gaius when he returned after sixty days in Africa. He was livid. Instead of giving up the idea of universal citizenship, he applied himself with greater energy. The first thing he did was to move from his home on the Palatine Hill, once Cornelia's beautiful villa, to a smaller home near the markets in Subura. Licinia protested, as did Cornelia, who saw the move as a sign that Gaius would seek a third tribuneship. But Gaius was determined. He hoped to gain the support of Rome's poorest people by living in their neighborhood.

He rewrote the citizenship bill and presented it to the Senate. During the three weeks of contiones and open discussion, he made regular appearances in the forum, speaking both for citizenship and against the duplicitous methods that Drusus had used to undermine his proposals. By this time, however, the Roman citizens had grown weary of wonderful promises made by demagogues. They lost interest in the ongoing battle of words and even Gaius' proposals rang hollow. The opitmates' strategy had succeeded. Drusus had entirely subverted Gaius. Words meant nothing anymore. Gaius Gracchus, the orator, was no longer the most powerful man in Rome.

A two-day gladiatorial exhibition was scheduled to take place in the marketplace south of the forum the week prior to the vote on Gaius' new citizenship bill. These bloody exhibitions were hugely popular among Romans of all classes and were as highly anticipated as any of the festivals or games that were a regular occurrence in Rome. Because of the certainty of drawing a large crowd, several of the magistrates took it upon themselves the day before the event to have wooden scaffolds built around the gaming area so the upper class would have good seats for the exhibition.

Gaius saw the grandstands being built. Clearly they would prevent the lower-class citizens from being able to watch the event except from a long distance off. With no way of removing the seating in a legal manner, he gathered twenty workmen from his road crew to dismantle and remove the grandstands that night.

When the first magistrates arrived in the morning to claim their seats for the opening of the exhibition, a huge crowd had already gathered and staked out standing room to watch the event. Nothing could be done to reverse Gaius' late night work. The average Roman could not have been more pleased, but the optimates saw it as another of Gaius' blatant efforts to garner votes.

Worse, however, was that it angered the majority of the tribunate. All but Fulvius stood with Drusus condemning Gaius' use of the tribunal workforce to serve his own purposes. At least he could have brought the issue to the tribunate to discuss. What he had done instead was beyond the authority of his position and little better than vandalism.

Cornelia came to his home the second day of the exhibition. She had so disapproved of his moving to the new home that this was the first time she had been inside the tiny but well kept home. Gaius was sitting in the atrium when Catalda opened the door for Cornelia. He immediately stood, surprised that she should be there at all. Licinia, seven months pregnant, came out of the children's room on the atrium's second floor when she heard Gaius greet his mother.

"They had no right to build those scaffolds," said Gaius as Cornelia reached the atrium.

"And tearing them down only made you look a bigger fool than them." Licinia later told me it was the first time she had ever heard Cornelia directly insult Gaius. "You have the biggest vote of your career coming up and you've disrespected the office of tribune."

"I didn't tear the scaffold down for votes, Mother."

"That's hard to believe, Gaius. In my mind you've become just another politician who buys his votes with favors. The clear sense of your vision for universal citizenship should be enough to carry the vote if the people really want it." She stalked, a little stiffly, across the atrium and back.

"It will be a close vote, Mother. Very close. What I did last night will help regardless of why I did it, no matter how foolish you think it was."

"You are a Gracchi," she said angrily. "If you are so determined to put your life on the line for the sake of the common man then your actions must match your high-minded ideals. I came to Rome this last year to watch how you went about your business—even though I wished, for my own personal reasons, that you were done with this ugliness. I have seen how hard you work and how hard others work against you—using some of the lowest and most despicable tactics imaginable. You must be better than them. I've done my best to keep my opinions to myself. But since your return from Africa, I've had a harder and harder time staying quiet."

Licinia listened from the second floor of the atrium. Cornelia was voicing the frustration she had often vented on me. Philocrates had heard the loud exchange and now stood almost out of sight at the edge of the atrium.

"If this is the path you choose, Gaius, it's better that I support you than ask you to desist, but it's almost more than I can bear. You have given me good reason to believe that the issue of citizenship is a valid one, and an important one. I felt just as strongly about Tiberius' land reform. I also recognize that you have come to politics with an even more articulate vision than your brother. I am proud of what you've accomplished and what you stand for, but with the removal of the grandstands, I see you losing out to thuggery. I see a man whose emotions are beginning to outrun his reason." Cornelia noticed Licinia watching from above, then she saw Philocrates partially obscured by the colonnade. She turned to Gaius. "Please, son, if you must break my heart, do it from the highest ground possible." She took a great breath, embraced Gaius, then walked straight out of the house to her litter and awaiting slaves.

Gaius stared at the atrium floor for a long time. Neither Licinia nor Philocrates moved. When Gaius finally lifted his head, he spoke to his wife. "Please forgive me, Licinia. I know what I'm doing is difficult for everyone." He looked at Philocrates. "And it will take all of your support to get us through it. Please bear with me."

CHAPTER 93

Three days before the citizenship vote Fannius ordered all non-Romans out the city. "No non-Roman," proclaimed Fannius, "shall stay in the city or approach within forty stades of it while the voting is in progress." This meant that the Latins, albeit with limited voting rights, the people who had the most to gain from the bill, could not take part. Gaius immediately called the law unconstitutional and announced that he would personally protect any Latins who came to Rome to vote. But Gaius had no capacity beyond his clients to protect people coming to Rome. His offer was an empty gesture at best.

The day of the vote the Latins were restricted from the city. But it did not seem to matter because everyone in Rome expected Drusus to veto the bill anyway. The tribes assembled, the auspices were taken, and Fulvius selected the lot to lead the Assembly. Gaius watched from the far left edge of the tribunal, Drusus from the center. When the herald stepped up to the podium with the scroll, no one spoke up to stop him. He read the entire citizenship bill from beginning to end.

The Romilia tribe drew the honor of being first to vote. As a vote on legislature, there was no ballot. The tribal representative would simply call out *yes* or *no*. The Romilia elder shouted a firm, "No." The second tribe reversed that with a yes. As Gaius had known, it would be close. The votes went back and forth almost evenly until the *no's* achieved a majority with three tribes yet to vote. It seemed to mark the end of Gaius' political run. The faction of senators who had worked behind the scenes with Drusus felt confident they had quieted the demagogue for good.

Gaius, however, had his spine up. Two weeks later he announced that he would be a candidate for the tribunate in the next election, one month hence.

CHAPTER 94

Although Gaius had defiantly announced after the defeat of the citizenship bill that he would seek a third tribuneship, as a returning tribune he was not allowed to register as a candidate. Again he would have to rely on write-in ballots.

Licinia, still trying to maintain a stoic face, suffered from the stress. Two weeks after the failed vote, she miscarried what would have been a third son. When Cornelia came to visit Licinia afterward, she confronted Gaius on his decision, repeating many of the same things she had written in her letter prior to his first run for tribune.

"And if you can't think of me, and the pain you're putting me through, at least think about your wife and your lost child. Licinia can't take the pressure. And it's not out of weakness—it's out of love for you, just as my grievances are."

"My work is not done, Mother. Only I can make the decision to go on or not."

"To that I can't disagree. It is your decision. However, it's idiocy to go on. Not only will it damage your relationship with me and place added strain on your marriage, but it will destroy your reputation. Accept that you have had two consecutive terms as a tribune, more than anyone before you, and that the work must be taken up by others. If you must continue in politics, having served as a quaestor, you will be eligible to become a senator in two years. Set your sights on that instead of this headstrong push to seek a third term as tribune."

Gaius, so used to success, had been piqued badly by the defeats of his second term. He wanted to hear nothing of joining the ranks of the men he had spent his entire political career fighting. "I will let the people decide, Mother. If it will assuage you at all, I will make no further show of my desire for a third term. I won't speak at the forum, and I'll refrain from making behind-the-scenes deals, but when the day comes for the vote, if my name is written-in on a majority of the tribal ballots, I will resume my efforts to make Rome stronger."

And that was how it ended. I sided with both Licinia and Cornelia, but I said nothing, again trusting that my brother had a destiny to fulfill.

While Gaius bided his time waiting for the upcoming election, Claudia Pulcheria, Tiberius' widow, announced that she had arranged a marriage for herself that would take place in the spring. Marcius Philippus, a conservative senator, would be her future husband. I was happy for her. Cornelia would have preferred she remain unmarried, but she kept her feelings to herself, being far more concerned about Gaius than her daughter-in-law.

During this same period of time, Laelia made her third appearance in court. Rather than file her documents in advance, she waited for a day that Manius Manilius was scheduled to be the judge and there were only two cases on the docket. I did not attend the court that day, but Laelia filled me in on the details afterward.

Manilius had denied Laelia's earlier petition for divorce because her husband, Quintus Scaevola, was not present in the court. Despite a summons, which the court refused to enforce, and all of Laelia's efforts, Quintus simply laughed at her attempt to divorce him and on the day the summons was delivered struck her.

On this occasion she tried a different strategy. She sent one of her slaves to the forum to observe the court and notify her when the second trial had begun. While the slave was at the forum, Laelia enticed Quintus into an early cup of wine by surprising him with an amphora of an expensive Falerian red. Quintus had little or no control over his drinking and after one cup, Laelia poured him a second. When the first amphora was empty, Laelia presented a second. After that had been drained, Quintus sought out a third. By the time the slave returned to tell Laelia that the second trial had begun, Quintus lay on a couch in the atrium too drunk to move.

Laelia called for two slaves to carry Quintus from the atrium to a litter waiting outside on the street. Quintus hardly even knew that he had been moved until they arrived at the forum just as the second trial was completed. Before Manilius could gather up his scrolls or disband the jury, Laelia had the litter placed before the table where Manilius sat.

The ex-consul looked up at her. "What do you want?" he growled, clearly not happy to see this woman back in his court.

"Senator, I bring you Quintus Scaevola." Laelia pulled back the curtains to the litter. "You have told me twice that you would not consider my petition for divorce unless my husband were present. Here he is. Will you now consider granting me a divorce?" She dropped her petition on the table.

Manilius frowned, glanced into the litter where Quintus was nestled with a cup of wine, then narrowing his eyes, turned to the jury and held up his hand to prevent them from leaving.

Manilius did not drink. He felt it weakened a man's body and mind, and had long spoken out about how much wine Romans consumed, claiming it would bring about the collapse of the Republic. Laelia had done her research and was well aware of all the above.

Manilius motioned to the court orderly. The orderly took hold of Quintus' arm and pulled him out of the litter and up to his feet.

"Quintus Scaevola," said Manilius, "your wife has brought you here to obtain a divorce. The court cannot proceed without your permission. What have you to say?"

Quintus, gripping his cup, and barely able to stand upright, eyed Manilius as though he were having trouble seeing. Quintus scrunched up his face, placed a hand on the table to maintain his balance, then muttered, "I could care less what this wench does or where she goes."

An unimpressed Manilius nodded. "Have you ever struck your wife?"

Quintus chuckled, then grinned. "When she needed it."

Again Manilius nodded. "Does that often happen when you are drinking wine?"

Quintus looked over his shoulder at the jury, like everyone was in on this great joke. "Invariably."

Manilius sat back and looked at Laelia, her expression grimly serious. He reviewed Laelia's petition, making sure it was properly filled out. Only the required signatures of the husband and the judge were missing. He pushed the petition forward and offered Quintus a stylus and ink. "Are you capable of signing your name?"

To Quintus this was a terribly funny question and he laughed drunkenly. "Of course I can. I'm no child." He bent over the table and hastily scribbled a mark on the document.

Manilius again looked at Laelia. He had no fondness for her, but Quintus' attitude had enraged him. "My apologies to the jury," he said, "I mistakenly bid you to stay. A signed petition for divorce needs no opinion from the jury." He signed the document. "I grant this divorce and give the wife custody of the children." He gave the petition to Laelia. "File this with the registrar. He will give you the forms necessary to have your dowry returned." He focused an ugly look at Quintus. "And make sure this man is quickly taken from the court before I find him in contempt."

Laelia instructed the bearers to help Quintus into the litter and carry him home. The divorce did not include a condemnation of manus, as Laelia had hoped, but it was a step in the right direction and she was free of Quintus.

CHAPTER 95

The Century Assembly gathered on the first day of the elections at Mars Field to vote for the consuls, praetors, and other military officials. Perhaps serving as an insight into the changing atmosphere in Rome, Lucius Opimius, a hardline anti-Gracchi, was elected to one of the consular positions. Quintus Fabius was elected to the other.

The following day the People's Assembly met at the top of the Capitoline Hill for the election of the ten tribunes. The incumbent tribune Mancius Acilius Glabrio was chosen by lot to preside over the election. Earlier in the year Acilius had worked with Gaius in the sponsorship of a bill to address magistrates taking bribes. Like the Rubrian bill to establish the colony of Junonia, the bill had passed with Acilius' name on it, not Gaius'. Unfortunately, Acilius was one of the tribunes who had been angered by Gaius' unilateral decision to tear down the stands for the gladiatorial exhibition.

Gaius' only hope for a tribuneship was as a write-in. Due to his failed push for expanded citizenship and the year-long dominance of Drusus on the tribunate, his name did not create the same kind of excitement it had the previous year. The faction of senators who had focused so much effort on diminishing Gaius' popularity had also instructed their various clients to make derogatory statements about Gaius in the forum and at the contiones prior to the election. Surprisingly, however, they did not confront him at the election or stage any kind of protest, leading Gaius to believe he had a reasonable chance to achieve a write-in majority.

When the ballots were collected from the thirty-five tribes, however, Gaius' name did not appear on a majority of the ballots, while only nine other registered candidates did, meaning there would be a second vote, but Gaius had not made the cut. This seemed impossible to Gaius because his clients had surveyed the tribal elders and felt that despite some loss in support Gaius would be elected. In the aftermath, Fulvius, who was part of the tribunate that day, accused Acilius and the other tribunes of deliberately falsifying the tally to prevent Gaius from receiving another tribuneship.

I know from my discussions with Gaius afterward that he had similar suspicions but had decided to resist Fulvius' push to claim foul. Instead he accepted the results, mostly due to Cornelia's request that he take the high road and stay above the fray. I was glad that Gaius listened to Cornelia's advice, but I also believed that the tribunate had deliberately stood in his way. The events that followed served to support this belief.

CHAPTER 96

When the new year began and the two new consuls were inaugurated and the new tribunate put in place, it became clear that my brother's enemies were not content to simply push him out of the political arena. They were intent on poisoning his name and all that he had done so that under no circumstances could he be elected to a government position again.

The first action of the new tribunate, a group of men who, in my view, had been bought and sold by the optimates, came from the tribune Minucius Rufus. He proposed a repeal of the Rubrian Law, which would curtail all efforts to establish Junonia as a Roman colony. Those in power chose to do this primarily out of spite, knowing it would infuriate Gaius who had spent two hard months in Africa to ensure the colony's success. Rufus' reasons for the repeal were the incidents that had occurred during the religious ceremonies in the first days of Junonia's founding. The ensign falling to the ground and breaking, the carcasses blown off the sacrificial altar, and the rumor that wolves had taken the boundary stones were once again characterized as fulfillment of Aemilianus' curse against Carthage, and signs from the gods that the colony should never have been placed there in the first place.

Gaius came to my house to talk to Cornelia the day he learned of Rufus' proposal. Since Gaius' failure to be elected to a third tribuneship, the tension in our family had greatly diminished. Licinia was happily under the impression that Gaius' involvement in politics was over, and Gaius had made several efforts to reestablish his rocky relationship with Cornelia, who planned to return to Misenum in two weeks.

I joined Cornelia and Gaius in the library when Nadia told me of his arrival. The discussion began with Gaius venting his frustration

325

over Rufus' proposal and admitting he held no official position that would allow him to stop the repeal. Yes, he still served on the land commission, and there were plenty of projects he had already set in motion that needed his supervision, including building roads and granaries, but this did not give him any power to confront the actions of the Senate or the People's Assembly. "What should I do?" he asked Cornelia outright.

Cornelia felt the insult just as surely as Gaius did, but she urged caution. "Be aware that this repeal was likely instigated to draw you into a conflict and further deprecate your reputation. Say what you must during the period of contiones and leave it at that. There must be a time when you accept that you are no longer the most influential man in Rome—and that's not such a bad thing."

"I'm inclined to agree with Mother, Gaius," I said. "Maybe your time is up."

"If I believed my time were up, I would accept it," Gaius snapped. "But I don't, and the way they pushed me out is almost as disturbing as what they are trying to do now. Yes, we lost an ensign, and the sacrifices went poorly, but they've added fabrications to circumstances that were already exaggerated. This thing about the wolves and the boundary stones is ludicrous. Whoever saw a wolf carrying a large stone in its mouth? I hate to see the populace so badly led astray and lied to. That's a bigger issue than my prestige."

"Let it go, Gaius," said Cornelia. "It's sad and disappointing, but you won't win against these people. The tribunate has become a collection of puppets, and the Senate holds the strings. For all the work you accomplished as a tribune, for all that you did to strengthen the people's position in the government, the optimates still use their money and influence to get what they want. It's time to let someone else do this ultimately very frustrating work."

"But I'm only thirty years old, Mother. Should I resume my military career or simply throw up my hands and give in to a life of wealth and leisure?"

"You've asked for my advice, Gaius. And as I said, give what speeches you must prior to the vote, but let it go at that. What you do next with your life is up to you, not me. You have a wife and two children. If you cannot stomach being a senator, bring your family to Misenum. Join my circles. Return to the sanctuary of arts and letters."

CHAPTER 97

I doubt Cornelia ever really thought Gaius would come to live with her. She probably understood that her advice to *let it go* was also difficult for him to accept. Like Licinia, I think she felt the worst of it was over and that his most likely career was in the military or as a senator. But that was before Gaius sat down with Pomponius, Laetorius, and Fulvius. Papirius Carbo had dropped off the land commission after Gaius' second term as tribune and was no longer part of Gaius' steadily shrinking stable of clients. All that remained of his inner circle gathered with him in Fulvius' home on the Palatine Hill, an elegant villa, decorated with all the most fashionable rugs and ceramics, but also containing Fulvius' vast array of military plunder—swords, shields, and javelins—collected during his years fighting barbarians in the north.

Pomponius and Laetorius were tremendously loyal to Gaius but not nearly as passionate about the politics as Fulvius, a man who seemed to become more stubborn and belligerent the more opposition he faced. From what I learned later, Fulvius dominated the meeting. He screamed at Rufus' affront. He ranted against Opimius and Fannius and any other senator he could think of. "They're asking for a confrontation, Gaius, and I believe we should give it to them. Rufus will speak about the proposal two days from now on the Capitoline Hill—before the entire Assembly. I say we go there with the strongest show of support we can gather and demand you be given a chance to speak. Rubrius proposed the law, but you made it happen. Junonia is your baby. You must be given a chance to defend it."

Gaius agreed to Fulvius' plan. He did want to speak to the Assembly one more time, and Junonia was as good an issue to address as any. It would be his final tribute to his brother's work for land reform.

CHAPTER 98

Gaius ascended the Capitoline Hill before dawn with his most loyal clients, nearly a hundred men including Fulvius, Laetorius, Pomponius, and ever-faithful Philocrates. The situation was reminiscent of the day Tiberius climbed the hill to seek his second tribuneship. Gaius' clients acted as bodyguards, surrounding him in three defensive rings. Cornelia, aware of what was happening, made her own contribution to the confrontation by sending another one hundred men she had gathered from the countryside to add to her son's safety.

Soon after this small army of unarmed men arrived, a herald and client of Opimius', Quintus Antullius, who was there to act as the crier for Rufus, saw Gaius standing behind the speaker's platform in the portico of the temple of Jupiter. Antullius, waiting for Rufus to appear, smugly walked over to the ex-tribune and casually remarked, "Let the bad citizens make way for the good." It was intended as an insult, and though ignored by Gaius, the comment enraged several of his clients standing nearby. One shouted at the herald, then another shoved him. When Antullius pushed back, ten men were on him, stabbing him over and over again with the bronze styluses used to mark ballots that sat in a box behind the tribunal. Gaius shouted at them to stop, but when the men stood back, Antullius lay dead on the temple porch.

Word of the incident quickly spread through the assembling crowd. Many of those in attendance hurriedly left. Others crowded in to see what had happened. Concerned that the murder would be linked to him, Gaius tried to explain what had happened and that he had tried to stop it, but he was treated as though he were covered with blood and had ordered the act. Before any further violence could take place, a sudden rain and windstorm blew in out of the west and scattered those who still remained.

While the men that Cornelia had assembled simply dispersed to their homes outside the city, Fulvius, a man to whom violence was a way of life, led Gaius' clients down the hill to his home to prepare for the backlash from the murder. A distraught Gaius, however, wandered off accompanied only by Philocrates. He was certain he would be held responsible for Antullius' death and everything he had fought for the last two years would be lost.

When Gaius reached the forum on his way to his home, he stopped at the statue of his father that had been erected on the south edge of the forum twenty years earlier. Gaius stood before the statue with tears in his eyes and his head bowed, as though conferring with his father. As Gaius sought solace, one citizen after another stopped and noted the extreme state of sadness that had overtaken the man they had once adored. Many of these citizens had heard about the death of the herald and realized that Gaius' life was in danger. While a few made derogatory comments, thirty of these men gathered around Gaius to protect him. When Gaius finally left, they followed him to his home and camped out around it, just as citizens had done for his brother the night before his death.

Gaius entered the house as in a trance. Philocrates came in after him, having said nothing to his master about the murder except to urge him to leave the Capitoline Hill. But now, within the safety of the house, he asked his master how he was.

Gaius simply shook his head. "Philocrates, I'm at a loss. I was only hoping to make a strong statement for keeping Junonia, and then," he took a deep breath, "you saw it. Those men overreacted. It's put me in a terrible spot. I have no idea what to do next."

Licinia had not expected Gaius to be back so quickly from the Assembly. She came through the atrium in time to hear his answer to Philocrates. "What's happened?" she exclaimed rushing up to Gaius.

"The very worst," muttered Gaius, moving on past her like a man groping in the dark.

Licinia turned to Philocrates. "What is it?"

"The herald was killed in a misunderstanding before Gaius had a chance to speak."

"By whom?"

"Several of Gaius' clients. Gaius had nothing to do with it, but he's likely to be held responsible."

Licinia paled. She watched Gaius slump onto a bench in the atrium, then ran to him, kneeling at his feet and wrapping her arms around his legs, tears streaming from her eyes. "Gaius, tell me now that you will finally give all of this up."

Gaius simply hung his head.

"Gaius, please talk to me. What can we expect next?"

Two knocks sounded on the front door. Licinia stood up fearful it was someone coming for Gaius. Philocrates opened the door for Laetorius and Pomponius. Outside the street was filled with the citizens who had followed Gaius to protect him.

"What's going on? Who are those people?" demanded Licinia.

Pomponius, as excited as the crowd outside, ignored her question and hurried to Gaius' side. "I've just come from the Curia. Opimius has called a special convening of the Senate for tomorrow morning. Word is they will accuse you of treason."

Laetorius was right behind Pomponius. "There's a gathering at Fulvius' home," he blurted out to his distracted friend. "They're plotting a strategy for tomorrow!"

Licinia fell to the floor and sobbed. Catalda came out of the children's room followed by Gaius and Publius.

"What's wrong with Mama?" asked nine-year-old Publius.

Laetorius spoke up. "Keep the children in their room."

But it was too late. The boys dashed down the stairs to their mother. Gaius finally looked up at his friends. "Fulvius may do what he wants. I will turn myself in tomorrow."

"No," pleaded Pomponius, "you will be executed—likely without a trial. You should stay here until the Senate makes a formal accusation, and then we'll prepare a defense. You know as well as I do, you had nothing to do with what happened."

CHAPTER 99

Shortly after the Senate convened the next morning, just as Opimius finished describing the previous day's incident in the worse possible light, the meeting was interrupted by the sounds of a large funeral procession coming across the forum toward the Curia. Opimius led the senators out to the porch as some two hundred mourners singing a traditional Roman dirge circled the comitium carrying Antullius' body on a bier. The corpse has been stripped of clothing so that the dozens of tiny wounds all over his arms and torso were visible.

Opimius called out to the mourners from the Curia steps. "Who killed this man?"

"The traitor Gaius Gracchus," shouted the mourners, who Opimius had paid to stage the funeral.

"The man is an enemy of the state," bellowed Opimius to his fellow senators. "He believes he's above the law. It's time to prove that he isn't."

Several of the senators came down the stairs and openly wept for the dead herald as part of the theatrics orchestrated by Opimius. One senator after another expressed his horror at the deed and indignation for the disrespect of Rome's long tradition of civil discourse.

A plebeian in a torn and dirty tunic stood on the rostra across the comitium from the Curia and let out a loud laugh like a hyena. "Frauds! You're all a bunch of frauds! You shed your crocodile tears for this lowly herald and let the body of Tiberius Gracchus be thrown into the river without any funeral at all. Now you plot the murder of his brother. May Jove strike you all down!"

Many of the people standing nearby cheered the rascal, repeating his words, "You're all a bunch of frauds."

Opimius dispatched five of his lictors to shut the man up, but the pleb jumped off the rostra and disappeared into the forum crowd before the lictors had a chance to circuit the perimeter of the comitium.

Opimius quickly reconvened the Senate, then laid out a long list of fabricated crimes committed by Gaius Gracchus and Fulvius Flaccus. He paced and gestured before the three hundred senators recounting the laws Gaius had passed and how they had impacted the Senate. "This man and his followers are trying to tear down the Republic. We are in a state of siege. Grant me the authority to see that the state takes no harm."

It was a request for martial law, and when the Senate passed the decree, Opimius immediately tried to rally the senators into action. "All of you come with me. Get two of your slaves and prepare them for a confrontation. We must rein these traitors in now!"

Despite the decree and all of Opimius' ferocity, several senators spoke out against such a hasty response. Opimius ranted and raved, but after a long, heated discussion, the majority decided to issue summonses to Gaius and Fulvius demanding they appear before the Senate the next morning. At the very least, they deserved a chance to defend their actions.

Later that evening, after couriers had gone to both Fulvius' and Gaius' homes to inform them of the Senate's order, Fulvius and a small contingent of bodyguards went to Gaius' house at the edge of Subura. Fulvius was welcomed by the ring of campers protecting the house, then ushered through the peristyle into the atrium. Pomponius greeted Fulvius and took him to the tiny library where Gaius had sunk into depression, refusing to talk to anyone.

Fulvius strode into the room his chest puffed out, all set for anything, then stopped cold at the sight of his friend's dark mood. Gaius looked up. "I plan to be at the Senate shortly after dawn tomorrow. I hope you will accompany me."

"No, Gaius, absolutely not." Fulvius came up close to him and put his huge hand on Gauis' shoulder. "Once we surrender ourselves our fate will be sealed. They're calling us traitors and Opimius wants only one thing—our lives."

Pomponius had already tried to impress this on his friend. Gaius just shook his head. "Do what you must, Fulvius. I'm going to tell them exactly what happened."

"No, think about it. They won't listen. They're thirsty for blood. Our only chance is to negotiate. I say we do what our ancestors did when the patricians occupied every position in the government."

Gaius looked up at his friend, his expression hopelessness.

"Come now, man. Listen to me," urged Fulvius. "We can assemble a thousand men if we make half a try. Then we go to the top of the Aventine Hill and fortify the temple of Diana. They will never be able to drive us out. We will force them to listen to us. Neither you nor I did anything wrong yesterday. Some men got out of hand. That can be explained. If we go to the Senate, we are at their mercy. We have no bargaining chip, no way to make our point."

Gaius just stared at his friend in wonder. "Do as you must."

"No, we must be united in this. We must confront them as one. It's no different than war. A well-defended position can't be overcome. It's the only way we can get a just hearing. That's all I'm asking."

Gaius tilted his head. "And will we arm ourselves like soldiers?"

"Yes, we have to. I have a house full of weapons. But we'll only use them if necessary—strictly for defense."

Gaius shook his head. "It's not for me."

Fulvius spun around in frustration. "But it is for *you!* That's why we've all done this. For you. You're the one with the vision and the passion. We can't allow them to take you from us. At least give us that, Gaius. Give us the chance to set this straight."

To a man like Gaius this argument had impact. What Fulvius was saying was true. Everything that had happened, good or bad, was because of his leadership. He did owe something to those who had remained loyal. Maybe there was still room for bargaining. After a long silence, studied hard by Fulvius, Gaius looked up. "Fine."

Fulvius grinned through his beard, then patted his friend on the shoulder to perk him up. "Gather everyone you can, Gaius. Bring them to the temple of Diana at dawn. We'll hold out until they give us voice."

CHAPTER 100

All of Rome knew Gaius and Fulvius had been summoned to the Curia. Anticipation for the confrontation could not have been greater. The forum began to fill with citizens just after midnight so that they could be there at sunrise. Gaius never went to sleep. He spent most of the night receiving runners who were connecting with Gracchi cells throughout Rome. The message was simple—be at the temple of Diana by dawn.

Long before dawn Gaius made a sacrifice to the family lares then offered a long prayer to his father and brother. Pomponius and Laetorius joined him for a breakfast of wheat gruel and goat cheese. Everything had been planned the night before. They would amass as many men as possible at the temple of Diana. Each man would arm himself in any way he could, if only a staff or makeshift bludgeon. Although uncertain of the strategy, Gaius owed his loyalty to those who still stood by him. He carried a small dagger.

Gaius went up to his bedroom just prior to leaving. A vague pre-dawn gray filled the room. Licinia lay in the sheets crying softly. He sat down on the bed beside her and placed his right hand on her shoulder. She turned her head to face his silhouette. He could not see her eyes.

"I'm going to the Aventine Hill," he said, drawing his finger lightly over her cheek, feeling the moisture of her tears.

"Will you be back?"

"It's the same as when I went to Numantia eleven years ago. Two people who have been so fortunate to meet have a destiny to fulfill."

"Are you talking about you and me or you and your brother?"

Gaius stared off into the dimly lit room.

"If you were going off to war, Gaius, if you were going to speak at an assembly of the people, I could accept whatever came of those honorable efforts, but today, you're ignoring a direct order from the

Senate and have prepared for violence. The honor of this is not so clear to me."

"Other forces compel me, Licinia. That's all I can tell you." His voice contained no emotion or energy. Licinia sat up and embraced him. He hugged her tightly.

Licinia whispered, "What is this I feel beneath your tunic, Gaius?"

One of the boys called for Catalda.

"What you think it is." He suddenly stood up. "I must be leaving."

Licinia caught the hem of his tunic in her hand. "Gaius, please."

He knelt beside her. They kissed with feeling. Licinia held him until he stood and strode out of the room. Publius grabbed him by the waist before he reached the stairs. "Where are you going, Daddy?"

Gaius picked up his son, tossed him in the air, then caught him. "To the temple of Diana."

"Why?"

"It's a place of sanctuary."

"From whom?"

Gaius shook his head sadly. "It's more than I can tell you now." He deposited the little ball of fire in bed with Licinia, then continued down the stairs where Philocrates was waiting to leave.

CHAPTER 101

The fifty or so men camped around Gaius' house had spent a quiet night and now stood at the ready. They formed a phalanx around Gaius as they hiked across the city in the dark to a path up the east side of the Aventine Hill. As they proceeded, more men joined them, swelling their numbers to several hundred by the time they reached the temple of Diana. Another hundred or more men were already there in the early stages of fortifying the temple with anything they could find.

The group at Fulvius' home had caroused through the night. Fulvius had a reputation for heavy drinking, especially prior to battle. He anticipated a fight and had prepared in the way he always did. He overslept and was so hung over he had to be dragged from bed. He staggered up the hill just after daybreak with both of his sons and a contingent of five hundred men, some who had stayed at his home, some who had joined him on the way, and many carrying trophies from Fulvius' campaigns in Gaul.

Midmorning runners came up the hill from Fulvius' and Gaius' homes. The Senate had sent two squadrons of lictors to demand their presence before Opimius. Though Gaius was willing to go, Fulvius, feeling badly from drink, argued as he had the night before. Their only hope was to bargain from a fortified position; otherwise they were strictly at the mercy of a man who had already made his position clear. He had called them enemies of Rome and had been granted permission to do whatever was necessary to protect the state.

After a long discussion, Gaius simply gave in to the warlike Fulvius. They decided to send Fulvius' youngest son, Quintus, a handsome boy of twelve years, to deliver a message written on papyrus to the Senate: *If Opimius wants to talk to us about the events of two days ago, he must come to the temple of Diana.*

The entire forum was filled with people waiting for Fulvius and Gaius to answer the Senate's call. Quintus, hefting a herald's staff to signify the importance of his chore, pushed through the anxious crowd and gained the Curia porch where Opimius received him and read the message. The consul immediately rejected the offer. "Taking a position on the Aventine Hill is proof enough of their guilt for me," he shouted to the three hundred senators fanned out on the Curia stairs and the onlookers beyond. He scratched his answer on the back of the papyrus—*Lay down your arms and come directly to the Senate or face the consequences.* He gave the note to the boy, saying not to return unless he came with both Fulvius and Gaius.

When Quintus arrived with Opimius' demand, Gaius again expressed his willingness to go to the Senate and make a plea, but by this time, his comrades, inspired by the bilious Fulvius, would not allow it. They were confident they could hold their position and believed that anything less than a direct confrontation would be dishonorable. Gaius, a man noted for decisive and dynamic action, seemed torn between being loyal to his clients and turning himself in. Fulvius became impatient and dispatched Quintus to the Curia a second time. The message was the same; they would not leave the temple.

When the boy arrived at the Senate, Opimius had him taken away and held. Then he turned to the collection of senators. "Have we not seen enough? These men are the enemies of Rome. It is my duty to protect the state. You denied me yesterday, but you can't today! Gather your arms. We're off to the Aventine Hill to rout these men out!"

Opimius had anticipated resistance. The night before he had contacted Caecilius Metellus, an ultra-aristocrat who had just returned from a successful campaign in the Balearic Islands. Metellus and his troops were waiting outside Rome for this current issue to be resolved before entering the city as part of a triumph. A cohort of Cretan archers was among Metellus troops. Opimius told Metellus to send these five hundred archers into the city at daybreak and have them wait in the cattle market for further orders.

With only a handful of senators refusing to take part, Opimius led some two hundred and ninety members of the Senate, each accompanied by two or three of their personal slaves, to the cattle market to join forces with the Cretan archers. The entire group, close to fifteen hundred strong, ascended to the top of the Aventine Hill and encircled the temple of Diana. Opimius had no intention of entering into a discussion with the men he considered traitors. He shouted orders to his comrades, then rushed the temple. The hastily built ramparts provided just enough resistance, and Opimius' men were summarily repulsed.

Instead of making another foray, Opimius deployed the Cretan archers into six positions around the temple then ordered them to launch their darts. Except for the steady rain of arrows piercing through the gaps in their fortress, the Gracchans could have held out all day against Opimius' forces. But one after another the men were struck by arrows. When the number of dead equaled the number living, Opimius signaled for another attack. His forces quickly surmounted the makeshift barriers, and the rout was on. Those still alive inside the temple made a break for it, simply trying to save themselves.

Fulvius and his other son, also named Marcus, raced down the east side of the hill scrambling through the homes and tenements with thirty men chasing them. Fulvius wound through the streets to the woodworking shop of a friend. The man ushered Fulvius and Marcus into a hiding place at the rear of the shop. Shortly afterward, the neighborhood filled with men searching for Fulvius. Every shop owner and tenant was questioned. When an old man told them that the woodworker was a friend of Fulvius', twelve of Opimius' militia burst into the shop and ransacked the place looking for the ex-consul. When they could not find him, they pressured the owner. Certain that his life was in danger, the woodworker said aloud that Fulvius was not there, but under his breath revealed where he was hiding

The twelve men positioned themselves around the hiding place, then called to Fulvius to come out. Rather than surrender, Fulvius leapt from his hiding place and tried to take the men on with only a gladius to defend himself. He was known as a dangerous man in battle, and he hoped to hold them off long enough for his son to escape. But against twelve men he had no chance. Four of them lunged at him at once. Two pierced his torso. When Marcus tried to come to Fulvius' aid, he was immediately struck down, leaving him in a pool of blood to watch his father brutally butchered.

Gaius, who had struck no blow in the foray, saw that everything was falling apart. He went into the temple cella instead of fleeing. He knelt on the stone floor beside the statue of Diana and issued a curse against those he had spent his life defending, "May the people of Rome never be freed from the shackles they refused to let me remove," then withdrew the dagger from within his tunic. He held it out to Philocrates. "Please, my friend, end this sad life for me."

Before Philocrates could take the dagger, Pomponius rushed into the cella. "No, Gaius! There's still a chance to get away."

Laetorius appeared behind Pomponius. "All of you, quick, come with me."

Pomponius grabbed Gaius by the wrist and pulled him to his feet. With Laetorius and Pomponius running interference, Gaius and Philocrates slipped through the ring of aggressors and followed their friends into an alley that led down the west side of the hill toward the Tiber River. One of Opimius' militia officers, Septimuleius, saw them enter the alley and called out for help.

On the way down the hill, now with ten men on his tail, Gaius tripped and twisted his ankle. Philocrates helped him to his feet and did his best to keep Gaius moving. Pomponius urged them go ahead. He would slow down Septimuleius and give Gaius a chance to get away.

As Philocrates, Laetorius, and Gaius passed through Trigeminia Gate, headed to the Sublician Bridge, they heard Pomponius shriek. Gaius stopped to look back, but Laetorius yanked him ahead, saying that he would man the bridge while Gaius and Philocrates made for the forest on the other side of the river.

Gaius limped ahead with Philocrates, neither of them sure where they were going or how they would get away. Gaius' life had fallen to pieces. He was running for his life but empty of all will to live. Laetorius blocked Septimuleius and now just six other men at the bridge. He killed two of them before he was trampled over, pierced with wounds. Philocrates beseeched passersby for help or the use of a horse, but it was too late to escape. They could already hear Septimuleius' voice.

Gaius directed Philocrates to the Furrina Grove on the west bank of the Tiber. The grove was a small grassy opening in the woods with a sculpture of the goddess Furrina and an altar. For a second time Gaius offered Philocrates his dagger. "My hesitation earlier cost the lives of my two best friends. Please, do it now, Philocrates, so that you might get away."

"No, I will take my life as well, master," he said accepting the dagger. "Your loss is also mine."

Gaius knelt before Philocrates and tore open his tunic to bare his chest. Before Philocrates could stab him, Septimuleius and four other men raced into the grove. Instead of killing Gaius, Philocrates fell on his master to protect him, but it was no use. Septimuleius and his comrades stabbed and hacked at both men until it was difficult to tell, except for their two heads, that they were separate corpses.

Prior to the attack on the temple of Diana, Opimius had placed a bounty on both Gaius and Fulvius, promising whoever killed either man a payment in gold equal to the weight of the man's head. Fulvius' killers came to Opimius with the ex-consul's head. Such was its condition, Opimius, a man of few scruples, refused to pay them, claiming he could not recognize the trophy as Fulvius.

Across Rome, Septimuleius dispatched his men, then took Gaius' head. He went to his home to remove the brain and fill the cavity with lead. He came to Opimius with the head mounted on a javelin. When the head was placed on the scales, Opimius became suspicious of its weight and quickly discovered what the man had done. He threatened to exile Septimuleius for trying to cheat a Roman magistrate, then had the head tossed into the Tiber with all the other corpses. Somehow, impossibly it seemed, Gaius' death was even more ugly than Tiberius'. Such was the horrible fate of my two brothers.

CHAPTER 102

Following the dispersal of the rebels, as they were being called, and Gaius' death, thieves and thugs went to both Fulvius' and Gaius' homes seeking plunder. Licinia learned of Gaius' death from the threats and insults shouted by these opportunists as they crashed through her front door and thundered in the back of the house through the peristyle.

Licinia managed to get out of the house before becoming part of the plunder. She ran through the streets in tears with Catalda and the two children trying to keep up. Cornelia and I were in the atrium anxiously awaiting news of any kind when Licinia burst through the door.

"Gaius is dead," she screamed, then threw herself on the entry floor, wailing and pulling at her hair. Cornelia rushed to her side. I trailed behind in my wheelchair as the horror descended upon us all like a family-specific disease.

There is little reason to detail the unspeakable agony we felt that afternoon. The children, the slaves, each of us women, simply gave into the tragedy of Gaius' death and cried, alternately embracing each other and ranting at the gods. Could a home fill with tears, mine would have. Although Opimius declared it illegal to mourn "the insurgents," no law could deny the grief that filled our lives in the following weeks, months, and, really, the remaining years of our lives.

In the month that followed the debacle at the top of the Aventine Hill, a place known since the first days of the Republic as a plebeian refuge, Opimius did all he could to rub salt into the wounds of our family and the families and friends of those who had died in defense of Gaius and Fulvius. In all, some one thousand corpses were carried from the temple of Diana and thrown into the Tiber. Another two thousand citizens were rounded up and executed without a trial. Everyday for weeks on end it seemed we heard of more men taken to the Tullianum, Rome's state prison, to be strangled. Quintus, Fulvius' young son, though only serving as a messenger for his father, was also executed. Opimius allowed him the great privilege of deciding how he would die. Additionally, all of Licinia's possessions, even her dowry, something always returned to a widow, were confiscated. When Cornelia left Rome, Licinia, her children, and the family's slaves traveled with her to Misenum.

As a final insult to my brothers, my family, and all those Gaius and Tiberius had given their lives to help, Opimius built a temple to Concord at the west end of the forum as a memorial to his eradication of the Gracchan movement, which he had denounced as a rebellion. Two weeks after the temple was completed, an unknown citizen defiled the temple by etching into the stone below the temple's inscription, *To Folly and Discord Concord's temple built.*

EPILOGUE

"Thus the sedition of the younger Gracchus came to an end. Not long afterward a law was enacted to permit the holders to sell the land acquired through redistribution; for even this had been forbidden by the law of the elder Gracchus. At once the rich began to buy the allotments of the poor, or found pretexts for seizing them by force. So the condition of the poor became even worse than it was before. By these devices, the law of Gracchus—a most excellent and useful one, if it could have been carried out—was once and for all frustrated. So the plebeians lost everything, and hence resulted a still further decline in the numbers both of citizens and soldiers."

-Appian of Alexandria, *Civil Wars*

The deaths of my brothers marked the beginning of a steady crumbling of the Roman Republic. In the eight years since Gaius' death, I have already seen the little cracks become big ones, along with the steady repeal of many of my brothers' efforts at populist reform.

Two years after Opimius' rash response to Gaius' political efforts, the then ex-consul was tried for his deeds. As an example of how things and people change, Papirius Carbo defended Opimius in court. He admitted that Opimius was responsible for Gaius' and Fulvius' deaths, but he used the Senate's order "to see that the state took no harm" as a defense for Opimius' actions. The Senate responded by denying all charges against Opimius. This awful and yet sensational trial catapulted Carbo to a consulship the following year.

Polybius died eighteen months after the trial at the age of eighty-two. Although I saw him three times subsequent to learning of Philocrates' part in Aemilianus' murder, I never told him what I knew and he never asked. I will always consider him a great and thoughtful man.

Two years after Polybius' death, Cornelia's longtime friend and suitor Physcon died in Egypt. He was sixty-six years of age. She was seventy-four. As it turned out, the last time they saw each other was the day Physcon requested a final parting kiss from Cornelia. It was the first thing she said upon hearing of his death.

My friend Laelia never remarried after her divorce. Although I would leave Rome and lose contact with her, she continued to study law and did finally argue several legal cases in the forum.

Cornelia spent the rest of her life in Misenum with Licinia, her children, and later me. She focused on the education of her grandsons and writing. She also continued and expanded her intellectual circle.

I showed this history to Cornelia shortly after completing it. She was not as surprised as I expected. "I knew you would be writer, Sempronia," she said when she returned the manuscript to me with a few pages of comments and additions. "Literature was your sanctuary after all." She embraced me, and I her, knowing she was right.

"I believe you elaborated on a difficult subject with remarkable grace," she said upon releasing me, "but I have one critical remark. A large part of this book is a portrait of me as a mother and an influential voice in Rome."

I nodded that this was accurate.

"But what comes across more strongly is your strength, not mine," she said. "I believe you did more to support your brothers than I did. Not only did you help them with their political struggles and give support to their wives, but you also took on Aemilianus and became an important political player in your own right."

"You mean as an assassin. No, Mother, that was not politics—that was self-defense."

"No, that was strength. If there's truly a woman of note in Rome, I believe that woman is you."

I do not agree with my mother's assessment. She was the one who made all of us who we were and was always there doing what a good mother must—support, defend, and, if necessary, criticize her children. I hope this is not lost in my history no matter how my brothers, or even I, are portrayed in the material. The influence of my mother is behind every bill my brothers proposed and every word I write.

Today, as I add this epilogue to my manuscript, Cornelia is one year short of eighty. She still remains a grand lady, who when asked about her sons refers to them as her jewels and recounts their deeds without a tear or a quiver in her voice, as though she were reciting from my history. Some have wondered about this. How could she possibly manage to talk about those twin tragedies with so little emotion? A few have said that old age has taken her mind and that she no longer has feelings to express. I have lived with Cornelia the past five years. I can attest that she has not lost any of her intellectual facility and that she still harbors deep and painful wounds from those difficult times. For the most part, I believe it is her elevated sense of dignity and her nobility that allow her to speak to others about those tragic events with such seeming distance.

When she and I talk about my brothers, however, the conversation becomes emotional and invariably leads to variations of the same question: *Had it all come about because of her?* Had her populist views infected Tiberius and Gaius with such a strong sense of duty that it became like an illness and drove them to an inevitable collision with the strongest forces in Rome? Cornelia would say yes. I always argued against that conclusion. Yes, she had educated her sons to the highest ideal. And yes, they had lived it. But as Gaius heard Tiberius tell him in a dream, "One life and one death is appointed to each of us, to spend the one and to meet the other in the service of the people." That was my brothers' destiny as surely as Tiberius Gracchus was their father.

In closing, it is worth noting that among the plebeians both Tiberius and Gaius will always be remembered as heroes. The locations of their deaths have become sacred places, and just last year a bill was approved by the People's Assembly to build a memorial to them. I hope it is completed soon so that I can take Cornelia to Rome to witness its dedication. Maybe one day they will build a memorial to her.

LIST OF CHARACTERS

Ada- Claudia Gracchus' Iberian housemaid

Aemilia Tertia Paulla- Cornelia Scipionis' mother

Aemilius Paullus- Roman consul, brother of Aemilia Paulla

Antullius- herald, client of the consul Opimius

Appius Claudius Pulcher- Roman senator, member of land commission, Tiberius Gracchus' father-in-law and Claudia Pulcheria's father

Aristonius- renegade Syrian King

Attalus- King of Pergamum

Blossius of Cumae- stoic philosopher, tutor of the Gracchi

Calpurnius Piso- Roman senator and consul

Catalda- Licinia Crassus' Sicilian housemaid

Claudia Pulcheria- Tiberius Gracchus' wife, daughter of Appius Claudius Pulcher

Claudia Crassae- wife of Publius Licinius Crassus, mother-in-law of Gaius Gracchus

Cornelia Scipionis Africana- daughter of Publius Cornelius Scipio Africanus the Elder

Coson- Cornelia Scipionis' Thracian male house slave

Diophanes of Mytilene- Greek rhetorician, tutor of the Gracchi

Elephantis- Greek poet and midwife

Eudemus- envoy from Pergamum

Fidelia- Cornelia Scipionis' Sabine housemaid

Fulvia- Pomponius Atticus' wife

Gaius Fannius- Roman consul

Gaius Fulvius Flaccus- Roman consul, brother of Marcus Fulvius Flaccus

Gaius Sempronius Gracchus- Cornelia Scipionis' youngest son

Gaius Gracchus- Gaius Gracchus' first son

Gnaeus Rubrius- tribune of the plebs

Hostilius Mancinus- Roman consul denigrated for campaign against Numantians in Spain

Laelia Sapiens- Gaius Laelius' daughter, Mucius Scaevola's daughter-in-law

Laetorius Antonius – Gaius Gracchus' friend from military service

Licinia Crassae- Gaius Gracchus' wife, daughter of Publius Licinius Crassus

Lucius Cornelius Scipio- Publius Cornelius Scipio Africanus the Elder's younger brother

Lucius Opimius- Roman consul, staunch opponent of Gaius Gracchus

Lucilius- Roman satiric playwright

Marcia- Laetorius Antonius' wife

Marcus Octavius- tribune of the plebs, opponent of Tiberius Gracchus

Marcus Fulvius Flaccus- consul, tribune of the plebes, member of land commission, close ally of Gaius Gracchus

Marcus Philippus- Roman senator, Claudia Gracchae's second husband,

Masinissa- Numidian king, friend of Publius Cornelius Scipio Africanus the Elder

Metellus Numidicus- Roman consul

Micipsa- king of Numidia, friend of Gaius' and Tiberius' father

Mucius Scaevola- Roman consul at time of Tiberius Gracchus' death, father-in-law of Laelia Sapiens

Nadia- Sempronia's Numidian housemaid

Panaetius- Roman stoic philosopher

Papirius Carbo- tribune of the plebs, member of land commission

Philocrates- Gaius Gracchus' personal slave

Physcon- King Ptolemy VIII of Egypt, suitor of Cornelia Scipionis

Pocuvius- Roman tragic poet

Polybius- noted Greek historian, wrote history of the rise of the Roman Republic

Popilius Laenus- Roman consul, led purge against Tiberius

Pomponius Atticus- Gaius Gracchus' friend since childhood

Porcius Cato- famous Roman orator and conservative politician

Publius Cornelius Scipio Africanus the Elder- Roman general and consul who defeated Hannibal to end the Second Punic War

Publius Cornelius Scipio Aemilianus Africanus the Younger- Sempronia Gracchae's husband, the adopted, grandson of Africanus the Elder

Publius Licinius Crassus- Gaius Gracchus' father-in-law, father of Licinia

Publius Gracchus- Gaius Gracchus' second son

Publius Satureius- tribune of the plebs, first to attack Tiberius Gracchus

Publius Scipio Nasica- pontiff maximus, senator, cousin, and adversary of Tiberius Gracchus

Phyllis- Claudia Crassae's Thracian housemaid

Quintus Metellus- brother of Metellus Numidicus

Quintus Mummius- client of Gaius Gracchus, brother of Spurius Mummius

Quintus Pompeius- Roman senator

Quintus Scaevola- Laelia Sapiens' husband

Quintus Tubero- son of Aemilianus' sister

Sempronia Gracchae- daughter of Cornelia Scipionis, narrator of story

Sempronia Gracchae- daughter of Tiberius Gracchus

Sempronius Tuditanus- Roman consul

Septimuleius- client of Opimius, murderer of Gaius Gracchus

Spurius Mummius- Roman senator, friend of Scipio Aemilianus, brother of Quintus Mummius

Tarus- Sempronia Gracchae's and Scipio Aemilianus' top male slave, once a Sardinian pirate

Tiberius Sempronius Gracchus (the younger)- Cornelia Scipionis' son

Tiberius Sempronius Gracchus (the elder)- consul, Cornelia Scipionis' husband

Tiberius Gracchus- Tiberius Gracchus' youngest son

Titus Annius- Roman senator, critic of Tiberius Gracchus

Tryphaena- Physcon's daughter

Veda- Sempronia Gracchae's Etruscan cook

GLOSSARY

advoate- lawyer

as (pl. asses)- bronze Roman coin, four quadrans make one as

cella- main room in a Roman temple

Century Assembly- voting group made up entirely of Roman citizens in the military service (active and reserve)

clients- active supporters of a politician

comitium- sunken amphitheater in front of the Curia

consulate- the pair of co-consuls

contio (pl. contiones)- public meetings for political discussion

coan silk- especially fine silk

Curia- Roman Senate House

curule chair- seat for consuls in Roman Senate, made of ivory

denarius (pl. denarii)- silver coin

equites (also equestrians)- second order of nobility in Rome, upper-middle class

flamen (pl. flamines)- religious orderly

gladius (pl. gladii)- double-bladed, short sword of Spanish origin

haruspex- priest trained to read entrails or actions of birds

hastatus (pl. hastati)- first row of soldiers in a Roman legion

ides- fifteenth day of the month

imagines- wax masks cast from a family's ancestors

imperium- authority to rule

iugerum (pl. iugera)- amount of land a man can plow with a yoke of oxen in one day

lares- small doll-like figurines representing household gods

lictor- bodyguard for Roman consul or other high magistrates

manus- type of marriage contract

mola- religious sacrament made from salt and ground wheat or emmer

mulsum- honey-sweetened wine

nones- the ninth of the month

optimate (pl. optimates)- conservative faction of Roman Senate

palla- shawl for Roman women

patria protestas- authority of father over family

patrician- highest class of Roman citizen, aristocracy

People's Assembly- voting group made up entirely of plebeians

peristyle- garden in Roman home

pleb (plebeian)- the lowest class of Roman citizen

penates- household gods of the hearth; traditional practice was to toss a bit of each meal into the fire to feed the penates

pontifex maximus- highest position in Roman religious hierarchy

poulterer- man who takes care of haruspex's chicken

popularis (pl. populares)- progressive faction of Roman Senate

posca- apple cider vinegar diluted with water

praetor- governor of Roman province

prorogue- to extent an official's term of service

quadrans- smallest denomination of Roman coinage, four quadrans equal one as

quaestor- military accountant, quartermaster

sesterces- Roman coin, four are equal to one denarius

sinus- the pocket formed by a toga draped over the wearer's left arm

stade- a unit of distance, about six hundred feet

stibium- black makeup, often used for eyeliner

stola- Roman woman's dress

subura- lower-class neighborhood in Rome

toga praetexta- toga trimmed in purple worn by Roman consul

tribunal- platform, stage

tribunate- the unit of ten tribunes of the plebs

triclinium- Roman dining room

umbilicus- the ornate knob at either end of a scroll

ACKNOWLEDGMENTS

I could not have written this book without the love and support of my wife Judith. My thanks to her is always and forever.

Thanks is also extended to the contingent of readers who helped me with this novel: Alice, Jim, Fast Eddie, Judith, Carol, Tom, Lora, and Steve.

Although the research for this book occurred over a period of several years and included the reading of many books and articles, Plutarch's *Lives*, Appian of Alexandria's *Civil* Wars, A. H. J. Greenidge's *A History of Rome During the Later Republic and Early Principate*, and David Stockton's remarkable book *The Gracchi* provided the historical basis for this novel.

For the most part this novel closely follows the Gracchi history as we know it. Some liberties have been taken for readability. The incident where Sempronia testifies in court against Lucius Equitius, which is a factual event, actually occurred ten years later than portrayed in the novel. Also, the teachings of Elephantis are largely lost or speculative, and her knowledge of Cornelia or her circles is fictional.

Other Sources:

Appian of Alexandria, *The Civil Wars*, translated by Horace White, Loeb Classical Library, Harvard University Press, Cambridge, Massachusetts, 1913.

Bauman, Richard A., *Women and Politics in Ancient Rome*, Routledge, London, 1992.

Bradley, Keith, *Slavery and Society at Rome*, Cambridge University Press, UK, 1994.

Cicero, *Complete Works*, translated by C.D. Yonge, Delphi Classics.

Cowell, F.R., *Life in Ancient Rome*, Berkley Publishing Group, New York, 1980.

Croom, Alexandra, *Roman Clothing and Fashion*, Amberley Publishing, Gloucestershire, England, 1988.

Duncan, Mike, *The Republic*, Herodotus Press, New Zealand, 2016.

Dupont, Florence, *Daily Life in Ancient Rome*, translated by Christopher Woodall, Blackwell Publishers, Oxford, 1989.

Everitt, Anthony, *The Rise of Rome*, Random House Trade Paperbacks, New York, 2013.

Greenidge, A. H. J., *A History of Rome During the Later Republic and Early Principate*, Oxford University Press, London, 1904.

Hemelrijk, Emily A., *Matrona Docta: Educated Women in the Roman Elite from Cornelia to Julia Domna*, Routledge of the Taylor and Francis Group, New York, New York, 1999.

Mackay, Christopher S., *The Breakdown of the Roman Republic*, Cambridge University Press, Cambridge, England, 2009.

MacLachlan, Bonnie, *Women in Ancient Rome*, New York, 2013.

Münzer, Friedrich, *Roman Aristocratic Parties and Families*, translated by Thérèse Ridley, John Hopkins University Press, Baltimore and London, 1999.

Nicolet, Claude, *The World of the Citizen in Republican Rome*, University of California Press, Berkeley, 1980.

Olson, Kelly, *Dress and the Roman Woman*, Routledge, New York, 2008.

Plutarch, *Lives*, translated by John Dryden, The Publishers Plate Renting Company, New York, 1937.

Polo, Francisco Pina, *The Consul at Rome*, Cambridge University Press, New York, 2011.

Scheid, John, *An Introduction to Roman Religion*, Indiana University Press. 2003.

Stockton, David, *The Gracchi*, Oxford University Press, Oxford, England, 1979.

Taylor, Lily Ross, *Roman Voting Assemblies*, University of Michigan Press, Ann Arbor, 1993.

Treggiari, Susan, *Roman Marriage from the Time of Cicero to the Time of Ulpian*, Clarendon Press, Oxford, 1993.

Warrior, Valerie M., *Roman Religion*, Cambridge University Press, New York, 2006.

The map of Rome at the front of the book comes from *Cambridge Ancient History*, Volume 9, page 70.

NOTE: The following passages in the novel were paraphrased or taken, nearly intact, from other books:

1. Tiberius Gracchus' speech from the rostra on page 31 of the novel comes from pages 111-112 of Plutarch's *Lives*.

2. Titus Annius' question to Tiberius Gracchus at the People's Assembly on page 90 of the novel comes from page 70 of David Stockton's *The Gracchi*.

3. Tiberius Gracchus' answer to Titus Annius' question on page 91 of the novel comes from page 117 of Plutarch's *Lives*.

4. Blossius' comments to Tiberius' clients on page 116 of the novel come from page 119 of Plutarch's *Lives*.

5. Blossius' exchange with Publius Nasica on pages 125-126 of the novel comes from page 121 of Plutarch's *Lives*.

6. Aemilianus' description of his dream on pages 159-162 of the novel closely follows Cicero's essay *The Dream of Scipio*.

7. Tiberius' words to Gaius in the dream described on page 208 of the novel come from page 123 of Plutarch's *Lives*.

8. Cornelia's letter to Gaius on pages 210-211 of the novel comes from pages 42-43 of Richard A. Bauman's *Women and Politics in Ancient Rome*.

9. Gaius Gracchus' speech to the People's Assembly on pages 239-240 of the novel comes from page 125 of Plutarch's *Lives*.

10. Gaius Gracchus' speech to the People's Assembly on pages 268-269 of the novel comes from pages 183-184 of David Stockton's *The Gracchi*.

THE AUTHOR

Dan Armstrong is the editor and owner of Mud City Press, a small publishing company and online magazine operating out of Eugene, Oregon. Information about his books, short stories, political commentary, humor, and environmental studies is available at www.mudcitypress.com.

CPSIA information can be obtained
at www.ICGtesting.com
Printed in the USA
LVOW03s1442050318
568694LV00002B/811/P

9 780999 321904